The Dragon Tree

This specially prepared edition, issued in 1959, is for members of The Popular Book Club, 9 Long Acre, London, W.C.99, from which address particulars of membership may be obtained. The book is issued by arrangement with the original publishers, Hodder & Stoughton Ltd.

VICTOR CANNING

has also written

VICTOR CANNING

The Dragon Tree

THE POPULAR BOOK CLUB

LONDON

MADE AND PRINTED IN GREAT BRITAIN FOR
THE POPULAR BOOK CLUB (ODHAMS PRESS LTD.)
BY ODHAMS (WATFORD) LIMITED
WATFORD, HERTS
S.559.SC.N.

1

AWAY to the left was the faint smudge of the French coast and below, shadowed by occasional drifts of cloud, the waters of the Bay of Biscay. In a little while they would hit San Sebastian and the dun-coloured, June-burnt ridges of the Pyrenees.

The air inlet above Major John Richmond hissed gently, the draught fretting at the edges of *The Times* which he was reading. The main article on the centre page was headlined —*Future of Cyrenian National Leaders*. And underneath, in smaller type—*Labour Dissatisfaction*.

John smiled at that. Sitting in the Strangers' Gallery yesterday he had heard the Labour members' dissatisfaction with the statement of the Secretary of State for the Colonies.

"... *the Secretary of State for the Colonies said in answer to the Opposition that the Government had not yet reached a decision on the future of the Cyrenian Nationalist leaders, Hadid Chebir and Colonel Mawzi, recently captured during operations against Cyrenian National forces.*

Mr. James Morgan (Llanryll, Lab.) said that as Hadid Chebir and Colonel Mawzi had now been in Government hands for more than two weeks the Opposition and, indeed, the country as a whole were entitled to know the Government's intention. Were they to be brought to trial, or did the Government intend to send them into exile? If this latter course were intended, as he suspected, then the Opposition could not too strongly condemn this further example of vacillation."

John Richmond lowered the paper for a moment, hearing the strong Welsh voice of Mr. Morgan still. He must have known that he was not going to get any satisfaction out of the Secretary of State. The Government had made up its mind all right, but until the thing was done no announcement would be made ... a *fait accompli* was the hardest thing to argue against. He smiled to himself as he remembered Mr. Morgan's next phrase, though this had not been reported in

The Times . . . "the usual brilliant Governmental demonstration of wishy-washy shilly-shallying."

The air hostess came down the gangway, holding a tray of drinks aloft expertly. She was a neat, anonymous figure, not a curve of her automatic B.E.A. smile out of place. She glanced at him as she passed and for a moment his smile shadowed her own, but he was hardly aware of her. He was a long way from the present, years and years back, and at Oxford. Hadid Chebir . . . He hadn't known him very well. But some of his memories stuck clearly, particularly one. The centre of the picture was vivid, the edges blurred . . . a hard winter's day, the muddy ground with a crisp meringue-top of frost and in the shower room at the back of the pavilion the whistle of water jets and a moving frieze of young men's naked bodies. One body, slim and long and pale coffee-colour, stood out against the Anglo-Saxon scrubbed pinkness of the others. What was it Chebir had said? "This passion for games! In my country you are a child, and then suddenly a man. There are no games." Someone had laughed and thrown a wet towel and the coffee-coloured arms had gathered it neatly and the towel had been smartly returned. It was odd how the isolated picture stood out in his memory.

When he had left the House and gone to the War Office to see Banstead, the memory had been with him. Banstead had been at his most pompous to begin with. You just had to sit and bear with him while he delivered one of his Royal Institute of International Affairs lectures.

"You have, no doubt, divined why I asked you to go along to the House?"

"I've twigged, yes." It amused him to see Banstead's frown when you put his words into the vernacular. "When do I leave and where do I go?"

"Tomorrow morning. San Borodon. Did the Secretary of State go into the historical and political background?"

"Not before I left. Mr. Morgan was giving him hell. But don't worry, I can see you mean to let me have it."

"This whole situation is very delicate and it's necessary to know where you are——"

"I'm going to be stuck on a small island in the Atlantic by the look of it."

6

"The climate is excellent. However, to come back to Cyrenia—the whole trouble there arises from the racial mixture of its peoples and its military importance in Arab-Afro and Mediterranean affairs. In a way, I suppose, it could be called the key to the Middle East strategic problem . . ."

The staff course lecture had gone on and there was no stopping it. The only time Banstead really relaxed was when you got him into a bar where he immediately became bawdy and soon given to horse-play.

". . . The Turks and the Arabs make up the larger part of the population, but there is a considerable Greek community."

"A hotch-potch."

"If you care to put it that way. In 1878, by a convention with Turkey, we took Cyrenia over on the understanding at that time that we did so in trust for the Sultan; but in 1914 on the outbreak of war between ourselves and Turkey, we annexed the country. Later, under the secret Sykes-Picot Agreement of 1916, the Government agreed not to open any negotiations for the cessation or alienation of Cyrenia without the previous consent of the French Government. This agreement was made public in the Franco-British Convention of 1920, and—by Article 20 of the Peace Treaty of Lausanne in 1923—Turkey recognized the annexation of Cyrenia."

"And since then the place has been nothing but a bloody nuisance."

Banstead's frown had deepened.

"Since then it has been a highly complicated problem. There's a Governor and a Legislative Council and eventually it will be granted autonomy, but the trouble is the Arabs and the Turks. They hate one another and the small Greek community is persecuted by both. Hadid Chebir's father started the trouble by raising a pro-Arab army and there was the uprising and massacre in 1935. Since then the Arab element has opposed any sort of reasonable constitution."

"When was it that the old man Chebir died?"

"In 1937. The name Chebir is a legend there. Since his death young Hadid Chebir and Colonel Mawzi have kept the Cyrenian National Army going and made trouble. There is

7

no doubt, too, that it has been supported by arms and money from interested outside sources——"

"No names, no pack drill."

"Precisely. We were very lucky to capture the two."

"And now you have them in the bag, you don't quite know what to do with them?"

"We—or the Government, rather—need a breathing space. In the meantime . . ." Banstead had smiled suddenly and lapsed into a more human manner, ". . . they are going to be your babies, and I'm bloody glad it's you and not me. The three of them are dynamite. And you've got to handle them with kid gloves."

"Three?"

"You're lucky. Madame Chebir has elected to go into voluntary exile with her husband."

"That doesn't surprise me." The English girl who had married Hadid Chebir and identified herself with Cyrenia was well known and through the press had become a sympathetic figure . . . Now, John Richmond thought, he would be meeting her and would know what she was really like.

"In the place of a heart she has a rock with the word *Cyrenia* carved on it."

"Judging from her photographs, she's damned attractive. Not the kind you'd expect to get mixed up in politics. Usually they're rather large and square-faced or——"

"Yes, yes," said Banstead, not pleased at this interruption of his lecture.

John smiled. "Sorry—carry on."

"All the arrangements have been made for you. Pick them up as you go out. There is one thing, however, I should explain. Both here and in the Colonial Office there's a kind of unhappiness about the whole affair. Some days before these two were captured one of our intelligence boys in Cyrenia was murdered. He was an excitable type, but sound, and he was on his way to report to the G.O.C. out there—after requesting a special appointment—because he'd got important information . . . He never did manage to spill it. But there's a general niggle around here that he really had something to say about Hadid Chebir and Colonel Mawzi that would have made a lot of eyes pop. Since you'll be more or less living with these people we want you to keep your eyes and ears open. Apart from the general report you'll make to Sir George Cator each week——"

"Is he still the San Borodon Governor?"

"He'll never be anything else until he retires. As I say, apart from your report to him, you'll also write direct and personally to me when you feel like it. But for heaven's sake don't step on Sir George's toes over this . . ."

John had smiled at this. His years in the Army had taught him how to avoid stepping on people's toes. And then, his mind going back to Oxford and Hadid Chebir, he had asked, "Is there any other reason, apart from the professional one, why I've been picked for this job?"

"None that I know. Is there something?"

"I suppose not."

If Banstead didn't know about Oxford there seemed no point in mentioning it. He had said wryly, "I must say you've sprung this on me pretty smartly."

"Every officer should consider himself at twelve hours' notice to move. You've got sixteen."

One short, Army word had been the only answer to that. Going out he had picked up his orders in an envelope red-sealed, top-secreted and addressed to Major John Richmond, M.C., and now . . . he leaned back in his seat . . . here he was.

The air hostess came back by his seat and he ordered a brandy and soda. Down below the pale lines of roads and tracks were spread out over the withered body of the earth like bloodless veins. It was only a fortnight since he had been in Spain on leave. They'd motored down through France and spent a few days at the Costa Brava . . . the place had been full of English and Swiss and the weather disappointing, and the whole thing had fizzled out, following the usual pattern. Another pleasant, but not important female personality had joined the few others in the shadowy gallery of his memory. He had a letter from her in his pocket now. It was the kind he had received before . . . resigned and faintly chilling. I'm nearly forty, he thought, and heading for permanent bachelorhood and too much whiskey drinking at the Bath Club. He smiled to himself at the picture.

The engine noise changed pitch and the plane began to

nose down, beginning the long run in to Barajas Airport.

There was an hour's wait for Gibraltar passengers. The Madrid passengers disappeared into the airport, to the customs check and the waiting coaches and taxis. John Richmond went to the transit restaurant and sat on the terrace in the sun watching the airport activity. It was hot and the air full of the sharp smell of burnt-up earth and Spanish tobacco smoke. A shadow fell across his table and a man's voice, pleasant and educated but with a slight regional background to it that could have been West Country, said, "Major Richmond?"

He looked up but gave no nod of assent. A dark-haired, good-looking young man of about twenty-eight was standing by the table. He wore a smart, well-cut dark blazer with monogrammed silver buttons, sharply creased flannel trousers and suède shoes. In one hand he carried a greenish-coloured, rather foreign-looking trilby hat. Standing with his back to the sun his face was in shadow but from its long, intelligent length two features refused to be subdued. The eyes were large, dark and well spaced with very fine lashes, delicately but firmly lined like a meticulous but not very inspired drawing, and the lips were broad and heavy.

"It is Major Richmond, isn't it?" he said, and with a flash of good-natured boyishness underlined with understanding he ran on: "It's on the passenger list. And, anyway, you passed me in the corridor outside Banstead's office the day before yesterday. I'm Grayson, A.D.C. to Sir George Cator."

"Oh, yes . . ." John Richmond stirred slightly and with one hand made a faint movement towards the empty chair on the other side of the table.

Grayson sat down and the thick lips parted showing small, very regular teeth. It was a wide, engaging, almost professional smile. He slipped his hand into his breast pocket and slid his passport across the table. John opened it. It was made out to Neil Grayson.

"Shocking photograph," said Grayson. John turned over the pages of the passport slowly.

Something about the deliberateness and caution irritated

Grayson. But he was careful not to show it. You got nowhere by showing your less flattering reactions to other people. He sat there watching John Richmond, matching the things he knew about him already—he had spent two hours the previous day briefing himself on Richmond—with his first impression of the man himself. He marked the comfortable tweed suit, so well cut that it would be worn a little untidily on the big frame; a gold wristlet watch with a worn strap, the lilies of the Magdalen College tie, the light-weight, highly polished brogues, the flash of a crested signet ring as the passport was returned to him, and then the fat, old-fashioned silver cigarette-case that followed it and was held open for him.

"It's quite a good photograph. Mine looks like a criminal with a hangover."

It was said easily, wiping away all formality. An easiness of manner, thought Grayson, which he had had to fight for and which came naturally to Richmond. And he had a wide sense of all the things which had come naturally to Richmond . . . education, the right friends, and position. But he had to admit that Richmond carried them all without a thought for their value.

"We've some time to wait, sir. Would you like a coffee?"

"Thank you."

Grayson called a waiter and ordered coffee. He spoke in Spanish and added some pleasant comment to the waiter just to show how good his Spanish was, and the moment he had shown wished he hadn't, and he knew then that he had written Richmond down in his book as someone worth knowing, someone who could be useful to him.

Over coffee Grayson said, "I've been on leave, but because of this business I've been called back."

"How are you travelling?"

"I came in on the London plane with you, but I was up forward so you didn't see me. I go on to Gib and then tonight I shall be with you on the destroyer *Dunoon*."

"I see." And then, making it quite clear that there was no wish to talk more about official business in an open café, "Do you know Madrid?"

"Not well."

11

"Pity we haven't more time here. We could have run in and had a look at the Prado. My mother used to drag me round it when I was a boy. Later on I found there was no need for dragging."

"Banstead tells me you've got quite a collection of paintings."

"I buy more than I can really afford. I tell myself it's an investment . . . I hope I'm right."

Without any envy—he'd long learned to keep that out of the way—Grayson thought of his own mother. She'd dragged him around too, not over the length and breadth of Europe pointing out palaces and paintings, but to help carry her shopping from the Co-operative Stores and to deliver her dress-making bundles to people's houses. He smiled to himself at the picture. Actually she had done very well from her wise shopping and the extra money she had earned to supplement his father's wages. Her ambition for him had been no less fierce than his own . . . a State Scholarship to Oxford —not Magdalen, though—and then a brilliant First and eventually the Colonial Office and now, but only as a further step in the ladder, A.D.C. to Sir George Cator. For that he could thank his father who had taught him to play a much better than average game of rugby football. An invitation to play in the Sir George Cator XV during an Oxford vacation had not been neglected. Cator had gone into the book, too, as someone worth knowing . . .

He said, "You're Royal West Kents, aren't you, sir?"

"Yes. But I haven't done Regimental duty for a long time . . . Not since the war."

"I missed the war. Too young. But I did two years after Varsity with the Coldstreams . . ."

John nodded. He was thinking of something Banstead had said about Grayson. "Grayson is a thruster. He's going to finish up in Parliament . . . the Cabinet. Maybe he even dreams of being P.M. in twenty years. He'll use any hold to climb." He wondered if he was looking at a future Prime Minister. Good luck to him, anyway, if that was what he wanted. At least he wanted something badly . . .

Somewhere a loudspeaker spat and crackled and then announced the departure of the Gibraltar plane. They walked out together on to the blinding white concrete apron to the waiting Viscount.

Grayson moved back to sit in the seat opposite John across the gangway. They talked for a while desultorily and then John went to sleep. He'd left his home at Benenden in Kent very early that morning to drive up to the Air Terminus in London by half-past seven. Normally he would have stayed in town the night, but this job had been sprung on him suddenly and there were last-minute details to arrange at Sorby Place with his farm bailiff and the housekeeper. The farm bailiff had driven up with him to take the car back and they had talked business most of the way. On a job like this he might be gone for a few months or it might stretch over into a couple of years . . . He shut his eyes seeing in his mind the early June dawn with a wisp of mist floating low over the smooth stretch of the village green and the dark plugs of the yews bold against the light grey stone of the church . . . He went away and he came back, and nothing seemed to change. Not even himself. It was a pretty, placid picture, dull, and at times even boring. Maybe what he lacked was the thing Grayson had, a burning ambition . . . or something like that.

Across the way Neil Grayson watched him sleeping. He was a big man, but nothing of his bigness sprawled or sagged. The kind of man who didn't have to exercise hard to keep in trim. The light brown hair was cut short—and without a doubt, Grayson guessed, by Mr. Trumper of Curzon Street—and there was a slight bleaching, it couldn't be called greying, at the temples. He was near forty, he knew. Some men have an optimum age which suits their bodies and temperaments and which they preserve. Major Richmond had just reached his and would stay with it for a long time. The face interested Neil. In his life people who might be useful or who might be opposed to him were put under a shrewd and careful analysis. It was the better type of Army face; square and with a strong sense of repose and deliberation. When this man gave an order he meant it and showed it without any touch of dictating. Drinking their coffee at the airport he had been intrigued by the alertness of the blue eyes when he smiled. Richmond was the kind of man, he felt, who had gone into the Army without much thought, but had found there something which satisfied him. He marked him as a man who obviously had influence in his Parliamentary constituency, a Conservative because it had never occurred to him that he could be anything else . . . a man whose friendship could be useful when the time came for influence. In his diary for the future he made a note that as soon as he and Richmond were back in England he would arrange an invitation for himself to Sorby Place.

Reaching for his briefcase and pulling a book from it he smiled at that thought of Sorby Place. Richmond had lived there all his life, and his family for donkey's years before him . . . one family and several centuries in the same house. Before he himself had left Oxford, his family had lived in over two dozen different furnished rooms and shabby houses. It takes all sorts, he told himself, to make a world, and the right sort to make the best of it . . . and that's going to be you, Neil Grayson. Keep at it, old chap.

He turned the book over in his hands and looked at the coloured wrapper. It was done in striking greens, yellows and blues and showed in the foreground a stiff, stylized frieze of banana trees and rising behind them, capped with a ring of cloud, the rocky cone of an old volcano. The title read— *The Islands of San Borodon, by Janet Harker*. He flipped open the cover. The fly-leaf was inscribed in a scrawling feminine hand—*To darling Neil, with love, Janet*. He made a little mouth as he read this and then pulled a penknife from his pocket and neatly cut out the fly-leaf. It wouldn't do to have the book lying around Government House with an inscription like that in it. Janet had been in Port Carlos two years ago collecting material for the book and he had seen her again this time in London. She made a lot of money from these gushy travel books of hers and she was generous with it and with herself. It was all very pleasant, but no more. When it came to marriage you had to pick the right woman . . . the right woman could spirit away obstacles and open the doors that a man wanted to pass through . . .

Having cut out the fly-leaf, he put the book back in his case. He had no intention of reading it. He knew all about the little colony of San Borodon, and, anyway, Janet's prose style

14

was like her love making, warm and caressing and full of breathless exclamation marks.

It was a still night. A pale slip of moon hung low over her own reflection on the smooth water. Dropping behind them, almost lost now were the lights of Gibraltar. The only sounds were routine and domestic, making of H.M.S. *Dunoon* a little world of contented isolation on the dark waters. Faintly from the mess deck came the soft sound of an accordion, under-scored with the low throb of the engines and the light-hearted, running *slap, slap* of the water along her sides that streamed astern in a brilliant, phosphorescent wake.

Sitting in his bridge shelter Lieutenant-Commander Edward Burrows, D.S.O., Teddy Burrows to his friends, said, "Don't pretend to understand the political ins and outs of this kind of thing. Got a feeling, too, that the big boys aren't all that sure of what they're doing. Mostly they just work to a rule of thumb and look wise."

"This situation is a pretty clear one," said John Richmond. He was changed now into uniform, bush shirt, drill trousers and a lightweight tunic. Because of the meeting ahead he wore his ribbons and a tie.

"Don't try to explain it to me. If a man's a nuisance get rid of him. Cut off his head or lock him up in the Tower. That's all there is to it." Burrows grunted and gave a horse-like, violent sniff. "Everybody doubled-up to make room for a lot of Wogs. Even bringing his damned harem with him. I'd like to hear the lower-deck on that one . . ."

He laughed, the sound breaking through the quiet night. He was a big man and when he laughed his body shook to its foundations. His face was square and there seemed to be too much of it even for his bulk. Shaggy eyebrows and crudely moulded cliff-sides of cheek, a large, good-natured mouth . . . his character and temperament matched his appearance, frank, sprawling, a man who didn't even notice the toes he trod on. His hands were massive, awkward and strong, adroit only on a boat.

"There's no harem, as you know," said John. "Only his wife, and she's English."

"So I heard. What's he doing with an English wife, eh?"

15

"Much the same as any man does with any wife, I imagine." John smiled. "She didn't have to come with him, you know. So far as she's concerned it's voluntary exile."

"Touching," snorted Burrows. "And what about this Colonel Mawzi? He's a first-class snake by all accounts."

John grinned. "He's a first-class soldier. I've talked to people who've operated against him. Getting him in the bag with Hadid Chebir was a stroke of luck."

"Hadid Chebir . . ." Burrows sighed. "They do have names, don't they? Sounds like Widow Twankey's milkman."

"His name's part of the trouble. When his father was killed the name and the old man's reputation couldn't be escaped. In a place like Cyrenia the name alone can put a couple of thousand men under arms——"

"Don't bother with the staff course lecture. I'm content just to ferry him to San Borodon. After that, he's all yours. Though personally, I'm sorry for you having to play jailer."

Later, lying in the cabin which he was sharing with Burrow's Number One, Lieutenant Imray, he found the word "jailer" sticking in his mind. That's what it was, of course. A high-class jailer. It wasn't the kind of job he would have chosen for himself, but then in the Army one didn't pick one's jobs. They were dished out and you accepted them. To-morrow morning, when the news broke in the papers, he could think of a lot of people he knew who would read of the deportation of Hadid Chebir from Cyrenia to San Borodon. They'd read his name, too . . . and he could hear the comments. "Johnny Richmond doing prison duty on an Atlantic island . . . Well, that'll shake the War Office creases out of him." There'd be a few, perhaps, who'd remember that he and Hadid had been at Oxford together and knew one another slightly. They'd find irony in that.

He got four hours' sleep and was back on the bridge at the first dawn light. Burrows was there with his Number One, and Grayson was wedged in a corner wrapped in a large tweed coat, frowning at the morning with the sour face of a man who hates early rising.

There was a lot of bustle and movement of men, orders being shouted and the *click, click* of an Aldis lamp. The sea had a dark, oily shine, no life in it.

16

Grayson said, "There she is, over there."

He nodded ahead and John made out a trail of smoke and the dark hull shape, still low down, about a mile ahead of them. They closed up rapidly and very soon the two ships were lying less than a hundred yards apart. The other was a steam yacht, flying the Cyrenian flag. Along her port bow ran the name *Khamsa*.

Burrows came over to them. "They've changed her name," he said. "She used to belong to one of these Greek shipping millionaires. Knew her as the *Pandora*. Lord love me, look at the way they're handling that launch!"

There was a great deal of shouting on the deck of the *Khamsa*, and a small motor launch that was being swung out on the davits suddenly went down with a run and was checked just before she reached the water, her bows about three feet higher than her stern. A gangway was lowered, the launch manned and for a while there was a passage of men up and down the gangway carrying cases.

"Why the hell do they need all that luggage?" asked Burrows.

Grayson smiled. "This may be a long visit, Teddy. One likes to have one's little bits and pieces around one."

"Well, this is a destroyer, not a bloody liner. Come on, Richmond, we'd better get down and make up the reception committee. Remember, old boy, this is your show and I'm leaving it to you. You know the lay-out. Where they go and what they do."

The sun came up over the rim of the sea as they reached the quarter deck. The *Dunoon's* gangway was down and the launch was bearing in towards them with a little white bone of broken water at her bows. The shadows of Burrows and his officers stretched long across the deck, and the little wind that had begun to come up with the dawn flirted gently at the wide collars of the ratings. The flat Portsmouth face of a petty officer twitched as he eyed the pile of suitcases in the stern of the launch and then grimaced as the launch came awkwardly alongside and took a six-inch score of white paint off her bows.

Richmond heard Burrows breathe, "Bloody wogs." He smiled to himself. For Burrows the whole world was split into the British and bloody wogs. There was no malice in the division. It was just a clumsiness of thought which he guessed spread right through the man, colouring all his attitudes and probably explaining why he would never get any real promotion in the Navy . . . The thought died in him as the party from the *Khamsa* came up the gangway.

The reception was very correct, very formal, but no honours were paid except a brief exchange of salutes and introductions.

Within ten minutes the *Dunoon* was heading west for the Straits with the San Borodon islands forty-eight hours ahead of her.

There were four of them. In the wardroom they made a silent, patently hostile group at the far end of the long table. Hadid Chebir sat with his elbows on the table, his face half-hidden by the cupped hands around his chin and mouth. He wore an old raincoat with the collar turned up and a green scarf was wrapped about his throat. Sitting on his left was Colonel Mawzi in khaki drill trousers and tunic, the tunic cut so that it buttoned tight against his throat. On his shoulder tabs were badges of rank unfamiliar to John, a scimitar surmounted by an eagle. The Cyrenian National Army . . . Only, John thought, it wasn't truly National. Just a bunch of pretty well-trained irregulars who knew all there was to know about sabotage and guerilla warfare. His hands, one of which held a cigarette in a dumpy bone holder, were spread across the forage cap on the table in front of him. To Hadid Chebir's right sat his wife. She wore a loose camel-haired coat over a white dress but John could see little of her face because her head was bowed. She seemed to be examining an ink spot on the brown table-cloth, appearing not to listen or even to be aware of anyone else. Behind them, his back resting against the sideboard, stood the servant they had brought aboard, a small, elderly man with a grey growth of stubble light against his brown skin. He wore a little black skull cap, a white tunic with unpolished brass buttons, and tight black trousers ending well above his ankles. His feet were bare. He gave the impression of having been to a fancy-dress party and now, caught by the dawn and his own fatigue, was feeling his age. He stared at the back of Hadid Chebir's head with the

18

same kind of intense interest that Madame Chebir was giving to her ink spot.

For the moment, to John, they were just a group of people without much separate personality, people who regarded him with no liking, whose concern with themselves left them no interest in others. Circumstance was going to force him to spend a lot of time with them . . . they would come alive and he would know them well. But at this moment they were just shapes with little more than the promise of personality. Even Hadid Chebir's face as he had come aboard and for a moment or two the new sunlight had fallen on it had been no more than a hazy extension of his distant Oxford recollection of the man.

Feeling the stiffness in him induced by their hostility, yet understanding it and, therefore, anxious to keep all parade ground manner from his voice, he said, "Captain Burrows and his officers and I will do all we can to make you comfortable while you're aboard. But you will appreciate that there is not much room on a destroyer, so things may be a little cramped."

Colonel Mawzi looked up. He held the cigarette and its holder in front of him vertically like a white exclamation mark and said, "Why do you assume that we understand English?"

"Your leader Hadid Chebir was at Oxford for four years. Madame Chebir, I understand, is an Englishwoman——"

"Was." The voice came muffled from Madame Chebir and her head did not stir.

"And you, Colonel, spent three years in America. However, if you wish only to speak your own language an interpreter can be provided."

Colonel Mawzi lowered the cigarette holder so that it became a pointing white bone of a finger. "It will not be necessary, Major Richmond."

"There is a cabin for Madame Chebir and her husband. And one for you, Colonel. Your servant will be looked after on the lower deck."

The Colonel stood up. He was a very short, neat-looking man, well into his fifties though the dark hair, brushed back brutally, showed no sign of greyness. His looks matched his reputation which John had refreshed himself about before leaving London. He was a hard, dedicated man, so full of purpose that one half-expected to hear the faint hum of some inner dynamo that powered him. Facing him one forgot his shortness, aware only of his quiet strength and the dark, unruffled intricacy of his thoughts. He was half Arab and half Turk and the lean, wedge-shaped face looked as though it had been sliced into shape with a dozen rapid knife slashes. The only softness was in the extraordinary length of his eyelashes that curled above his dark eyes gracefully and took even more emphasis from the fact that his eyebrows were practically non-existent.

"The cabin arrangements must be altered," said the Colonel. "Madame Chebir is very exhausted and would prefer to be on her own. I will share the cabin with Hadid."

"As you wish. Your meals you will take here alone. Your servant will attend to you. As the weather is hot Captain Burrows has given orders for a small portion of the deck to be reserved for you and an awning will be erected. . . ."

I might, thought John, be a sea-side landlady crying up the advantage of my lodgings. There wasn't any doubt in his mind that they were going to be awkward prisoners and that a great deal of his time was going to be spent smoothing out troubles. Well, that's what he was paid for. . . .

"How long will it be before we reach San Borodon?"

It was the Colonel again. The other two might have been dead for all the interest they were taking.

"Roughly two days to Port Carlos."

"And then?"

"The arrangements for your . . ." John hesitated, rejecting the word "detention", and before he could go on Colonel Mawzi without humour or charm said:

"Let us call it accommodation, Major."

"All this will be explained to you by Sir George Cator, the Governor. I am not at liberty to say more than that I shall accompany you wherever you go. Anything which it is in my power to do for you——"

John got no further than that. At this moment Madame Chebir stood up quickly.

"For God's sake," she cried, "let's finish with all this! All right, anything in your power you'll do. You'll be nice and

20

polite to us and if the bath water's cold we complain to you. And if we don't behave you'll put us on bread and water——"

Hadid Chebir's hand came up and gripped her tightly on the elbow. He didn't say anything, he just held her, his fingers biting into the material of her coat sleeve. She was breathing heavily from her outburst. John could see that she was close to tears. She was a tall woman, little more than thirty, and more attractive than her photographs. She was no longer dead, a shape without speech. She stood there, her face alive with emotion. This was the almost legendary Madame Chebir, John thought. The woman with "Cyrenia" carved on her heart. Well, obviously she was pretty worked up at the moment. She had reason to be, he thought—things had crumpled around her and Hadid Chebir. He liked the look of her face, it had force and feeling. It was a pity he was going to be her jailer—a fortnight in Spain would have been more the mark. Nevertheless, he had no intention of being bullied by her.

"I can't promise about the plumbing in Mora," he said easily. "But I'll see you don't get bread and water."

Hadid Chebir smiled and his hand dropped slowly from her elbow, but he still said nothing. It was Colonel Mawzi who spoke.

He said, "Madame Chebir is overwrought. She has had a very difficult time."

"I understand," said John.

"He understands!" She laughed and raised her eyebrows with a sudden comical expression. "The very correct Major Richmond understands." She turned away from the table and moved towards the door. "I should like to go to my cabin."

She walked easily, the coat swinging away from her dress. John drew back the curtain from the doorway for her. Neil Grayson was standing outside.

John said, "Madame Chebir is going to her cabin. Would you show her? The one which was to have been for Colonel Mawzi."

Grayson gave Madame Chebir a little bow as she came to the doorway. She stopped for a moment and looked at John. Her eyes were tired and he could see she needed sleep. Momentarily her hand went up and touched one temple with a weary gesture. He saw the glint of a plain gold wedding ring and the glitter of heavy stones from two other rings. A little turn of sudden anger twisted in him . . . She was out of place, shouldn't have been mixed up in all this. Hadid Chebir and Colonel Mawzi knew what to expect . . . they were hard and understood force. The bitterness of defeat only made them more dangerous.

For a moment he thought she was going to speak to him, saw her mouth partly open to begin something and then she thought better of it and went through the doorway to Grayson.

Colonel Mawzi said, "Abou!"

The servant padded across on his bare feet and followed Madame Chebir to attend to her.

When they were gone Hadid Chebir pushed his chair back and stood up. As he did so Colonel Mawzi moved back a foot to stand slightly behind him and to his left. It was a movement that took John's attention, as though the man were falling back instinctively to a defensive, guarding position, taking up a station which was familiar . . . This way they had walked warily through the night along the bare ridge paths of their homeland, ready to strike, sustained by a passion which had burned out all others in them. For a second or two, surprising even himself, he was aware of the futility of trying to contain men like this with troops and tanks.

Hadid rested the tips of his fingers on the table before him and his head was lifted for the first time full towards John. It was a fine face, lean, intelligent, the eyes deep sunk, the skin taut and healthy with a fine grain to it and lighter now than John remembered from Oxford, but the same face grown older, the remembered vitality replaced by a severe nobility. He loosened the scarf at his throat with a little gesture and said in a slightly husky but pleasant voice:

"We are men, Major Richmond, and understand what is happening. But my wife . . ." Just for a moment the shoulders lifted and it marked all the distinction he drew between men and women. "Her decision to accompany me voluntarily was a difficult one. She feels strongly for me and shows it. You must not think her rudeness to you was personal." He smiled for an instant and went on, "She does not understand the politeness and respect men often feel for their enemies. What is your regiment?"

The question didn't surprise John. All the time the man had been speaking he had waited for some shadow of recognition. It would have been out of place in the circumstances for him to bring it forward, but he had wondered whether Hadid would remember. But although the dark, deep-set eyes had been full on him they weren't recognizing him as any other than a soldier in uniform, a figure of authority and restraint. For Hadid yet he was less a man than a rank and a regiment.

"The Royal West Kents," he answered. "I quite appreciate Madame Chebir's feelings."

Hadid nodded and said, "It is a good regiment. We have met them in Cyrenia. And now we should like to go to our cabin, Major Richmond."

Forward of the bridge on the small space of deck above the wardroom Petty Officer Grogan, with the Portsmouth face, was with a party of three seamen rigging up an awning for the new arrivals. He was thinking without enthusiasm of San Borodon where the *Dunoon* had now been stationed for six months. It had been good to come back into the Med. for a change, even if it was only bloody brief. It would be better still to get back to Portsmouth, though he couldn't see that coming off for a long time. The old woman had written saying she was papering the sitting room. Sure to make a muck of it. She fancied herself at that sort of thing. Last time he'd gone back it was to find the kitchen with a yellow ceiling and blue walls. Nearly singed his eyeballs. But there it was. No stopping a woman. Once they made up their mind to a thing . . . Look at this Chebir woman. The buzz had gone round that she needn't have gone with her husband. English, too. That was a rum one.

He walked under the awning and reached up a hand and smacked at the taut canvas.

"Tight as a pig's belly," he said.

"You think she'll sunbathe out here, chief?" one of the men asked.

He looked at the man and said nothing, but the men

23

laughed. When Grogan looked and said nothing it was very expressive and not usually complimentary.

Close to A turret Lieutenant Imray and Neil Grayson had their backs to the port guard rail. A couple of seamen in overalls were slapping grey paint over the armour casing of the gun and whistling gently. The sun was well up now and there was a growing strength in it.

Imray, young, and not long engaged to a doctor's daughter in Herefordshire, was very much in love and not yet through the delicate pomposity of a man handling a new and fascinating possession. A year ago he used to wake up feeling excited and pleased and realize it was because he was thinking of a new sports car his father had given him. Now the doctor's daughter had taken the place of the car. The behaviour patterns of men and women in love were like a newly discovered parlour game to him. Grayson who had known him for six months at Port Carlos thought he was an engaging half-baked adolescent.

"I'm not surprised at what she's done," Imray was saying. "She loves her husband, so she sticks by him and goes into voluntary exile with him. Anyone can understand that. What I do find odd is why she should have married a man like that . . . You know, not European? Must cut her off from her family and friends."

Grayson chuckled. "She hasn't got any family and friends. Not the way you understand things. Her father's a window cleaner in Swindon or somewhere like that. He'll get free beer at the pub on this story for a week and maybe a few guineas from some London rag for his story. She was on her own from about the age of sixteen, worked at a draper's in Swindon and then went to London and was a ribbon girl at Harrod's——"

"How do you know all this?"

"Oh, wake up, Imray. You don't think the authorities would dump this lot on San Borodon without briefing us. She was at Harrod's store when she first met Hadid. He was at the London School of Economics. They never looked back. I don't blame him. She's a damned fine looking girl and she's learnt how to talk and walk and dress and behave——"

"But that's the point. She's so attractive she could have done well for herself——"

Grayson gave a little snort of impatience. Really, some of these blokes were practically still in the egg.

"Listen, Hadid Chebir is a highly cultured, intelligent man. He's not a native as you would call it. And he's worth half a million. Show me a girl with a counter job and a Swindon accent who can do better than that. And don't forget"—his mouth gave a humorous twist as he fired the shaft—"she loved him. Love conquers all, colour, race and creed. Or maybe that hasn't seeped through to the wilds of Herefordshire yet?"

Imray frowned, annoyed. "There's no need to be like that. The people of Herefordshire are the same as anyone else. Delia, for instance, has the most advanced views about—— "

Grayson put on a listening but not hearing face, shuddering inwardly at the thought of Imray's Delia who probably had thick legs and smelt of horses.

There was a water reflection through the porthole dancing on the wall above her bunk. In a row of ugly pipes at the top of the wall water made an intermittent clanking sound. For a moment or two in the wardroom Marion Chebir knew she had been on the point of letting go. She had felt battered and nervous and ready to scream. Hadid's grip on her arm had stopped that. Two years . . . and everything had changed. The Hadid who had taken her to Cyrenia, taken her everywhere, Europe and America, opened a new world for her and given her a new personality, had gone. The Hadid whose hand came out, fingers biting into her flesh, had nothing for her.

She stirred and kicked off her shoes. They fell from the end of the bunk with a thud. She reached out and drank the rest of the water from the glass which Abou had brought her for her aspirin.

Hadid had no real need of her now. They meant nothing to one another. But Mawzi had insisted that she came. Politically her presence with them was important. Mawzi had assessed its emotional and propaganda advantages. He saw it in terms of men and arms and world opinion. But Mawzi didn't trust her. In the past it had been different. She had worked for Cyrenia, lectured abroad, been a courier

25

and an agent for them, entertained and turned on the charm
when they wanted money from someone, and once or twice
she had even shared their campaigns, riding hard with them
and living rough. She had obeyed the two of them; hypno-
tized by the past and by her power of a dedication still alive
in her, and unable to deny the force behind the great loyalty
of her love for Hadid as he had once been. What would have
happened if she had stuck out against coming, refused to
budge from Tunis to come to them? As though she could . . .
she laughed drily to herself. When Hadid and Mawzi wanted
something they took a lot of stopping. The British were
finding that out. The British! God, she could even think of
them as though they had nothing to do with her.

She lay back and put her palms under her head and her
hair pushed up by her fingers in disorder lay dark against the
white pillow. If anyone had ever told her as a girl that she
would be here, that so many things would have happened to
her . . . but, come to think of it, somebody had. With another
girl from Harrod's she had gone to a fortune-teller once.
Somewhere in Montpelier Square, and she remembered how
the two of them had gone giggling up the stairs, and then the
woman, her breath smelling of pickled onions, saying
banally, "You'll travel far, like a bird, but it will be long
before you find a place to rest. But don't worry, dearie,
happiness is waiting . . ."

Happiness, she supposed, was always waiting at the end or
the fortune tellers would be out of business. And the next
week she had met Hadid and she was swept off her feet and
up to the skies with happiness. Nothing her family could say
made any difference. She could see them sitting round the
kitchen table in the Swindon council house. Already she was
a stranger to them with her London ways and her voice
almost free of the Wiltshire accent. Dear Mum, how worried
and anxious she had been, with that little tremble of the
upper lip which meant she was near to tears, the movement
they all knew and which brought her father's hand out to
give his wife's arm a rough caress. "Cheer up, Ma. Why
shouldn't she marry him? He's a nice chap and he can't
'elp 'is colour. What's colour anyway? He ain't no more than
a nice sunburn."

But Mum couldn't see it. With her nice ways and talk she could have married a bank clerk, done well for herself, and they would all have been proud of her before the neighbours. But the neighbours couldn't understand Hadid. He was a foreigner, a native . . . Didn't they have half a dozen wives? Hadid had never known how close she had come to not marrying him because of her mother . . . the childish, anxious woman, full of courage although she was so fearful, who kept her little bits of household budget money in envelopes on top of the kitchen mantelpiece . . . the insurance, the rent, the shoe repairs, the grocery and the meat; and the holiday envelope that never had more than enough to take them for a day's outing to Eastbourne. Bread and dripping when Dad was out of work, and herself going off to school in a gym frock bought secondhand and too large for her, turned up, tucked in, so that she could grow into it with the years. The agony of not having clothes like the other children . . . All this, an age away now. Maybe she should have married a bank clerk and had a daily help and two children and her Mum over to tea once a week.

"I like him, yes, and he couldn't be more respectful, but . . ."

"He's all right, Ma. Stands up in the local there with us all and takes 'is beer just like the next man. He's a fine chap and God gave 'im 'is colour. Don't you worry, Ma. He'll look after our Marion."

And her sister in the shared bedroom for the week-end. "Really, sis, I don't see how you could let him touch you." That had made her angry.

And her brother, older and already married, working in the railway shops, hard but kind. "You marry him, kid. If that's what you want. But it won't be a bed of roses. Ma'll get over it. You know her. Has a good cry Monday mornin' for all the milk that's goin' to be spilt durin' the week. Marry 'im and give yourself a leg-up. No one else will do it for you."

They'd all seen it differently. Not one had seen it her way. But Hadid had seen it her way and their way and every way. For that alone she would always be grateful . . . loyal.

"Your family is the same as hundreds in my own country. They are the people who make countries . . . poor and honest

27

and proud. They suspect strangeness because they must. They have enough troubles without inviting new ones. They have their fears and their hardships, but they understand them. Why should they take on strange ones? But already you have left them and you cannot go back . . ."

What would they say now, she wondered, when they read the news? Not a great deal, perhaps. But the feeling would be there. Her mother, older now, but not so active, putting on her hat and taking up her shopping bag and going down to the butcher's shop . . . and that upper lip tight to stop the tremble as she faced the other women who would have read the newspapers over the uncleared breakfast tables . . . She was suddenly, bleakly full of homesickness as she pictured it. It was so far away and yet so near. Nothing you could do could stop that ache that came for them . . . you sent them money, but they wouldn't take much. You wrote but your letters never said the things you wanted to say. You couldn't go back. Marion Heath was dead. Long ago. Marion Chebir, now. And now part of Marion Chebir was dead. Quite clearly now she understood that she should never have come from Tunis. But it was too late now. She was committed to her part.

Staring at the deck above she said aloud, "Damn Hadid and damn Mawzi. I hate them both." And then she turned over and pressed her face against the pillow, feeling the tremble, too, in her upper lip, and the wet softness of the tears she tried to keep from her eyes.

2

THEY gave no trouble. They had their meals alone in the wardroom and then left. Most of the time they spent in their cabins or else under the deck awning. Even when they were all three together under the awning there was little conversation between them. Madame Chebir read a book she had picked up in the wardroom and Hadid, his throat wrapped in a scarf, spent most of the hours sleeping.

Colonel Mawzi seemed the least affected of them all by their present circumstances. He neither read nor slept during the day. He sat, watching with interest everything that went on around him. Sometimes as though the restlessness in his short active body was too much he would get up and walk the small length of deck allotted to them, going to and fro like a caged animal. The other two took no notice of his restlessness, as though they had known it too long, were so used to it that it no longer had any power to irritate them. He was always, too, the last to retire to his cabin. After dinner he would come back on to the deck and the glow of his cigarette could be seen in the purple darkness.

The first night, after dinner, John went to the cabin which he shared with Imray and wrote his official diary of the day's procedures and after that a longer, more personal document which he intended eventually to send to Banstead. He had been asked to keep his eyes open and, since he didn't know in the slightest what it was that he was expected to see, he had decided to record everything which seemed of any interest. Reading over his notes to Banstead, trying to put himself in Banstead's place and wondering what would interest him most, he could pick out nothing except his comment about Madame Chebir.

> Her manner I found a little puzzling. She wasn't with Hadid or Colonel Mawzi when these two were caught in the El Geffa hills. That they should be exhausted and played out after being on the run for a week I can understand. But they show little signs of it. Madame Chebir, however, gave the impression of someone under strain. Yet we know she was in Tunis when they were caught and immediately flew back to Cyrenia to join her husband and chose voluntary exile with him. As you know, I'm not very hot on female psychology, or any other, but when you sacrifice yourself, choose to go to prison on principle, it seems odd to be immediately bitchy to the first prison warder (me, old boy) that you meet.

John locked the report away in his brief-case and sat back, thinking about the girl. All the afternoon she had sat under the awning in a yellow linen dress and a light scarf round her shoulders. At one point he noticed that she had kicked off her sandals. It was a small thing but it put her comfortably for a moment back into the category of so many other women he had known. They were always kicking off their shoes, under restaurant tables, in theatres . . . and then you had to get down on your hands and knees with a cigarette lighter to

look for them. Suddenly a little spasm of irritation took him.
She was a damn fool. No English girl with an ounce of sense
should have married Hadid. By the time he'd left Oxford and
gone on to the London School of Economics it was quite
clear what was in store for him. Cyrenia had killed and made
a martyr of his father and he couldn't avoid the mantle
falling on him. No matter about his money, his good looks
and charming personality, only a girl who never took the
trouble to read the newspapers could have missed what was
going to happen.

He got up and went out on deck for a breath of fresh air.
It was a warm, mild night with a slight north wind blowing.
They were well through the Straits and heading into the
Atlantic on a south-westerly course. Carried on the wind
John imagined he could smell the land away on their star-
board quarter . . . a vague smell of Spain, scented, a little
pungent. A school of porpoises was running abreast of them,
cutting the water into creamy green flares of phosphores-
cence as they surfaced. There was a glow of subdued light
from the bridge and a plume of smoke from the *Dunoon's*
stack flared away low and heavy across the dark waters.

Abreast of the deck awning he saw the sudden glow of a
cigarette and Colonel Mawzi's face was illuminated for a
moment. The man was leaning on the guard rail, his face half
turned to the sea.

He said quietly, "Major Richmond."

John stopped a yard from the man.

"Yes, Colonel?"

"Hadid's throat is very sore. It is an infection he gets from
time to time. The prescription is very simple . . ." His hand
went to his tunic pocket and a piece of crumpled paper was
held out.

John took it.

"I'll send it along to the sick bay. They'll look after it."

"Thank you."

John would have passed on, but the Colonel turned fully
towards him and tipped his cigarette holder in the direction
of the gun turret. In the shadows an armed sailor was
standing.

"It is necessary, Major, for these guards? Outside our

30

cabins, outside the wardroom when we eat, and here?"

"I'm afraid so."

Colonel Mawzi laughed gently. "What do you think we would do? Sabotage the engines, or jump overboard?"

John smiled. None of the questions was serious. There was no hint of complaint behind them. He guessed that Colonel Mawzi just wanted to talk.

"If you were in my place, Colonel, would you withdraw the guards?"

"Of course not." It was said with amusement. And then, as he fitted another cigarette to his holder, "And if you were in my place, Major, would you commit suicide or try to escape?"

"I can't see that suicide would do you much good. Escape, yes. But the *Dunoon* is hardly the place for it." Most of his instinct told John not to get into this kind of talk. He had a place and a distance to keep, but he had also been given an over-riding instruction to get to know all he could about these people. He couldn't do one without sacrificing the other. But he had every intention of preserving a careful balance between them.

"Some years ago," said the Colonel, going easily off on another tack and by that ease acknowledging that John was prepared to talk for a while, "a battalion of your regiment, the West Kents, was in Cyrenia."

"I know."

"They were good soldiers. It is curious about soldiers . . . the military life is almost a form of religion. Although we fight, you and I, there is little hatred. In fact, some sort of love. Only behind the soldiers stand the things and the people we hate."

"This applies to both sides."

"Of course." He had a way of saying the phrase, curtly but without offence, that seemed to wrap a subject up and dispose of it. "One of your officers was a prisoner of ours for a time. A Lieutenant Rawford. He escaped after four days, stealing my own jeep." He laughed. "The jeep, of course, had been stolen by us originally from one of your dumps outside El Geffa. He also took my own personal bottle of whiskey. For this I had paid highly. You know him?"

31

"No. But I read his intelligence report on his capture and escape. He made no mention of the bottle of whiskey."

Colonel Mawzi chuckled, and then suddenly the sound was cut off and he came forward a step and the movement seemed to take him out of one character into another, as though mentally and physically he had crossed some border. He stood stiff and alert and his voice was abrupt. "You cannot hold down half a million people who want to run their own country. Not by force, not by bullets nor by imprisonment. To deny it is to deny history. We shall win."

For a moment the change surprised John. Then he understood. The man's passion was a pain inside him. Just for a while the pain had gone. Now it was back and he had to voice it. It was a fanaticism which he had to follow. And it was just that which made him dangerous.

"We shall win!" he repeated.

John said, "I'll go and see about this prescription for you. Good night, Colonel."

Andrews, sick bay attendant, filled the medicine bottle with the greenish looking liquid he had made up and slapped the cork home with a firm smack of his hand. He was a pale, freckle-faced young man with a pugnacious mouth.

"See what I mean," he said with mock anger. "The moment any bloody foreigner gets among the English he starts to take advantage of the National Health Service!"

"Poison is what he wants." One of the cooks who had scalded his hand was taking an easy cigarette in the sick bay. "My brother-in-law caught a packet in Cyrenia."

Andrews took up the prescription and fastened it round the bottle with a rubber band. "Linctus-tinctus and a squirt of hocus-pocus, colour it green and shove it down their throats and they think they're cured. Medicine, cookie, is illusory."

"Sure, I'll take half a pint of that. It's a treat to hear you talk. I'll bet your girl gets her fill of it."

"She gets it all right. But not often enough by me. Well, here we go. I wonder who served Napoleon on the *Bellerophon* with his laxatives."

He went out carrying the bottle and made his way forward. There was an armed guard a little to the right of the door of the cabin which Hadid Chebir and Colonel Mawzi shared. He raised his eyebrows at Andrews who held up the bottle and said, "Night-cap for their Highnesses. You look damned silly standing there, 'specially as your fly-buttons are undone." When the guard looked down at his trousers, Andrews went on with a snort of disgust: "Blimey, still don't know that navy slacks don't have fly-buttons."

He stepped by the guard and knocked on the cabin door. Someone said, "Come in", and he entered, looking as though a lozenge wouldn't melt in his mouth.

Colonel Mawzi was standing in the centre of the little cabin and Hadid Chebir had already turned in on one of the bunks.

"Throat prescription, sir."

Andrews handed over the bottle to Colonel Mawzi.

The Colonel took it and with the movement managed to isolate Andrews in the centre of the room, saying as he did so, "How is it to be taken?"

"On the prescription, sir. Four times a day in water."

"Ah, good. Perhaps you would be kind enough." He placed the bottle by a water container at the side of Hadid's bunk.

Andrews had no choice but to take the glass by the container and prepare a dose. Hadid took no notice of him. But Colonel Mawzi, his back against the cabin door, lit a cigarette and said pleasantly:

"We are grateful to you."

Andrews grunted as he measured out the dose into the glass. Behind him Colonel Mawzi went on conversationally:

"You have been away from England a long time?"

"Too long," said Andrews with sudden feeling and then added, "Sir."

"But you will be going back soon, no doubt? The ship on duty at the San Borodon station is changed from time to time?"

"I don't know, sir." Andrews poured water into the green throat solution and, since neither Hadid nor Colonel Mawzi could see him, stirred it with his forefinger. What he did know, he told himself, was when he was being pumped. He turned to Hadid, holding the glass for him to drink.

Hadid raised himself from the bunk a little and smiled over the top of the glass. It was a great flash of charm and warmth and he said, "You have a good face. If one had to choose whose prisoner to be one would always choose the English."

Andrews who was a Scot and held a different opinion made no comment. Hadid drank and handed him back the glass, and behind him Colonel Mawzi said, "Mr. Chebir is still suffering a little from an old bullet wound in the leg. The muscles stiffen frequently. Perhaps it could be arranged that you come tomorrow and massage it for him?"

Andrews said, "You must clear that with the Captain, sir." And he thought to himself, where do they think they are, bloody Harrogate Spa? Now, if it was Madame Chebir who wanted her legs rubbed . . .

Outside he was so occupied with his thoughts that he was hardly aware of the guard until that gentleman put out a foot and tripped him as he passed, saying:

"That'll teach you to be saucy with me, you lousy pill-roller."

Inside the cabin Hadid, sitting up now on his bunk, said, "You will get nothing from him. They invented the Geneva Convention. Rank, name and number. I know them better than you, Mawzi. They are clams."

Colonel Mawzi shrugged his shoulders. "We have nothing to lose. Everything is worth trying. Every little thing we learn will help. Neglect nothing . . ." And going to the porthole he stared out and suddenly said again but with a surprising ferocity in his voice, "Nothing!"

The next morning, following a request made to the Captain by Colonel Mawzi, John Richmond came into the wardroom just as the three were finishing their breakfast. He gave them good morning and then addressing himself to Hadid Chebir said evenly, "Commander Burrows' compliments. He regrets that he has no qualified masseur aboard. He suggests that if your leg troubles you either your wife or Colonel Mawzi could render you as adequate a service as anyone else on this ship. By tomorrow morning we shall be at Port Carlos. If you have need for skilled medical attention I will put your request to Sir George Cator."

Hadid looked at Colonel Mawzi and the other, after a

34

moment's pause, made a brief motion with his hand and said, "It is nothing. We shall forget it."

"Very good."

As John turned away to leave the room, he saw Madame Chebir watching him and there was a faint smile about her lips. And he knew why she was smiling, too. His formality made him sound like a head waiter. His "Very good" could not have been bettered by anyone at the Savoy. Well, that was all right. If they got a little satisfaction from it all he didn't begrudge it. A lot could be learned from a good waiter. He knew how to deal with awkward customers. And unless his bet was wrong, these three were going to prove just that.

Later, Burrows said to him, "It was a try-on, of course. Bloody nerve. Thought they could pump something out of Andrews."

"It shows the temper of the man," answered John. "Mawzi's no fool. He'll neglect nothing. If you don't try to pump people you'll never find the one with the loose mouth."

Burrows grinned. "Andrews' mouth's loose all right. But not that way. If you ask me Hadid and company don't intend to settle down peacefully. If they can get away and back to Cyrenia, they will."

"That mustn't happen. The effect of a successful escape and return would be tremendous in Cyrenia, probably bring in all the waverers to them and they'd ride through."

"Napoleon and Elba, eh?"

"In a way. The name of Hadid Chebir is like a battle flag."

"Well, I wouldn't like to have to get off Mora." Mora was the name of the smaller of the two islands composing the San Borodon group. "Napoleon never beat St. Helena."

"Maybe not," said John. "But I wonder if he ever thought of it. You can't return twice. What are the chaps like on Mora?" It was the first time he had really thought ahead to Mora and to the details of the job that waited for him. So far it had been nebulous . . . something that could wait. But now with the *Dunoon* cutting through the calm summer seas, bringing the San Borodons nearer every hour, Mora and his life there began to encroach on his thoughts.

"There are about a dozen of them. The Forgotten Force

my blokes call them. Other things, too, they get called. They're a lot of odds and sods. Most of 'em have found a niche in some local home. Gone a bit native, you know. There'll be new blood in the Borodon group. They're all right, but they want jerking together. The sergeant's the best of the bunch. Benson. Good chap, but it's uphill work. I wish you joy of them." He leaned over the bridge, a big, comfortable, unhurried man and watched Colonel Mawzi, Hadid Chebir and his wife come out on to the quarter deck and go forward to their awning. As they disappeared under it, he said:

"She's an attractive girl. But they're all skinny these days, aren't they? Egg and steak diet." But he wasn't thinking of Madame Chebir, he was thinking of his wife, Sir George Cator's daughter, who lived with her father at Port Carlos. He'd never approved of that since he was stationed there. Gave him an advantage over the other officers and the ship's company which he didn't want. Still, old Cator wanted someone to be hostess for him . . . Not that they did much damned entertaining in a hole like Port Carlos.

Grayson came onto the bridge in light fawn trousers, a silk shirt and a foulard round his neck. Burrows disapproved of Grayson and the get-up. Damn it, this was one of Her Majesty's destroyers doing a job of work. He made it look like a Margate steamer.

"Did you hear the B.B.C. news this morning? Nothing but the San Borodons and Hadid Chebir. We're right on the map for once. The Opposition is kicking up a fuss—in pretty poor taste most of it—about high-handed interference in Cyrenian affairs. All the usual stuff. There's a motion for a debate tomorrow and the P.M. is going to make a full statement."

Grayson didn't look at them as he spoke. His eyes were way ahead, watching the sun sparkle on the blue-green waters, and he was imagining the scene in the House. Sometime it would come. He would be there . . . right at the heart of things.

"These bloody Labour people," said Burrows.

John said nothing. Actually the whole affair was highhanded, he thought. But it had to be. That was the dilemma

36

of politics. You made up the rules of the game as you went along; you kept in sight some large, rather shapeless idea of good, but to achieve it you were forced a long way from morality, even from justice . . . He was glad that he had nothing to do with that part of it. I've got three prisoners . . . no, detainees, if you wanted an awkward word . . . and I've got to keep them on Mora until fresh orders come through. As simple as that. At least, he hoped that it would be as simple as that. But it was a soldier's hope in which nothing was taken for granted.

The San Borodons consisted of two islands, San Borodon, the larger of the two, which was roughly an inverted pear-shape, about fifty miles long and nearly twenty miles broad at its widest point; and Mora, which was circular in shape and lay about ten miles due south of San Borodon and formed a full stop below the rather plump exclamation mark of its parent island. Geologists stated that at one time the two islands had been connected by a narrow isthmus. Both were volcanic in origin and Mora, not more than five miles in diameter, was little more than a long-dead volcano rising steeply from the sea. The position of the islands was latitude 34 South and longitude 22 North; that is to say about two hundred miles north-west of Madeira, two hundred and fifty miles due south of the Azores and nearly eight hundred miles due west of the nearest point on the African coast which was Casablanca.

Their early history was obscure. Some historians placed the date of their discovery as early as 1351. Some said they formed part of Pliny's *Purpuriae*. However, most authorities were content with the date of 1421, and named their discoverers as Zarco and Vaz—the famous Portuguese navigators of Prince Henry—who the year before had discovered Madeira. But whereas Madeira had been uninhabited, the San Borodon group was inhabited, like their distant cousins, the Canaries, by an indigenous population—the Guanches—whose ethnological status still presents a problem.

Where the Guanches came from is anyone's guess. Some say—because of their custom of embalming the dead, a practice shared only by the Peruvians and the Egyptians—

that they came from Egypt via the Canaries. Others say they came from Africa and are Berber in origin. Although there are few traces of them left because of the heavy admixture of Spanish and Portuguese blood, the argument still continues. Archaeological research has traced their occupation of San Borodon back to the Stone Age period, and fifteenth and sixteenth century Spanish and Portuguese records describe them as being strongly built, though not tall, good-looking and of a fiery temperament. A type of physique and temperament easily absorbed into the Iberian race.

The Guanches resisted the Portuguese and were only conquered after an intermittent series of invasions that spread over fifty years. The last attack, which finally subdued the island, also practically exterminated the Guanches. The islands which were at that time heavily wooded were set on fire. Those who did not capitulate were smoked out and killed. The fire, which contemporary records say burned for over two years, although the death pyre of the Guanches, was the economic salvation of the islands. The bare hill slopes were terraced and cultivated and bananas, sugar cane, and vines took the place of virgin forest.

In 1580 when Portugal came under the domination of Spain, San Borodon passed to the Spaniards until 1640 when it reverted to the Portuguese. In 1662 on the marriage of Charles II to Catherine of Braganza it again changed hands. Over the matter of Catherine's dowry Charles drove a hard bargain with the Portuguese. To a settlement of half a million pounds in silver, the concession that British subjects could trade with Brazil (until then a jealously guarded Portuguese right) and the transfer of Tangiers and Bombay to the British Crown the little islands of San Borodon were added as a *bonne bouche*.

At first San Borodon was administered by a military governor and a few British troops. During the Napoleonic wars the garrison was strengthened and fortresses built at Port Carlos and also on Mora. After the Congress of Vienna a civilian governor was appointed and the garrisons withdrawn. Eventually its administration became a direct responsibility of the Colonial Office.

During the 1914-1918 war it was bombarded for ten

minutes by a German submarine and three houses at Port Carlos were destroyed and ten people killed. A plaque to their memory is let into the wall of the main square. Between the two world wars Port Carlos was established as a small naval refuelling point. Shortly after war broke out Port Carlos and Mora were nominally garrisoned and a certain amount of arms and ammunition were stored, a provision that was felt necessary in case Spain abandoned her neutrality and attempted to occupy the islands from the Canaries. Men from the islands went into the Navy, the Army and the Merchant Navy and thirty-seven of them never came back. A very fine memorial to them is in the San Borodon church at Port Carlos.

Economically the island of San Borodon had few troubles. There was a thriving banana export trade. Most of the bananas were grown in small holdings and the export handled by a Co-operative of Banana Growers. Vines, tobacco and sugar were the second important crops and at one time there had been a valuable export of cochineal from the colonies of cochineal insects harboured on the cactus all over the island, but the development of synthetics had killed this. From the sea the fishermen as well as catching enough for local consumption also drew large catches of cod which were salted and dried and eventually sent as *bacalao* to Spain and Portugal. The island of Mora was much poorer and less developed. Most of the island was inaccessible by road and the soil much poorer than San Borodon's.

An attempt had been made to attract tourist traffic to the islands but it had failed. Chiefly volcanic in origin, the coast-line rose sheer and broken. With a few exceptions the only beaches were short, rough stretches of crumbled lava or coarse black lava sand. The roads were bad and there was only one hotel in Port Carlos which, although good enough for the people who had to visit the island on business, was not the kind of place to attract holiday folk. Also the smell of drying cod when the wind was in the south took a little getting used to. Only after a couple of months' residence was it no longer obtrusive. Some people never got used to it. After two weeks Sir George Cator had forgotten all about it. But to his daughter, Daphne—Lieutenant-Commander

Burrows' wife—its pungency seemed never to decrease.

The day before, a Sunderland flying-boat of Air Force Coastal Command had arrived at Port Carlos. It lay now, moored to a buoy in the southern curve of the harbour. The outcurving point of land that ran protectingly towards the mouth of the harbour was continued by a short stone breakwater backed by half a dozen oil refuelling tanks. Close to them was the berth where the *Dunoon* lay when she was at Port Carlos. Further round the sweep of the harbour, and closer to the town, were the fish curing sheds and the rows of wooden jetties with their bamboo frame-works, rather like a series of clothes horses, where the salted cod was hung in the open to dry. This morning, because the wind was in the west, the town and harbour were spared the smell of fish.

But wind or no wind Daphne Burrows could smell it. It was the kind of odour which clung. There were times when she imagined that everything smelt of it . . . her clothes, the bed linen, the food she ate and even her skin. Those were the bad times . . . the times she knew when her own sense of frustration, of being held down when she desperately wanted to spread her wings and fly, made her particularly nervous.

Although the flying-boat had no regular schedule, it usually came in once a fortnight with official mail and despatches and the flight from Southampton was used as a training detail for new crews. The captains of the flying-boat changed from time to time.

Looking down now from the terrace of Government House where she was having breakfast with her father, Daphne could see the boat on the far side of the harbour. Last night, with the heat of the day still radiating from the ground, she had driven out with the captain of the flying-boat to Dancey's Hotel and had had dinner with him. Dancey's was no longer a hotel, it was a restaurant used by the handful of people who could afford it on San Borodon. It lay in a small bight of the coast five miles north of Port Carlos and a terraced garden dropped to a concrete swimming apron from which one could dive into three fathoms of clear water. Her companion was a young Squadron Leader and on top of four pink gins they had swum before dinner, both of them

40

exhilarated. In the darkness of the water they had kissed and his hands had been on her body, but that was all that was allowed. She'd come out of the water knowing that she could do what she liked with him, and knowing too that he wasn't what she wanted. To take the edge off the boredom of Port Carlos she permitted herself so much. It was a thing she had drifted into because of the disappointment of her own marriage. But she was already tired of it. Marriage with Teddy Burrows had promised her everything—but when he had decided to stay in the Navy things had begun to fall apart. It was odd, really, because she still had love and affection for him . . . but something had gone.

And because she was fundamentally a forthright person who the moment she saw a thing clearly had an impatience to do something about it, she was wondering now how she could tell her father that she meant to leave Teddy Burrows . . . not just a separation, but a divorce. Her father would be shocked at first. He was easily shocked. And also he was very fond of Teddy and imagined that their marriage was a great success. However, his fondness for her was stronger than any other feeling in him. All her life he had spoiled her. Given the right moment and the right approach she could get anything from him, and she had no intention of handling this in any way except that which would leave their relationship as it had always been.

For a moment she was uneasy with the frankness of her thoughts. She loved Teddy, as much as she could, and she had a very deep love for her father. She wouldn't want to hurt either of them—but what could she do? She had her own life to think about and if it had to be re-shaped then she must do it, tactfully and cleverly. Sir George was a man with a rare but violent temper. She mustn't risk arousing that . . . He gave her a generous allowance, and he was a man of considerable wealth. It would be idiotic to jeopardize either his affection or support.

These morning breakfasts on the terrace were a ritual with them. It was then that they talked things over, made their confidences and their plans. But this morning she knew after five minutes that it would be useless to try and talk to him about herself. She saw that he was excited about this Hadid

41

Chebir affair. He was the Governor. They would be his responsibility and he loved responsibility and importance. He was slapping more marmalade on his toast than he usually did. Normally he confined himself to one cup of coffee. He was already on his second, and with it he lit a cigarette. It was rare indeed that he smoked before lunch. If I mentioned divorce now, she thought, he wouldn't even hear me.

She smiled as she listened to him. Despite all her own shrewdness and management of him, she really loved him.

He was saying, "You're not really interested in politics, Daphne, but since these people are coming here you ought to know a little about their background. If only"—he cocked a white-eyebrow at her and smiled fondly, teasing a little—"for conversational purposes."

What he meant, she knew, was that nothing was going to stop him giving her a political lecture. He'd sat up half the night with his despatches and memoranda.

"Of course," she said and, fixing her eyes on the far peak of Tower Hill away south of the town, she stopped listening.

Sir George Cator was a short, stocky man of about sixty, and with a surprisingly ugly face. He looked like a kindly, but distinguished baboon. There was nothing frightening about his ugliness: in fact it was oddly endearing and he was a great success with children. With adults, however, he had the ability to be forbiddingly stiff and formal if necessary, a man who put his public duties before everything and yet managed to ensure his own comforts and pleasures unobtrusively. With his own money he had built a nine-hole golf course out of impossible terrain on the slopes of Tower Hill, and with his own money he had presented and maintained an admirable public library and natural history museum in Port Carlos. He was bald, except for a few long strands of dark hair that streamed in a curious sweep over the top of his scalp, and he had a habit when talking of reaching up with the palm of his hand and patting them as though to ensure himself they were still there.

". . . the Opposition, of course, are making all the trouble they can in the House. Any stick to beat a donkey. Everyone wants self-determination for Cyrenia, eventually . . . but it's got to be worked out harmoniously, and there must be justice and security for all the national elements involved . . . Are you listening, Daphne?"

"Of course." Her eyes travelled down the slopes of Tower Hill, an ugly volcanic plug, patched with neat rectangles of green banana trees, swept across the town and then out to sea. The *Dunoon* was due in sometime that morning.

Sir George went on talking, his voice full and authoritative . . . "The Cyrenian National party is illegal and while it exists, and as long as Chebir's followers are so intransigent, there is little hope of any lasting solution . . ."

He stopped for a moment and leaned forward. There was a lizard moving slowly up the stout stem of the bougainvillaea that spread over the terrace. He watched it stalk a small butterfly, watched the lightning stroke of the tongue as it took its prey . . . and somewhere, deep inside him, he gave a little sigh. Pretty soon now he would be retiring and then he would be free to indulge his love of natural history. That's what he'd always wanted to be, an entomologist . . . the butterfly had been a Rawson's yellow, particular to the islands and named after a Waterloo general who had been the first Civil Governor here. And then, becoming aware of his own silence, he noticed that Daphne was not even conscious that he had stopped talking. She was staring down at Port Carlos, its pink and yellow walls vivid under the morning sun, and her face was blank. He smiled comfortably. His girl. Day-dreaming again.

He watched her for a moment, taking pleasure in his appraisal of her. He might have a face like a monkey . . . (Oh, yes, he'd heard that said. No surprise to him, though, because he'd been christened Monkey Capers at Wellington and it was still used affectionately by very old friends at the Carlton Club) . . . but he'd produced a damn fine girl. Well, his wife had had a hand in it, too. But she hadn't been any beauty and, up to the day of her death when Daphne was only twelve, had shared his wonder at the pale, blonde-haired creature they had produced. What was Daphne now? Twenty-seven? She was tall. Maybe her shoulders were a little narrow, a little stooped forward, but he was told that was fashionable . . . a model's figure . . . and her skin was jewel-clear. But that light-blonde hair was the thing. You could almost hear the sunlight purring over it. He saw her reach absently for a cigarette from the box on the table and he held out his lighter.

As she looked at him over the top of the flame they both smiled suddenly and he said affectionately, "You were miles away."

"Sorry, Daddy."

"No need to be. It's dull stuff. Don't see why any woman should be concerned with it. Though I must say we were lucky to put Hadid Chebir and Mawzi in the bag. The wife's English you know."

Daphne made a mouth. She didn't give a damn about any of the three. "She'll love Mora," she said, and went on, "What's this Major Richmond like?"

"Don't know him. Knew his father. Billy Richmond. He was at Sandhurst with me. Great point-to-pointer. Broke his spine hunting when he was forty. Finished him . . . for the service I mean. He died a few years back." He pulled a letter from his pocket, cleared his throat a little to indicate a change of subject and handed it to Daphne. "This was in the mail. It's confidential . . . between us of course. You know how I value your opinion on this kind of personal thing, and you've had a fair chance of summing young Grayson up. Like your views on this."

Daphne took the letter and reached for her sun-glasses. She read it carefully. It was from an old friend of her father's, the chairman among many other things of a large group of chemical industries and also an extremely influential man at the Central Conservative Office. He wanted a frank report on Grayson from her father. The young man had been noted, made himself felt . . . he had ambition tempered by a wise control and a diplomatic manner. A constituency could be found for him . . . It didn't matter that he had no money. If he came into politics there would be no trouble in finding him something with the chemical group. One had to look to the future, and young men of real promise must be helped along . . . etc. etc., thought Daphne.

She handed the letter back to her father and was silent for a while. She liked Grayson. She guessed that he liked her. Just now and again she had caught a look from him, but he had always been very proper, polite, helpful, but never playing a card wrong. She knew that was because of her father. Her father thought the world of him and the last thing—she lapsed comfortably into a slanginess of thought —Grayson would risk doing was playing around with Sir George's married daughter.

"Well?" Her father questioned.

"You know the answer," she said. "And I agree with you. I'd give him ten out of ten for everything. No," she corrected herself, "there's only one thing. He does tend to be just a little flamboyant at times."

"Yes, yes . . . but time will take that out of him. Or maybe the right wife. He's come up from nothing, no background. A man like that needs the right kind of wife perhaps more than money."

Daphne said nothing. But behind the long, pretty face with its firm, rounded chin an ice-cold thought had suddenly formed. She saw Grayson now more vividly and realistically than ever before. It was the obvious thing. She was the kind of wife he needed. They both had ambition, but she had background. She could take him wherever he wanted to go, take him where she had once hoped to take Teddy.

Instinctively, she knew that she could put it to Grayson, coldly, like a business deal and he would appreciate it, being neither shocked nor offended. She knew she would do it, but . . . the other things had to be right. Teddy was inclined to undervalue that side and was easily embarrassed by her passionate nature. If they were going to be man and wife, then it had to be complete . . . Anyway, that was easily found out.

She stood up, stretching her arms against the sun, a tall figure in green canvas trousers and a loose silk shirt, and she smiled at her father as she bent to kiss him.

"You won't mention this letter to Grayson, of course?"

"Good Lord, child, no. It must come from the other end after I've written about him. But I'm glad for the boy's sake."

"So am I."

He patted her hand as she stood by him. She was a good girl, warm, generous-hearted and a great comfort to him. It would have been a great shock to him if he could have

45

had a transcript of her thoughts in the last few minutes.

It would have been less of a shock to Lieutenant-Commander Burrows. On the bridge of the *Dunoon* now he was watching the distant cap of clouds that for more than six months of the year hung over San Borodon. It was this cloud formation, it was said, which had first attracted the attention of Zarco and Vaz and brought them to a discovery of the islands. Seeing the clouds and the low haze of the island sharpening up slowly as the *Dunoon* made her way across the long sea swells, Teddy Burrows was thinking of his wife. Quite early on things had gone wrong between them. Not enough for other people to notice, perhaps. He'd married her when she was twenty-two. At the time he had decided to leave the Navy and go into the city with his brother who was partner in a wealthy firm of stockbrokers. At the last moment —in fact on the return from his honeymoon—he had baulked at the idea. He stayed with the Navy because it was the one thing that meant anything to him. Daphne hadn't liked it. For a while, she'd privately been damned unpleasant about it. She'd been very young but not so young, he realized, that she hadn't been influenced in her choice of him by the fact that he was going into the City, that she could carry on with her London life . . . That, and then, of course, there was the other thing.

He loved her, wanted no one else, but somehow, even though he was happy and contented with their love he could feel she wanted more . . . Hell, maybe that was his fault . . . Still, if he wasn't exactly a wizard in the bedroom he'd never had any complaints on the occasions before his marriage when with other women . . . He grunted softly in his throat, disliking his thoughts.

At his side Imray said with an ironical nod towards San Borodon, "Catches you by the throat, doesn't it, sir? Home sweet home. And a smell of dried cod."

"Never bothers me," rumbled Burrows and for a moment regretted that he sounded a little gruff and bad tempered. He liked Imray. His thoughts went back to Daphne. Maybe in the end it would all sort itself out. Sir George had been delighted at the marriage. His own father had been at school

46

with the Governor and the families had known one another for ages. Daphne would never do anything drastic like leaving him . . . Upset the old boy too much. Anyway, she was too fond of him for that, and he of her. It would all work out eventually. He didn't mind her occasional flirtations. One thing he'd say for her—she was damned discreet and she knew when to draw the limit. His eye fell on Marion Chebir coming out from the awning to stare at the growing shape of San Borodon on the horizon. Lord, women . . . they were odd creatures. This girl must be wishing surely that she'd kept her nose out of all this trouble. But you couldn't tell. Could be that she was enjoying it. They loved importance. Loved to be in the centre of the stage.

Marion Chebir, passing along the deck, looked up and saw him watching her. For a moment she held his eye boldly to show him that she was not intimidated, not oppressed by the thought of exile. It was a gesture of defiance made for her own satisfaction more than his and she felt a little touch of triumph when he finally avoided her look. A bluff, grumpy good-natured man, she thought . . . comfortable and well set in his life. Some day he would tell his grandchildren how he took Hadid Chebir into exile, tell them about Hadid's English wife. What could he tell them that was anywhere near the real truth? However, it wasn't the truth that occupied her at this instant, it was a sudden sharp picture in her mind of the continuing future she sensed ahead of him, so certain, so even, running through his remaining days of service to a retirement in the country and the occasional trips to London. She'd served many like him in her days at Harrod's, shopping with their wives . . . Pleasant, elderly retired service officers with a twinkle in their eyes and that inevitable air of gallantry when they spoke to a pretty girl . . . His future . . . But what about hers? So far as she could see at the moment it was coming up fast in the growing shape of San Borodon and beyond that she could assume nothing.

As she turned off the deck to go to her cabin Major Richmond who was about to come up the gangway saw her and stepped back, waiting at the bottom for her to come down. As she negotiated the last three rungs, he put up his hand and took her by the elbow to help her.

She said, "Thank you."

He gave a slight movement of his head, but instead of passing on she stood there.

"Do we go ashore at San Borodon, Major?" she questioned.

"No, madame. The Governor will come off in a launch. The *Dunoon* will be leaving for Mora this afternoon."

It was odd how when some people called her "madame", it made her feel about sixty-five, but this man threw it away, gave it no emphasis.

"The Governor comes with us to Mora?"

"No. Just me." There was the slight rise of an eyebrow and the hint of a smile as though he were humorously apologizing for the paucity of ceremony.

Marion Chebir smiled, too, but with intent and said: "I understand you were at Magdalen with Hadid?"

Just for a moment John showed his surprise. So Hadid had remembered.

"Yes, I was. I only knew him slightly."

"He remembers you. Perhaps I ought not to mention it, but it's unlikely that he will acknowledge the fact to you. Understandably," her face momentarily became unfriendly, severe, "he is in no mood to recall his past in England . . ."

"I quite understand. And thank you for mentioning it, madame."

He was very correct, very British, she thought. This was what his class had above everything else, good manners. She'd gone out with young men in London who by now had also grown up like Major Richmond and Lieutenant-Commander Burrows; polite, even when they were wild, the kind whose attentions were the same to a shop-girl as they were to a débutante—except that the débutantes knew their families and the shop-girls never would.

"Also," she said spontaneously, "I apologize for losing my temper when we met."

"Please . . ."

To avoid his embarrassment and her own, she moved on towards her cabin. She would like to have stopped and talked to him about Hadid at Oxford . . . that was before she had met him. He'd come straight down from Oxford to the London School of Economics and she had met him while he was there.

Hadid had a good memory. He never forgot a face or a place. She opened her small travelling case and pulled out a thick, limp leather-bound notebook. Its pages were filled with a close short-hand script. It was her own short-hand but one would have needed a knowledge of Arabic to transcribe it. Hadid had insisted on her learning Arabic, and it was one of her few achievements in which she took pride. She sat on the edge of the bed and began to read at random from the notebook and the pleasure of the past came refreshingly and soothingly back to her.

3

THE *Dunoon* dropped anchor just inside the harbour mouth at noon, and ten minutes later Sir George Cator came out in a launch. He was piped aboard and a guard of honour mounted for him. The Governor liked ceremony and he was in full dress uniform. With him was the Chief of Police and one of his secretaries.

Accompanied by Burrows, John, Grayson and the Chief of Police he went to the wardroom where Hadid Chebir, his wife and Colonel Mawzi were waiting for him. Two sentries with fixed bayonets—Teddy Burrows knew the old boy would like that touch—stood outside the room. Inside when they were all assembled it seemed rather crowded.

John announced formally, "His Excellency, the Governor of the San Borodons, Sir George Cator, K.C.M.G."

The formal introductions were made, Sir George, stiff and very correct, giving the impression that while he had no intention of hurrying things he did not regard this as an occasion for anything except strict protocol.

John listening to him, remembered that Sir George had known his father. His father had been very fond of him. Sir George started to read the formal notice of exile and detention himself, the weighty phrases trundling out like heavy boulders being rolled over resounding boards.

"Her Majesty's Britannic Government under the powers vested in it by . . ."

Colonel Mawzi, John noticed, was staring at a patch of reflected sunlight, his lean brown face immobile, only the long curved lashes of his eyes flicking now and then.

And then their individual names which somehow made all three seem even more strangers and more remote.

"Hadid Ben Sulamon Chebir, merchant——"

That, thought John, was unnecessary, almost a calculated gibe. What jackass in Whitehall had tacked that on? The Chebirs were merchants, at least the father had been, it was true, but they were also a family of rank.

". . . his wife, Marion Edith Chebir . . ."

He saw the girl glance at Hadid, but Hadid stood stiff and as uncompromising as Colonel Mawzi, remote from the whole thing and in this little wardroom they both achieved a tremendous dignity.

". . . Fadid Sala Mawzi, farmer——"

The bloody fools, John felt anger stir in him. Mawzi was a fighter, a born soldier, that he owned ten acres of orange grove meant nothing. To call Mawzi a farmer was stupid and insulting to anyone who knew Cyrenia or the Arab world. John was full of sympathy as Mawzi glanced at Sir George and said sharply:

"My rank is Colonel, your Excellency."

Sir George looked up from the proclamation paper in his hand and John had an idea that he, too, realized the stupidity of this, but he gave no sign.

"In what Army?" he asked curtly.

"The Cyrenian National Army."

"Her Majesty's Government does not recognize its existence."

Colonel Mawzi shrugged his shoulders and smiled briefly. "Odd. Her Majesty's Army has been fighting it for the last six years or more."

At John's side Grayson whispered, "Christ, what fool drafted this . . . ?"

But Sir George was going on with his reading.

"To be detained at Her Majesty's pleasure in the Fortress of San Sebastian on the island of Mora in Her Majesty's colony . . ."

Marion Chebir was staring at the row of medals on Sir George's tunic. Just above her head was a coloured print of Queen Elizabeth and Prince Philip, and across the cabin their representative, whatever his own feelings, was reading away . . .

"And whereas it has, for the reasons hereinbefore appearing, seemed expedient . . ."

That was a good word, thought Grayson. Expedient. You couldn't do without it in political life. He was going to use it a lot.

". . . Now therefore, Her Majesty with the advice of the Privy Council is pleased to order . . ."

Lord above, thought Teddy Burrows, shifting his feet a little, what a time it takes them to get down to brass tacks.

". . . Notwithstanding that Her Majesty may from time to time revoke, alter, add to or amend this Order . . ."

Which means, of course, John decided, that if they ever decided it would be wiser to bring Chebir and Mawzi to trial instead of isolating them in the Atlantic, then they could. But at the moment a trial of the two would cause such a rumpus in Cyrenia that they daren't risk it. Tuck them away and forget them and, with luck, time might produce a settled answer for Cyrenia. He couldn't see it. He was sure that these two had no intention of being tucked away and forgotten.

Sir George Cator finished, folded the paper and looked up directly at the three.

"Major Richmond here is the Commandant of Fort San Sebastian. He will act as my representative and you will be entirely under his orders." He paused for a moment and then in a shade less formal voice asked, "Any questions?"

For a while none of them said anything. Then Hadid Chebir said, "What freedom of movement shall we have at this Fort?"

"That is for Major Richmond to decide. Naturally it will be conditioned by security measures and the terrain."

"And any communications we wish to make?"

Colonel Mawzi had dropped back to his familiar position

51

a little behind and to the left of Hadid. Hadid stood out, tall, untouched, full of calmness, his voice still a little hoarse now deepened with the impulse of some inner dignity.

"Official communications will be made to me through Major Richmond. All private letters will be forwarded by me to London for censorship. They may or may not be passed. This is out of my hands."

"Do you mean I can't even write for a fresh supply of silk stockings? That some Whitehall clerk may decide I can't have them?" Marion Chebir spoke gently.

John raised a hand to cover the smile that betrayed itself on his face.

Sir George coughed, embarrassed by this frivolity as he saw it.

"I have no doubt, madame, that adequate arrangements will be made for legitimate personal items."

It's the first time, thought Grayson, that I've ever heard silk stockings called "legitimate personal items". And very nice legs she has, too. He went off into a brief daydream about legs.

Hadid, who appeared hardly to have been aware of his wife's remark, said, "Your Excellency, I would like to point out that in the statement you have just read our removal from Cyrenia is stated to be for reasons of good government and the maintenance of order. If there are specific charges against us they should be brought and we are willing to stand trial in Cyrenia. Until such time as this happens we must regard our detention here as illegal, unjustified and a direct infringement of our rights as individuals. I wish this protest to be made to Her Majesty's Government."

"In that case you must put it in writing and I will see that it is forwarded to the proper authorities."

It won't do you any good, thought John, and you know it. For all their United Nations and Hague Conventions and Habeas Corpus Acts (theirs, why do I say theirs, when I mean ours?) in the end there was only force. And there had to be. For the moment Hadid Chebir was playing the martyr. But don't forget, he told himself, the killings in Cyrenia, the little Turkish shopkeepers and farmers who were burnt out, the British troops shot in the back and the police jeeps that went sky-high from landmines. Chebir had that side to his discredit.

They left them, confined still to the wardroom until Sir George should leave the *Dunoon*, and went forward to the deck awning where the wardroom mess steward had laid out a table with drinks. Sir George was given a large pink gin and relaxed.

Sir George said to Burrows: "Teddy, you stay at Mora until Richmond has had a look round and settled himself in," and then, turning to John, went on: "Unofficially I've been told to allow them a reasonable amount of liberty. They're not prisoners to be locked in a cell. But any privileges you grant them must be in line with security . . . We don't want them flying the coop." He grinned, his ugly face massing with wrinkles. "I'm too near retirement to want that to happen. It would blot my copy book, and wouldn't do you any good. You're Billy Richmond's son, aren't you?"

"Yes, Sir George."

"We were very good friends. You won't find much on Mora to amuse you . . . Shooting's not bad. There are a few quail and the odd wild pig. When you're squared up over there, I'll come over for a couple of nights and have a look at things. Burrows here will make a weekly visit with the *Dunoon*. There's a direct telephone line between the islands, too. Though it's a very old marine cable and always going wrong. Personally, I can never hear a damn thing on it." He put his glass down and Neil quietly took it and handed it to the steward to be refilled.

Teddy Burrows said, "I should think they'd find it difficult to get away. They'd have to have outside help. Not so easy, that. Most of the shipping around here is regular stuff . . . banana boats and the odd liner on the South America run. We've got a patrol pattern worked out for the *Dunoon* . . . We'll have our finger on everything."

Grayson put the filled glass by Sir George's hand.

"Escaping is an art. The last war taught us all that. Even if you put them in chains you couldn't be certain. But I imagine that Madame Chebir would be a bit of a handicap."

"Maybe, maybe . . ." Sir George ran a finger around his

tight tunic collar. "All right then, let's go ashore. I'll take you, Neil. Get your things aboard the launch."

"They're on, sir."

"Good." Sir George turned to John. "It's all yours, Richmond. Use your discretion and take what action you think fit. I'll back you up."

In five minutes he was gone, a small, white figure sitting in the stern of the launch talking to Grayson. The anchor chain of the *Dunoon* began to grumble aboard.

Two hours later the *Dunoon* dropped anchor off the little village of Mora from which the small island took its name. Mora clustered to one side of a shallow indentation at the northern tip of the island. On a clear night, looking north, the revolving lighthouse beam on the southernmost point of San Borodon could be seen.

As they ran in Imray stood with John by the rail pointing out the features of the island.

The whole island was dominated by the great peak of the dead volcano, rising about five thousand feet and sliced off untidily at the top like an egg. Two great ridges ran down from it to meet the sea in tall cliffs. Within the rough flanks of these ridges a wide, rather broken valley ran back from Mora and John could see that every inch of it was cultivated.

"The volcano is called La Caldera," explained Imray. "There are three other ridges like those two you can see, but they run down to the south of the island. In fact the thing's like an octopus squatting up there with its tentacles reaching over the island. They call the valleys in between *barrancos*. But this is the only one that's really cultivated . . . The rest of the country is pretty rough.

"That's the church. The tower with a sort of onion on top of it, behind those palms at the back of the houses. And that's Fort Sebastian on the headland to the right of the town."

As the *Dunoon* swung in, John saw a crenellated tower on the seaward side, and a shorter one close up against the sheer face of the hillside. Between them ran a tall wall cut with embrasures. Built of blackish stone it looked neat and tidy like some toy fortress. The entrance was hidden by a shoulder of land but he saw a dusty road running down towards Mora and picked out the haphazard movement of goats on its surface.

"It was built in the Napoleonic era," Imray was saying. "Lord knows why. They did the one at Port Carlos the same time. They really had the wind-up about these islands. The water's deep. You can lay right up alongside the wooden jetty there. Though there's precious little shelter if the wind's anything but south. The old man won't risk going alongside today. Too much swell running."

A few boats were pulled up on the narrow crescent of beach, and more lay at anchor just off the jetty. Behind the beach was a row of palms, masking most of the houses and John could see a small crowd of people gathering.

Turning away from the rail to go to Burrows, he saw Hadid Chebir, his wife and Mawzi. They were under the awning, all of them standing up and watching Mora. The hot afternoon sun blazing down put them in deep shadow and he couldn't see their faces well. They stood very still, like people waiting on the lip of the future, facing it with hostility.

But whatever front they put on, he thought, the strain was there. They lived for an idea. There was nothing tranquil about their lives. In his opinion Marion Chebir was showing the strain more than the others. Then, almost like an answer to his thoughts (but coming from the least expected of the three) he saw the tall central figure of Hadid Chebir slowly sway forward and collapse to the ground. John was there before the other two seemed to have realized what had happened. Momentarily, as he knelt by Hadid, he saw Marion Chebir's face. She was staring down and there was a little furrow of creases above her eyes. Then he forgot her. Hadid was lying on his side, one cheek against the deck and his mouth was loose and half-open. His eyes were shut and he was moaning a little and sometimes saying a few words that sounded like Arabic, but it was less speech than incoherent sound. John rolled him over and began to loosen his collar as Imray came up.

"Get some brandy," John said.

"No. It's not necessary."

It was Colonel Mawzi. He was on his knees by John. He

pushed John aside and slid his arm under Hadid's head, raising it a little. "It is the heat, Major. Sometimes this happens, always with the heat and strain . . ."

As he spoke he raised his right hand and with the flat of the palm slapped Hadid's face. It was no gentle slap, but a hard, violent blow the sound of which was like a paper bag bursting. Three times he slapped him, cradling his head all the while. Hadid stopped moaning, lay still for a few seconds and then very slowly opened his eyes. He looked at John, his eyes blank, and then his head shifted until he saw Imray. The blankness was still there, and then he saw Colonel Mawzi's face hanging above him. He took a deep breath, shut his eyes for a moment and then opened them. There was no blankness in them now. He knew where he was and who was with him.

"Madame Chebir and I will take him below," said Colonel Mawzi. "No, there is no need for anyone to help. We are used to this."

Marion Chebir bent down and put a hand under Hadid's left armpit. With Colonel Mawzi she helped him to his feet and he stood, swaying a little. Then without a word he turned slowly, making a little gesture with his hands for his wife and Mawzi not to touch him and he walked away. The two went with him, not helping him, but escorting him closely.

Imray turned and barked an order at the one or two men who had gathered and as they went back to their duties he said to John, "Well, what do you make of that? Went out like a candle."

"He's been through a lot, I suppose. And then this heat . . . I don't know . . . "

"I'll go up and let the captain know about it."

"Don't bother. I'll tell him." John turned and moved off. But the thing that stuck most in his mind was Colonel Mawzi. He had spared nothing when he had slapped Hadid's face, putting all he knew into it, his lips drawn tight back from his teeth. He'd hit him as though he hated him and welcomed the chance safely to show his hatred . . . Or was he just imagining that? Could be that Mawzi knew the treatment and he'd obviously handled this kind of incident before. But John couldn't get out of his mind the sound of those ringing blows, and the sight of Mawzi's face, taut with ferocity, and the eyes shining with satisfaction as he struck.

Burrows on the bridge as they slid in towards the island said, "Poor bastard. Took one look at Mora and it was too much for him. It isn't as bad as all that, though. Still, I must say I'm surprised. Doesn't look the type to keel over with a fit of the vapours."

John went ashore with Lieutenant Imray. He wanted to have a look around Fort Sebastian and settle where the quarters of Hadid Chebir and his party should be before he brought them ashore.

There was a jeep waiting at the end of the little wooden jetty. A sergeant in drill trousers and shirt and with a Royal Ordnance Corps badge in his cap stood alongside the jeep. Behind him, but at a reasonable distance, a little crowd of the people of Mora stood under the palm trees and watched the landing with interest.

The sergeant came to attention and saluted smartly.

"Sergeant Benson, sir."

John returned the salute and said, "Glad to meet you, sergeant."

He was a fresh-complexioned man of about thirty-five, stocky, his drill trousers carrying a knife-edge crease, the sergeant's stripes on his shirt sleeve whitened until they almost hurt the eyes under the strong sun. He looked good-natured and competent, and not likely to stand much nonsense.

A man pushed his way from the crowd behind the sergeant and took off his panama hat. He was a large, loose, hot-looking man in a tight black suit, his face brown and smiling. In rather stilted English he said:

"Señor Andrea Aldobran, Major. At your service. I am the manager of the Wine Co-operative here. If you need anything, please call on me. The people of Mora are very honoured to greet you."

"Thank you, Señor Aldobran."

Señor Aldobran smiled, pleased by his momentary prominence before the rest of the islanders, and said, "We are not many here, Major, but we have big hearts for the British. Also in my office I keep a very good sherry."

"I'll come and try some one morning, Señor Aldobran."

They got into the jeep and Sergeant Benson backed it, edged his way through the crowd, ignoring the smiles and nods that came his way, and then began the short, rough rise of road to the fortress.

"How do you get on with the islanders?" John was sitting beside him. Imray was in the back.

"They're all right, sir. Friendly, bit childish, and some of them very light-fingered if you leave anything around. Aldobran's the head man." He spoke carefully, beginning the careful process of assessing an officer. This one looked all right, but that was nothing to go by; some of the worst looked all right.

"I want to have a quick look round, so that I can settle the quarters for these people. You can explain the layout as we go. You know what all this is about?"

"Yes, sir. We had a signal from Port Carlos. And one of the boys here has a short-range set and we've heard the London news. I was a year at a base depot in Cyrenia."

"How many men have you got here?"

"About a dozen, sir. Including myself. One corporal, a lance-jack and the rest . . ." He hesitated. "You'll see them, sir. We don't get the cream of the army here . . ." He flushed for a moment, realizing that he might have put his foot into it and tried to save himself by adding, "That is, sir, not as far as the men are concerned."

John laughed. "It goes for officers, too, sometimes. I'll have a word with them when I've finished looking round."

The jeep slowed for three goats that were straying across the road and a small boy in charge of them raised a hand and shouted a greeting to Benson. He frowned, changed gear noisily and as they topped a slight rise said, "That's it, sir."

The road ran down gently to a wide, dusty plateau, hedged on the seaward side by tall spikes of cactus and agave. Beyond the cactus was a steep, hundred-foot drop to the sea. Fort Sebastian sat on the end of the headland with the taller of its two round towers overlooking the water. A long stretch of crenellated wall faced them, and in its centre was a tall, arched entrance with its double wooden doors drawn back.

58

A sentry with a fixed bayonet came to attention as they drove through into a narrow, rectangular courtyard.

For the next half-hour John was busy going over the place. The fort had been built around the inner courtyard. At the seaward end was the main flag tower and, at the other end but on the opposite corner was a smaller, fatter tower, called the bell tower from an old-fashioned warning bell that was mounted in a gallows on its courtyard face. The bell tower looked out over a narrow strip of ground to the sheer face of the long ridge of mountain that ran down from La Caldera two or three miles away. A wide parapetted walk ran right around the top of the four walls. Built into these walls were barrack rooms, store rooms, an armoury, various offices and kitchens, officers' quarters and a fine panelled mess room above the main gate. The place had enough accommodation for about three hundred men. Large parts of it, damp and echoing, were now shut up and Sergeant Benson's party had their quarters in a group of small rooms on the far side of the courtyard, opposite the main gate.

The bell tower, John decided, was the place for Hadid Chebir's party. It had three large rooms which would serve as bedrooms, a bigger room above them for a mess room. There was a primitive bathroom and toilet built under the curve of the stone stairs between the level of two floors. The only entrance to the tower was from the parapet level, reached by a stone stairway to the courtyard. For his own quarters he chose a couple of rooms in the main gate wall, close to the large mess room.

Over the years a great deal of furniture and fittings had accumulated in Fort Sebastian, most of it army pattern stuff, but there was also a fair amount of ordinary furniture. The lighting came from a small plant which thudded away gently in a room in the basement of the flag tower.

John gave instructions for the rooms to be fitted out as comfortably as possible and then, before he left to go back to the *Dunoon*, he had Sergeant Benson call his party on parade and he spoke to them.

For the moment he didn't try to isolate any of them. They were just eleven men and a sergeant. In a little while he would know each one. Just now he was content to accept them as a unit. From their cap badges he could see they were a mixed lot, R.E.M.E., R.A. and some infantry men. Standing at ease as he talked to them their faces were wooden, showing no interest, parade faces behind which there wasn't a single thought that would have surprised him. In time they would either be with him or against him. Briefly, and as simply as he could, he explained the Hadid Chebir business, and he finished, "These people are not prisoners in the strict sense of the word. They've been exiled and it's our job to look after them here. They'll be under guard at all times, but they will be allowed a certain amount of liberty of movement. Sergeant Benson and I will get out the Standing Orders about that, and also a detail of the guard duties. But I want you to remember that they are to be treated with courtesy at all times. On the other hand you must not talk to them outside the line of duty. Keep your mouths shut and your eyes and ears open. Hadid Chebir and Colonel Mawzi are clever men. They don't want to stay here and they'll use any advantage they can. Our job is to keep them here. So, if at any time you see or hear anything which strikes you as out of the ordinary—not only here—but in Mora or anywhere else on the island, you must report it at once to Sergeant Benson."

Driving back to the *Dunoon*, he was worried about the guard position. With twelve men it stretched things much too tight. During the day there had to be a guard on the main gate and one at the bell tower. At night the main gate could be shut and a man could sleep in the gate room while the bell tower guard could patrol the parapet. In addition Sergeant Benson slept in a small room through which the armoury was reached. Stored in the armoury was a large quantity of ammunition and weapons which had been placed there during the war and never removed.

"In fact, sir, they're really the only reason for keeping any men here at all. I can't think why they haven't been shifted. There's a lot of stuff, too, from a liberty ship that ran aground beyond Mora, but except for the tinned stuff, half of that's no use now. That's stored in a room under the flag tower and kept locked."

Out of his men, too, there was the cook who would not be

available for guard duties. So far as John could see he needed at least another six men, and even then if his men were to have any free time off it would still be less than comfortable. On the *Dunoon* he wrote a letter to Sir George Cator, explaining the position to him, and asking that six men be drafted to him from the Port Carlos police force while in the meantime a request was made to the War Office for proper reinforcements. But until extra men came, he knew he would have to do what every officer in every army of the world had to do most of the time, make do and still try to keep the men happy. As for why the War Office kept men and ammunition stores senselessly on Mora long after the war . . . well, he knew from his own work in the War Office that it had more than once been decided to withdraw the lot, but at some higher level the decision had been made against it. It was useful to have a place like Fort Sebastian just in case one had to deal with people like Hadid Chebir.

The three of them came ashore before it was dark and were driven up to the fort. In addition to the jeep, the Government detachment possessed a three-ton lorry. This was sent down to the Mora quay to bring up their luggage. The baggage caused a certain amount of trouble.

With Sergeant Benson in attendance, John went to Madame Chebir's room after her cases had been carried in. She was standing at the barred window looking out at the steep cliff face a hundred yards away. The evening shadows were scarring it with dark fissures. In the sky above it a few stars had begun to appear.

She turned and looked at him and then around the room. Against one wall was an old-fashioned bed, its frame full of brass knobs and ornate iron work. A table, a cane arm-chair, and a stout green barrack-room cupboard made up the rest of the furniture. The only touch of brightness was a small Spanish rug on the bare boards of the floor by the bed.

Seeing her eyes moving round the room, John guessed what she was thinking.

"I'm afraid it's pretty rough at the moment. You'll need a dressing table and, of course, a mirror. Sergeant Benson will do something about that."

"Thank you. Also"—she nodded towards the cupboard —"some hooks to hang my clothes on."

"I can send someone up to fix that this evening, sir," said the sergeant.

"There's no hurry; they can stay in my cases for tonight."

"About your cases . . ." John hesitated. He hated having to do this but it was necessary. If he didn't and anything went wrong then he'd have to take the responsibility.

"What about the cases, Major?" Maybe she sensed what was coming for her voice had become wary.

"I'm afraid I shall have to search them. I regret this, of course. But it is a necessary precaution."

Her mouth tightened and she made a quick little movement away from the window and then, as though the futility of any protest was clear to her, the movement became an indifferent shrug of her shoulders and she half-turned her back on them.

"All right, sergeant." John nodded to the cases which were stacked on the floor. There were three of them in expensive but by now well-worn pigskin.

As Sergeant Benson lifted the first one on to the table, Marion Chebir crossed to the bed and picked up her handbag. She flashed in it and said, "You'll want the keys." But instead of handing them across she tossed them on the end of the bed and turned back to the window. John picked them up and gave them to Benson who for a moment let one eyebrow begin to cock in reply to the quiet smile that touched John's mouth.

They went through the cases carefully. She had a very comprehensive selection of clothes. Good ones, too, John noticed; Balmain, Dior, and shoes from Ferragamo in Florence. For a moment as he went through a smaller case, the feel of silk in his hands embarrassed him with the sudden memory of the last time he had seen a woman in her underclothes. For a man who liked women, he told himself, even if he didn't seem to be able to settle on any particular one, it was too long ago. A man his age should be married. Not only because of women and their bodies and their underclothes, but for all the other things . . . the sense of belonging, companionship and family. He caught Benson's eye on him and

62

hastily folded the nightdress he had been holding. As he put it back his hand fell on a couple of limp, black leather-bound notebooks. He flipped one open.

"What are these?" he asked.

She turned.

"My diaries."

"You write shorthand?"

"Obviously."

He dropped them back in the case and shut it. She was staring at him so hostilely that it annoyed him. Damn it, she must see that he had a job to do. He crossed to the bed and picked up her handbag. A little ruthlessly, piqued by her attitude, he tipped the contents on to the bed. A purse, a compact, some more keys, a silk handkerchief, a small bottle of aspirin, sun-glasses and a few more odds and ends . . . he gathered them up and put them back in the bag. On the bed also was her jewel case. He went through this and when he had finished he closed the lid with a snap and stepped back.

"All right, sergeant," he said. "That's the lot." And then, as Sergeant Benson moved towards the door, he said to her, "I apologize for this, but unfortunately——"

She gave an angry jerk of her head, rejecting his apology, and said quickly, "I wonder you don't finish the job and search me. I might have a file sewn into my waistband."

John let his mouth twist into a smile and hoped that it would irritate her. All right, so she had spirit and she had no reason to like him; nevertheless he could sympathize with her although he had no intention of showing it. And it wasn't going to do her any good to taunt him.

"The bars," he said, "are over two inches thick. They'll take you a long time to saw through and they'll be inspected morning and evening. There's also a hundred-foot drop and the combined length of your bedclothes is about twenty-five feet when knotted, say, fifty if you tear them into double strips . . . You'd still have a long way to drop. I'd be very concerned if you were to break your neck."

Looking straight into his eyes she said with a lack of emphasis that somehow gave the words more force than anger could have done, "As far as I'm concerned, Major Richmond, you can go to hell."

63

He said calmly, "In the circumstances I can see that it's a reasonable attitude."

Sergeant Benson opened the door of the room and stood aside for him to pass.

"Also," she halted John as he was half out of the room, "I'd like a key for the door. I notice there is none."

"The keys from all rooms have been withdrawn on my instructions," John said briefly and went out.

Sergeant Benson closed her door and for a moment he and John looked at one another.

"She's quite a woman, isn't she, sir," said Benson. "I thought we might get something thrown at us."

"She'll settle down."

"Why'd you take the keys away, sir?"

"Because, sergeant, I don't want any of them locking themselves in so we can't get at them. We'd be in as much trouble if they committed suicide as if they'd escaped. She's not likely to, but Hadid Chebir's an unpredictable bird. I want to be able to get at him and the others if I want to."

Together they went through the rooms of Hadid Chebir and Colonel Mawzi, and finished up with Abou the servant who had a small room without a window on the parapet level quite close to the main tower door which could be locked and bolted from the outside and was always to be guarded.

Colonel Mawzi made no objection to the search. He had his tunic off and sat on the edge of the bed smoking as his cases were searched. He watched them in silence until they had finished, then he stood up and tossed Sergeant Benson his tunic.

"You'd better look through that, sergeant."

He turned to John and raised his hands above his head. John ran his hands over him and made him turn out his pockets.

"All this was done in Cyrenia, you know, Major," he said.

"That was over a week ago, Colonel. You have friends there. Even on the *Khamsa* perhaps. You might well have acquired a few things."

With Hadid Chebir it was much the same, except that he lay on his bed and watched them. He seemed quite recovered from his attack. John had to ask him to stand up to be

64

searched. He did so, taking his time, ignoring them, his thoughts apparently miles away. He gave the impression of a man obsessed quietly with some large question that excluded everything else from his mind and made him only automatically aware of the things that were happening immediately around him. When they had finished John turned to Benson and said, "Sergeant, wait outside for me a moment."

"Very good, sir."

With the sergeant gone, John turned back to Hadid Chebir. The man was staring at him blinking. For a moment the long, intelligent, handsome face was stiff and uncompromising. Then very slowly the fleshy lips flexed as though they were trying to remember how to smile and he said, "It was a long time ago, wasn't it, Richmond?"

"A long time, yes."

"So long that I prefer to imagine it never was. This is the only time I shall refer to it."

"As you wish. I just want to have one thing clear. I regard you as responsible for the behaviour of your party. I want you to be as comfortable here as you can. Anything I can reasonably do I will. I shall give you all the liberty of movement I possibly can. But if there's trouble of any kind, I shall clamp down hard. To be quite honest, this isn't the kind of job I would willingly choose for myself. It's entirely up to you whether you want to make it comfortable for yourself or not."

"I think you've made yourself clear."

"Good. In the morning I will explain the regulations for your movements."

Colonel Mawzi had one inner window frame drawn back and was leaning with his elbows on the stone sill, looking out through the thick bars at the night. It was a warm night and there was little coolness in the slight movement of air. From outside came the shrilling of cicadas. On the crest of the steep hillside facing the tower a fixed navigation light burned. It was a marker for the entrance to Mora. He was smoking and deep in thought.

So far everything had gone just as he had imagined it would. It was too soon yet for anything to happen. It would be some days before there would be any sign. In the meantime patience was easy. Of the three or four places the British had to choose from they had picked Mora. That had been his guess, too . . . Not entirely an inspired guess. Not all the members of the Cyrenia legislature were pro-British. When some of them had information it came to him. The only real danger had been the chance that they might be held in Cyrenia and made to stand a trial. Hadid had worried about this, but not he . . . The British, he had decided, would not want to stir up so much publicity and propaganda. Tuck them away quietly and forget them for a while, that was their decision, and he had seen it coming. Hadid was a fool as well as a puppet. Without him he had no life. His thin lips tightened . . . Hadid. He had intelligence and he had courage of a kind, but he was a fool not to have seen the unspoken, ultimate step that lay beyond all their plans. To be sent into exile, to escape and return with all the driving ferocity that their homecoming would bring . . . to sweep back into Cyrenia and enflame the waverers who until now had held them back . . . All that Hadid saw. Saw, too, the need not just for a quiet escape, but an escape full of triumph for them, rich with humiliation for the British . . . Yes, Hadid understood all that, but the one thing he couldn't possibly see was the last step. Cyrenia needed another martyr, and Hadid was going to provide it. Colonel Mawzi would return alone to tell the story, to raise every village and *souk* into revolt and to take over.

He contemplated the future without excitement. It was planned. It had to be. Hadid would go.

He stared at the night, confident, a small, wiry composed man who knew exactly where he was going. There was a knock on the door behind him. He called "Come in" and turned as Marion Chebir entered.

She wore a simple green frock. He noticed that her face was made up a little more than usual with a different lipstick. She was, he had noticed in the past, always particular about her appearance, the more difficult the crisis, the more attractive she had made herself—for Hadid. But that was past. The habit remained. Mawzi had a great admiration for her. This was a woman who knew how to love a man and a cause . . . a woman who needed love. All she had now was a fervent love of Cyrenia. But even that fire was dying in her, he guessed. A woman would take a husband's cause to her heart, be more ruthless than he in fostering it—but when love died . . . then she became a woman again.

She came over to the window.

"The major searched your cases?" she asked.

"Yes."

"Mine, too."

She held out her hand and gave him a long flat parcel.

"I brought it from Tunis as you said. Hadid had the jewel case made for me years ago. The major would have been very clever to find it. I am worried about Hadid."

"There is no need to be."

"On the destroyer today——"

"Just sometimes the strain hits him. You have seen him faint before. As for this——" he tapped the parcel— "he has used it all his life. But if necessary he can do without it. He is happier with it, that is all. His greatest need for it is before he has to take action."

"When will that be?"

Colonel Mawzi shrugged his shoulders. "It is arranged, but one cannot always name the day."

"Yes, but how long roughly? A week, a month, a year?"

"I cannot say, but not too long. If we are too long we shall be forgotten. That must not happen."

"Was it necessary for me to come?"

"You are a legend. Hadid Chebir's British wife. All the world knows your name and what you have done for Cyrenia. Not to have come would have made bad talk and propa ganda against us."

"In the old days it was different. I would have done everything."

"I understand this well. You have done much . . . maybe enough. All that is asked now is patience—and you will see our victory in Cyrenia." Colonel Mawzi smiled. "There are ways of making oneself comfortable. Hadid needs nothing, except for this occasionally," he held up the parcel, "but you and I . . . We are made of blood and spirit as well as hopes."

67

"We have had this discussion before."

Colonel Mawzi dropped the parcel on to the table by the window and moved towards her. She stood her ground, watching him.

"We have. But in different circumstances. Now we are shut up together. A man and a woman. For you Hadid is a shadow. But I am here. See."

He stepped close to her and put his arms about her and his lips touched the side of her neck. She put up a hand and placing it on his chest pushed him away. He moved back easily, without struggle and the dark eyes in the wedge-shaped face watched her curiously.

"I don't need you," she said calmly. "The only thing that keeps me here is my loyalty to Hadid. You know that. If you were stupid you could make me forget it."

"I am neither stupid. Nor do I forget." He half-turned away. "But the need is here, in me and in you, and sometime it will have to be acknowledged. A woman cannot love a shadow for ever."

She put up her hand and touched the side of her neck where Mawzi had kissed her. "In the old days," she said evenly, "Hadid would have cut your throat if he had seen you lay a finger on me . . ."

"The old days, yes. He would have spilt my bowels on the sand . . . He was a man. But shadows have no strength, and I am content to wait."

She said nothing. She went out, leaving him by the window, not even watching her going and she knew that it was his form of arrogance. What he had decided should be was, for him, something that would certainly happen. If his faith in himself ever broke, it would either kill him or shrivel him to the dimensions of a bazaar beggar . . .

Going down the stairs to her room she paused for a moment outside Hadid's door. She was tempted to go in and see if there was anything he wanted. Then she turned away. There was nothing he wanted, nothing she could give him or he could give her. Mawzi was right. He was a shadow. And God, how she had begun to hate living with a shadow on one side and a fanatic on the other . . . What a relief it would be to be ordinary, humdrum, to have a future that was a husband

and a family, the worries of little things and the uneventful joys of being loved and accepted, scolded and caressed.

For that, she thought, I should have married one of my own kind. The Hadid she had loved was gone. But all her need for love remained and she couldn't help it if the need, physical and emotional, built up inside her like a slow rage.

She had a longing now, a great tenderness for ordinary things . . . to lie in bed in some English town, to hear the whistle of a passing express train as she had when a girl in Swindon . . . a hot stuffy English night with a day coming full of ordinary things . . .

Sergeant Benson had a small room next to the Armoury. It was neat and comfortable like the sergeant himself. There were three framed photographs on the wall. One of a Cumberland farmhouse with his mother and father standing at the door, the woman's hand touching the ruff of a collie dog; another of the sergeant leaning out of the cab of a tank transporter with a background of sand and sky, and the last of a rather plain-looking young woman sitting on a pebble beach holding a sunshade, and written across the bottom of it—"Hilda, Brighton, 1952". One day Sergeant Benson would go back to England and marry Hilda. She was neat and comfortable like himself.

Hilda was certainly no oil painting, Corporal March was thinking as he sat talking to Benson. But maybe that was a good thing. The serg. didn't have to worry about her while he was away, as he had to worry about his girl. She was a cinema usherette and if he thought too much about her and what she might be up to it made him hot under the collar and very short-tempered.

He said, "What's the major going to be like, Serg.?"

Sergeant Benson jabbed a couple of holes in the top of a can of beer and filled their glasses.

"I don't know," he said thoughtfully.

"Not easy?" Corporal March tipped his chair back and held his glass to the light that pulsed gently from the unsteadiness of the distant generator. Bloody stuff, he thought, frowning at the beer. He'd give a lot for a pint of the real old mainline, drawn from the wood by Ma Jones whose charlies were so big she could hardly reach around them for the beer handle . . . Good old Ma Jones, and all the other lucky so-and-so's who right at this moment were all knocking it back in the *Rose and Crown*.

"Not easy in the way you want," said the sergeant. He didn't really like March, but he put up with him because he was closest in rank. He was a thin, dark-haired fellow, a bit unhealthy looking like a great many of these Londoners, and a bit flashy in his manner. But not a bad chap right down so long as you didn't expect too much from him.

"Well, it can't be all work. Why even you——"

"That's enough."

March smiled. The sergeant seemed to be less worried about it than most of the others, but even he liked an occasional afternoon down in Mora. He had a nice little widow down there, but no one knew whether they just played cards and drank a little wine, or . . . if he knew widows it didn't stop at that.

"Sorry, Serg. Still, I just wanted to know."

Benson drained his beer and said forcefully, "I know what you want to know, and I'll tell you. So far as you're concerned, my lad—and the others—there's no more sleeping out of barracks. No slipping off to Ardino for you while we've got this job on."

"Trust an officer to muck everything up."

"It's not him. You try and figure out a twenty-four-hour guard rota with the handful of odds and sods we've got. You'd better make it clear to the rest of the boys, too. In barracks every night. Your girl friend over at Ardino is just going to be lonely at nights. Anyway, they're a bad lot over there. Everyone knows that. You'd do well to keep clear."

Corporal March stood up and went to the door. "They're no worse than any of the others. Arianna's a smasher." He said it a little pugnaciously as though he wanted to convince himself. "I'd do anything for that girl."

Benson grinned. "You probably have. But you'd be wise to keep it from that dog-faced brother of hers, Torlo. He doesn't know how to talk unless he's got a knife in his hand."

Corporal March made an angry noise in his throat to cover

his sudden sense of anxiety. The sergeant didn't mean anything by it, but he was damned near the truth.

Outside, he paused in the warm darkness of the enclosed yard, and lit a cigarette. From somewhere beyond the cookhouse came the sound of men's voices. He caught the flare of a match being struck. They were sitting outside the dormitory, a favourite place on these warm nights. A shooting star flared briefly across the patch of sky above and the sound of a mouth organ started up hesitantly and then firmed into "Che Sara Sara". Corporal March turned away from the group and strolled towards the main gate. Any other night and he would have been out and away before this. It was four miles to Ardino and on the unit's bicycle he could make it in forty minutes. Yes, old Benson was perhaps nearer right than he knew. There was no holding back with Arianna. She wouldn't let you. They'd had scares before, of course. But this one . . . it was well over three months now. Even Arianna was beginning to look a bit glum about it, and he wouldn't put her down much as a girl given to easy worry. Well, what the hell anyway? Still, he would have to get over there otherwise she would start thinking things. No good trying to explain about a new officer, guard duties and this bleedin' Cyrenian mob. If he didn't show up she'd begin to squawk, and then that flaming brother of hers . . . Dog-faced was about right. Ought to have been strangled at birth. How Arianna could have come out of the same litter . . . He began to whistle gently to cheer himself up. You'll be all right, Marchy boy. Buy 'em off with corned beef, or if they were awkward her brother would settle for a rifle and some ammunition. Do anything for meat or a gun, and he could always lay his hands on them. He rattled the bunch of keys in his pocket and suddenly felt better.

Burrows and the engineer officer from the *Dunoon* had walked up for drinks after dinner and were now gone. John Richmond's room was still heavy with the fragrance of Teddy Burrows' cigar. He sat now by the open window, writing. The window was in the outer wall of the fortress to the right of the main gate and he could look down the rough stretch of hillside to Mora. A few lights were showing and then, detached from them, floating on the darkness of the sea were the riding lights of the *Dunoon*. Somewhere in the room a mosquito pinged fretfully and an occasional moth came banging clumsily through the window.

I got the impression that Colonel Mawzi really hated Chebir's guts. I may be wrong, but you know how those things pop into the mind before you know it. No one likes to do all the real donkey work and then watch the other take the plums. Metaphor a bit mixed, but you know what I mean.

He paused, seeing again Mawzi's lean face, deep cut and the thin lips tight with pleasure as he struck.

Marion Chebir seems now to be much more self-possessed, though not prepared to accept anything lying down. Do you know anything about her personal relationship with Chebir? They insist on separate rooms which seems odd to me since she's come here of her own free will and out of love for him. Could be that their marriage has gone bust and it's now simply a matter of policy to carry on. If she left him it would be bad publicity for him.

He got up and fixed himself a whiskey and water and carried it back to the table. He stared out of the window, caught for a time by the sense of remoteness around him. A few lights showing from a huddle of houses, the night air full of new scents and the fiddle-fiddle-fiddle of the cicadas' mad orchestra . . . At home now, almost at this hour, he would have called up the dogs and taken a stroll around. The dew on the grass, the dogs racing into the darkness, the screech of a little owl and high above maybe the drone of a Paris-London plane . . . But whether he was here or there made no real difference. He frowned as he thought this. In the last year or so a sense of aloneness had deepened in him, almost unwelcomingly. It was as though he were trying to ask himself some question but couldn't frame it, couldn't give a body to the question. The nearest he could get to it, when he let himself dwell on it, was that he felt he wanted something . . . Something more than he had, something of importance. As simple as that could it be? He wanted something. But what?

He made a quick gesture of irritation and went on writing his log for Banstead.

The men in Fort Sebastian are pretty much as one would have expected. Most of them have had more than a year here with only local leave to San Borodon. I fancy most of them have got dug in

72

with local families. Not that I'm against these contacts. If Hadid and Co. are really planning anything it won't hurt to have my blokes keeping their ears and eyes open while they have their feet under the kitchen tables of Mora. But if this is going to be a long business, I suggest you start twisting someone's arm for more bodies to be sent.

Just how long would it last, he wondered? And, when it was over, back he would go and another job would turn up. Well, he didn't want that. When this was over, he'd ask for regimental duties again. It was about time, and with the Regiment, at least, he'd have a feeling of being as much at home as anywhere.

4

H.M.S. *Dunoon* stayed three days at Mora. During that time the garrison at Fort Sebastian settled into an orderly routine. At night the three prisoners and their servant, Abou, were locked in the Bell Tower and a sentry was always on duty outside the doorway which gave access to the parapet walk. During the day the three were allowed the liberty of the parapet and were free to move along the stretch between the Bell Tower and the Flag Tower. This gave them a view westwards to the steep dropping headland and the coast which almost immediately began to curve away sharply southwards. Again a sentry was always on duty on the parapet.

None of the prisoners, except Abou, was allowed down into the main courtyard or into any other part of the fort. Abou, however, was allowed to move freely between the Bell Tower and the kitchen quarters in order to fetch and carry the meals for the other three. It was curious, though not unexpected, that while most of the men showed little continuing interest in the three prisoners, accepting them, and then relegating them into the impersonal status of the *raison d'être* for the new tenure of their lives, they all took to Abou. Within twenty-four hours they had given him that teasing, fondly bullying affection which troops bestow on those who excite their imagination or touch their sympathy and which is always marked by one or two nicknames. Abou, padding about bare-footed in his tight black trousers, white jacket and black skull cap, smiling when spoken to but not, they were all sure, understanding a word, drawing his thin shoulders in and making a slight, old man's bow when any kindness or service was done him, became their pet. He was "Ali-Bloody-Baba", "Abou-Ben-Stinkpot", and finally "Abby". In the kitchen while he waited to collect the meals, he was instructed in the rudiments of the English language, beginning as troops always do with those simple, barrack-room obscenities which in the uncomprehending mouths of foreigners always convulse the British soldier. To see Abou bow gently in the kitchen and say, "I come fetch f———g food for bastards," or some other gently mouthed scurrility made the cook, Jenkins, reel against his stove, weak with laughter.

Unknown to them Abou enjoyed it too; for he had a very competent understanding of the English language which Colonel Mawzi had instructed him to keep to himself. Abou fetched and carried, but not only food. The name and duties of each man were noted, the layout of the men's quarters and the details of the duty rosters . . . all these went through Abou-Ben-Stinkpot, through tight-trousered Abby, to Colonel Mawzi.

The cook, a Royal Army Catering Corps private, with the Welsh name of Jenkins, but born in Sussex and not a touch of the Welsh now in his speech, a fat man of about twenty-eight whose skin shone like a seal's and whose eyes were bright black buttons, took Abou under his wing. In Abou he found someone unmoved by his temperament, someone who, given a glass of beer, would stand or sit patiently for all time and listen to him talk. Within two days it had become a ritual that, bringing back the dishes from the evening meal to the kitchen, the two would adjourn to the courtyard and sit in the last angle of sunlight as the sun went down beyond the Bell Tower and the hill sweep of La Caldera and talk. Jenkins, as a change from cooking, had taken on the duties of gardener. Before joining the Army he had been an under-gardener to some estate in Sussex. In the centre of the court-yard was a large, stone-edged circle, half as big as a tennis court, in which grew shrubs, azaleas, oleanders, syringa and a shrub with a white trumpet-shaped blossom which the

74

people of Mora called *flor de campina*. All these Jenkins tended, watered, hoed between and cherished. If any man from the garrison walked unheedingly across the circle, snapped a twig or tossed an empty cigarette packet on to the tidiness, Jenkins' voice would bellow from the open cook-house door. It must be said, few men ever did trespass on his garden, for only the biggest of fools in the Army ever gets on the wrong side of a cook. Around the edges of the circle were a fine show of canna lilies. In the dead centre of the patch was Jenkins' joy, and indeed Mora's pride. This was a tree.

Its trunk, which was a good fifteen feet in circumference at the base, was a distinctive light grey colour, rough and grained like old elephant hide. At about six feet from the ground the trunk divided into a mass of upthrusting smooth grey branches, leafless until their very extremities, a good forty feet from the ground, where they were tipped with narrow, spear-like leaves, two or three feet long. The thing looked like a great candelabrum, the maze of grey branches twisted and involved, reaching up and spreading out into a gigantic mushroom shape.

Jenkins, the cook, was fascinated by it. From the family of his girl friend in Mora he had learned its history, and he had also written to the secretary of the Royal Horticultural Society in England for botanical details. Sitting with Abou now, peeling potatoes for the next day's meals, Abou helping him, the two smoking and occasionally refreshing themselves with beer, Jenkins was happy to give Abou a lecture about it, not caring whether he understood or not.

"You see, Abby, you po-faced heathen, it ain't a true tree, not really. It's really a lily—that's what the botanical boys say. *Dracaena draco,* they call it. Round here it's called the dragon tree. Just think of it." He cocked an eye to the spear-pointed leaves which were catching the last of the evening sun. "A bloody lily, forty so-and-so feet high. Not even Kew Gardens could go better than that. And I tell you something else, for the ignorant heathen should always be instructed, it don't have sap. It has blood. Like a human being. Yes, blood. You cut it with a knife and it bleeds—but don't let me catch you tryin' it!"

Abou smiled politely and his eyes were on Jenkins, and the cook shook his head despairingly.

"The tree I'm talking about, you silly bastard."

"Ha, yes, bastard . . ." Abou nodded his head.

Jenkins wiped his wet hands on his apron and took a draw at his cigarette.

"Blood, real blood, and it's about a thousand years old. Know what they say around here? When the islanders made their last stand against the Spanish or the Portuguese, or whoever it was, they fought it out under this tree, and as they went down the tree began to weep blood. Blood, you understand, blood?" He pinched at Abou's arm and then drew a finger across his own throat. "Blood. Buckets of it. Every once in a hundred or so years it begins to weep blood and when it does, look out Aly-Bloody-Baba, for it means trouble. But it ain't a tree. It's a lily, though I must say I don't go much for its flowers. Little tiny, pinky-white things . . ."

Corporal March came across from the little guard room by the main gate in webbing belt and anklets, a rifle over his shoulder and standing beside them said:

"All right, Sinbad. Time to lock you up for the night."

March was guard commander for the night. Abou looked up at him and rose to his feet. For a moment he pretended not to understand, and Jenkins said, "Time for bed. Sleep." He laid his own head expressively on the pillow of his hands to explain and Abou smiled.

March's thin lips grinned. "Come on. Get up them stairs."

He followed behind Abou as the servant crossed the yard and began to climb the flight of steps that led up to the parapet by the Bell Tower.

Jenkins tipped his kitchen chair back and eyed the tree. It really was something. A thousand bloody years and still going strong. Made you think. When he'd had his lot and was in civvy street again, he'd go back to gardening. At least you had something to show for your work when it was over. But cooking for this mob . . . ! You sweated your guts out over a stove with the temperature in the eighties and then they shovelled it into their stomachs and the only thing left to show for it all was a few belches or a lot of lousy complaints.

John went aboard the *Dunoon* before she left at noon to give Burrows his report. Coming ashore, instead of going back to the fort, he went round to the office of Señor Andrea Aldobran.

Aldobran was at his desk in his shirt sleeves, a fly-swatter in one hand and a glass of sherry close to the other. He was delighted to see John and rose hastily to put on his jacket and to get out another sherry glass.

"This one," he said as he poured, "is very fine, maybe a little too dry for your palate?"

John tasted it, nodding to him over the rim. "No, no . . . just as I like it." In fact it was very like the Tio Pepe his father had in his cellars . . . His father? Himself now, and he had a sudden vision of the cellar at Sorby Place and the racked port that his father had put down. He thought of the time his father had shown him how to decant port, a solemn, religious rite and the first time his father had taken him into his London wine merchants . . . all the solid, sensible mystique of wine. He ought, he thought, to be putting down port now . . . But whom for? His son . . . He smiled at the thought and Señor Aldobran took the smile for his pleasure in the wine.

"Good? These islands, there is no fine wine here. It is good only to wash the mouth with. No more."

"Señor," said John; "you understand about the prisoners at the fort?"

"Yes, señor major. From the radio, from the newspapers when they will come. I have read much about Cyrenia. You understand, I live really on San Borodon, at Port Carlos. But here I spend much of my time. In Port Carlos, we have a political and historical club. Oh yes, I understand much about Cyrenia and its problems. Something troubles you perhaps about them?"

"Well, in a way. My job is to keep them at the fort. But both of the men, Hadid Chebir and Colonel Mawzi, are not the kind to sit down and accept this situation. They have friends, money, a political and military organization. If they can escape, they will. It would be a great feather in their caps . . . and a bad thing for us."

"Oh, yes. All this I understand. But this is a tiny island, major. How could it be?" He refilled John's glass.

77

"It's a possibility I have to face."

"Naturally. Yes, naturally, I see. But what is there to do?"

"That's why I've come to see you. You know all the people on this island. You get around. I want you to ask them to keep their eyes open. If they see anything odd, see any strangers, I want to know."

"So you shall, major. I shall speak to them. You take your work very seriously, and that is good that you should. It is the duty of a soldier to be a soldier. Just as it is the duty of a wine merchant to be a wine merchant. At the desk at the desk. In bed in bed. This I often say."

And enjoyed saying it, too, John could tell. He liked Aldobran, and he guessed that little passed on this island that he did not come to know about in quick time.

When he left the office, he walked back along the open water-front under the shade of the palm trees. Alongside the little wooden jetty a small schooner was loading up with a cargo of bananas from the terraced plantations that ran back from Mora. Each bunch was carefully wrapped in a swaddling of thick brown paper stuffed with pine needles. A couple of old lorries and a handful of ox-drawn carts shuttled between the jetty and the town. Nets were spread to dry along the narrow crescent of beach and the wind made a thin noise in the green palm fronds.

The largest buildings in Mora were the church of San Sebastian and the wine-growers' co-operative buildings, an ugly grey concrete structure at the back of the town where the houses gave way to the wide upsweeping valley.

As John topped the slight rise leading up to the Fort he turned and looked back. The *Dunoon* was under way, streaming a white wake behind her. He stood, watching her head northwards. As she grew smaller and smaller he had the sensation a man might have who faced the moment of being marooned, who watched his ship draw away and knew that the moment had come when he was entirely on his own. The sensation had the effect of abruptly changing his conception of the island of Mora. Suddenly it was the world, his complete world and everything took on a series of new dimensions. The small pink and chrome washed houses of Mora were no longer picture postcard façades, but solid and large, and he was aware of the land running back into the interior, miles and miles of country which, because of his charge here, had a special significance for him. This, in effect, was his domain. It was not just an army command he held, but a trust, difficult and far from straightforward. Looking inland he saw the long slopes running sharp and sheer to the jagged rim of La Caldara. The mountain seemed immense now, and the cap of piled cumulus cloud over it seemed to spread and dominate all the sky. In Whitehall, he thought, they would soon be coming back from lunch and sinking into their desk chairs, relaxing for a moment before making the somnolent effort to face the afternoon until five o'clock. At home, his farm bailiff would be starting to make the afternoon round of orchard and fields and the dogs would be with him, their long spaniel ears knocking the pollen from the swollen grasses as they hunted through the ripening hay. Banstead might give him a thought, the farm bailiff and a few other people . . . but he knew that with none of them would he persist in their minds with any special affection or regard. Liked, yes . . . John . . . John Richmond . . . Major Richmond . . . each placing him exactly. But not a single soul would be really aware of him, vividly, importantly, maintaining a consistent flow of sympathy which was for him alone. Not since his mother had died had there been anyone like that. And it was odd, he thought, as he turned slowly and went on up the hill, how until now this sensation of lacking a special line to a special person had never worried him. He had a packet of friends but not one of them—and this was no reflection on them since their relationship could not include it— would regard his obliteration as more than a temporary shock. Faced suddenly with this, though he sensed that it had been a long time aboiling up, he didn't turn from it. If a problem existed, it had to be tackled. The thing fresh and clear with him, he set it up squarely and examined it, and it took no time at all to find the answer.

It was as simple, he told himself, as A.B.C. You can't live alone and you can't live for yourself. In a crude sort of way that's what he had been saying every time a new woman seemed to promise an answer. But each woman was no more than a promise. Some fellows found a woman without any trouble, but finding the right one . . . they said a bell rang, you fell in love, bingo, like that. It never damned well happened like that with him. Sometimes you thought you'd found the right one, just as sometimes you thought you'd cured your driving slice at golf. You played round brilliantly. Then the next day, hooking, slicing, topping . . . ! Yes, there was always the next day with the women he'd felt were right. Almost certainly the fault was his. Up to now, maybe, the thing had always fizzled because he wasn't entirely convinced of the truth that a man's self-sufficiency and isolation were undesirable . . . Before they had seemed to contain a large element of freedom and happiness; no ties, no obligations, appealing widely to a selfishness which was natural in him as it was natural in thousands of others. But not now. He just knew that he didn't want to go on alone. And with a military pragmatism he decided that when this job was done he would marry, have children, put down port for a son, and be glad to lose the isolation of his own personality in the only composition which was armed against catastrophe. The boy would go to Marlborough of course, though he hoped to heaven they'd modernized the plumbing since his time . . .

He wasn't surprised at his decision. Given the facts clearly, he was used to making up his mind quickly. It was a faculty which often surprised many of his friends into thinking that he acted on impulse. But in this they were wrong. He was a good soldier because he was not a dashing one. But as a man, he took into his personal life the faults of a military training. Here was a staff course problem . . . all the facts and, swiftly produced, came the text-book answer. He would marry and have children. It was a good answer, but—he smiled to himself—incomplete.

Marion Chebir, who was leaning over the inner wall of the parapet and looking down into the courtyard, watched him pause beside Jenkins who was watering the shrubs in the courtyard. They spoke for a moment but she couldn't hear what they said. But abruptly she heard John laugh. The lifted, tanned face was suddenly bright and open and boyish. The sound of the laugh gave her an unexpected pang. Just to raise your head like that and laugh, free, without a shadow. It was a long time since it had happened to her.

He crossed the yard and came up the steps by the Bell Tower to the parapet. Every morning and afternoon he came up to have a word with the sentry, to pass on to his charges, to show himself, to offer himself to them if they should want something. He was correct, she thought, but the moment he began to climb the steps to face them he left part of himself behind down there.

He saluted her as he came on to the parapet and she turned away from the wall, facing him, feeling the sun strike full across her. She raised her hands and made a little movement to dust from them the scraps of lichen and moss which rested on her palms from leaning over the stones.

"The *Dunoon's* gone," she said.

"Yes, she's gone."

"So, you're all alone. Master of Mora." She said it with a light note, and before he could say anything she went on, "I watched her go out round the headland. There's always something sad, I think, in watching a ship leave. Not, of course, that I've any special affection for the *Dunoon*."

"I don't think I should have either, if I were you," John answered.

She laughed. "Can you imagine yourself in these circumstances? A prisoner. It's a new way of regarding oneself."

"I shall try to make it as comfort——"

She raised a hand swiftly and cut him off. "No, no . . . don't start being a warder for the moment. Down there you could laugh and be natural. You might spare a little for these regions. Ah, now you look surprised."

She couldn't have told herself why this mood had suddenly come over her. Perhaps it was just a reaction to the whole solemn business of politics . . . but she felt strongly the need unexpectedly to pretend that the situation was different.

"I am," he said frankly. "I thought you only saw me as a warder."

She nodded, remembering her arrival at Fort Sebastian. "Yes, I was rude. I apologize for that." She smiled, dismissing the past. "What was it that the cook said which made you laugh?"

81

John grinned. "If I told you, you would be shocked."

She shook her head lightly. "I doubt it. I worked as a shop-girl for years before my marriage." She paused, silent for a while, the word "marriage" taking her back over the years, and from the way she looked at him John could guess that she was looking through and beyond him. In the bright, hard sunlight she made a colourful splash against the grey-black parapet wall in her green skirt and white blouse, the gold clasps on her wrists moving gently as she stretched her hands out touching the wall behind her. She gave the impression of being taller than she actually was, partly from the way she held herself, the fine shoulders carried proudly and from the long line of her body, narrow at the hips, which had a firm, controlled grace. The kind of woman, John told himself, who would look right anywhere . . . on a dance floor, or mucking about in a boat; Claridge's or Cowes . . . but not mixed up in all this Cyrenian business. She'd come into that through Hadid Chebir . . . but he couldn't see her as having a distinct passion for Cyrenia by itself . . . Political women, he smiled at the thought, just didn't look like this . . . they ran to fat, to stumpiness, or to scragginess.

All the fatigue and anger seemed to have gone from her, she looked young, fresh and, he didn't even try to ward off the thought, the kind of attractive creature a man would find running easily through his first, second and a great many succeeding thoughts. If she'd been standing alone like that against a hotel terrace in Cannes a man with the need for company would have tried to find a way to her . . .

"Tell me," she said breaking into his thoughts, "did you know Hadid well at Oxford?"

"Not very. We played rugby together sometimes. And once we spent a week-end walking in Wales. We were in two parties. I didn't see much of him."

"You find him changed? But, of course you do."

"Well, it was a long time ago. He's been through a lot since then."

Marion nodded. "Hadid in those days was like . . . like quicksilver. All movement and fun and just a bit crazy. Now he has become Cyrenia." She made a sudden expressive gesture with her right hand which he realized was characteristic and indicated the brushing away of one set of thoughts and a turning to pleasanter lines. "He was popular at Oxford?"

"Yes. He was liked very much. But, to be quite honest, he moved in a set that was too fast, too expensive for me ... I didn't really see much of him."

She moved forward from the wall abruptly. "I saw him change. I didn't understand much about it in those days. But I learned." Firmness was back in her voice and the easy friendly creature of a moment before was gone. "It was terrible. He used to love the British. And then he hated them. For a time he tried to have both things. Love and hatred for them. But it wouldn't work. So he chose. And I chose with him because I was his wife and loved him ... A wife has to do that if she wants to go on." She stopped and her head which had been lowered came up quickly and, full of a dark beauty, she looked fully at him, seeing him now, speaking directly to him. "I'm sorry. I shouldn't talk about these things. It embarrasses you ..."

Before he could say or do anything she walked away, shutting him off completely from any connection with her, and went past the sentry through the doorway of the Bell Tower.

The sentry, whose name was Hardcastle, watched Major John Richmond turn and move along the parapet towards the Flag Tower. Somewhere inside the tower he heard a door close sharply and he was completely unconcerned with Marion Chebir or Major John Richmond. He stared at the sky above the Flag Tower and he was thinking to himself that it was Saturday. Saturday afternoon. Some time to go yet before the close of play at the Oval ... Well, not really, 'cos you had to make an allowance for the difference in time out here. He'd get the news when he came off duty on the B.B.C. Overseas radio ... If Surrey were still there with some decent wickets in hand they'd have a chance ... Yes, the bleedin' Oval and bleedin' cricket. Not this bleedin' hole where there weren't a bit of ground flat enough to play rounders on, leave alone cricket.

Abou came padding up the stone steps to the parapet and went past him into the tower, his face cat-smiling, his white jacket flapping in the rising on-shore wind.

"Whatcher, Abby," the sentry greeted him cheerfully. "Why don't you tuck your shirt tails in and keep your mahogany arse warm?"

H.M.S. *Dunoon* although she headed north from Mora for San Borodon and Port Carlos did not continue long on this course. Four miles out when all that could be seen of Mora was the distant cloud-capped snout of La Caldera she altered course to port and began to make a wide sweep right around the island, but well out of sight of it.

By the time she was three-quarters of the way round her circuit of the island the evening was closing in and long before she was back on her course again for Port Carlos it was dark. Her radar and lookouts had picked up no sign of shipping whatsoever except one cargo vessel, the *Oldenburg* of Hamburg, twelve miles south-south-east of Port Carlos just as darkness came down.

Teddy Burrows knew the *Oldenburg*. She ran between the Canaries, Madeira and San Borodon, taking on general cargo, bananas, tobacco leaf and timber. Burrows knew all the regular shipping around the islands, even down to the smaller fishing boats. He had strict Admiralty instructions to patrol all the shipping in the San Borodon waters. To do this effectively, he knew, meant that the *Dunoon* would spend precious little time in Port Carlos. In a way he was glad of this because it was always an embarrassment to him that, while his own officers and men slept aboard, his wife Daphne expected him to sleep at Government House. He disliked pulling his rank to claim any personal privileges. At least, now, he thought, he wouldn't have to make excuses . . . On the bridge, the warm night air full in his face, he stared at the far loom of the lighthouse beam from the southern tip of San Borodon and felt comfortable and relaxed. If he hadn't changed his mind in time he might now be committed to a daily grind in the City; catching the eight-thirty, bowler hat and rolled umbrella, nothing but grimy air to breath and no exercise to work off expense account lunches . . . He gave a soft little growl to himself at the thought of how near he'd come to that fate.

Aft he heard some of the crew talking and laughing and

occasionally, as one of them flicked a cigarette end overboard, the bright red tip made a wavering parabola against the velvet dark sea.

On the poop deck, a little forward of the depth charge racks P.O. Grogan and S.B.A. Andrews sat a little apart from the others. Between the freckle-faced young man with the pugnacious mouth and the stolid Petty Officer there had grown a quiet friendship, unspoken and undemonstrative, except on shore leave when they drank together to excess.

Andrews said, "Why'd we have to go all round the houses like this?"

"We'll be going all round the houses for a long time. Just so long as that mob are on Mora. Nobody's going to slip in and whip them away."

"Rule Britannia." Andrews' mouth twisted into a grin. "Send a boy to do a man's job. I was talking to Sergeant Benson before we left. He's got a dozen men. A dozen! They're going to be so stuck up with guard duties they aren't even going to have time to go to the heads."

"Do 'em good. They've had it easy for a long time . . ."

As Andrews opened a packet of cigarettes, Grogan reached out and took one, lit it and leaned back. There should be mail waiting for them back in Port Carlos. There'd be a couple of letters from his wife. She was a good letter-writer. Wonder what she'd been up to this time? Always up to something. Re-decorating the kitchen, re-organizing the front garden, digging up the plants to see if they'd got roots . . . he saw her affectionately in his mind's eye. A firm, well-set-up woman with a smile nothing could shake. Pity they couldn't have kids, but there it was. She could have spent her time organizing them. The only time he'd ever seen that smile go, seen real misery in her face, was when she had been told . . . Suddenly he felt very close to her. So far as he was concerned she could take the roof off the house and put it back upside down if it pleased her.

At his side Andrews stared up at the sky and thought of nothing, or at least tried to and found it hard work. It was something he'd read about in the *Reader's Digest*. Yoga, or something. You just concentrated on infinity or nothing and if you did it hard enough your spirit left your body. Trouble

85

was the body took a lot of leaving. You bet, the good old body . . . Infinity receded and with a snort of disgust he found himself thinking of Port Carlos and a girl who worked in one of the cod drying stations. The humorists on *Dunoon* used to hold their noses when he came aboard from a shore leave . . . Very funny, ha, ha, he said savagely to himself, and tried infinity again only this time to be distracted by the sound of a plane high above the light pocking of small clouds. Just for a moment he caught a glimpse of navigation lights high, high up. . . .

At his side P.O. Grogan said, "That's the Iberia plane. Madrid, Lisbon, Bermuda, Havana . . . She's late, too. But did you ever know a Spaniard that wasn't?"

But it wasn't the Iberia plane for Havana. That had passed over an hour before and dead on time. This was a flying boat working under Spanish charter for a company whose real nationality it would have been difficult from the books to unravel with any truth. She'd begun life at the Short Brothers works on the River Medway in Major John Richmond's county of Kent, but she had done a lot of travelling and changed hands many times since her keel had first hit the muddy Medway flow.

She was flying at eighteen thousand feet and had been at that height since she had left Aargub in the Bahia de Rio de Oro on the coast of Spanish Sahara five hours before. Aargub was the kind of place where curiosity was a dangerous form of bad manners if it were shown openly. The six men in the plane, too, were the kind who didn't ignore curiosity. They dealt with it unemotionally. None of them found this difficult for their careers had conspired to reduce their normal human complement of emotions to about three simple ones which served them well.

Apart from the pilot they were all members of the Cyrenian National Army. The highest in rank and the leader of the party was Walter Mietus. He was a major and his loyalty to any organization was governed by the money it paid him and the work it expected him to do. More than once he had turned down good money because the work struck him as routine and unexciting. He needed excitement as a substitute for a whole series of emotions and physical outlets which were denied him. He was German, with a Greek mother. His first sight of the Mediterranean had been as a young Ober-leutnant in a Panzer Division of the German Afrika Korps; twenty-three years old, married to a girl in Munich and with two young boys. His tank had been hit by an armour-piercing 3·7 in. shell from a British anti-aircraft gun which formed part of the tank defence at El Alamein. His crew were killed but he, with a throat wound, climbed out of the turret and jumped clear, but not clear enough. The tank, canted on a slope, was hit by two more shells and rolled over to one side, trapping him by the legs and across his lower stomach. He should have been crushed to death but the soft sand giving a couple of inches under his body and the tank settling back a fraction of an inch saved him. He was held instead in a powerful vice. He should have bled to death, but he managed to get his free hands to the throat wound when he recovered consciousness and staunch it with the field dressing from his tunic breast pocket . . . From that point on life contrived to lead him to the edge of many agonizing moments when death would have been kind and welcomed, but always he was spared. His wife and boys were killed in a bombing raid while they were visiting relations in Dusseldorf. He learned this while in hospital in Italy. He wept—for the last time in his life. The doctors had made it plain that while his legs would carry him again he would never have the power to satisfy any woman . . . He never went back to Germany and, for the love which was denied him, he substituted violence.

He walked with bowed, awkward legs and his body was hard and shock-proof with the strength of a deformed oak. Now, at forty, his blond hair was white and thinning and scurfy, and his squarish, not unpleasant face, had the rough, sand-and-water bleached colour of a pine plank that has lain on a beach for months.

The others were all close to the same age as Mietus; Lorentzen who had been thrown from some limbo into the French Foreign Legion, deserted, pimped for an Algiers brothel, drifted half-way around the world and then back again, a soldier of fortune (as they all were, but not caring a damn for fortune because fortune needs tomorrows to enjoy it and they lived for each second as it came); Plevsky, out of Russian captivity to the Polish Army of General Anders, to become a deserter in Cairo, and finally a guerilla in Cyrenia; and Roper who spoke English with a gentle voice and what could have been the authentic echo of an Irish accent, who loved reading and music as Lorentzen loved horses, and practised an absorbing dedication to the violence-releasing now—and last of all Sifal, dark-skinned, the only true Cyrenian among them, and here because he was Colonel Mawzi's choice as a first-class radio operator. After his capture Colonel Mawzi, by bribing and dark influence, had found means to have Mietus come secretly to his cell, and had briefed him. Each man had been chosen for some particular need, and all of them for the common reason that not for the last fifteen years had any of them known a moment's hesitation in killing, whether it was man, woman, child or beast so long as their pay was not too much in arrears. Plevsky, alone, still had a few moments of regret for the past, still could find a little compassion for others though he was careful never to let his companions suspect it.

Of the pilot, Max Dondon, little need be said, except that he was half the age of Walter Mietus, but granted the same luck and the same disturbed world would turn out much the same as any of the others by the time he was in his forties.

All of them, too, except Max Dondon, wore much the same dress, brown light-weight leather jerkins, dark shirts, dark canvas trousers and rope-soled shoes.

Now, as the plane droned its way westwards, Mietus, Plevsky, Lorentzen and Sifal played a quiet game of bridge using the top of a packing case hauled out on to the catwalk of the stripped fuselage; Roper lay on his back reading a German translation of Sir Winston Churchill's first volume of *A History of the English Speaking Peoples*. Roper was always reading. It was a quiet, relaxed, contented group. Everything ahead of them was long rehearsed. Each man knew what he had to do, and each of his companions knew that he would do it.

For an hour after passing over H.M.S. *Dunoon* the plane stayed on her westerly route. Then Max Dondon with a glance at his watch brought her round slowly in a circle and headed eastwards losing height gently until he was well under the thin cloud canopy and about a thousand feet above sea level. Three-quarters of an hour later he picked up the distant gleam of the San Borodon light. The plane turned south-east and began to draw in towards the west coast of the island of Mora. Max said something over his shoulder and Roper put down his book and went forward to stand behind him. Slowly ahead of them the dark loom of Mora against the light sky began to swell from the sea.

"Lights," said Roper.

Max threw a switch and all the lights in the flying boat, except the dim cockpit glow, went out. The bridge players sat in the darkness. They went south another couple of miles. The flying boat dropped to the waters like a great bird. Gently they taxi-ed in. Roper touched Max on the shoulder and the engines died. They lay there rocking slowly on the long swell.

Each man then moved with the sureness of long drilling. The hull doors were opened and the fresh air swept into the tobacco-fogged interior. An inflated dinghy bloomed suddenly alongside and lay tugging at its painter in the drift. Mietus slid down into it and stood, reaching up for the packs that were lowered. When it was full Sifal joined him. The dinghy was paid off on a long line. Another dinghy was dropped to the water and swelled slowly with faint protests of the expanding rubber to its full size. This, too, was loaded and then crewed by Roper, Lorentzen and Plevsky.

Their only goodbye to Max was Plevsky's raised right hand as Max stood on the lip of the doorway looking down at them. He slipped the dinghy painter and they drifted away into the darkness, hauling in on the line which linked them with Mietus' dinghy.

The doors of the fuselage closed. The engines coughed and turned and across the waters a furrow of white bow wake was scored like a long rent in the fabric of the darkness.

None of the men in the two dinghies watched the flying boat. They had left it and because it was now the past they had no interest in it. They had their paddles out and without hurry were making for the coast a few hundred yards away.

They came ashore on a small beach at the foot of a rough black pinnacle of cliff. The dinghies were hauled clear of the water and without a word Mietus and Roper, free of all encumbrance, except the revolvers in their hands, moved away into the darkness. The others half-circled the dinghies, their backs to the sea, each pair of eyes, each pair of ears concentrating on different sectors of the dark cliffside ahead of them. They expected nothing, feared nothing, but they gave no trust to any of the succeeding seconds.

Mietus and Roper came back, materializing suddenly from the gloom, their rope-soled shoes soft on the rough lava rubble of the beach. The dinghies were deflated and folded, and then, each man burdened with a heavy pack, they moved away from the sea. It still needed two hours before midnight and the rising of the moon and by that time they would be well inland high up on the slopes of La Caldera.

The garden of Government House ended on the seaward side in a small promontory topped with a little stucco-and-tile gazebo that looked down across the Port Carlos harbour. It was a wild part of the garden, deliberately left to itself by Sir George who had a dislike of too much formality in gardens. A fleshy-leaved *monstera deliciosa* wreathed its way up the walls of the gazebo and spread across the tiled roof, fighting with plumbago and bougainvillaea. Azaleas, oleanders and a stiff frieze of prickly pear cactus backed the little building in a rough semi-circle, and before it was a wide terrace of flat, rough stones from whose cracks grew a collection of heathers and herbs, each planted by Sir George.

Teddy Burrows and his wife, Daphne, were sitting on the terrace just outside the gazebo. Teddy Burrows, comfortable from two glasses of the Governor's port, one of his cigars now in his hand, sprawled a little, the stiff front of his mess shirt bulging gently, a polished white shield in the darkness, and felt at ease. Daphne, for a change, was being very reasonable about his sleeping aboard. It was, he thought, the beginning of a proper understanding in her . . . After all it took a few years for married people to settle down and understand one another. Give and take on both sides, of course . . .

He put out a large paw and took her hand.

"It's a nuisance. Lordy, there's nothing I'd like better than to be up here with you all the time, but you know that wouldn't go down well on the *Dunoon*. One of the responsibilities of command is that you have to deny yourself more than you deny others. I don't like it any more than you. But there it is."

Daphne nodded. "I understand. What Mrs. So-and-So in Portsmouth must do without so must I——"

"Daphne . . . Really old girl!"

She laughed. "Don't be such an old prude, Teddy. That's what it boils down to."

"Maybe . . . but put like that. Anyway, this is only a matter of sleeping ashore at night. I do see you and have some time with you."

"Oh, yes. That's where I'm luckier than Mrs. So-and-So."

She laughed again, seeing his face in the sudden glow of his cigar. Embarrassed, he made a rough noise in his throat and said, "H.E. was in a good mood tonight. He had the Croft's '27 out."

He sat there talking about port, enjoying his cigar and, although he wouldn't have said this to her, enjoying her company. For a long time now he had sensed always the edge of resistance, of discord between them. But tonight it was gone. It was his first night in Port Carlos for many days and he had expected her to be annoyed that he had decided to sleep aboard. After all, they had to pull out at four in the morning. But she had taken it easily, reasonably . . . Taken it so well, in fact, that it almost made him want to change his mind and stay.

Actually, Daphne was thinking to herself, the poor dear's got it all wrong. Since she had made her decision to leave him this business of sleeping ashore had become unimportant. Earlier, when she had first come to Port Carlos, she had been annoyed because he wouldn't. But that annoyance sprang from her own pride. She was his wife, she was attractive; he should want to take every opportunity to be with her, even if when they were together it wasn't all it should be. Curiously, her decision which had nothing to do with four legs in a bed —in the privacy of her thoughts she had a natural bluntness that sometimes spilled over into her speech—but was concerned with her ambition to have the kind of life and husband she wanted, had provoked unexpectedly an added fondness and affection for him. Now that she knew she was going to leave him there was a new tenderness in her. He would do better without her, would find himself someone more suited to him . . . In a way she was doing him a favour by her own ruthlessness. Married people should have the courage to recognize their failure and the will power to cut loose from their disappointment in each other.

She stood up and the stiff under-petticoat of her dress swung the skirt out in a wide flare that brushed against his knees. The movement stirred the air and it was touched with the fragrance of her scent. Teddy held her hand as she stood above him, tall, slim, her hair like a wan flame. She was a damn fine-looking woman, damn fine. He was a lucky man. He stood up, put his arms around her and kissed her. Just for a moment his bulk, the strength in his arms and the rough, cigar odour and his masculinity moved her. She kissed him warmly, her affection for him taking her much nearer passion than she had ever known with him. Maybe, she thought, every goodbye kiss, the real goodbye, held that promise, the promise that could never be fulfilled.

"If the *Dunoon* goes out at four you'd better get back and have some sleep. How long will you be away?"

"Depends. It's a heavy patrol schedule."

They walked back to the house, hand in hand. A few minutes later he was walking down the hill to Port Carlos by himself. It was near midnight and the moon was rising far out at sea. The wind he noticed had changed a little, veering to the south and the smell of drying cod was stronger. He smiled at this, thinking of Daphne. Even that she was getting used to . . . hadn't heard her complain about it for a long time. She was a good girl and he was damned lucky to have married her . . . They all had their fads of course, and you had to weather them. Just for a moment in his imagination she was in his arms again and her lips warm and stirring gently against his . . . Damn the *Dunoon,* he said to himself suddenly. Why should he be such a stickler for discipline and good example? He paused, surprised by this inner rebellion, and half inclined to go back. But as he stood there a taxi came

92

down the hill behind him and drew up. A side window went down and Lieutenant Imray's head poked out.

"Evening, sir. Can we give you a lift?"

In the car with Imray was his engineer officer and Teddy could see that they were both a little, but pleasantly, tight.

"Where have you two scallywags been?"

"Dancey's Hotel, sir. Celebrating our return to this demi-semi-Eden, this little jewel, this something . . ."

"If you're going to quote Shakespeare get him right," growled Teddy, but he was full of good-humour. He opened the door of the car and slid in beside them. As they drove on, the two of them chattering away to him, laughing, he relaxed against the leather and knew that it was a good world, full of fine fellows, good chaps, and he acknowledged the simple, honest pleasure of feeling himself lucky to be alive and to be himself with all he could ask for already his, a fine wife, a fine ship and pleasant ship-mates.

In his little office which was next door to the library on the ground floor, Neil Grayson had done two hours' work after leaving Sir George and Teddy Burrows over their port. He was in the middle of making up Sir George's annual report, and there was now also Sir George's weekly report to be sent to Whitehall on the Hadid Chebir affair. In effect this was little more than a suitable transcription of Richmond's report which Burrows had brought back. As he had charge of all the diplomatic mail which went back on the Sunderland flying boat to Southampton each week, he had gone through the mail which had come from Mora. A bulky letter addressed to Banstead at the War Office from Richmond had not escaped his notice. He would have given a great deal to have been able to read it. He knew Banstead and he guessed that he had asked Richmond for some sort of informal report to be sent confidentially to him. And he knew that sometimes this kind of private comment very much affected other people's careers.

He went into the library and fixed himself a large whiskey and soda. At the side of the deep leather arm chair by the window was a neatly folded pile of copies of *The Times* which Sir George had been reading through. The old man was in bed now. Grayson went out onto the verandah, put his feet up on a cane chair and relaxed with his whiskey. It was a warm, airless night, the edge of the rising moon just beginning to show. He watched the headlights of a car probe down the hillside towards Port Carlos. He undid the front of his dinner jacket to make himself more comfortable and sipped at his whiskey.

Daphne Burrows came round the far end of the verandah and stood under one of the shaded lights. Her hands resting on the top of the wrought-iron balustrading, she looked down towards Port Carlos. He watched her, knowing she hadn't seen him. It was a new dress, or one he hadn't seen before, and the full skirt running up into the tight sheath of bodice emphasized her height and slimness. Momentarily he contrasted her with Marion Chebir. They were both beautiful, striking women. But Daphne's elegance was brittle, delicate. A high wind on a cliff-top would have cut her down, but the Chebir woman would have leaned into it, taken the wind in her face and breasts and laughed at it . . . bloody poetical he was getting, he thought as he sipped his whiskey. Anyway, Daphne was much more his type . . . He watched her, aware of her as he always was not as Sir George's daughter, as Teddy Burrows' wife, but as a woman, and as usual his curiosity was stirred. Because she was Sir George's daughter she had no place in his world, but because she was a woman, and the kind of woman who normally he felt himself drawn to, she had a large place in his fantasy . . . that pale hair, that clear pink and white complexion and the lazy, yet somehow noble elegance of her body challenged an infallible instinct in him for knowing those who would burn and tremble into an abandon that would complement his own. You could always tell . . . at least, he could. It was like a bell ringing. But there were some bells you had to ignore.

She turned, sensing perhaps his thoughts about her, or warned by the aura of his presence, and she came down the verandah towards him. He stood up as she dropped into a chair. She looked at his glass and then at him.

"A large whiskey and soda is what I want too, Neil," she said.

He brought her the drink and put it on the table at her side. As he sat down she reached for it and drank and they sat

94

in silence for a while, a silence dictated by her and respected by him.

Then very calmly she said, "Teddy's gone back to the *Dunoon*."

"I know."

She held up the glass and twisted it a little in her hand. The distant light made the glass facets sparkle a little.

"It would be easy," she said, "if a whiskey and soda were the answer to everything."

He knew then that she wanted to talk to him. He was quick to mark the inconsequent phrases that people spread before them to cover the approach of a confidence.

When he made no reply she laughed quietly and put the glass down. "I know that's a silly remark. But it isn't always possible to go straight to the point."

"Before you do, it's better to make sure that you really want to go there."

She shook her head. "No, I don't want to be let out. That's what you mean. No . . . it's too late. I've finally made up my mind. I'm going to leave Teddy." Something in the way she said it isolated the last sentence and gave the impression that not until she had said it had she begun to talk.

He was silent for a moment, his mind working fast. She'd never made any confidence to him before. They called one another "Neil" and "Daphne" but that was the limit of their informal contact. But he knew that she was clear-sighted, determined and not without ruthlessness. It was easy to recognize in others the things you possessed yourself. So that now, in this pause, he knew that everything was calculated and deliberate in this confidence and he was trying to see beyond this moment.

"Divorce?"

"Yes. It'll be arranged somehow. In a few weeks I shall go back to England."

"Does Sir George know about this?"

"Not yet. Nobody knows, except me—and now you."

He didn't miss that either, but it was less of a surprise to him.

"Not even Teddy, yet," she added.

"Sir George won't take to it kindly."

"He will after a while. I can manage him."

"I don't doubt it." He smiled and she answered it with her own smile and this movement of expressions between them was the first of their intimacies. "You can manage most things, I imagine."

"Most. But not all. There are some things a woman can't be by herself. You know what I mean?"

He nodded. "Clearly." He leaned back in his chair and fingered his glass, looking at her. The attractiveness of her body and her personality he acknowledged to himself by the distant tremor of excitement within him, but just now it had little importance.

"How clearly? I don't altogether trust you, Neil. I think you pretend to a wisdom you haven't got. Everyone says you understand women. But do you? Just cocking an eyebrow, smiling and keeping silent isn't understanding."

"You want words?"

"Yes."

"All right. But you should see that because of some words I haven't given you that I understand. I haven't asked you the first question most people would have asked you. The first thing Sir George will ask you is why. Why are you going to break with Teddy?"

"But you know."

"I think so. You're like me. You laid down a plan for yourself. An ambitious plan. When you married Teddy he seemed to fit into it, seemed to be the man who would make your plan possible. But when he stuck to the Navy the whole thing flopped. If he'd stuck to the Navy because one day he might become an admiral, that would have been all right. But he'll never be more than a lieutenant-commander. Now, you've decided to make a fresh start. Good for you."

Very quietly she said, "It could be good for both of us. And it could be everything you want."

Neil laughed pleasantly. There was no surprise in him.

"I've no doubt that some parts would be wonderful. I've never had any doubt of that. But, quite frankly, if you've got a plan for yourself, so have I. It includes a woman, a wife, but she must be much more than just that." He pulled out his cigarette case and held it towards her. She'd been outspoken,

96

dropped every inch of pride to speak so frankly, but he knew that as far as he was concerned he still walked a tight-rope. The wrong word or phrase could destroy everything. As he lit her cigarette, his face was close to hers over the flame. "Tell me," he said, "what it is that you're offering which I can't find elsewhere?"

"Money. I have an income of my own and father will . . . well, you know."

"Other women have the same."

"Family, the right connections, knowing the right people."

"That by itself isn't enough. It might not work for me. For a man like Major Richmond it would work automatically— but not for me."

"I shall make it work. I can get you a directorship in Talloid Chemicals." She smiled to herself as for the first time she saw his face grow serious. "The chairman isn't unknown at the Central Conservative Office. You could have a constituency, maybe a safe one right from the start. In ten years you could be in the Cabinet. It's bad luck, maybe, to put a name to the ultimate thing you want. But if you want it, so will I and . . ." she stood up, ". . . and I think you know now that when I want a thing I don't stand about dreaming and hoping for it to turn up."

"This I admire, of course. There is the divorce, though. I don't want to limit my place in politics. Some people are still old-fashioned."

"Teddy won't make any trouble. It'll be done as I want it. Quietly, decently . . . Divorce means less and less. You know that, and by the time you're ready. . . ."

"No doubt. Still . . ." He frowned suddenly. "Hell, there's nothing wrong in being ambitious."

"Nothing, or in speaking frankly." She smiled. "Usually, in my set, parents more or less arrange a marriage. Yes, even now. Is there anything wrong in re-arranging one's own?"

"No." Neil stood up. Suddenly the seriousness went from his face and with an unexpected, boyish grimace he said, "Well, that seems to be settled."

Daphne shook her head. "No, not quite. There is one other thing. I don't want any lady travel writers in our plan. Oh

97

yes, I know about Janet Harker. Everything has to be right. Everything."

"You know it will be. You wouldn't have spoken to me if you didn't think so."

"That's true. But I want to be certain."

"Well, there's only one answer to that."

She moved a little towards the library door and then looking back at him said, "My bedroom door is never locked. The maid comes with my tea at seven."

He sat there for an hour after she had left. Then he went slowly up to his own room and undressed. It was two o'clock when he left it and five minutes to seven when he returned. Everything had been perfect.

5

BEYOND the town the road ran straight for a while across the level skirts of the valley. Half a mile inland where the *barranco* began to rise steeply the road split into a fork. Corporal March brought the jeep to a halt.

"Which way, sir?"

In the angle of the road was a rough finger post. The left-hand sign read *Torba*, and the other *Ardino*. John Richmond spread the map on his knees, smoothed out its dirty creases and studied it.

Corporal March stared ahead at the rising cone of La Caldera and hoped that Major Richmond would choose the Ardino road. If they went there, he might get a chance of a few words with Arianna. Not once since H.M.S. *Dunoon* had brought her prisoners to Mora had he had a chance to slip out and see his girl. Arianna would be in a fine old state. It would be like his luck, though, if Richmond chose the Torba road that ran part way round the eastern side of the island. It was a hell of a road, too; worse than the Ardino one, which was bad enough. They'd both have their guts shaken out. He was seeking some way to put this over when the officer said: "Let's have a look at Ardino."

Corporal March put the jeep in gear and they began to

98

climb steeply up the side of the valley towards the crest of the radial ridge that ran down from La Caldera. The road twisted and curved around small gorges and gradually the wide Mora *barranco* was spread out below them, terraced and patterned with green strips of banana plantation and tobacco patches. Now and again they passed some small cabin, each with its neat square of garden quarried and terraced out of the rough hillside, the age-old lava stone broken down by the centuries into a friable, fertile soil and rich with maize, tomatoes, pimentos and beans. Alongside of the road, sagging and untidy, ran a continuous length of small-gauge water-piping, joined here and there by tributary pipes that looped down the side cuts and hanging valleys. Away below, in the Mora valley, the round concrete water reservoirs, green with scum, that the pipes fed lay scattered among the plantations like a handful of verdigrised pennies. The morning sun was hot and high so that when they ran into the sudden chestnut-shaped bends under the hanging hillside it was like being plunged into cold water.

For the first time in several days since the *Dunoon* had left, John had felt that things were sufficiently well organized at Fort Sebastian for him to take some time off and have a closer look at the island. It never hurt, he felt, to have the feel of the lie of the land. Now and again a turn in the road brought him a view of the far crater of La Caldera. The broken lip was rough and cliff-slashed but lower down there was a soft covering of pines and stunted oaks. Higher this morning than he had ever noticed it before hung the soft cloud cap.

Apart from Mora, Ardino and Torba were the only other settlements on the island. Neither of them amounted to more than a handful of houses, and at both of them the road came to an end, leaving the whole southern sweep of the island inaccessible except on foot and along the few goat tracks.

From the top of the ridge—the one which ran on two miles further to the north to end in the steep bluff above Fort Sebastian—they could look down the western slope of La Caldera to Ardino. With the exception of one or two slopes that were planted with new vines, the country was wild and broken, tumbling away to the cliff edge and the blue-green

Atlantic waters. The road down was steep and rutted and Corporal March took it in low gear. The road ended about two hundred yards from the sea in a wide circle of bare, hard-packed earth. A few houses crouched squalidly round the circle and over one of them in faded blue letters ran the words *Bar Filis*. On the seaward side was a small church with broken lengths of iron railings around it. A few dogs, a pig, and a handful of scraggy bantams occupied the circle. The two men got out of the jeep and Corporal March seeing Richmond look around, puzzled, said, "There won't be any-one much about, sir. They'll all be working. Most of the men down on the beach and the women up there." He jerked his head towards the hillside.

"They fish?"

"Yes, sir. Got a few boats down there. Fish, and chestnuts and maize . . . they live on them. They're a pretty tough lot and keep to themselves."

John looked around, at the shabby church and the single-storey houses, paint and plaster flaking from them. The whole place looked sullen and unkempt. A dog came up and walked suspiciously around him. He could see patches of eczema in its pelt.

"The wine's not too bad, sir." March jerked his head towards the bar. "I could get a bottle for our haversack rations."

"All right, Corporal, do that. I'll stroll down and take a look at the beach."

"Blanco secco or rojo, sir?"

"Get one of each."

"Very good, sir."

March watched him move away past the church and take the path to the beach. He turned and went over to the *Bar Filis*.

It was dark inside and his eyes took a little time to accus-tom themselves to the gloom after the hard light of the day. An unshaven man in shirt sleeves was leaning with his elbows on the bar, picking his teeth and reading an old magazine. Four young men, smoking long brown cigarillos, were playing cards at a table by the wall. March couldn't remember a time when he had come into the bar and the grouping had been much different. They were a lazy, dirty lot of so-and-so's. Too lazy to scratch their own lice.

The card players looked up briefly and nodded to him. He was Arianna's soldier. They accepted him but no more. It wasn't the first time Arianna had got pine needles in her hair through lying out in the dark with a man. It wouldn't be the last and, anyway, this one brought corned beef, sugar and tea from the fort supplies. And if one wanted more he could easily be frightened into it.

The barman said, "Is that the new officer?"

March nodded.

"He is good to thee?"

Although he spoke a rough Spanish that had improved since he had known Arianna, March said in English, "He's a bloody officer." His tone made the barman laugh.

"And the others? I hear there is a woman."

"Don't talk to me about them. A man could get out for a breath of fresh air before they came."

"Fresh air. Ah, yes." The barman scratched his stubble with dirt-rimmed nails.

"A bottle of white and a bottle of red. Not that turpentine either. The good stuff."

March reached out for the cognac bottle at the side of the bar and filled himself a glass. A little covey of flies went up from the sticky bottle top as he lifted it and he grimaced. Why they didn't all die of dysentery or typhoid was beyond him.

The barman brought the bottles and as March handed him some money he said, "Where's Arianna?"

The barman shrugged.

One of the card players said, without turning or looking at March, "It is her day for the church. Maybe there."

March took his bottles and went back to the jeep. He put them in a locker under the back seat and then walked over to the church. He knew what she would be doing there. For all their slovenliness these people had a passion for flowers. Even the scruffiest house always sported a vase that would have made a hole in a couple of quid if you had to buy the flowers in a London shop. It was something in their favour, but not much. Arum lilies grew wild like daisies in the shaded gullies and every backyard had a clump of hibiscus.

He went in by the side entrance, into the little room which the priest who came from Mora used once a week. An old cassock hung on a hook behind the door and a rough wooden table was covered with vases. Flower stalk ends lay on the table where they had been cut. The floor was wet with slopped water and a couple of buckets held an assortment of blooms. He pushed open the inner door to the church and stood there, close to the altar. A blue and white wooden madonna with a tinsel crown backed the altar and great banks of flowers were arranged on either side of the altar steps. There was a smell of old incense. Crude wall paintings of shipwrecks and other disasters, each with a saint treading air above it, ran down the far wall. The rafters of the wooden roof were painted a cold blue and one of the windows, long broken, was half-boarded up.

Arianna was with another girl close to the altar. She turned as the door creaked and saw him. Her arms were full of madonna lilies and just looking at her March felt his throat choke. She was a little over twenty, a rough apron covered her faded cotton frock and a handkerchief was tied across her dark hair. She was well built but slender at the waist, and her skin was an even warm brown. She had a young face, childish, and with an expression of heavy, almost petulant sensuousness. Seeing him, she put the flowers down, said something softly to the other girl and came across to him quickly. He took her arm, pulling her into the little room and he closed the door.

She came into his arms and they kissed. It was a long kiss and left them both shaking when she pulled away from him.

She held his hand still and said, "Why hast thou been so long?"

"We have a new officer. He keeps us working hard. It is very difficult."

"Even at night?"

"We must keep guard on these prisoners, even at night." He paused, letting his eye travel from her face down the length of her body. He felt ashamed of the thought, but as far as he could see there was no change in her. "How is it with thee?"

"I do not know."

"Why not? There's been time."

"No, I cannot tell. When we work hard it alters things sometimes. All the women know that. For a month now we have been on the hill staking the new vines, hoeing . . . it is hard work, and from the first time I have never been regular. Sometimes I fear. When I am alone I fear. But now with thee the fear has gone." She came back to him, her full bosom just touching the front of his bush shirt. "The flowers are finished. We could go——"

He shook his head violently. "I can't go anywhere. I'm here with the officer. He's on the beach but soon he will be back."

He saw her face change, the disappointment hardening the heavy passion in it. She might be afraid when he was not with her, but when he was, all her fears, every shred of thought about the future, vanished so long as they could go down into the pine woods and make love. She forgot so easily then that he sometimes wondered whether the rest of it wasn't an act just to string him along.

"Ask this officer to let thee come back. Tonight."

"Arianna," he rolled his eyes, "things aren't like that in the army."

"But thou wilt come?"

"Yes."

"Tonight?"

"Not tonight. Maybe tomorrow."

"My brother asks why we don't see thee. He says the British soldiers take what they want from a woman and then look for another. It is a matter of his pride."

Privately March knew what her brother, Torlo, could do with his pride, but he said gently, not wanting a scene, "Tomorrow or the next day, I will come. Now I must go to my officer."

He kissed her again and his hand slid into her bosom and for a while they were close together, each made hungrier by the brief liberties that the time and place allowed to their hands and lips.

As he went to the outer door she said, "My mother says to tell thee that she has need of sugar and coffee, and it would be well to bring something for my father."

March nodded. Sometimes he wondered why they didn't write out a list and post it to him.

When he got outside it was to see Major Richmond standing by the jeep.

They drove back to the fork road and then out to Torba. The country was much the same, and Torba almost as slatternly and dead as Ardino. They ate their haversack rations on a ridge top a mile north of Torba and drank half a bottle of wine each. Afterwards Richmond told March to park the jeep in the shade somewhere and have a sleep. Himself, he set off along the ridge towards La Caldera. He knew he had no hope of reaching the top. It was a good two-hour climb from this side, and, anyway, from this ridge he could see that eventually he would be faced with a tall rock face two hundred feet high. But he was in need of exercise. It was a long time since he had stretched his legs against a stiff climb. It was hot and he was soon sweating. He saw no one except a couple of women, knitting and watching a herd of goats on a stretch of pasture below the first of the pines. He went through the pines and found himself, half an hour later, on a wide moraine of old lava. It ran upwards from him in a dark, broken fan to the black face of the cliffs that crowded around the crater. He hesitated at the foot of the lava, wondering whether he would go on to the foot of the cliffs and then decided in favour of returning to the jeep by fetching round in a wide detour to the far side of the pine forest.

Although he didn't know it, his hesitation at the foot of the lava stream had been marked by Walter Mietus and Roper. High up on the lip of the cliffs they had watched the jeep go to Torba, then come back and halt on the ridge, and without a word they had seen Richmond begin his climb. There was no concern in either of them. No one could climb the cliff face at this point.

Mietus focused his glasses on Richmond as he moved along the edge of the pine forest.

"He wears a major's crown," he said.

"Does he walk with an object, you think?"

"Why should he? He is English. They are dedicated to

104

exercise, to sport. In the African campaign I saw two officers sailing a sand yacht . . . a sand yacht within two hundred yards of our leaguer!"

Roper took the glasses.

"He goes well. They haven't sent an armchair officer. What would he say, you think, if he knew he was probably due to have his throat cut some day in Fort Sebastian?" Roper laughed.

With the palm of his hand Mietus deliberately flattened a beetle that walked across the smooth rock face under his nose. "He would cock an eye at you and you would be wise not to count the thing as done until it was done. I have a great respect for the English." But he used the word "respect", grinding it from between his teeth, as though he were saying "hatred".

Roper rolled over on to his back and lit a cigarette. He had a sudden picture of a sand yacht rolling across the hard, flat desert.

"You think the two officers had made it themselves?"

"Made what?"

"The sand yacht."

"We did not ask them. Our machine gun put an end to their sport."

Roper had another sudden picture, of the hard flat desert spurting into a moving line of sand blooms as the bullets swept across the yacht. He sighed with pleasure.

Two hours later John was back at Fort Sebastian. He took a shower and changed his clothes. Sergeant Benson came into him before dinner, saluted and then said, "While you were away today, sir, I had a request from two of the prisoners. Colonel Mawzi and Madame Chebir. They want to know whether they can be allowed to bathe from the beach below the fort."

John was silent for a moment, then he said, "What do you think about it?"

"Well, sir, it's hot enough. They've only got that parapet to walk on. Most of my chaps slip down sometime during the day and take a swim. They can see them at it from the parapet. Probably what put it in their heads, sir."

"All right, Sergeant. One guard on the beach and a man

105

standing off in a boat. But if one goes down they all go down, Abou as well, even if they don't swim. I don't want the party broken up. Haven't got enough guards."

"I can stand off in the boat myself, sir. That'll ease things a bit."

"Good. Has Corporal March got a girl at Ardino?"

Sergeant Benson's bluff face showed his surprise. John smiled. "It's all right, I'm not a thought-reader. He came out of the church over there and I saw a girl standing in the doorway behind him."

"I believe there is a girl over there, sir."

"All right, Sergeant. That's all. I'll see Colonel Mawzi myself later and tell him about the bathing party."

Ten minutes later he was called to the telephone in the garrison office, which was a small room to the right of the main gateway. For once the line from Port Carlos was as clear as a bell.

Grayson was speaking. A signal had been received from the War Office that within the next eight or ten days a detachment of six men was being flown out to supplement the garrison at Fort Sebastian.

"Six isn't enough."

"It's all you're getting. I've talked to the chief of police here and he was prepared to spare you two of his chaps—he's only got a small body, you know, but when he heard of this detachment coming he stuck his toes in. I could twist his arm, if you insist."

"Don't bother. We'll manage until the six come."

"How are things?" Grayson sounded alert and cheerful.

"Running smoothly so far. Tell H.E. that I'm giving them permission to visit the beach. If he's against it, let me know."

"Seems O.K. I'd like to see Madame Chebir in a swim suit."

John smiled. "I imagine a lot of my chaps are looking forward to it, too. When's Sir George coming over here?"

"Not yet awhile. He's up to the eyes on his annual report. Unless you want him, of course."

"No. What's the news from home?"

Grayson knew what he meant. "The Opposition are going to force a vote of no confidence over Chebir. It's the usual

106

line. Exile is no way to solve any problem in Cyrenia. Some pressmen have arrived here, but H.E. won't give them a clearance to go to Mora yet."

"I don't want 'em, either."

"You'll have to put up with them when Sir George comes over to you. He'll probably bring a couple."

He shied away from the thought of pressmen. He'd had some of them before. They drank your whiskey and smoked your cigarettes. They were friendly, intelligent people who kept you up until all hours talking and then they went away and produced stuff which turned simple facts into astonishing revelations. They saw everything dramatically, black and bold like their own headlines. They'd dramatize this grey hulk of a fortress, and they'd wring everything they could out of his three prisoners' situation although they would never pass a word with them. They'd even dramatize the drains if it gave them a good paragraph. He didn't dislike them. It just was that he couldn't stick their lack of proportion.

He was reminded of them again the next afternoon when he went down, a little after the bathing party left, to see how things were going. The scene would have made a press photographer happy.

The beach lay at the foot of the cliffs on the far side of Fort Sebastian. A rough track zig-zagged down to it, loose and slippery with stones. The patch of coarse black sand, little larger than a tennis lawn, was flanked by two horns of dark cliff. The Atlantic swell came in with a regular smack and roar and then a long suck-back over the beach. Sergeant Benson stripped to the waist, wearing one of the wide-brimmed hats the islanders made from palmetto, sat in a small rowing boat fifty yards offshore, dipping his oars now and again to keep station. A guard with a rifle, leaning back against a boulder in the shade, came to attention as John jumped to the beach, his feet sinking into the loose sand. The guard relaxed as John passed.

Colonel Mawzi was in the water, a few yards from the boat, lying on his back and kicking a little now and then with his feet. Hadid Chebir sat on the near side of the beach, cross-legged on a rug, a book balanced on his knees. He wore linen trousers, and a silk shirt open at the neck. He looked up as

John's shadow fell near him and for a moment his face was relaxed, almost pleasant, as though he had left much of himself behind in the fortress.

"You don't bathe?" asked John.

"No, Major. But it is pleasant to sit down here and be cool. We are grateful to you." He turned the book over to keep the pages from flying in the breeze and reached for cigarette and matches from the rug at his side. "How long," he asked, "do you think they will keep us here?" He lit a cigarette.

"I do not know."

"Officially, of course not. But privately, what do you think?"

John shrugged. "Unless we have a change of government, I do not think you will see Cyrenia for many years."

"Perhaps never again?"

"Perhaps."

Hadid shook his head. "The easiest way to alter the course of a river is to go to the mountain and divert the small spring. That is what your people think. I am the spring, the source. But block one spring and the hillside is broken by others because water must flow. Water must flow."

"Sometimes," said John, "it lies about, stagnant in ponds, until the sun evaporates it——"

Hadid threw back his head and laughed, and then suddenly silent he gave John a quick look, shook his head and turned abruptly to his book.

John passed on, not understanding the man, and abruptly touched by a sense of irritation. The whole thing was a mess. Everyone knew that, and everyone worked like a beaver throwing up new dams to stop the flood of confusion, but one by one the dams were swept away. He'd read History at Oxford and he had always taken an intelligent interest in his international politics. He'd been as earnest and sincere as any young man in his time . . . but with the years the whole thing had gone sour. You couldn't keep up with it. The jigsaw couldn't be sorted out because people kept knocking the table and spilling the pieces. That's why he liked being a soldier. Do this. Do that. Soldiering gave you a limit. You could work comfortably within it. Guard these three and see they don't escape. That was something he could understand.

But when someone said, work out a just constitution for Cyrenia and make it acceptable . . . Well the thing was doomed from the start. Just was. You might as well plant boiled potatoes and expect a crop. Maybe this kind of thought made him a defeatist. Antediluvian. Well, if it did, it did. Inwardly he stirred with a swift revulsion for the whole hotch-potch.

A voice said, "You look very serious, Major."

He stopped walking. Marion Chebir lay stretched out on a large towel. She lay there in a white costume, all woman under the sun, and one hand was raised a little to shade her eyes as she looked up at him.

"Maybe I am."

He lowered himself on the sand at her side and there was no surprise in him at his action until he was sitting there with his hands clasped round his knees, looking at her. The salt water from her recent swim was wet on her legs.

"And yet you can make Hadid laugh?" She sat up and jerked her head backwards to throw the loose dark hair from her forehead.

"Is it so hard to do that?"

Her legs were brown and long and polished and he had no interest in Hadid at all. Quite suddenly it was as though someone had warningly struck him gently across the throat with the edge of a hand making him swallow quickly.

"It is very hard. You must have said something very funny." She leaned forward and ran her hands down her legs sliding away the water from her skin and her nails took the sun and he saw the evenness of her half-moons and the shadow of veins across her knuckles, and in his own hands he could feel the sensation of how it would be to hold her hands.

"I said peace could be stagnation." But he wasn't interested in his own words.

"Maybe it is funny for Hadid. I don't know." Her hands came back and just for a moment, as she raised them to smooth her hair, they hesitated at the top of her costume and she gave the edges of the white silk a little tug to settle it more comfortably about her breasts. It was a gesture he had seen many women make, but seeing her do it now it was new and left his eyes watching the column of her throat. It was something he had never had before, this kind of wanting that struck without warning.

"You like talking politics?" she asked.

"Sometimes. But I don't think we could ever agree about Cyrenia . . ." His eyes were on her.

"I know all the arguments," she said. "I've heard them all so often before." She turned her head a little.

Ten minutes ago, he thought, if anyone had asked me I would have said her eyes were brown. I notice things like that; the rings on a woman's finger and the graining of the skin that smooths away below the ear, but now her eyes are not brown and I am seeing them for the first time. Hazel tints with a richness of gold and green in them. I ought to get up and go away because this isn't the kind of thing I care to have happen to me without warning.

"So have I," he said.

"Years ago I heard it all from Hadid. Hadid put all the words into the mouth of Cyrenia . . . The large nations are doomed to withdraw before the small ones. France, Britain, the United States have bound themselves to UNO and tied their hands from all-out violence. But the little nations are free to yap and bark and bite and run wild, and little by little the big ones must give them what they want. That is the whole policy of every country that seeks self-determination. I've heard it so often. I believe it. Oh, I believe it . . ."

She lay back and stretched her arms, and he guessed that she was only thinking of herself, of her own weariness and that he scarcely existed. But she existed for him in the long length of her legs, in the smooth salt-damp coolness of her flat stomach, in the curves and warm unendlessness of her blood, and her body that lay all woman, all brown and white and black tangled hair in the sun on the dark beach which had once been a molten, white-hot lava spew from far Caldera.

He said, "You remember it very well." And he had an amazement in him at the thought that no matter what she and Hadid had been in the past there was, so far as he could tell, nothing of man and wife between them now. How could that be, feeling as he did, which was simply feeling as a man, for she was a woman that he could not conceive any man not wanting with this same sudden rebellion of the body that he

110

knew? My backside, he thought, must be concreted to the sand otherwise I would get up and go and with my first movement destroy all this. But he sat there and watched her flex one leg and dig her toes into the black sand, all without any coquetry or real awareness of him.

"I am all memory." She sat up then and looked full at him and for the first time in their talk she smiled a little, bringing him wanly to life in her own mind and she said, "It is odd that I find it easy to talk to you now sometimes. And then sometimes I hate you because of all this . . ." Her hand lifted and the movement of her arm swept across the sea and back to Fort Sebastian. And he didn't care a damn whether she was all memory, whether she hated him yesterday, found him easy to talk to today and would hate him tomorrow, for the only thought and sensation in him, just as it had been a little while ago in his hands, was the shaking sensation of his lips as they imagined themselves pressed against the bare white hollow of her armpit as her hand swept by him.

For God's sake, he told himself, I must have heat-stroke. He raised his hand and let the black sand trickle through his fingers and a few grains drifted to the white stuff of her swim-suit. That contact from his hand to her body, though no real contact, seemed to close his throat and finally awakened real anger in him at his damn-foolery.

Marion stared at the sun-glittered sea, narrowing her eyes against it. This man, Richmond, had a difficult job. Privately she was aware of sympathy for him. He must hate it. You could tell that. Whenever he came near them he was correct and formal. It was hard to imagine what he was really like. What was he like, for instance, when he took too much drink in the mess? At a theatre with a woman . . . or with a woman? There must be that part of him, a warm, natural John Richmond somewhere. He was about as natural to her as she was to him . . . She shut her eyes and deliberately imagined herself on some Mediterranean beach with him . . . swimming and sunbathing, laughing and somewhere behind them the sound of ice against glass. So many things seemed to have gone from her life . . . dancing, she liked to dance, to let herself go to music; to laze, to potter about on some verandah, watering the plants; to come into a room wearing

111

a new evening frock and to see some man rise, the pleasure on his face a rich compliment . . . God in Heaven, what a grubby, angry thing all this politics and national aspirations made of life. Give me, she thought vehemently, a four-roomed villa, a loving husband with twelve pounds a week, and it would be paradise. . . .

A shadow went across the sun and Colonel Mawzi was standing before them, bitten with the sun like a pearl diver, his waist thin and wiry above the red triangle of his briefs, and the face polished with wetness.

"You've come to join us, Major?"

John shook his head and rose. The thing was broken in him.

"The major," said Marion, "takes his swim early in the morning. I have watched him from the parapet. He likes the beach all to himself. That much I remember from when I was British. They can't bear to share a beach with anyone."

She smiled up at him, her white teeth showing between her red lips. But the softness and wetness of her lips as her pink tongue flashed across them did nothing now for him. The thing had gone like the shadow of a quick passing cloud.

"The water was good," said the colonel. But the words meant little. His eyes were on John, and he could sense the disturbance in the man. He saw the tiny, rapid flicker of a vein in the other's left temple. He looked back at Marion, wondering, but she had lowered her head and was running sand idly through her hands . . . He turned towards the cliffs and shouted sharply, "Abou!"

Abou came out of the far shadows, carrying a towel.

John moved away and as he passed the guard on his way back he turned and saw Mawzi towelling his head. Marion had turned over to take the sun on her back and one leg was raised lazily in the air.

The guard watched his major climb the steep cliff path. He was Hardcastle, the cricket enthusiast. But cricket was out of his mind just now. He was thinking of men and women, what women did to men and what men would do for women, and particularly of Corporal March. Smoking a cigarette with Corporal March in the courtyard before lunch, the corporal had said:

112

"You sleeping in the gate-room tonight, right?"

"Yes."

"Well, if you hear anyone slipping out about one and coming back about five keep your eyes and big mouth shut."

"You can't do that. You know the sergeant's orders. No one leaves at night."

"Marchy-boy can do what he likes and if you shove your oar in I'll bust your face, and a lot more beside."

He didn't like it but there was nothing he could do. March was a wizard with keys. He'd made one for the stores where the liberty ship stuff was and now and again he let him have spam and tinned coffee to take down to his girl's family in Mora. He had other keys, too; including one for the small wicket door in the main gate. Oh, yes, he was pretty fly about keys, but he'd bloody well land himself in trouble, and others with him . . . He stared out at sea where Sergeant Benson sat in the rowing boat. If he split to the sergeant about March then old Benson would drag everything out of him and he'd get it in the neck about pinching stuff from the liberty stores. And the bloody major, too. He'd know, and he looked the kind of correct bastard who wouldn't stand for any nonsense. Women . . . ! Why the hell did March have to have a girl right over at Ardino? If she'd been in the town like his, he could have slipped down for half an hour in the afternoon. Not that his girl was worth slipping down for. Not much. For all the spam and tinned coffee he gave her folks she still shied away from him if he started to get fancy. The longest innings on record he told himself gloomily. Four months and not a single run scored.

Out at sea Benson blew a whistle. Hardcastle heaved his back from his supporting rock and looked military as the party on the beach began to gather themselves together. Well, old March had better be back before the sergeant got stirring in the morning. He wasn't going to carry the can for him if he was late.

It was a quarter to one when Corporal March moved quietly into the dark shadows under the main gate arch. It was a warm still night and he wore only a shirt with his two full corporal's stripes on the arm, a pair of drill trousers and

113

plimsolls. Over one shoulder he carried a light haversack bulky with stolen stores.

The door of the gate room was half open. He looked in and by the light of a hurricane lamp turned down to a glim saw Hardcastle's figure stretched out on a camp bed. Hardcastle was asleep and snoring gently.

At the main, double gate, now locked and cross-bolted, March took a key from his pocket and opened the small wicket gate cut in the large frame. Outside he locked the gate and then moved away to the right, giving the angled walls of the Fort a wide berth and working his way up the slope to the foot of the long ridge that ran down from La Caldera.

It was handy, he was telling himself, to be able to make a key. The Army was careless with its keys and if you were a corporal in the Royal Army Ordnance Corps there was nothing easier than making a key. And anyway, seeing that he wasn't on duty again until eight, why the hell should he be locked in all night?

He puffed a little as he set himself to the steep climb, and frowned as the haversack bumped awkwardly against his rump. If he could have risked taking a bicycle he would have followed the road down to Mora and up through the valley. But this way, when time was short, was quicker. He began to slant across the face of the ridge end towards the sea and finally struck a small track that followed the edge of the cliffs. Half an hour's hard going along this would take him to Ardino. He stopped once for a breather and looked back towards the fort. It was in darkness except for a single light which shone narrowly through one of the windows of the Bell Tower. One of the prisoners unable to sleep, he thought. Well, neither could Marchy boy sleep. The night was a good time for not sleeping. His eyes growing used to the darkness he picked his way along the path, feeling pleasantly excited because he was out and on his own and going to Ardino. He thought of his London streets and the moon coming down coldly over the rows of narrow houses . . . the times he'd waited outside the Odeon for his girl to come out and they'd walked up the hill from New Cross to Blackheath. It was good up there, especially on a summer evening. People passed in the darkness and there was the murmur of voices and

114

quiet laughter and away, ringing the darkness, the great glow of midnight London. God, what would he give to be back. It was summer now, July . . . and if he knew her some other fellow waited for her to knock off and come out and walk home to Kidbrook Park Road, her French heels tap, tapping on the hard pavement. The good Old Smoke; they could keep their so-and-so country, and their so-and-so Mora, and that went for the Army as well.

The track swung out taking him to within a few feet of the cliff edge. Down below, unseen, he could hear the rush and draw of the swell against the rocks. If anyone wanted the sea, Margate or Southend was good enough with the whelk and cockle stalls and half a dozen boozers to choose from within a hundred yards. The path moved through a patch of heather and gorse and then into a clump of chestnuts and tall palms. Palms, he thought, were unnatural. Not trees. Just like overgrown brussels sprout stumps. He began to sweat gently and loosened one of the buttons of his shirt front.

Fifteen minutes later, against the moon-lit sky, he saw the bell turret of Ardino church lift itself from the hill slope and, remembering Arianna standing with her arms full of madonna lilies, he blew the breath through his nose with a sudden snort of pleasure.

Her father's house was just down the slope from the square. The only light was from the open door of the *Bar Filis*. He crossed the open space by the church and went into the bar. There were two tables of card players. They looked up at him briefly. The air was thick with cigarette smoke.

At the bar counter he nodded to Ercolo, the proprietor, and said, "A bottle of *fundador*."

Ercolo handed him the brandy and winking said, "It is good afterwards to be under the pines and drink."

The card players, hearing him, laughed. March turned and went out. One of these days, he told himself, he'd push a few faces in.

He went back across the square and down the slope to Arianna's house.

He moved round the side of the low house, cocked his leg over a crazy wattling of bamboo slats and stepped knee high through a patch of melons. The house was in darkness.

115

He threw a handful of soft dirt against her window. The third time she heard him and he saw her face, white against the grey gloom of the dirty glass. He raised a hand and then went round to the front door. It was unlocked and he pushed it open gently and stepped into the darkness.

His nose wrinkled against the smell, sour wine, garlic, strong cigarillo smoke and the familiar herby, musty stuffiness of poverty.

He heard her cross the room but he couldn't see her. Then he felt her hands on his arms. He kissed her, both of them clumsy and awkward, easing the first shock of pleasure.

"Hullo, ducks," he whispered.

"Amore mio . . ."

Then she came to him again and there was a gentleness in them both. Under his hands he could feel she had slipped on a raincoat but from the way it moved he knew that there was little beneath it. Why do I fuss, he thought, about what that slut from the Odeon is doing? Arianna's worth a million of her. No "Don'ts"; no "Be careful nows".

He held her away from him, feeling her quick breath just touch his cheek.

"Here?"

"No, amore. Outside."

He unswung the haversack and dropped its contents gently to the floor.

"For your old lady."

Holding her arm he slid out of the door and she closed it gently. They went down the hill slope, towards the path which he had travelled.

This is Colonel Fadid Sala Mawzi, Commander-in-Chief of the Cyrenian National Army, at half-past one in the night, leaning with his elbows on the stone sill of his narrow window. He is a man who has gone past needing real sleep, gone past observing the customary distinctions between night and day. He is fully dressed and, for each night he has been on Mora, the light has shone in his room. Between the hours of twelve and three he has stood, his elbows on the hard stone sill, and his mind set even harder than the stone against the thought that his vigil may prove futile. This is a man with two snakes

116

in his bosom. One is ambition and the other is Cyrenia, and they are intertwined so closely that they are one serpent with two heads, and the two heads strike his flesh and goad his body ceaselessly. If you do not understand this, you cannot understand Colonel Fadid Sala Mawzi whom one of Her Majesty's civil servants called "farmer" and thereby detracted from Her Majesty and forsook civility. This is a man who, trapped by his enemies, now waits to humiliate them and from that humiliation to find freedom and surcease from the venom which is in his blood.

He stood there smoking and thinking of Walter Mietus. Days before he had said to him, "Wherever they take us, and the choice is limited, you will come. Watch our place and you will find my window always lighted. Watch for three nights before you do anything. After that we will plan."

His eyes were on the darkness of the hillside. He had great faith in Mietus. By day and by night he would watch first before he moved. When his light came it would be placed so that the sentry at the Bell Tower parapet door would not see it.

The door opened behind him and he heard the soft shuffle of Abou's bare feet. He did not turn.

Abou said, "The cook who likes me has given me coffee and a little stove. I shall make coffee for the Colonel?"

"No, Abou. Go to your sleep. Sleep for me."

Abou bowed, but before turning to the door he said, "There was talk in the cook's place tonight of more men coming soon to be guards."

"They could send a hundred and it would make no difference."

"They send but six. There is much grumbling about it."

"When do they come, Abou?" His eyes were still on the darkness outside.

"No one knows, Colonel. But it is not thought soon."

"Six is nothing, Abou. If they come in time then there are six more bullets to be used."

"The cook's death will grieve me."

"Death is always a grief to someone, Abou. But it is death just the same." For a moment he turned, his dark eyes on Abou, his face like a meanly fleshed skull, the hair brushed

117

hard back until it seemed no longer hair but shadow and the clefted face knifed with sharp creases. Abou, too, he trusted but not as much as he trusted Walter Mietus. "If I put the knife into your hand, Abou, would you take death to the cook?"

Abou made a little bow and his old hands went up in a slight gesture. "Put the knife in my hands, Oh Colonel, and I will bear with my grief."

"Then go to your sleep."

He turned back to the window and, five minutes after Abou had gone, the light for which he had waited suddenly sparked faintly away on the hillside far to his right so that he had to slide to the left of the window embrasure to see it comfortably. The light winked and winked and then went. Colonel Mawzi waited. The light came again, winking faintly in the darkness for a while and then went again. He walked to the door and switched off the room light. He waited, and then switched it on, waited and then switched it off again and walked back to the window without hurry or excitement. There was no surprise in him or elation for this was how he had planned it. He pulled a small hand torch from his tunic pocket and began to signal. It was a small torch, as slim as a pencil and no longer, and from the hillside one would have needed binoculars to pick out its tiny glow. It had travelled to Mora in the back of the long handled clothes brush which Abou had brought to look after his master's clothes.

Walter Mietus and Colonel Mawzi communicated for half an hour and, at the end of that time, Mietus knew essentially as much about Fort Sebastian and its garrison as Colonel Mawzi did.

When Mawzi had finished signalling, he switched on his room light, waited a little while and then went down to Hadid Chebir's room. He entered without knocking and, in the darkness, crossed to the bed. Hadid Chebir's sleeping breath was gentle and regular in the darkness. Colonel Mawzi sat on the edge of the bed. Sitting there, not yet waking the man, he suddenly remembered something which Marion Chebir had recently said to him.

"In the old days Hadid would have cut your throat if he had seen you lay a finger on me."

118

And his own reply:

"The old days, yes. He would have spilt my bowels on the sand . . . He was a man."

In the old days, yes. Hadid had been as quick with a knife as he was with his tongue or brain. Out of his mood of triumph, his sense of confidence because Mietus had arrived just as he had planned it, there was a quick torsion of regret in him. It was better in the old days when Hadid had been everything in his life, when Hadid had signified to him Cyrenia and all his own ambition. Now he was the master. But fundamentally, he knew himself utterly; he knew that he was born to serve; there lay all his talent. But to serve well a man must have a master ten times as strong as himself, ten times as subtle and devious in thought . . . All that had changed . . . This creature who slept now was a shadow, a shadow that drew courage from drugs, a husk without fire even to warm a woman like Marion Chebir. In the darkness his face stiffened with scorn. He put out a hand and shook the sleeping Hadid by the shoulder and when he woke, clumsily, enquiry confused in his throat, Mawzi touched his lips with two fingers, feeling their dryness and said gently:

"It is I."

The bed creaked as Hadid sat up. He breathed thickly through his nose and cleared his throat.

"Mawzi?"

"Yes."

"What is it?"

"They have come."

"They?"

At the question contempt was strong in Mawzi. In the old days one touched Hadid on the shoulder in his sleep and he was awake, his brain clear, and the knife or revolver already in his hand.

"Mietus and the others." His voice showed none of his feelings. "Roper, Lorentzen, Plevsky and the good Sifal."

There was silence between them for a moment, then the sound of Hadid easing himself back against the pillows.

"So," he breathed. "What is arranged?"

"Nothing yet. How could it be? But tomorrow we talk

119

again. And the next day. There are many things they must know now in detail."

"And when will it be?"

"This I have considered. More men for guards come to the island soon. It would be better that it should happen before then. But for success the Governor must be here."

"You still think that is necessary?"

"Yes. It is not enough to escape. The thing must be an explosion. Its noise must carry around the world to put our names in every mouth and to rouse the madness in our people's blood. Just once we need this madness . . . just once and nothing can stop us. For this we need the Governor."

And he was thinking to himself, also we need your death to add the blood of a martyred son to that of his father's. Your blood and the person of Sir George Cator to give my people the mockery of the British which must run with their madness.

"To escape is not enough," he said evenly. "Escape is nothing. But to take the Governor with us is everything—for that is humiliation."

"I agree. But when does he come?"

"Who can tell? But come he will. If it is not soon we must find a way to bring him."

"You have thought of something?"

"Yes; but maybe it will not be necessary. If he is a good Governor, which I think he is, he will come to inspect soon."

Hadid Chebir suddenly breathed deeply and a hand reached out and touched Mawzi's tunic, affectionately, like the hand of a child seeking reassurance from the dark.

"Sometimes I think we play with madness and death unknowingly. Like a child who sits in the wadi bottom and innocently reaches out to stroke the head of a puff adder. Sometimes I think I live in a dream. These are bad moments and then I need to reach out and feel your strength. This then I know is the woman in me, the blood of my mother, and I am ashamed. Be my strength, Sala Mawzi."

"I am thy strength," said Mawzi, despising him. To himself he added, "And I am thy death and thy victory and the honour that shall live always around thy name for everyone except myself."

120

He stood up. "Say nothing to Marion. When the time comes I shall tell her."

Mawzi went out, closing the door quietly. For a moment he stood on the stone-flagged landing. A few steps below him was the door to Marion Chebir's room. Did she lie sleeping or awake? He stood in the darkness, knowing she was there, only a few yards from him, and his imagination was strong in him. And the desire for her, running swiftly alongside his own elation, released now that Mietus had come, was like a thirst in his throat that cried for coolness. He stood there for ten seconds, feeling the small kick of a throbbing vein on his temple. Then he turned and went back to his room and he was thinking of Major Richmond who that afternoon had risen from beside Marion on the beach and had stood in the sunlight with the blood high in his face and had raised a hand to touch that side of his temple where a small vein kicked. He, too . . .

What fools some men were.

"This then I know is the woman in me, the blood of my mother, and I am ashamed." What kind of man was it that did not know that the strength of a woman was beyond any man's?

6

THE moon was well up. In the pines above them the warm night breeze sighed occasionally. They lay across the old raincoat, her head cushioned against his outflung left arm, but their bodies now apart. The bottle of brandy was untouched on the ground by his side. Usually they had a few drinks as they talked, but tonight there was no desire in them for drink. They both smoked, watching the thin drift rise and shred into the night.

Arianna said, "In thy country the women work as they do here? In the fields and with the goats?"

"They work. Mostly in factories and shops."

"Even when they are married?"

"Sometimes."

"To bring more money?"

"Yes." He was used to this kind of practical questioning. She had a great appetite for facts. He flexed his left hand and played with her ear.

"I would like to see thy country. Only twice have I been to Port Carlos ... My brother has been once to Teneriffe. There was a great confusion of people and cars and many ships in the harbour. I should like that. The time is soon for thy return?"

"I don't know."

"In thy country there is a girl who loves thee beneath the pines like this?"

He laughed, and she laughed with him, and rolling over a little lay with her cheek on his arm and blew smoke at his face.

"I am not jealous. It is too far away. Here, I would be jealous."

He saw the fall of her bosoms under the shift and the image of her body beneath the thin cotton was a tenderness in him. She was simple and straightforward and he was full of a sudden need to do many things for her.

"In my country," he said, "it is often cold and raining. And London is so big. It is not easy for lovers." And he was thinking of the close, crowded stuffy atmosphere of cinemas, and the shine of rain on wet bricks in alleyways; and he was also thinking that when he was with her all the dirty jokes of the chaps back at Fort Sebastian fell away from him, and that, feeling for words in her language, he didn't even sound like the Marchy-boy who knew his way around the houses better than anyone. The way that "thee" and "thou" and "thine" passed between them made him a different person.

"I love thee," she said, "and if thou should ask me would come back to thy country. But there I would be jealous. Ask me to come back with thee."

He didn't say anything. His face a few inches from hers he looked into her eyes. It would be a smack across the snitcher all right for some people he could think of, some people who played fast and loose with a fellow and went tap, tapping along the pavement in their high heels, waggling their tight bottom about as though it were stamped twenty-four carat gold and not another like it between New Cross and Waterloo

122

Bridge. Oh, Marchy-boy (he smiled and she smiled back not knowing the reason for his smile); and then he thought of his Ma and Pa, and the others down the street when he turned up with a flashing-eyed Spanish piece. Dressed up, she'd knock the stuffing right out of any other girl.

"There is thy family," he said, aware of the idea growing in him, puzzling him because it was suddenly fitting into something inside him as though made to measure, and not even sparking a protest from the fly, smart, know-your-way-around Marchy-boy he was so proud of.

"That to my family." She made a vulgar gesture with the whole of her body and he giggled.

"My country would be strange for thee."

"It would be strange. But there would be much that would not be strange. Our loving would not be strange and children are born the same be it London or Mora." She sat up, her face serious and held out her hands towards him, palms up. "These know how to work. In a factory if it should be that we need more money. I would keep thy house and be thy woman through all. For thy faults I do not care that much——" One hand made a quick turning movement, like the spurt of a bird's wing as it shakes water from its feathers. "Am I not used to the drunkenness of my father and the wickedness of my brother? Against these thy faults are small. I speak seriously for I love thee and it is in my mind that I might carry a child for thee, though it is not because of that that I speak so. Other men have been here with me, but to none have I had the desire to speak as I do now. One must say what is within one, but whatever thy answer do not be afraid of angering me. Marriage is a word that frightens many men. It is of my own willingness that I have loved thee, not to find a husband, for that would be shameful."

He sat there listening to her; and he thought, when she talks, it is all God's honest truth. Not a twist or a wriggle in her. What is there comes out straight. Compared with the girls he had known she was Johnny Walker against their fizzy lemonade. He touched the palm of her still open hand and he could feel the smooth callouses that came from hoeing between the maize and vines, but the hand was small and a woman's hand, too, and without looking at it he was aware of

123

the richness of her body and the straight, young simpleness of her. And quite suddenly he got the hard, choked-up feeling in his chest which he had when he wanted her badly, but this time it was not from wanting her but just from her being there. And then, without any thought of ever regretting it, without a word to the old Marchy-boy who should have known better, who had no flies on him, he knew what the score was.

"I love thee, too, Arianna. When I go back to my country we will be married. It is with me now that I want no other woman."

Will you listen to me, he told himself, shaken by the force in him. I must be off my rocker; but I mean it. But she does this to me, and what I say I mean. Yes, I mean, he told himself fiercely, and if anyone says a word out of place when I tell them I'll kick their guts out.

She raised her palm and put it against his cheek and then leaning forward she said, "It is a good moment, amore. Such a good moment."

He laughed, awkward with the newness in him, and then to cover it pulled her towards him and they lay close together, not making love, but just being close and sometimes laughing quietly as though their happiness was a new joke which would never lack relish.

He was happy when he left her. She wouldn't let him go back to the house with her. It was hot in the house and she preferred to sleep the rest of the night under the pines. He left her sitting on the old raincoat, turning again and again as he followed the path to see her sitting there, raising his hand silently and in salute, hers going to her mouth to send him kisses. And then a turn of the cliff path took him out of her sight. The untouched bottle of brandy was in his haversack, bumping gently against his back as he walked. No point in leaving it with Arianna at Ardino. She'd only give it to her brother, Torlo, to guzzle. He'd stick it by Hardcastle's bed— a present to him for keeping his mouth shut about his visit to Arianna. He moved along, noiseless, in his plimsolls, and his thoughts were full of her.

It was a good thing. He wondered he'd never thought of it before. She'd stick to him through thick and thin. They were like that. And he'd stick to her. That's what a chap had to have, really. As for the baby . . . Well, it was no shock to anyone in his parish if the woman cleared the vestry door just in time to call the midwife. Yes, marriage was the thing. He didn't even have to worry about having a baby now. Oh, she knew she was going to have it, but it made no odds now. Marchy-boy, the proud pa. He'd show the little buster . . . Teach him to use his fists, make him smart. Might, in time, start a little business. March and Son, newsagents, greengrocers, something like that.

Yes, that was it. Family man. And with a wife that would knock their eyes out. She'd pick up the lingo in no time. He followed the path automatically. He could see them going into the boozer of a Saturday night. Arianna dolled up to the nines, the kid left with the old people . . . No harm in putting it about that her father was a big banana grower in her own country, fair bit of money, old Spanish family, right back to Christopher Columbus. Oh, you're lucky, Marchy-boy. You've got a winner on your hands. All this time and you never knew it until now. Real lucky, and let me see anyone who tries to say different.

He smiled with the happiness in him and skirted a tall outcrop of rock that shouldered across the path. As he came round it he found himself facing three men who were following the track in his direction. He stopped dead, surprised at the meeting, and confused for a moment at the reaction of the three men. They had been in single file but before he had seen them almost the file was broken, swiftly and silently, and now there was a man facing him dead across the path and the two others were on his flanks, close to him, crowding him, and all of them very still, watching him.

They stood full in the light of the moon. The man facing him wore a dark leather jerkin and canvas trousers. Bareheaded his faded blond hair moved a little across his forehead in the night breeze. He stood with an awkward stance, body thrust forward and his legs bent outwards, bowed but planted strong and sturdily on the path. His eyes which had been on March's surprised face moved, drawn by the bone-white corporal's stripes on the soldier's arm, and the square face, serious until now, broke with a little smile.

March didn't look at the others. They were there. He could half-see half-feel their bulk close to him. He felt crowded and he didn't like it.

"Evenin' chums, nice night for a walk." He spoke his own language and forced good-humour into it. Who the hell were these? He'd never seen any of them before. "A lovely night, but I'm in a hurry to get back to barracks or I'll lose my stripes." He gave a little laugh and made a move forward.

Walter Mietus put up his hand and March stopped at once. He knew a knife when he saw one and he knew what a knife could do.

"Here, what's the bloody malarky?" He let his anger go freely to ease the fear in him.

"A moment," said Mietus in English and his voice sounded apologetic. Then, his eyes still on March, he spoke to the other two, ignoring March, the half-raised knife holding the soldier in the path. He spoke in German.

"He is from the fort. He would talk."

"If he doesn't return, that will talk, too," said Roper from March's right, answering in the same tongue.

"But not so loud or so clearly," said Sifal who stood with his back to the sea and the cliff drop not ten yards away.

"Sifal is right," said Mietus.

"Then finish him. We waste time here and it's dangerous to stay on the path. A dead soldier is a dead soldier in any country."

"I would like to use the knife but it would look wrong. You do it, Roper, when I move."

March had had enough. Who the hell did they think they were and what was this Dutch talk?

"Put that bloody knife away and let me pass. Who the hell——"

He said no more. Incredibly swiftly Mietus' right foot came forward and thudded into March's groin. He screamed chokingly and began to fall. As he did so Roper stepped in, swung one arm round his neck and with the flat of his free hand struck the back of March's head violently. There was a noise like the crack of a sappy branch breaking under strain.

Roper took his arm away from March's neck and let him drop to the path.

126

Mietus said, "Search him, Sifal. Take what a thief would take."

Sifal dropped to the ground and went through March's pockets and his haversack. When he had finished Mietus and Roper picked up the body and carried it to the cliff edge. Holding it by the wrists and ankles they swung it three times between them for momentum and then let it go out into the darkness of the cliff shadow.

Jenkins, the cook, was hosing the plants in the centre of the courtyard. Breakfast was over and he liked to get this job done before the sun rose high enough to flood the courtyard with light. One thumb over the end of the hose to increase the water pressure he walked slowly around the circle directing a great fan of water over the plants. He liked the sound the water made as it hit the leaves, liked to see the dry earth turn chocolate colour as it was damped down. Now and again he flirted the spray high to the leaves of the dragon tree and paused to watch it cascade down. It was going to be another scorching day, but for the moment all was damp and cool and growing in the courtyard. Bully-beef stew and a currant roll . . . that's what he'd give 'em today. Quick and easy. Look at that camellia, would you? Opened up since yesterday. He frowned and bent down to pick up an empty matchbox from the earth. Untidy bastards.

Private Hardcastle came across from the gate and stood at his side.

"Seen March this morning, cookie?"

"No."

"He went out last night and he ain't back yet. He's on guard duty in a few minutes."

"More fool you to let him go, man."

"You know what Marchy's like."

"Like the rest of you."

"What shall I do?"

"If he's on duty right away you can't cover him any longer. Tell the sergeant. If old March loses his stripes it'll do him good. Out of my way will you." He jerked at the length of hose and moved farther round the circle.

Unhappy, Hardcastle went to Sergeant Benson's room.

Benson was doing his hair in front of a small square of mirror on the wall. Flicks of water came from it as he pulled the comb through leaving it in a smooth chestnut brown sweep, the parting as straight and sharp as the crease in his drill trousers.

Hardcastle reported the absence of Corporal March. Sergeant Benson lit a cigarette and frowned.

"How'd he get out? Your key?"

"No, Sergeant. He's got one of his own. You know that."

"I don't know anything of the sort, officially." He spoke sharply, angry at March for being such a bloody fool. "I suppose he's got shacked up with that girl and can't tear himself away."

"You going to shop him, Serg.?"

"That's my business, but we'll give him till ten and see. I'll fix the guard. What time did he go?"

"About one. I heard him, but I was asleep, officially. You know what he's like, Serg. I didn't want to get across him."

"I'll fix him when he comes back."

But at ten March was not back and Sergeant Benson who was prepared to cover a man for a reasonable period could hide March's absence no longer. He went up to the officers' mess and reported the absence to Major Richmond.

John, standing by the window that looked down the hill to Mora and the small harbour, let the sergeant finish. There was no surprise in him. Men were always going absent in the army, and these men were being worked hard. He didn't question the fact that Benson had waited a few hours before reporting the absence. A good sergeant was entitled to use his discretion.

"How did he get out?" he asked when Benson had finished.

"Through the wicket gate in the main gate, sir."

"That's locked every night."

"Yes, sir."

For a moment John didn't say anything. He turned full from the window. He could see the unhappiness in Sergeant Benson.

"Did he take Hardcastle's key?"

"No, sir. Hardcastle was sleeping fully dressed according to standing orders and the key was in his pocket."

"Hardcastle didn't hear him go?"

"No, sir."

"I see. It looks as though he's got a key of his own then, doesn't it?"

"It could be, sir."

"I'm damned sure he has. He's an ordnance man. All right, get the jeep out and go over to Ardino. He probably made a night of it and is sleeping it off somewhere."

"Very good, sir."

"Take another man with you, if you think you need one."

"I can manage him, sir. Drunk or sober."

Sergeant Benson drove over to Ardino by himself and went straight to the *Bar Filis*. He knew his March. If he was out for a night's spree there'd be a bottle as well as a woman in it. Somewhere the stupid bastard was still sleeping it off. He'd cooked his goose this time. He was angry with March now and looking forward to getting his hands on him.

Summoning up his rough Spanish he demanded brusquely of Ercolo:

"Was Corporal March here last night?"

Ercolo scratched his chest through his dirty shirt and nodded.

"Drinking?"

"Not here. He bought a bottle of brandy and went out." He winked at the sergeant. "Under the pines it tastes good. Puts a fresh flame back in the body."

"All right, that's enough of that. Do you know where he is now?"

"No, Sergeant."

"If you know you'd better say." Benson felt truculent. Sweating around in this heat looking for a scab like March; everyone working double-time at the fort and March off wenching and drinking like some bloody lord.

"I do not know where he is, Sergeant. You doubt me?"

"You're bloody right, I do."

Benson turned and left the place. He went down the slope to Arianna's house. She was sitting outside the door cutting up a pailful of beans for soup. Standing in the doorway behind her was her brother, Torlo, sleepy-eyed and smoking,

129

the cigarette drooping like a piece of chewed string from his under lip. He wore a singlet and a pair of patched trousers. Dried fish scales stuck to his bare forearms like sequins. His hair was dark and tight-curled and he had a narrow, unpleasant face, the nose long and pointed and the eyes close-set. His mouth was large and the lips thin and broken with sun and cigarette sores. Dog-face, March called him, thought Benson, and dog-faced he was. Like a whippet or a greyhound in bloody bad shape, but not all the condition powders in the world would do him any good.

Sturdy, neat, his face shining with sweat Benson stood before them. They looked at him and said nothing.

"I'm looking for Corporal March," he said.

"Not here," said Torlo.

"He was here last night. He told me he was coming."

He saw Arianna look up at her brother and then turn back to her work with the beans.

"The whole night I was fishing," said Torlo and his voice was full of indifference. He let his eyes move slowly over Benson, marking the sharp trouser crease, the freshly laundered khaki shirt, the neatly tied sweat rag round his neck, the brilliance of the three arm stripes . . . The smartness and compactness of this soldier stirred him to a curious hostility.

"He was here all right," said Benson. He moved a little to make Arianna look up at him. "You know he was here."

"No, I have not seen him," said Arianna. If March was in trouble she had no intention of helping this sergeant.

"Don't beat about the bush with me," said Benson vigorously. "He came over to see you. He bought brandy at the bar. You both made a night of it and now the stupid fool is sleeping it off somewhere. Where is he?"

"I do not like the way you talk of my sister," said Torlo.

"That's too bad," snapped Benson. He moved closer to Arianna. "Where is he? It's for his own good I'm asking." The girl was all right; it was her brother who put his back up.

"Is he not at the fort?" asked Arianna.

"You know he isn't. Where is he, inside, sleeping it off?"

Benson made a move towards the door. God, he'd let

March have it for this caper. Who wouldn't like to spend a night out? But anyone else would have cut down on the bottle and got back in time. But not Marchy-boy. Oh, no—to hell with everyone was Marchy's motto.

Torlo made no move from the door. One hand on the frame he blocked the way.

"My sister said he did not come last night. Also I say he is not within." His voice was insolent, hostile. What were they, dogs? This big Englishman with the red face and the neat uniform, what was he to come here and talk like this to him and his sister? These soldiers were all the same. His sister was a fool to go with one.

"I'll see for myself," said Benson, anger and the heat rousing him.

Torlo smiled. "Here is the door. Try to enter."

His hands dropped towards the belt at his side. As he moved so did Benson. He stepped forward with astonishing quickness and had Torlo's wrist in his grip, holding his hand from the knife. For a moment they stood close together, their faces almost touching.

Behind them Arianna rose. Fragments of chopped bean fell from her skirt. Her face sullen, but full of dignity, she put out a hand and touched Torlo.

"Let the sergeant enter, Torlo."

Torlo frowned.

"That he should enter!" Arianna's voice was suddenly sharp, commanding.

Torlo shrugged his shoulders and Benson released his grasp on the man's wrist. Torlo stepped aside, leaned against the house wall and stared down at the distant sea, all interest gone from him.

Benson went into the house with Arianna and looked round. Coming out, feeling that he had let himself go too much, even a little ashamed, he said to Arianna, "I'm sorry. But we are worried about March. If you see him tell him to hurry back and I will try and save him from too much trouble."

As he moved away Torlo, still leaning against the wall, spat at the ground.

At midday Benson was back at the fort without March.

131

"He's not at Ardino, sir," he said to John. "Or any of the places. But he was over at Ardino last night. Bought a bottle of brandy at the bar."

"Did you talk with the girl?"

"Yes, sir. She swears that he wasn't over there last night. Or at least that she didn't see him."

"Do you believe her?"

"No, sir. She's covering up for him."

"I see."

John lit a cigarette. On stations like this men could get so fed up that they just walked out with no other object than to keep away until such time as someone found them and brought them back. It was a spontaneous, hopeless revolt. He didn't know much about March, but six months in a place like this could take the common sense out of the steadiest man.

"He's probably hiding out. If he doesn't show up by to-night we'll have to go after him. Maybe we could get some help from the men in Mora. Anyway, just in case anything's happened to him, you'd better send a couple of men out along the cliff path to Ardino. That's the way he would have gone, isn't it?"

"Yes, sir."

"Tell 'em to have a good look round. He could have slipped and be stuck somewhere. Especially if he'd been drinking."

The first person in Fort Sebastian to learn exactly what had happened to Corporal March was Colonel Mawzi. Walter Mietus signalled to him at two o'clock that night and gave him the news. The information which Colonel Mawzi passed back to Walter Mietus was equally interesting. Abou from his evening chat in the courtyard with Jenkins, and from keeping his ears open all day, had learnt that Corporal March was missing, that it was known he had slipped out at night to visit his girl at Ardino, and that he possessed a key to the small wicket gate in the main door. Colonel Mawzi flashed this news to Mietus. The key had been with others which Sifal had removed from March's pockets. The question of an entry to Fort Sebastian had been one of the most difficult for Walter Mietus to handle. Now it looked as though it would turn out to be the simplest.

The next morning, as they took a stroll on the parapet after breakfast, Colonel Mawzi told Hadid Chebir and Marion. It was the first mention he had made to Marion that Mietus and his men were on the island. They leaned over the parapet, looking down towards the small beach where they bathed. When Mawzi had finished Marion said:

"So, Mietus is here?"

"Naturally. Without his help we cannot escape. It was all arranged long ago." Mawzi fitted a cigarette into his bone holder, lit it and filled his lungs with smoke. He sent the smoke from him in a long sigh of pleasure.

Marion could see that he was happy. Not relaxed, for she had never known him to be that, but happy.

"Mietus," she said, "is a monster. Was there any need to kill this poor soldier?"

"There was every need," said Hadid sharply. "Would you have had him come back and report that he had seen three strange men. Don't be a fool!" He spoke sharply, not looking at her.

Marion knew that Hadid was neither happy nor relaxed. She could vaguely recall the face of Corporal March from his guard duties on the parapet, but he was a shadow to her. Now he was dead. It was a bad thought, but then she had got used to such bad thoughts, had learned to accept death to some extent in the same fashion as Mawzi and Hadid accepted it. There was a point beyond which one became hardened to grief and to shock. The only thing left then was anger at one's own indifference . . . a bastard emotion in the place of the true one.

"When this escape comes, will there be more deaths?"

"Why do you ask?" Mawzi looked across at her sharply and then let his head travel further to check the position of the parapet guard, to be sure they could not be overheard.

"Because I know Mietus. A plan can be a good one—I do not ask you for details of the plan because I know you won't tell me yet, or perhaps ever fully—but with any plan Mietus will embroider it with violence. Unnecessarily. You know that."

"Who is there here you would have us save?" asked Mawzi

and he watched her closely, remembering the tiny drumming of the temple vein and the movement of Major Richmond's hand to it. Had she noticed what had happened to him? Maybe not. Sometimes women had a great blindness; but sometimes they only pretended to it.

"They are British," said Hadid simply. "Why should any be saved?"

Marion straightened up from the wall. "I have been with you in the past. I am with you now. You all know that. No one has ever questioned my loyalty. But"—she faced them, her face shadowed and stern—"I am sick of killing. Sometimes it seems to me that you have no interest in what is to come. You want a peaceful, happy future for Cyrenia. It is for this that we all work and fight. But now I begin to think that you are concerned only with fighting. You delight in that. You will be unhappy and lost when you have got what you want for Cyrenia."

"You are a fool," said Hadid quietly.

Marion's lips tightened with anger. "And you? Would it be hard to find the right names for you?"

Hadid would have moved towards her, but Mawzi's hand fell on his elbow. He was smiling.

"There is no need for names. What Marion says is right. In battle it is not easy to think beyond battle. And being men it is hard not to delight in battle. But it would be wrong to think we have lost sight of the future. And it would be wrong to think that there is any virtue in killing a man without cause. The death of this soldier is unfortunate, but it was necessary."

"And when we escape?"

"It is not planned that there should be much killing. See, I do not lie to you. To make wine it is necessary to tread the grapes."

"Let it be soon then, and see that Mietus understands."

She spoke stiffly, with an intense authority which roused Hadid to anger, but before he could do more than stir, tugging at the restraining hold of Mawzi's hand, the other had spoken.

"You speak like this with a purpose?"

"You know I do. I have said I am sick of violence. Now I

134

say more. I am sick of Cyrenia and both of you. Until we escape I am with you. I've loved Cyrenia and I've worked for it. I have done more than most people for Cyrenia; and all this out of love ... but I can't live always for the past. I see now that I should never have come here."

"Your being here has meant much for our cause—all over the world it is admired," saw Mawzi.

"There is an end to everything, and since I have been here I have understood this. When we are back in Cyrenia I shall leave. You will need me no more. I shall go to some other country and be forgotten." She was trembling a little, touched with an amazement at what she was saying for until she had begun to speak she had not known she was going to say this. She saw Hadid biting his lower lip with anger and Mawzi, calm, smiling a little, and she knew that it was Mawzi who really understood and who was the more dangerous of the two. But what she said was true; she was sick, sick, sick, of the whole thing, suddenly, finally and with a spreading sense of weariness. They took the good thing, the clean thing which was Cyrenia and the destinies of thousands of small people, and in their hands it became something unclean and quick with violence ... Only now she had come abruptly and amazingly out from the shadow of these two men and seen the truth. She wanted a life that had nothing to do with Cyrenia.

Hadid said harshly, his voice rough with threat, "If you do anything against us you will not live."

Marion laughed contemptuously. "There would be a way to cut my throat? Maybe, but it would be Mawzi's hand that held the knife, not yours. It takes courage to kill a woman."

Mawzi slid forward between the two. "What you ask for is just. You have done much for us. There is a little more to be done. I know you will do it. When we are back in Cyrenia you shall be free and we shall be generous. And now let us finish this talk for the guard is watching us. I give my word that when you are in Cyrenia again you shall be free."

He turned away from her and began to walk slowly along the parapet. In every truth, he was thinking, there is a deceit; and with her as never before with anyone else I am able to feel some unhappiness at the deceit. There was only one freedom waiting for her in Cyrenia. He saw her, in his mind's eye, standing before them, speaking with the fierce tongue of a woman whose emotions are stronger than her wisdom, standing there like a young cypress, still, and yet full of movement, and he was beyond understanding how in two years Hadid had never wanted to touch her. In two years, he carried the thing like a certainty, diamond-sharp in his mind, no man had ever known her. A woman could not be for ever held by the past. This outbreak proved it. She wished to shake off the past. There must be a new budding and a new blossoming. He regretted now that he had turned away to his own room from the top of the stairs on the night when Mietus had first signalled.

John Richmond coming on to the parapet from the stone steps of the courtyard saw the three of them. Mawzi was at the far end of the parapet close to the Flag Tower, smoking and looking out to sea. Hadid Chebir was half-way along the parapet, sitting in one of the embrasures, his legs crossed and a book on his knees. He was rapidly going through the limited library at the fort, reading everything that came to his hand indiscriminately. Marion Chebir was just beyond the Bell Tower, elbows on the wall top, looking down to the small beach. Something in the wide spacing of the group struck him as odd.

The guard at the head of the steps came to attention as John approached.

"Everything all right?"

"Yes, sir."

"All right; stand easy. Where's Abou?"

"In the tower, sir. Just come up from helping the cook."

"How are our friends this morning?" John tipped his head towards the parapet length.

The guard smiled. "Much the same, sir. Though it did seem to me that just now they was having a bit of an argy-bargy over something. Mrs. Chebir seemed to have said something to upset her husband."

John smiled. "It's a habit wives have."

He moved on down the parapet walk. He could see the

136

slight hunch of Marion's shoulders where she leaned on the wall, and the long line of her back. Her legs were bare and she wore white sandals. But he could look at her this morning calmly. Thank the Lord for that. And in the calmness there was a detachment which he welcomed because he could regard her less as a distinct personality, than as a representative image of some future woman. He was sure now that when he went back to England he would marry. Somewhere, in a few years' time, there would be a woman; somewhere in the future that woman would lean over a wall like this and he would walk towards her in the hot morning sunshine knowing she was his ... Where would it be? Antibes, or that little place at Aiguebelle? Hot sun, the smell of pines, the flash of the sea against red rocks, and he would go up to her, put his arm across her shoulder and without a word she would half-turn and smile at him and they would need no words. In the last few days this anonymous figure had begun to live in his mind, faceless with a hundred different faces, beautiful with a changing brilliance of fancy ... Now and again he embarrassed himself with the vividness of his vision and the images it trailed ... She would walk with him through the glasshouses at Sorby Place, admiring old Johnson's display of perpetual carnations. He could see the old gardener cutting one for her, always a Royal Crimson, and she would hold it to her face, loving the clove scent, and charming the old man ... He'd even quarrelled with her over the refurnishing of the long sitting room at Sorby Place. But there was a calmness in it all. The figure was still too anonymous to create the illusion of passion, and there was no need. That could be taken for granted.

Thank the Lord, he thought, for the privacy of the mind. If some of the chaps at the Bath Club, or the soldiers here could follow his fancies they'd laugh their heads off or be embarrassed. But that didn't matter. Privately he rather enjoyed the thing ... building up a future for himself, arranging it, keeping his specifications within reasonable limits, knowing that he was asking for no more than a man might reasonably find.

Marion Chebir, hearing his footsteps, swung round and said, "Good morning, Major."

"Good morning." He stopped.

"We're all here," she said lightly. "Three lost souls, marooned in the middle of the Atlantic. What a wonderful morning. Do you know what I'd like to do?"

"What would you like to do?"

"I'd like to put on a pair of stout shoes and go for a walk. Up there, perhaps——" her head moved towards the far slopes of La Caldera.

"It's pretty rough going."

"Oh, don't be so dull. I don't care what it's like. Anyway I can't go, can I?"

"I'm afraid not." He smiled.

"It's ages since I really walked. And I suppose if you would let me go, which you can't, I'd get tired of it before long. It's just the idea of walking. When I worked in London I used to do it some week-ends with other girls. Take the train on Sunday mornings down to Sevenoaks or Lewes and just walk. Bread and cheese in a pub for lunch and then tea at some cottage. God, that all seems a long, long way from here. Just think, right at this moment there are girls behind the counter in Harrod's, the same kind of girls, looking forward to the week-end, and tonight they'll dash home to some shared flat to cook something in a frying pan over a gas ring. I loved London. A few weeks ago you were there?"

"Yes, I love it too." Something has upset her, he thought, or she wouldn't be talking like this.

She looked at him steadily, her head tilting a little.

"What are you thinking of now?" he asked.

She couldn't tell him, but it had suddenly occurred to her than when they escaped—and she had implicit faith in Mawzi, knowing it must happen—then he would be in trouble. He'd take all the blame. She didn't know much about the army, but it would probably affect his career . . . Poor Major Richmond, the man who let Hadid Chebir slip through his fingers to make the British a laughing stock for the world. Spontaneous sympathy for him flooded through her . . . nothing could stop it. Whatever you did in this fight had to hurt someone.

"Is it so serious?" he asked lightly.

She shook her head, chasing away her thoughts. "I was

138

wondering . . . I was trying to picture you in a War Office bowler and a dark suit."

"It's a homburg and pin-striped trousers."

"Do you carry a cane or an umbrella? I can't imagine you out of uniform somehow."

"A malacca cane with a silver handle, belonged to my father."

"It would," but there was no malice in her voice. "And you belong to the right clubs, of course?"

"The Bath and the Carlton." He lifted his eyebrows humorously.

"And you always use the same restaurants and the head-waiters have known you for years so that you get just the table you want?"

"Yes. Do you want their names?"

"No. But I still can't see you out of uniform. You're like Mawzi. You're a soldier. And Lord help me, I'm tired of soldiers!"

She turned away from him, and the turning and the tone of her last sentence was like a blow in the face. He stood there, surprised, and suddenly angry, but before he could do or say anything she as quickly turned back to him and said gently, "I'm sorry. I shouldn't have spoken like that. And anyway, I wasn't thinking of you. I was just being sorry for myself."

Momentarily he wanted to put out his hand and touch her arm, to show her that now he didn't mind. Instead, he said, "I only wish I could let you put on your walking shoes. Or, better still, your best hat and take you out to lunch at the Caprice . . ."

He saw how the words had touched her more surely than any movement of his hand could and her eyes were full on him for a moment. Then she turned away and almost inaudibly he heard her say:

"Thank you . . ."

And then, beyond her, drawing his attention, way down the steep slope to the beach he saw the movement of men. A small fishing boat had run hard up on to the black sand. Three men hauled it higher and then leaned over the side lifting something out clumsily between them. Even from this distance, as they rolled it to the sand he knew it was a body. For a moment he stood there, seeing one of the men look up towards the fort and the two others haul out a square of canvas from under the stern thwarts of the boat.

Without a word he turned and hurried down to the court-yard.

7

ARIANNA was sitting under the pines in the spot where she and March had last made love. The morning sun between the pines was hot. Yesterday she had heard of the death of March. Yesterday and all night her grief had hardened in her until now it was a kind of calmness. She would never see him again, she would never go to England. As though with a knife a great part of her life had been cruelly carved away from her.

Since March's death she had realized how much she loved him. What had begun out of passion, and with her, too, an eye for her own advantage, had become much more. She knew now that she had truly loved him.

She sat there with her elbows on her knees staring through the pine trunks towards the cliff edge and the distant sea whose movements broke the sunlight in rough ridges and scars.

There was the sound of feet over the thick pine needles and Torlo passed her and sat down a few yards from her, his back against a pine.

He rolled himself a cigarette and lit it.

"It is time," he said, "that thou should return to the house. The officer comes to ask questions in a little while. Also it is time that we should speak for I know what is in thy mind."

Arianna's eyes watched the flare of his match.

She said, "There is much in my mind. There was always hatred between thee. If his death came from thy hand I will kill thee."

"It is true I did not like him, or any of these soldiers. Their eyes on our poverty are full of insult, and their eyes on our women are full of——"

"If his death came from thy hand, then I will kill thee. He was not like the others."

"But I did not kill him. This I swear. I would have killed him if he had made thee unhappy. But it was this I waited to know."

"He made me happy. I have his child. I would have gone back to England with him as his wife. This he promised the night he left me. If his death was not from thy hand it was from another."

"This I have thought of, too."

"Though the sergeant does not believe me, it is true that when he left me he had not drunk. How can a man in bright moonlight slip over a cliff? He was sure on his feet and knew the path. It is not believable. Thou art my brother. For my unhappiness thou would kill. It is now that I am unhappy."

"Then I will kill. But there is much that I do not understand. There is no other man in Ardino who would have done it for love of thee. This, I know, because all knew that thy happiness was my concern."

"He was killed."

"This I have thought about. I have talked to the men from Mora who found him. I have found the place on the cliff where he fell and have found his haversack fifty feet down. At the top the path is three yards from the cliff edge and there is no sign of slipping. But on the path there are many signs of other men."

"What men are these?"

"I do not know. It is to be discovered. But on La Caldera three days ago I found the remains of a fire in a gully. The fire was not built the way our people would make a fire. There was also the remains of two cigarettes which are not our cigarettes. It has been in my mind that because of the prisoners at the fort there could be strangers on the island."

"For the prisoners I care nothing. For these men if they killed him I have only one wish."

"Assuredly. Now, come back. The rest is with me."

He stood up and she rose obediently and they went back along the path together.

For the Court of Enquiry John took Sergeant Benson and Señor Aldobran with him to Ardino. Aldobran was to act as interpreter for neither his own nor Benson's command of the language was good enough for this purpose.

On the way over in the jeep he asked Aldobran:

"What are these people like? They don't seem very co-operative."

Aldobran spread his hands. "They work hard, Major. But they . . . we," he smiled, ". . . we are an island people. With strangers we are always suspicious. Not always frank. With these people more so. They do not come into Mora much even."

"So far as I can see," said John, "it was a pure accident that he fell over the cliff; he was drunk and stumbled over, or . . ." he paused.

"Somebody pushed him, sir?" asked Sergeant Benson.

"Yes."

"You're thinking of the brother?" asked Aldobran.

"Is he the kind?"

Aldobran shrugged his shoulders. "He and many others. Their morals are nothing, Major. But their pride . . ." he rolled his eyes.

A small group of villagers was waiting for them as they drew up outside the *Bar Filis*. Inside the card players were at their table. Aldobran spoke to them and they got up reluctantly and left. Ercolo, leaning on his bar, watched the three settle round the table.

Aldobran said, "Go to the door, Ercolo, and call them as we need them." Untidy and unshaven, Ercolo shambled to the door.

"The girl first," said John, and then to Benson, "You get it all down."

"Arianna Zarate," Aldobran called to Ercolo.

"Arianna Zarate!" Ercolo's voice was surprisingly loud and commanding and John glancing at him saw that he was smiling, pleased with his authority and position at the door.

She was a long time coming. When she did John saw that she was not in working clothes like the other women outside. She wore a black dress, black stockings and a black, thick mantilla over her hair. The clothes, dowdy and ill-fitting

made her look dusty and shapeless. Only her face, handsome, set, and with a slight puffiness under the eyes had a
grave, controlled dignity. Through Aldobran, John spoke to
her.

"Señorita Zarate, you were a friend of Corporal March.
His death is a great sorrow to you and I do not wish to make
things harder for you. But for the sake of his parents in
England and also because he was a soldier, I must ask you
some questions. I hope you will help us."

"Yes, señor."

"Three nights ago Corporal March came to Ardino to see
you?"

"Yes."

"At what time?"

"Late."

"How long was he here?"

"A long time."

"Where were you? In your house?"

"No. In the pines below the village."

"When he left you he went back by the cliff path?"

"Yes."

"Was he sober when he left you?"

Arianna's head rose a little and her mouth stiffened.

"Yes."

If he had been drunk, thought John, she wouldn't say so.
He was dead, and she was not going to speak ill of him.

"Can you think of anyone who might wish him harm?"

"No."

"You think he slipped and fell over the cliff? A man who
was sober and knew the cliff path well? There are no signs
of slipping on the cliff anywhere that we can find."

"He is dead, señor Major." Her dark eyes were full on him.
"He is dead. What does the manner of his death matter?"

"It is my duty, señorita, to discover the truth for many
reasons. If you think anyone did him harm you should say
so."

She was silent for a while. All these questions meant
nothing. He was dead and now only one thing remained.
Torlo had promised to take care of that. This major was
kind, he treated her with respect, not like the sergeant, but

if strangers on the island had killed March and the officer was told about them then Torlo might never get his chance. The strangers would be taken away and punished elsewhere. She wanted to know that March had been avenged, here on Mora, and by her brother who in this matter she could trust.

"Señorita," said John, "we are waiting. Do you know of anyone on this island who might wish him harm?"

"No, señor Major. I could not name anyone."

John let her go. Every moment she stood in front of him he realized was heavy with anguish for her. There was no doubt in him that she had loved March. Odd, he knew nothing of the man except his face . . . She'd get over it, but for her the thing was existing now, and there was nothing anyone could do.

The bar room was hot. Ercolo brought them glasses of water, lukewarm and a faint brown colour. He gave evidence that he had sold brandy to March. Torlo was called and John saw at once from the man's attitude that he hated their guts. He stood before the table, shoulders forward a little and one hand thrust into the top of his belt. Most of the time he kept his eyes on Sergeant Benson.

On the night of March's visit he had been out fishing with two other men from dusk until dawn. There was nothing he could tell them about March's death. His manner began to irritate John, but he kept his temper. The man stood slouching in front of them and he longed to bark at him and pull him up, but he could see that it would do no good.

Finally, John said, "Corporal March's death may have been an accident. But it may not have been. Can you think of anyone who might have wanted to do him harm?"

Torlo smiled, sucking at his teeth. This officer was wearing a gold watch. The brown shoes that he could see under the table were brightly polished and of fine leather, good, close grained leather. A man would be proud to have a pair like it. A lot of things this officer knew and owned that he, Torlo, would never know or own. But there were things Torlo knew. For all their cleverness, he, Torlo, knew more.

"Answer, man!"

It was Aldobran who spoke, but the words and the tone came from the officer.

144

That is how they spoke to you, thought Torlo. We are poor and we work hard and are of no importance, and so we are spoken to like this. They think us stupid and imagine that our women are easy . . . It would be a good thing to show them that others were better than they in some things. In his mind, tickling his pride and his vanity, he knew suddenly what he would do. If there were strangers on Mora and they had killed March, he would kill them. That for Arianna, and then he would load their bodies on a cart and drive them to the fort and call out to the officer to come and see. There was an importance about strangers on Mora, he knew that from Aldobran. If he brought them dead to the fort, then there would be an even greater importance about him, and this officer and the sergeant would have to recognize it. His name would be known and the Governor would speak to him and there would certainly be a reward.

"Do you know anyone, Torlo?"

Torlo stirred and straightening up he said, "If he had dishonoured his promise to my sister I would have killed him. But I did not. If he had taken my sister from some other man, that man would have killed him. But he did not."

"Thank you. That's all," said John.

Torlo went. They thanked him now. But they would thank him for much more later. He went back to the house, collected his shot gun, a corner of bread and a bottle of wine and left the house, making his way up the slope towards the lower oaks and pines that fringed the first approaches to La Caldera. As he went he saw the jeep with the officer and the others raising a small cloud of dust as it went up the road. As he climbed higher the crescent of harbour at Mora came into view and he saw that the destroyer from San Borodon was coming in. If it ever had to be, Torlo thought, he would be a sailor rather than a soldier. Maybe, when he had his reward he would go away as Arianna had wanted to go away. He would get a job on one of the boats from Port Carlos. Everywhere he went people would know that he was the man who had killed the strangers on Mora who were there because of the importance of the prisoners in the fort of which the radio in the *Bar Filis* spoke often, and his own importance would be great and lasting; and if he ever met the sergeant in some place where they could be alone he would spit in his face instead of at his feet. Oh, Torlo, that it should happen thus. He whistled gently and happily to himself.

Someone about the turn of the century had panelled the long mess room over the main gate with pine wood, large panels with a now faded line of gold leaf marking the pilastering. Along the walls small electric light sconces with white silk shades clung like long-dead, frayed and gigantic moths. Mice had eaten into the wiring behind the panelling and only a few of the lights worked. Over the baronial fireplace which now housed an army stove was a dark, obscure picture of a General Cutts who at one time had been Governor of the San Borodon Islands. Four small windows, stone mullioned and barred heavily, looked down towards Mora. In one of them there was a small leather-topped card table and John Richmond was sitting at this writing. Two pewter holders with lighted candles stood on the table and he only had to lift his head to see the lights of H.M.S. *Dunoon* where she stood off Mora. She had arrived that afternoon, making her weekly call with stores and mail.

John liked this long, shadowed room. It reminded him of the dining room at Sorby Place, and on a hot evening like this, with the windows open, it was cooler than the garrison office or his own bedroom. The breeze drifted straight in from the sea, making the candles flicker and sway gently.

He wrote to Banstead:

> "Burrows came in on the *Dunoon* this afternoon with the weekly stores and mail. He's off tomorrow morning and can take this, and my other reports, with him. There's a Sunderland going out of Port Carlos tomorrow evening and this should be on it."

For a moment he saw the Sunderland coming down out of the cloud over Southampton Water and the greenness of the Isle of Wight, the white cliffs and the high summer swarming of yacht sails in the Solent. At dinner here in the fort that evening Teddy Burrows had been talking about Uffa Fox and a boat he was designing for him. The lieutenant-commander had brought a couple of bottles of claret from Sir George Cator as a present to John. Chateau Durfort-Vivens, a Margaux second growth. They should have rested it after

146

the sea trip, but they sacrificed one bottle. Burrows had been in a good mood and had taken too much brandy later, not by any means drunk but confidential, leaning over the table wagging a finger that looked like a rowlock peg. In the silence now of the long room the memory of his voice echoed noisily:

"Boats and women. Just the same, Richmond. Just the same. A boat looks a beauty on the drawing board. Everything you can want. But the moment her bottom touches the water she begins to play tricks. Got to handle her; got to make adjustments, got to get to know her faults. Same with a woman."

"And what happens to a woman, the moment you get her off the drawing board and her bottom touches water?" He'd had his share of brandy, too.

The roar of Burrows' laughter had shaken the dry, brittle silk of the light sconces.

"Same thing. You pick the right one, you think. Pedigree, good movement, good dresser, looks like a good breeder and full of show points. But she'll play the same tricks and you've got to learn to handle her. My advice to those about to marry. Don't." He roared again and then shook his head seriously. "Don't mean that. Happily married meself. But the happiness don't come wrapped in cellophane like a packet of Players. Got to work for it. You'll find out when you marry. If you do. Got you marked down, though, as the bachelor type. Too fond of your little comforts, eh? Well, there's something to be said for that."

He'd gone out of the main gate, laughing still and Sergeant Benson had driven him down the hill in the jeep.

John went back to his writing.

"By the way, you'll see from H.E.'s official report that a few nights ago we lost one of our chaps. A Corporal March. The whole thing's unfortunate, but in a way the silly young fool asked for it. He slipped out at night to visit a girl friend at a village down the coast. Coming back along the cliff path—and the cliffs are about two hundred feet high—he went over the side. A couple of fishermen from Mora found him while they were going along the inshore rocks for octopus. He was badly smashed about by the fall and had most of his clothes ripped off him. Not a nice sight. She swore blue he hadn't been drinking, but I think she was lying. Women and

147

vino go together in these parts. However, it's a nasty thing to happen, and you know what hell it is writing to the family."

He put down his pen. He could see the girl, her face puffy from tears. Poor kid . . . and poor March, too. It was a beastly way to finish up.

They had buried him that afternoon in the little military burial ground which was on the cliff top just below the Flag Tower. It was the first burial there for a good fifty years and in all there was only a handful of graves. A few people from Mora had come up. John had read the burial service. The girl had been there, standing by herself, a scarf over her head and most of her face. After the salute and as the earth and stones had begun to fall on the rough coffin top she had turned away and gone down the hill to Mora.

John finished off his letter to Banstead. He went out on to the parapet for a breath of fresh air before turning in and found Sergeant Benson taking a turn of guard duty at the Bell Tower. He was a good sergeant. With March gone they were shorter than ever of men.

They chatted for a while and then John moved on as far as the Flag Tower. For a moment he looked over the seaward side. The fresh earth on March's grave stood out clearly against the hard ground. He'd seen plenty of men buried quickly and roughly. One never lost, he thought, that sense of desolation that came when the thing was done and there was only the fresh earth to mark a man's passing. This was what they would all come to, a loneliness and an unimportance. But while waiting for it, each man assumed an importance that really deceived no one. It'll all be the same in a hundred years. Was it true? Just now there was Mora and this Cyrenian business. Important. Filling the headlines. But in a few years it would mean nothing. He turned away towards the inner parapet and saw the moonlight striking the silver-grey leaves of the dragon tree. He knew all about the tree from Jenkins, the cook. Over a thousand years old, renewing itself, growing all the time, and ready to weep blood at moments of tragedy . . . Well, some of the things that went on in the world today were terrible enough even to make trees weep. But men were past weeping. Death and torture began to have little meaning when there was so much

148

of it. March was dead, buried in the afternoon, and in the evening he had sat down to a bottle of claret with Burrows and they could find laughter in themselves. Hungary, Poland, the slow death of Arab refugees, the Suez fiasco, and Cyprus and Cyrenia violent with sudden deaths and murders . . . at times they were all too much, and the spirit became too tired to respond sincerely. The events of the world were deadening men's susceptibilities . . . they piled themselves on top of one another too quickly for weeping. He stared gloomily at the tree. It was hard not to imagine that that was the way it was. It was hard not to shrug one's shoulders and withdraw into one's own tight little circle and accept the fact that, instead of trying to weep for others, it was easier to write a cheque for a relief fund and then forget. Maybe that was the trouble, you could buy off your discomfort with money. The Lord Mayor's Fund for the Relief of Hungarian Refugees had become, with a hundred other funds, an easy way of dispensing with one's obligations. It certainly seemed like that . . . In that moment, leaning over the parapet, he felt depressed and lonely and out of harmony with himself. Things should be different, and to be different there had to be a start with individuals and the only way a man could start was with himself . . . He straightened up suddenly, shaking the thoughts from himself and began to move back along the parapet. But he knew what he was doing. He was escaping, just as everyone else escaped, had to escape because it was so impossible to know what else to do.

On the *Dunoon*, anchored just off Mora, Petty Officer Grogan and Andrews were in the sick berth with the door locked and a flask of island wine between them. Andrews had brought it back when he went ashore that afternoon. They were both very mellow and at this moment very silent. Andrews sprawled on the examination couch and Grogan sat on a chair, elbows in his knees and a cigarette burning idly between his nicotine-stained fingers.

Andrews drained his glass and reached out to the stool between them for the flask.

"The more you drink of this stuff," he said, "the worse it tastes. Like turpentine and scent." His voice had the slightest

149

edge of a slur in it, and the sound pleased Grogan. He'd heard it so many times when they had been together on shore leave. Good old Andrews. He was young and he couldn't hold it so well, and they were both bloody fools to be drinking aboard, but what the hell . . . A man couldn't always live by the book.

Grogan took a draw on his cigarette, blew a fog of smoke and staring at it said, "I am thinking of a large glass of Guinness. Three-quarters of the way up the glass it is as dark as a negress's leg."

"And on top," said Andrews who'd heard it before, "it's got a head of froth like a tart's fancy garter. Don't you ever think about anything but drink and your old woman?"

"Mrs. Grogan to you."

"Mrs. Grogan to me. I'm glad I'm not married. I don't have that kind of worry."

"What kind of worry?"

"That kind. Oh, where is my wandering girl tonight?"

"Mrs. Grogan don't wander. And you know it. She's too busy putting new lino on the bathroom floor. God bless her."

"God bless her," said Andrews. "You are a lucky man to have a paragon."

"What the hell's that?"

"It's a wife that don't wander."

"That's good. Just for a moment I thought I might have to knock you off that couch."

"If I have any more of this stuff I'll float off it. You want to know something?"

"Tell me anything. Only keep the words simple."

"No, perhaps I'd better not. I don't trust you. You know, if you drank enough of this stuff it would be better than an anaesthetic. I'll bet you could cut my leg off right now and I wouldn't feel it."

Grogan cocked an eye at Andrews. He was gone further with wine than he had imagined. But there wasn't only that. He knew his Andrews from Portsmouth to Port Carlos; he knew him in beer, in rum, in whiskey and in wine, and he knew when something was on his mind.

"Yoga's the same thing," Andrews went on staring

straight above him. "Takes you right out of your body. That's me up there, look. Floating about like a bloody seagull."

"Well, come down and tell me the thing you won't trust me with."

"You know that girl I got in Port Carlos?"

"Smelly Nelly?"

"Ha, ha, very funny."

"Don't tell me she's a paragon."

"No, but she can split and gut a cod with anyone. Also, she's got a sister."

"No thank you."

"It wasn't offered. But this sister works at Government House."

"So what? Umpteen other servants do."

"That's right. But this one is a maid. Very smart she looks in her uniform. And she looks after Mrs. Burrows."

"The old man's wife?"

"That's right. You'd never have guessed there was trouble there, would you?"

Grogan stirred uneasily. The old man was the old man and much as he liked Andrews he wasn't taking any loose talk about the old man.

"Careful, Andy," he said. It was an old warning, always given on the rare occasions when they fought.

"All right, I'll shut my mouth. I've been with the old man almost as long as you. They don't come any better."

They were silent for a while and Grogan thought of his wife in Portsmouth. Thank God, he didn't have that kind of trouble. And then he thought of the times when he and Andrews had drunk and fought in Naples, Durban and a score of places, and then he thought of the old man and his wife and he said:

"What about this girl?"

"She takes up the early morning tea. She knows what a bed looks like when it's had two people in it. She's seen him, too, slipping away. How could a woman want to do a thing like that to the old man? Makes you want to puke."

"Grayson, is it?"

"Yes. We could get him one evening, if you like. Rough him up. No one would ever know."

"That wouldn't do any good." Grogan stood up, frowning. "Think the old man knows?"

"How the hell should I know? But get this into your head"—because of his affection and regard for his captain he was shocked into anger—"you breathe one word of this to anyone else and——"

"What do you think I am? Taken me two days to make up my mind to tell you. I don't trust my girl's sister, though. She don't like Grayson or Mrs. Burrows. She's all for the old man. She might tip him off—anonymous letter or something. I've promised to brain them both if they do . . ." He took a drink and sighed wearily. "You wouldn't think it to look at her, would you? Or would you?"

"I don't want to think about it."

"Then sit down and have another drink." Andrews raised his glass solemnly. "For those in peril on the sea. You know there's a nice little bar around the back of the church here. Found it today. Kept by an old bloke with a funny right hand. Very interesting hand, twisted right round at birth. Always got his palm up as though he's waiting for you to put something in it. Anatomically . . ." he took the word slowly, "speaking, it's very interesting. Oh, yes, very." He stared at the deck above him and said deliberately, "By God, I know what I'd like to do to that bastard, Grayson. The old man's too good to have——"

"Shut up," said Grogan fiercely.

Marion lay in bed in the dark, wide awake. Outside now and again she could hear the scrape of the guard's heavy boots on the parapet stones. All about her in this fortress were people of her own blood, a people she had schooled herself to regard as enemies in the past years. For Hadid's sake she had done that. When you began to think of people as enemies they lost their true character. They became figures and symbols. For years she had had very few contacts with the British. Always there had been Hadid and Mawzi, and in Algiers, Tunis and Cairo, in Cyrenia, wherever they went it was never to be with her own people. She knew the Arab and Turkish mind, found herself thinking like an Oriental, as fatalistic and callous as Hadid's own people. How had she been able to do that? Out of love for Hadid originally . . . Loving him it had been easy. When she had first married him she had been an empty-headed shop-girl with little more than a capacity for love and loyalty, and over the years he had dominated and changed her. For the first few years she had had no idea of the ambition and dedication in him. They had just enjoyed themselves, idle, rich, and she learning all the time. And then when he had begun to take her into his confidence she had seen a new Hadid and known her love increase, so that anything he asked she did, counting herself lucky to have him for a husband.

She reached out, found a cigarette and lit it. In those years there had been no question in her mind that what he said and did had been right. But her strength, she knew, had been in her love for him. In the last two years that had gone, and she saw now that it was inevitable that with its going she had changed. That's why she had spoken to them as she did on the parapet. She wanted no more of Cyrenia. Out here that had become clear to her, and she wondered how much the desire had been quickened by having her own people about her. The heavy robust faces of some of the guards, the way the cook sang in the courtyard and watered his plants . . . this English passion for flowers and gardens. Time and again in the past few days her thoughts had gone back, far back, to Swindon and London, to her father and his garden, cramped between tall brick walls, seeing him putting out the empty halves of oranges to trap the earwigs from his dahlias, seeing him sitting in his shirt sleeves at the kitchen table reading *Amateur Gardening* . . . These were her people and she had only been able to turn from them by the power of her love for Hadid and his for her.

The two years had marked her and, finally, killed all love. She could feel it in her mind and in her body. And in many ways they had destroyed her because now, when she reached Cyrenia, her freedom would mean nothing except the permission to hide herself. Where could she go and what could she do . . . ? She had money, but where would it take her? What would she become? One of those anonymous women moving from hotel to hotel, or withdrawn behind the walls of some Spanish or South American villa. Drying up slowly, beginning to drink too much, or pathetic in her pretence that neither body nor spirit had withered. Would she take lovers to begin with and then with the passing years find them hard to discover . . . ? She stubbed the cigarette out vigorously, her body suddenly tense as she thought of the emptiness of the past two years.

Just as the great shadow sweep of Hadid and Cyrenia over her had moved away so that now she could see her own people clearly, so too there was a growing rebellion in her body, a crying out for love, and if at first it came only as a longing for the vivid passionate presence of another it carried much more with it. She thought of the men in this fort with the photographs of their wives and sweethearts stuck over their beds, of the pin-up girls cut from coloured magazines, and their wallets with the dog-eared snapshots of children . . . All that comfort, all that richness which was part of loving, was kept from her, and the thought of it was a great ache in her.

To herself she said fiercely, I was a fool not to have ended it two years ago. I should have walked out and my grief would have passed and I could have lived. Some man would have loved me and love would have grown again in me. Somewhere a man would have put out his hands and gripped my elbows and I would have known from the shake in his hands, in the tightness of his grip all that was passing in him . . . and in the darkness there was in all her senses the ache for the hard, muscular strength of a lover, and the imagery in her mind was so strong that she turned over in the bed, forcing her face into the pillow, stiffening her body to keep back the almost overwhelming desire to let go and find relief in sobbing.

She sat up suddenly, angry with herself. She kicked away the bedclothes and slid out of bed. In the darkness she walked to the switch by the door and turned on the light. She crossed to the barrack cupboard that Sergeant Benson had installed for her and opened it. From the bottom of her suitcase she pulled out two black leather-covered notebooks and took them to the small fireplace set in the far wall beyond the bed.

Very deliberately she opened them and began to tear out

154

the pages. When she had a small pile in the fireplace she reached back to the bedside table for her matches.

She set light to the pages and as they flared up she tore more from the notebooks, feeding the flames. After a little while all the pages were burned. She went to the window, opened it, and threw the leather covers out between the bars.

The closely written shorthand record, entirely personal, of the last ten years was gone. Until now there had always been pleasure in going through it, always some memory of the happy past to drive away the misery of these years of change. But now it was all gone, happiness and unhappiness, and she sat on the chair before the fire where a last few threads of sparks ran along the blackened pile of leaves and felt free. She was neither happy nor unhappy, but disburdened; not Marion Chebir, not even Marion to herself so much as a nameless, uncertain person, awake from a long sleep yet still, for a while, held down from movement and thought by the fading memory of long dreams. She lit a cigarette, drawing hard on it, closing her eyes against it, and wishing that she could have a really strong whiskey and soda. A whiskey and soda. It was odd how much she wanted that just now. She smiled to herself. All she had to do was to walk out of the room and call the guard and send him to Major Richmond. Tell him I want a whiskey and soda. Yes, at three o'clock in the morning. Wake him and tell him I want a whiskey and soda. She could see him, sitting up in bed, his hair ruffled, frowning, almost hear the half-blasphemous thoughts in his mind. A whiskey and soda, Major Richmond! A whiskey and soda! Wake up, wake up and stop looking so stupid and surprised.

The picture was so funny that she began to laugh to herself, rocking forward on the hard chair, her shoulders shaking . . . A whiskey and—No, it was too funny. Oh, Lord, oh, Lord, oh, Lord, what was happening to her? She hadn't felt like this since the days when she shared a flat with other girls and they would suddenly go off into mad giggles over nothing.

8

SIR GEORGE CATOR came into Neil Grayson's office and waved a hand at him to prevent him from rising from his desk.

"What have we got this morning, Neil?"

"It's pretty much the usual run of stuff, sir."

Sir George went to the window of the room and let his eyes travel slowly down the slope to Port Carlos. In the bay the sun glinted on the grey and silver shape of the Sunderland flying boat which had arrived at first light. The London despatches the boat had brought were on Neil's desk.

"I've been thinking, Neil. It's time I went over to Mora. The *Dunoon* will be in this evening. Teddy can take me over the following day. You might send a signal to Richmond and let him know I'm coming."

"Yes, sir. How long will you stay?"

"Oh, a night, maybe two. He can fix me up at the fort. I hate sleeping on the *Dunoon*. Gives me claustrophobia."

"What about the pressmen, sir?"

"Two of 'em, aren't there?"

"Yes, Sir George. They're getting rather restless."

"All right. I'll take them, but they can stay on the *Dunoon*. Richmond won't want them at the fort . . . though no doubt they'll want to have a look round there. You'd better sort that out with Richmond."

"I'll do that, sir. Oh, by the way, there is this which you may like to look at now." Neil picked a sheet of paper from the pile before him and held it out.

Sir George came back from the window and took it from him. As he read it, Neil stood up and lit himself a cigarette.

There were only about twenty lines of typescript on the sheet but Sir George seemed to take an age in reading it. No matter what self-interest coloured Neil's attachment to Sir George there was also a natural affection in him for the man. He was kind and considerate and there was a rough, almost bashful gentleness in him. The last person he wanted to hurt was the old man. Plenty of people he would have no hesitation in hurting if they got in his way. But Sir George was not one of them. One of the things he knew would hurt

156

him most was a lack of respect for the proprieties. No power on earth could stop a man from falling in love with another man's wife; (Sir George, of course, would never know how far that had gone already) but if it happened . . . Well, Sir George, even though the truth wasn't evident at the time, would expect that man to leave his house.

Sir George cleared his throat noisily and dropped the paper back on the desk.

"Lot of damn wishful thinking, I'd say. What do you think?"

Neil's face was serious and he frowned a little. "I don't know, sir. Except that it would be foolish to take anything for granted." He picked up the paper. It was an intelligence report from the Colonial Office. Rather baldly—almost as though the person who had drafted it shared Sir George's view that it was wishful thinking—it stated that in Cyrenia in the last week a very definite rumour was alive in the towns and villages that Hadid Chebir was returning, that the National Army—re-grouped and in greater strength—was waiting for the return, that this time nothing could stop them.

"It could be just skilful propaganda carried on by Chebir's people to keep things alive."

"That's all it is, surely?"

"One would think so, sir."

"I'm sure that this is just bazaar talk, However, doesn't do to be complacent." Sir George smiled and cocked an eye at Neil. "Send this through to Richmond. He's the man on the spot and he's no fool."

Sir George began to move towards the door. "Let me have the rest of the stuff up as soon as you can."

"Yes, sir. There is, however, one other thing."

"What's that?" Sir George turned, his hand on the door knob.

"It's something which I find very hard to say. Very hard, indeed."

Sir George came a step back in the room.

"What is it, Neil?"

"Well, sir . . . I've been with you a long time now, and I'm grateful to you for the many things you've done for me."

"Nonsense, Neil. You're a damned good A.D.C. I'm

grateful to you for the way you take things off my shoulders. Anyway, what is it? You want to move on? Fresh fields. Eh, is that it?"

"Frankly, yes, sir."

"Don't blame you. What have you got in mind?"

"Well, sir . . . I thought I'd go into industry. I've some friends in London who'd help me. And then . . . well, you know my political ambitions, sir."

"Of course . . ." Sir George rubbed his hand slowly across his mouth as though he were hiding a smile. "Well, why not? Could help you, too. My brother is in Talloid Chemicals. I'll write to him. I don't have to tell you who his chairman is. When do you want to go?"

"That's rather up to you, sir."

"But the sooner the better, eh? All right, we'll get this visit to Mora over and then we'll fix things up."

"Thank you, Sir George."

When the Governor had gone Grayson relaxed in his desk chair. The question of his resignation had gone very smoothly, more smoothly than he had anticipated. Sometimes the old man could be awkward and probing, and he had a way too of knowing a great deal more about the things that went on around him than he ever showed. That's why he knew that it was dangerous for him to stay here with Daphne any longer. It would be so easy for something to go wrong. The way they felt towards each other now made it more and more difficult to hide the liberties of thought and attention which were between them.

The door opened quietly and she came into the room. Every morning she did this now, to smoke a cigarette with him and talk. It was innocent and natural, but a new habit and the kind of thing which Sir George might easily notice.

He stood up as she came across to him, tall and lovely and smiling. Her hands came out to him and just for a moment he touched them. Without a word he lit a cigarette for her and watched her settle herself on the corner of the desk.

He went to the window and sat on the sill, facing her, letting his eyes hold her.

"I've just spoken to your father," he said.

"About leaving?"

158

"Yes."

"How did he take it?"

"Very well."

"I don't want you to go."

"I must. You can follow later."

"I don't want to be separated from you."

"I know that. But I'd only stay if we were going to go to him together and explain things——"

"No, I must do that. By myself."

Grayson nodded. If anyone had told him three weeks ago that this was going to happen he would have laughed. He had it all cut and dried, one way or the other, one wife or the other. But not now. That was something he must remember when he really got to work in London, that there was always this intangible, unexpected element in life that had a habit of slipping into the best calculated plans, sometimes for the good as now, and sometimes for the bad. However hard you schooled yourself there must always be the daemon that would twist loose.

"You didn't come to my room last night."

"No."

"Why not?" Her eyes were on him and there was a gentleness in her face which touched him deeply. She knew why not. Maybe she hadn't put it into words and action as he had yet. But she must know it if only as a feeling.

"You know why not. Because I'm in love with you."

"Yes, I know. But I wanted to hear you say it."

He laughed gently. "I think we're both a little scared by it. I know I am. We'd got it all arranged, a nice blueprint for the future. My work, your money, my ambition, your friends, we're both young and we both understand one another, by day and by night. And now this happens!"

She laughed a little at this. "But it doesn't change anything. It makes it better."

"It makes it right. But it changes things for the moment. Now it isn't a question of my wanting you and you wanting me. We're in love and suddenly there's something inside me that won't let me do things against that love until I can claim it out loud and in public. That's why I can't come to your room. That's why if I stay much longer under this roof with

159

you I'll burst a blood vessel or shout the whole thing out loud."

She slipped off the desk and came over to him and their hands met again. "I'm glad you said that. Oh, I'm so glad you said that."

He lowered his head and kissed one of her hands. Lord, it was true, he thought, that people sometimes got more than they had ever deserved. He knew about himself, had always seen himself clearly and chosen his path deliberately. As far as the virtues were concerned he didn't come very high in the list. Any of Teddy Burrows' friends could have found the right words to describe him. And they'd have found a word for Daphne too. And yet, now, within himself, and within herself, too, he knew that the thing had happened which made it right. Don't question it too much. Just accept it. And keep it right.

He stood up. "I must phone Richmond," he said. "We're going over there tomorrow for a couple of days."

For a moment she put her arms around him, holding him closely to her, resting the side of her face against his. This is the thing, she thought, that is in so many people's mouths, shrieking at you from hoardings, headlines in the papers, clumsy little paragraphs in magazines, the thing you giggled about in the dormitory at school, the thing that was just a word meaning bed for so many, the unknown, not understood until it happened thing, and when it happened it was like nothing that had ever been in print or words or thoughts before. It just was and it was hard not to be frightened that any morning you might wake and find it gone.

He put his arm round her shoulders and went to the door with her.

"Outside with you," he said. "I've got work to do." His voice was full of tenderness.

After Grayson's telephone call, John called in Sergeant Benson and told him about the Governor's visit. There were a couple of bedrooms on the near side of the long mess room over the main gate. These were to be prepared for the Governor and Grayson. The pressmen could sleep aboard the *Dunoon* or find quarters in Mora.

The last part of Grayson's conversation was concerned with the Colonial Office intelligence report. Although his prisoners could not have been better behaved, John knew that this could mean nothing at all. To treat the Cyrenian rumour of Hadid Chebir's return as bazaar talk did not entirely satisfy him. Chebir and Mawzi had left very able men behind them in Cyrenia. This talk of a return could be propaganda, put out to keep up the hopes and spirits of their adherents. Possibly it was no more than that. But it would be foolish to overlook the other possibility. He decided to walk down to Mora and have a word with Señor Aldobran of the Wine Co-operative.

Aldobran was in his office in the warehouse that looked out over the small run of beach. The *Dunoon* had gone early that morning. Fat, perspiring, his loose shirt sleeves flapping around his hairy wrists, Aldobran gave John a warm welcome and set a bottle of sherry and two glasses on the desk. John told him about the Colonial Office report.

"It may be nothing at all, but as Commanding Officer here I can't ignore it."

"Naturally."

"When I first came here I asked you to pass the word to all your people to keep their eyes open for strangers."

"So they have, Major. So they have. But there is nothing they have seen. But then . . ." He lifted his glass of sherry, spinning it by the thin stem.

"But then, what?"

"You know the south part of this island. It is very wild, and no one there. Strangers could stay there without being seen. Also up on La Caldera . . . There are many places to hide. Only this I say, if there were people here and they started to move about on the northern part of the island, well, then somebody would see them and tell me."

"I've been thinking about that too. The trouble is that I've got such damn few men. I can't take them away from the fort for patrol work, but I would like to go through that part of the island . . ." John paused for a moment. "The Governor's coming tomorrow. He'll be here probably a couple of days. The *Dunoon* will be lying off Mora all the time so I shouldn't imagine anything could go wrong until he's left.

But after that do you think you could find me twenty men? I'd like to go right over the island."

"Easily, Major. There are wild pig there you know. We could make it a little sport, too. But personally I think that is all you will find. Just wild pig."

"I hope so."

Walking back to Fort Sebastian he felt happier. Considering the odds strictly against an escape he felt that the whole thing was very unlikely, but as the officer directly responsible for the prisoners he knew it was no good being complacent. His quiet, professional pride suddenly writhed as in imagination some anonymous voice said, "I see old Richmond made a balls of that Mora affair. They got away right under his nose. The trouble with these War Office warriors is . . ."

Hell, he didn't want anything like that.

Back at the fort he sent for Sergeant Benson. Excluding the cook he had ten men. He split them into two guards of five men each, and each guard was to do a twenty-four duty.

"At night one man on the tower guard, one on the gate and to patrol the courtyard, three sleeping, fully dressed in the gate-room. They'll grumble like hell about it, but it's got to be done. On the beach guard there must always be three men ashore. You and I will manage the boat between us."

"It's pushing them hard, sir."

"I know it is. But it won't be long before we have the fresh men we've been promised."

"Are you expecting trouble, sir?"

"Not in the way you mean it, Sergeant. But that's what we're here for. To expect trouble. Don't think this is a lot of bull to impress Sir George Cator."

"I don't, sir, but that's what the men will say."

John smiled. "I can imagine all the things they will say. But the fact is that we can't take the risk of just a tower guard at night and a man sleeping in the gate-room."

"No, sir." Sergeant Benson put his hand inside his tunic pocket. "While I'm here, Major, I thought you'd better know about these. One of the men keeps a few chickens outside the fort, up against the wall under the Bell Tower. Found them in the run this morning, sir, and brought them to me."

162

He laid two black leather covers on the table in front of John.

"The run, sir, is right under Madame Chebir's window."

John picked up the covers and flipped them open. All the pages were gone. He remembered seeing them when he had searched her private luggage. He leaned back in his chair fingering the covers. Her name was written inside both of them.

He looked up at Benson. "If I remember right she said she kept her diary in these?"

"That's right, Major. I was with you when she said it. Looks like she's given up keeping a diary, sir."

"It does, doesn't it. Who keeps the chickens?"

"Carmichael, sir."

"Then give him a pat on the back from me."

As Benson left the room John tucked the covers under some papers on his desk. He lit a cigarette and went to the window. Why the devil should she have done this? For the moment, with the thought of escape strong in his mind, he wondered if there were a connection. A woman planning to flit might want to destroy some of the things she would have to leave behind, things she wouldn't want to have fall into other people's hands. But that hardly applied to her diaries. He knew she had them. At any time in the last weeks he could have confiscated them. He hadn't because all their effects had been combed through in Cyrenia before they left for the *Dunoon*. If Military Intelligence hadn't considered them important . . . No, they were probably just personal stuff. She could leave them behind without doing any harm. And, anyway, this kind of clearing up, if there was an escape in the air, would not be advertised by chucking things out of the window. Something else was afoot. It was very odd. Why would he, for instance if he kept a diary, decide to destroy it? Because it contained military or political facts he wouldn't want anyone to read. But she had brought her diaries openly with her. She would never have done that unless they had no importance except to herself.

He left the room, walked down the corridor but before he reached the long mess room went up a short flight of steps that led to the parapet walk. After the shadowed coolness of

163

the corridor the afternoon glare of sun struck down at him like a great white hand. He stood there, blinking for a moment and feeling for his sun-glasses. Each day now the weather was getting hotter and the cap of clouds over La Caldera was thinning and rising higher.

Down in the courtyard a couple of men were working on the fort's three-ton lorry. Jenkins and Abou were seated outside the cookhouse door, peeling potatoes. On the far parapet walk were the three prisoners. Sergeant Benson had rigged up a small awning for them. John walked slowly round the parapet, past the guard at the Bell Tower.

Hadid Chebir lay on a mattress under the awning. Colonel Mawzi sat in a canvas chair at his side. Neither of them spoke. Hadid seemed to be asleep and Colonel Mawzi sat with his chin in his cupped hands staring over the parapet wall to the sea. At the end of the walk, isolated in the shadow thrown by the Flag Tower, Marion Chebir sat by herself reading.

She looked up from her book as he neared her. Behind her sun-glasses he was aware that she had smiled for a moment; as though, for a fraction of time, she had forgotten where she was and who he was, naturalness escaping from her. She wore a silk dress marked with a paisley pattern. She was relaxed in her chair with an easy grace and he saw that she had kicked her sandals off.

He said, "Good afternoon."

Her book came down, resting on her lap and she returned his greeting in a tone that carried no finality, that had no hint of wishing him to move on.

He said, "I've asked for some more books to be sent over from Port Carlos."

"Hadid's the reader," she said. "He'll be glad."

"What are you reading?" he asked, but at the back of his mind the question he wanted to ask was *Why did you destroy your diaries?* But he couldn't do that.

"It's an old guide book of the San Borodon Islands. I've been reading about the building of this fort and how the islanders insisted that the dragon tree in the courtyard should not be touched."

"The tree that weeps blood?"

"Yes. It doesn't happen very often apparently."

"That suits the islanders, I imagine." He smiled but away at the back of his mind was the thought that he should have checked the books in the fort library. A guide book for anyone who planned an escape could be useful. It would almost certainly have maps. One never knew. Inside him, equally distant, was a sigh of weariness also at the thought. He liked her, acknowledged her attraction and would have been glad to sit down beside her in the shade and just talk idly, but there could be no real easiness between them because of this kind of thing. *Why did you destroy your diaries? What is it that rests uneasily between you and the two others? Are there any maps in the book?*

He said, "May I see?"

She handed the book to him and he flipped through its pages slowly. There were no maps. Handing it back he said casually:

"When you've finished with it, I'd like to read it."

"Of course."

When he passed on the book lay unregarded in her lap. She watched him move down the parapet on the seaward side, a tall, trim figure, his body carried easily with just enough military brace to the shoulders to hint at the vigour and authority in him. They were lucky in him, she thought. They could have had some strutting, pompous, red-faced martinet . . . Yes, they could have had a lot worse. She saw him pause for a moment in the middle of the walk and look down towards the cliffs. Instinctively she knew that he was looking at the grave of the soldier, March. A stronger instinct made her look away from him. She didn't want to think of March. In the old days a man's death had been impersonal to her. She'd forced herself to suppress all feeling about violence and death, justifying it for a cause, for Hadid's cause. It wasn't so easy to do that now.

Her eyes, turning from him, caught the gleam of the sunlight on the lance-tipped leaves of the dragon tree which reached up just above the inner parapet wall level. The tree that wept blood. Everywhere blood and death. There would be other deaths before she was free. Colonel Mawzi had promised that. Although he would give her no details he did not hide the wide truth. The price of their freedom meant other deaths. And now, suddenly, a new thought went coldly through her; abruptly and vividly repellent, she realized that it could be that the death of this Major Richmond might be inevitable. Men were going to die . . . the whole gallery of faces in the fort was before her, the solid dependable and not unkindly sergeant, the cook with his passion for gardening, and the silent little man who kept a chicken run under the walls of the Bell Tower . . . and finally this man, this tall, brown-faced major. She swallowed hard, shocked, as though the thing had already happened. Suddenly she saw them all lying under the hot sun and the ugly detail of death was in her mind from so many memories. She put her hands up under her sun-glasses and rubbed at her eyes as though she would rub the images from her mind. And when they were dead she would go free, she would go far, far away, forget it all, force herself to forget . . . and then she knew that she could never forget. Death wasn't a thing you forgot. She took her hands from her eyes and saw that he was now on the far side of the parapet walk, directly across the courtyard from her, and turning to go down the small steps that led to his quarters over there. All I have to do, she thought, is to get up and run round to him, call to him, see him turn, his face puzzled, run up to him and begin to tell him . . . tell him everything and stop death. She could see herself there, her hands on his arms, shaking him a little as he talked, explaining that tomorrow when the Governor came, tomorrow, tomorrow, tomorrow . . . But there was no movement in her. She was clamped to the chair and her hands were holding the arms with a fierceness that held captive the passionate rebellion inside her.

The daylight was going fast. Standing just inside the door of Colonel Mawzi's room Abou could see the great wedged and jagged shadows on the steep scar of the hill outside. Colonel Mawzi stood with his back close to the wall by the window, one hand on his chin, his lean face lowered a little in thought so that his eyes were hidden from Abou. Hadid Chebir sat on the bed, one leg swinging nervously.

Abou kept a hand between the door and the frame, holding

it open an inch or two so that he might hear if anyone should begin to come up the stone stairs.

Colonel Mawzi looked up suddenly and smiled at Abou.

"You are certain of these details, Abou?"

"Nothing is more certain, my Colonel. The Governor comes tomorrow morning. He stays one night for certain. Maybe two. This morning I have helped two of the soldiers to carry things to the rooms which are for the Governor and his A.D.C. I have been right through that part of the fort."

"It must be tomorrow night then?" said Hadid.

"That is agreed," said Mawzi. "One night he stays for certain, it must be that night. All the spare men sleep in one dormitory on this side of the courtyard. The sergeant sleeps by himself. Then there is the guard at the gate, and the guard outside the tower here. Mietus will have to move quickly. What about the lorry, Abou? There were men working on it today."

"It is a routine maintenance they do. The lorry is good."

Colonel Mawzi moved slowly forward into the room.

"Yes, Mietus will have to move quickly, but then we can rely on him to do that. With luck the guard up here will move to the top of the steps when he hears the noise below. He should be easy for them to deal with. And the key to this tower, Abou?"

"At night the guard carries it in his pocket and hands it over to his relief."

"Whoever Mietus sends up to release us must bring arms. We can then go to the parapet steps that lead down to the long mess-room corridor. Mietus's people will take them from the other end of the officers' quarters. The door to those stairs is not locked?"

"No, Colonel."

"The men sleep with their arms by them?"

"In the barrack room, Colonel, they are in racks by the door. In the gate house each man has his rifle by him."

"And Major Richmond?"

"This morning I looked into his room. His belt and revolver hang on the wall by his bed."

Hadid stood up. He was restless and impatient.

"It is the destroyer that worries me."

167

"Once we have the fort the destroyer will do nothing. But we must have the fort. It is here, in this first move, that everything should go without hitch." Colonel Mawzi faced Abou and held up his left hand, fingers spread. "Think, Abou, for it is of importance that not one man is out of place. The guard up here." He began to tick off the points on the fingers of his left hand. "The Governor, Major Richmond and the A.D.C. in the officers' quarters. The gate guard. The sergeant in his room next to the cookhouse. The rest of the men in their dormitory."

"That is so, Colonel."

"The cook sleeps also with the men?"

"No, Colonel. In a room next to the sergeant."

"If one man is out of place, one man unexpectedly somewhere else we could fail."

"It is as I say, Colonel."

In the darkening room Hadid stirred by the window, but he was a shadow. Colonel Mawzi and Abou seemed unaware of him. And as though to assert himself, anxious to have a rôle in this scene, even though his mind was on larger and more telling scenes to come in the future, he said, "But are you sure in fact that the destroyer will do nothing?"

Almost without turning Colonel Mawzi answered, "Nothing is certain, Hadid, but I am sure. This about the destroyer I have explained so often and yet you still question it."

"Two shells from her guns could destroy everything."

"There will be no shells."

Hadid opened his mouth to say more, but Abou put up his hand, his head cocked towards the crack of the open door. Suddenly his thin, old body relaxed and slowly he drew the door open.

Marion came up the last two stone steps and paused on the threshold.

Abou stood aside and she came into the room. He closed the door to its old position and stood behind her. Marion looked from Mawzi to Hadid. She had no need to ask what they had been discussing.

Her glance came back to Mawzi.

"It is tomorrow night for certain?"

"For certain. Just before dawn."

"What is required of me?"

"Nothing. You will stay in your room and wait."

"Nothing . . . So there is no need to tell me more?"

Mawzi smiled and spread his hands a little, his shoulders jerking like the wing shoulders of a lean bird settling its plumage.

"Nothing," he repeated. "In a few hours Mietus will be signalling. Before then I shall have made our final plans and will pass them to him. What is there for you to know except that soon you will be free?"

She was silent for a while. Now that she had said she would leave them once she was free she knew she could expect no confidence.

"There will be violence. I know this is inevitable. And some will die."

"Some will die," Mawzi echoed her words.

"It is known which?"

Mawzi shook his head. "How can it be known? One man quicker than his brother will be first to raise his rifle or sten gun. He is marked for death and the others will profit from seeing him die. But how can such a man be named? There shall be no wanton killing. This I promise."

"And the Governor?"

"He comes to Cyrenia with us. But the British will not want him to die. Should we either, since he will be a weapon in our hands? No, he will live and one day write his auto-biography, telling of his experiences as a prisoner of Colonel Mawzi and pretending to a great knowledge of Cyrenia affairs."

It was a joke, and since he did not often make jokes he turned, looking from one to the other to show them his pleasure. But, as he half smiled at Hadid, coming to him last, he was thinking, *He does not even notice that I say a prisoner of Colonel Mawzi where another would say the prisoner of Hadid Chebir*. And then turning back saw Abou's eyes on him like dark grey stones and knew perhaps that one in the room had noted the form of his words.

"And Major Richmond?" asked Marion and she held herself tightly, forcing herself to put casualness into her words because, sitting in her room below, she had been thinking of him, not understanding why her concern in this affair should seem to centre around him, but knowing it did, and now, after it had brought her up here, anxious that none of them should mark it as any different from her concern for the death of an unnamed soldier.

"Who cares who dies? What is this kind of talk between us?" said Hadid.

"There is more importance in this escape and return than in anything else that has ever been done for Cyrenia," said Mawzi steadily. "It is right to consider everything. Major Richmond," he moved a step closer to Marion and ran one hand slowly over his tight, smooth hair, "will come with us as far as the beach at Ardino. While we are on the island he is as much a hostage as the Governor . . ." He paused with a deliberate cruelty for he had not been deceived by Marion. A lesser man who wanted her, he thought, might have felt jealousy. But there was no jealousy in him. It was natural that as she neared freedom she should awake again as a woman. She began to look around and the major was there, the only man with whom she spoke outside her party. He was a man who would hold a woman's eye. "But on the Ardino beach," he said, seeing the thinning of her lips as she waited to know, "we shall leave him." He smiled again, brilliantly, turning away towards the window with a rapid movement and saying: "But let no one think that one day he will write his autobiography, too. He is not the kind." And with his back to them all, he said to himself that since Marion was now so much awake he would try her once again. If she refused him, then as simply as the Cyrenian women instinctively balanced the patterns in the carpets they made, so he would see that Major Richmond died on the beach before he left.

Hadid said, "That beach will have a place in history. My people, who will never see these places, shall have their names in their mouths as familiar as the names of their own villages. The beach at Ardino. Fort Sebastian. The destroyer *Dunoon* . . . Ha, yes, the destroyer *Dunoon*." And with the mention of that name the sudden vitality in his voice flickered and waned and he seemed to fade into the deepening shadows of the room. None of the others thought it odd or wondered

170

at this sudden flaring and dying in him because they all knew that he was inwardly a man of many fears and little courage. Tomorrow and tomorrow night he would be brave, but only because he would help himself to more courage. And Hadid was thinking to himself, *What if the commander of the Dunoon should be a fool and impetuous and fire?* The long, high whine of shells . . . He bit his underlip fiercely.

"Forget the destroyer," said Mawzi. "Think only of Cyrenia and of our people as they rise." But he said it without passion, cynically; and again he saw Abou's stone-grey eyes on him and he knew that Abou understood that Hadid would never see Cyrenia, that Cyrenia had to have another martyr.

Hadid said, "That is in my mind always, but also it is not easy to forget the noise of a shell."

Marion made a quick movement of disgust at the open fear in him. She turned swiftly and left the room.

After a time Mawzi said gently to Hadid, "You are a fool to talk of some things." He put an arm lightly over the other's shoulders and walked with him to the door. "I have much to work out and plan before Mietus signals. Leave me."

Hadid went down to his room. When he had gone Mawzi stood for a time by the door, close to Abou. Neither of them spoke for a while and then Mawzi said calmly, "It is not like the old days, Abou."

"No, Colonel. But it will be soon."

"Yes, Abou." Mawzi's eyes were frankly on him and there was an unspoken understanding between the two men. "It will be soon as it was in the old days."

Abou smiled, making a little obeisance with his head so that for a moment he could see his bare feet, pale at the ends of his tight, dark trousers, and he thought, "My feet itch for the feel of hot sand, and my fingers are lonely for the company of a rifle and my right shoulder longs for the thrust of a stock as the bullet burns the throat of the barrel."

"Go," said Mawzi, "but come back when it is time for Mietus and sit outside the door. This night nothing must go wrong so that tomorrow night everything shall go right."

Teddy Burrows walked through the garden to the point

171

where it narrowed above the headland that overlooked Port Carlos.

Against the darkness he could see the lights of the town, and those of the *Dunoon*. Hands in his pockets, he stared down at the bay. Distantly, from the house behind him, he could hear music. Above the music suddenly he caught the sound of Daphne's laugh . . . He shut his eyes, his face tightening.

The last three hours had been terrible for him. Before dinner he'd come up to the house from the *Dunoon* in time for drinks and, being early, had gone into Grayson's office to collect his mail. In a cheap envelope, unstamped, addressed in pencil the letter had awaited him half-way down the pile of London mail . . . The phrases in a mixture of Spanish and bad English stuck in his mind . . .

With a movement of swift revulsion he turned away from the sea and lit a cigarette. God, the thing was a filthiness in the mind. Only a fool would take any notice of an anonymous letter . . . some servant who'd been sacked, or someone Daphne had offended . . .

He sat on the bench outside the summer house, drawing fiercely at his cigarette. Damn it, Teddy, he told himself—you know better than to take any notice of a thing like this. Nobody's telling you anything. You know perfectly well that Daphne kicks over the traces now and then . . . dinner with some of the flying boat captains and a moonlight bathe . . . And, what the hell, a kiss or two might pass. She's a damned attractive woman. But nothing more. Not with Daphne . . . And Grayson of all people. The bastard wouldn't dare even if Daphne were willing. Too damned careful about his career . . . no scandal.

He threw his cigarette away suddenly. Forget it, he told himself sharply.

But it wasn't possible to forget, no matter how much you told yourself you should. The poison was there and proof against logic . . . All through dinner he'd watched the two of them, and he had to admit that there hadn't been a word or a look out of place. But wouldn't that be how they would keep it in front of him if there were any truth in—Blast it! There you go. Why damn it, he loved Daphne and she loved him—

172

she flirted sometimes, but that was all. He trusted her. Yes, he damned well trusted her. In the past they'd had their ups-and-downs . . . she'd never wanted him to keep on with the Navy . . . He'd been firm about that . . . Still, she'd accepted it. Why, lately she'd been even happier and easier with him than she'd ever been——

He stood up, disturbed. Maybe she had. But, maybe, the happiness came from . . . God in heaven! Grayson of all people—that fancy-dressing pip-squeak who'd fall to pieces if salt-water touched him! If it were true he'd—— He clenched his fists and growled softly to himself.

All through dinner . . . with old Sir George bumbling about some plant he'd discovered . . . and not a sign. For Christ's sake, Teddy—pull yourself together. If you really believe it, go and tackle Grayson. Get it over. But if you don't believe it—forget it. It's just a dirty, filthy letter with no truth in it——

He walked slowly back to the house. He didn't believe it. He wouldn't believe it. Maybe he'd ridden roughshod over some of Daphne's wishes . . . Yes, he could have humoured her more. There was no doubt about his love for her . . . Although there was no truth in this letter, at least it made him think, made him see that he ought to consider her a little more. Damn it all, if she really wanted it he would leave the Navy. He'd never make more promotion, anyway . . .

A burst of laughter from the house terrace greeted him as he went up the steps. Sir George was reading, a glass of whiskey at his side. Daphne and Grayson were on opposite sides of a small cane table, playing some gambling game with dice and a shaker.

"Teddy——" her voice, gay with pleasure, greeted him; "—come and sit in on this!"

"Yes——" Grayson stood up. "You play her. I've lost all I can afford, and I've got work to do." He smiled as he slid away from his chair. "Watch her—she cheats like fury."

"That's all right—so does Teddy. Come on, darling——"

She reached up with one hand towards him, and under the terrace lights he thought she looked more lovely than he had ever known her to look. For a moment he held her hand

173

before sitting down and suddenly he was calm and happy. The truth was here, in the way she smiled at him.

"All right, you shark," he said affectionately. "See if you can fleece me. I was born with silver dice in my mouth——"

9

FROM the afternoon of the previous day Torlo had been up on La Caldera. This mountain and its deep crater he had known since he was a boy, and there was no track in the great southern sweep of wild country unfamiliar to him.

The first afternoon he had walked and climbed openly around the rim of the crater, knowing that most of the time he was sharply silhouetted against the skyline to anyone who might be down in the crater. He had shot two quail and the great crater bowl had rung with the echoes. Later, he had dropped off the edge of the crater and, out of sight, had worked his way to the southern side of the mountain and then climbed until he was on the crater lip.

The rim was broken and craggy and the pines on this slope ran right up to the lip. He worked forward through the pines and finally lay between two boulders on the edge of a four hundred feet drop. Until sunset he had watched the crater below him. Nothing had stirred. The bottom of the bowl was broken with loose stone slides, clumps of bushes and a few wild fig trees. To the north-west of the crater there was a small pool, the glitter of its water almost obscured by the growth of rushes that spread over it. He had watched the pool with more interest than any other part of the crater. Men needed water and this was the only water on La Caldera. No one had gone to the pool during daylight.

When darkness came he ate some of his bread and drank half of his bottle of wine. He left his hiding-place an hour before the moon was due to rise and went northwards along the crater rim until he was above the pool. Here, he slipped off his boots, and went silently down the side of the crater, moving easily in the darkness as though he were in his own house crossing a darkened room without once touching

174

furniture. Waves of warm air rose from the rock faces baked by the sun all day. A handful of fireflies flickered and signalled over the myrtle bushes and the night air in his nostrils had a rich, dry smell.

For two hours he had waited on a ledge thirty feet above the pool and finally his patience had been rewarded. On the far side of the pool there had been the sound of movement. The dark mirror surface of the pool was broken and against the moonlight, which was just beginning to break over the distant edge of the crater, Torlo had seen the bulky shape of a man rise and turn away from the pool. Torlo had followed him, guided mostly by the sound of the water slopping about in a half-filled can. After fifty yards Torlo had stopped and turned back to the pool. He knew where the path led which the man was following. A hundred yards further on against the foot of the crater wall was a small cave, the front barricaded with a bamboo palisade.

Years ago the people from Torba, the village on the east of the island, had pastured their sheep and goats in the crater bottom. The cave had been used as a shelter for beasts and men. But for years the pool which flooded the bowl in the rainy season had been shrinking and now the floor of the crater was poor in pasture and shrubs and the people of Torba never used it.

Torlo went back to the pool. He drank the rest of his wine from the bottle and then filled it with water. When dawn came he was lying hidden four hundred feet above the cave and not five yards from the track which men would take if they wanted to leave the cave and travel north to Mora.

Now, as the last of the daylight went, he was still in his hiding-place. All day he had watched the patch of ground before the cave but no one had moved across it. He was not surprised. If these men wanted to keep their presence on the island a secret they would move only by night.

Although Torlo was an impetuous young man, he had great patience. It was no hardship to him to wait. There could not be many men in the cave and it was settled in his mind that he would kill them, and he knew how he would do it. That they would be all together in the cave made it easier. But first he had to return to Ardino. If they were to be killed he had to have the means to do it. Also Arianna should be present. It was for her that he killed. She should see it done. This he knew she would wish. That it should be done this night, or the next night or the next made no difference. But for Arianna's sake it was better done as soon as possible; and for his sake, too, for then he could go down to the fort and tell what he had done. If he did it tonight, then tomorrow he would go down. The Governor would be there . . . He lay on the hard ground, the great bowl below him a maze of grey and indigo shadows. He saw himself in the fort and the Governor was saying proud things of him and he was standing there, very straight and still and full of pleasure which was better than any woman could give, and the sergeant was full of envy and the officer with the polished shoes and the gold watch was probably saying to himself, *This man Torlo is a man and I have been mistaken,* and the Governor would say, *Tell us again Torlo, how thou hast done this thing. Tell it again and with every little detail for there is no story so good as the story of a brave killing.* And Torlo heard himself telling the story and the pleasure inside him was again sharp and clear like the sudden electric run in one's hand from a line when the big bass strikes and the world for a moment is all wonder.

In the midst of his wonder there came the sudden sound of a stone rolling for a moment on the path far below him. It was a small sound but it came clear through Torlo's pleasure of the mind and he was abruptly very still and watchful and without thought. He lay there listening and watching. After a time, although there was no more sound of stones or any sound of feet on the ground, there came gently to him the noise of men breathing. The way of their breath made a picture in his mind for this was the way every man in Ardino breathed as he bent to a steep patch from the beach. In his mind he could see the men coming up from the crater, setting their back muscles to the slope, their hands knuckling on to their knees to give them purchase.

He moved his head slightly and marked the place at the crater edge where the dark ground gave way to the less dark night sky. After a while he saw a shape rise from the ground like a small cloud and pass. And then another shape. And

176

another. And yet another. Torlo waited. Four men had passed. Torlo rose and went silently to the lip of the crater, staring down into the darkness. There was no sound from below. Four men and they had passed going in the direction of Mora.

He turned and followed them. It was not difficult. He had been without tobacco himself for thirty-six hours and his nostrils were keen. The smell of tobacco from the men's clothes was like a thick swathe along the path. As the ground began to slope away towards the sea, the track running down the long rib of high ground towards Mora and Fort Sebastian, he had the lightening sky ahead of him and the shadows were dark and long under the moon when they were free of the high belt of pines. The four men moved slowly and carefully. Torlo had an admiration for their movement, for there was one man ahead on the track and two others on each flank of the track, about twenty yards out, and the last man on the track a good fifty yards behind. They let nothing alter their formation, going over spur and rock break, dropping down terrace walls and through the patches of cactus and scrub oak without once breaking the pattern and, although they never stopped, there was always, it seemed, one man without movement, his head casting round until another would stop to watch and he would move on. There is no animal, thought Torlo, with the cunning and craft of man when he has got wickedness in him, and his lean dog face worked with pleasure at his own craft as he followed them. If their movement was like that of the fox coming down to the hen roosts his passage behind them was like the brown floating of an owl, all silence and velvet. That it would be a pleasure to kill these men . . . since for all his skill he would be treading on the spring of danger.

It took them two hours to reach the cliff edge a little way back from the fort. Once they all stopped and then, without signal, melted into the night so that for a while Torlo lost them. This was just after they had crossed the Ardino-Mora road, and the crossing of that road had been a pleasure to watch for they had drifted across like puffs of dust raised by a turn of unexpected wind. With their going Torlo discovered what had alarmed them. Somewhere on the far side of the road a man's voice had come loud and clear, and then another answering it, and out of the chestnut trees above Ardino two men had appeared. Across the still night Torlo could hear what they said. They were men from his own village, two fishermen who lived in a small cabin on the slope with their old mother, and they were on their way down to the beach for the night's work. They were swearing and arguing about which fishing ground they should use that night. Torlo smiled to himself, his thin lips tightening back from his large teeth in a movement of contempt, for they were worthless fishermen and would be so until they died unless the world turned upside down and talking could lure fish to a net.

When they were gone it was a long time before the men ahead of him moved, so long that he thought he had lost them. Then they were back like four small cloud shadows and moving.

At the cliff edge they did not move down so far as the path but converged together in a small clump of oleanders, coming together like four shadows, making one large shadow and then being swallowed by the darkness of the bushes. Torlo stayed fifty yards behind and above them and to their right. A quarter of a mile away was Fort Sebastian and beyond it Mora. There were few lights in the town for it was now long past midnight, and fewer lights in the fort. Two rooms were alight in the Bell Tower and another beyond the tower and inside the courtyard. From where he sat he could look right down into the courtyard. The solitary light there came from a bulb that hung naked in the gate entrance. For two years, when he had been a boy, there had been no soldiers in the tower, only a civilian caretaker, Barjes, an old man a little soft in the head, who had let boys into the place. Barjes was dead now but he remembered the man's fondness for boys and the way they had taunted and jeered at the old man, knowing well his weakness, but it was a different matter if Barjes ever caught you in the Bell Tower or one of the store-rooms. Just in time he refrained from spitting in disgust at the memory. The sound of spitting would carry in this still night.

After a very long time one of the two lights in the Bell

178

Tower went out. A little while after that he saw the small needle eye of a torch flick on and off from the darkened room. Below him for a moment until a hand cowled it he saw the answering flick of a torch from the oleanders. Again he had admiration for these men. The *flick flick* of their torch was no more than the dance of a fire-fly and the one from the tower was such that only from this angle could it be seen. He sat there, hugging his knees, his body balled tight against the bole of a palm and there was a great satisfaction in him, so great that there were times when he forgot that he was doing this for Arianna. He was doing this now for his own sake, for the sake of not always being Torlo of Ardino and unknown. Somewhere in England was the Queen whose enemies these men and the prisoners in the tower were. Two years ago he had been in Port Carlos when the Duke who was her husband had come there in the Royal Yacht . . . What a boat . . . and he smiled to himself as he remembered how he, among the waiting crowd on the quay, had seen the Duke's face twitch at the smell of drying cod as he came ashore. This was his Queen, too. He did this for Arianna, yes, and for the Queen.

It was good to do things for women. He heard himself saying to the Governor, *That these men were thine enemies was clear, that they talked to the ones within the tower of escape or bad things was clear . . . I, Torlo, was clear in my thoughts and knew that to hunt with many breaks too many silences, so by myself I did it lest these men should escape to return again and work some other wickedness.* And the Governor would hear him out and then say, *Torlo, thou hast done well. There is no other man who could have done so well against our enemies. Choose something now for thyself, something good and reasonable and it shall be yours . . .*

His face grew serious at this thought. In the matter of a reward it was necessary to be serious and to choose right. It was necessary, too, to be ready when the time came and speak firmly. Maybe he would ask to be given a job on the Royal Yacht. That would be a proudness no other San Borodon man could ever claim.

Torlo rose and went along the cliff path to his house. He had no need to watch the men any longer. He pushed open the door and went into the darkness of the main room and

179

then quietly, for he had no wish to wake his mother or his father, up the stairs to his sister's room. Her door was half open. He entered and reaching her bed went softly on to his knees and stretched out his hand and found her arm. He held it gently above the elbow and at once he knew that she was not asleep.

"Torlo." Her voice had the relief of someone who has been awake a long time, and tiring of her thoughts, welcomes company.

"I have come," he said, keeping his voice low, "from the cliffs by the fort. The men were there. Four of them. It is there that thy soldier must have met them and they killed him to keep the secret of their being here. Everything is clear to me. They signal to the fort."

"Is it done yet?" There was a quiet impatience in her voice and his hand left her arm as she sat up.

"Not yet. It is for that which I come to thee, but there is need not to wake the old ones for they would not understand."

"Is it to be tonight?"

"While it is still dark, before dawn. Thou wouldst be there?"

"Who else has the right? I wish to see them die and to spit on them. How is it to be done? With thy gun?"

"No."

Torlo stretched out in the darkness on the floor boards, supporting himself on one elbow and rolled himself the first cigarette for many long hours. He lit it, drawing hungrily at the smoke.

"No," he said thoughtfully. "This I have gone over in my mind. With a gun nothing would be certain against four men. But I have thought of something which pleases me." In the darkness he chuckled a little.

From the bed came Arianna's voice, sharp and angry. "That thou canst laugh or be pleased means nothing to me. I do not like the sound of thy pleasure. There is only one need in me."

"And in me, too," he said, ignoring her rebuke. And then, talking more for himself than for her, he went on: "These are men of great cunning. One has only to see the way they move at night to understand that. They live in the old cave in the crater and do not leave it by day. At night they come out for water and to go to the fort to signal. By now they will be back."

"How is it to be done?" Arianna asked.

"With the hand grenades," said Torlo.

"Ah, yes," sighed Arianna. "It is right that it should be thus."

"More than right," said Torlo. "For it was thy soldier who brought them to us. Remember how when he first came to know thee we would go fishing together——"

"I have no need for the memory," said Arianna quickly. But all the same the memory was with her. March, to win favour with them, had brought the hand grenades from the fort and they would row out along the cliffs beyond Ardino. He had shown them how the grenades worked, how to arm them and then, withdrawing the pin with their teeth, how to toss them out into the water. One counted five as they sank and then the water would convulse itself with an agony of noise in its bowels and then spout high, drenching the boat with spray, and in a little while the fish would float around them like palm leaf ribs, white and limp.

"There are four left," said Torlo, "but two will be enough. Before dawn we shall go up there."

He was silent, seeing himself standing in the early morning gloom before the cave, a grenade in each hand, felt his teeth on the pin, the grenade alive in his hand, and his arm swift with the movement of throwing. And with the throwing his teeth would bite on the pin of the other grenade . . . He lay full back on the floor, sucking at his cigarette.

"If I should sleep," he said, "wake me in an hour and we will go without disturbing the old ones."

Marion came out of her sleep slowly. She had been dreaming and much of the dream was still with her. She had been walking on the downs above Newbury and the day had been hot, a fierce heat without a trace of breeze, and after a while she had noticed that on the path ahead of her a man also was walking. Not wanting to overtake him she had slackened her steps but in some odd way, although he had made no alteration in his walk, the distance seemed always

181

to remain the same between them. Whatever she did she found herself walking with the man a steady two hundred yards ahead and after a time, maybe because he was the only other moving figure in the great green sweep of hills and the wide, empty arc of sky, his figure had seemed familiar, though she could put no name to him. Slowly there had grown in her a need to overtake him, to pass and turn and see his face, and the need had become an urgency in her. But though she hurried her steps she could not shorten the gap between them. The heavy heat around her was like a burden that she was forced to carry and that always held her back. And then ahead, the man had disappeared into a clump of tall beeches that marked the top of a smooth groove of valley running down to the field-checkered plain. She had hurried into the trees and found a great coolness amongst the silver grey trunks and the pale shadows and her feet on the dry leaves and beech husks had made a gentle, comforting noise. It was so calm and cool under the trees that she had stopped, looking round, knowing, too, that the stranger once in this haven from the heat would be forced to linger, but she could see him nowhere. Then, as she moved round a tree, he had been standing with his back to it and he put out a hand and took her gently by the arm just below the short sleeve of her silk dress. Looking up into his face, although she had still no name for him, she heard herself say, "Yes, of course. Yes, of course . . ."

She woke now, slowly, lost for a while in the amorphous darkness, but feeling his hand on her arm. She lay there very still and slowly her mind made shape and sense of the darkness. She was on Mora, in Fort Sebastian, and this bed was against the stone wall of the room, the head towards the window.

The grip on her arm tightened a little and then the hand left her entirely and a voice said, "You are awake?"

She said, "Yes," recognizing the voice as Colonel Mawzi's and the word she spoke sounded strange because of a sudden clot of nervousness in her throat. She heard his body move and the creak of her bedside chair on which he was sitting.

He said, "A little while ago I finished talking to Mietus. Everything is arranged. Tomorrow, sometime, Sifal will radio instructions for the flying boat. Everything is within everything like a walnut into its shell. You are pleased?"

"Yes," she said, "I am pleased." But she knew, too, that she was frightened. Although Mawzi kept his voice low she could hear the excitement in it, like a fine tremble that beat at the darkness between them and his hand had come back to rest lightly on her bare arm. "You have told Hadid?"

She heard him breathe contemptuously through his nostrils at the name. "A jackass could bray in his ear without waking him. You know how he is when he has need to kill his fears before danger. Tomorrow he will be as brave as a lion."

"I am sorry for him."

His hand was moving on her arm now, caressing it, and there was dismay and exhaustion in her almost to the point of apathy.

"He is not a man. To think of him is a waste."

"But you need him."

"Yes, but he is still a waste and an emptiness. I know that and you know that. Let us forget Hadid."

His hand now had gone under the strap of her nightdress and was on her shoulder, held very still and the warmth of it against her skin was like a soreness.

There is a way, she thought, to handle each man, even Mawzi, but her mind was too tired to discover it.

"There is a greatness for you and Cyrenia," she said, "and I can see that for you this is no time for sleep. If you wish to talk, talk. But that is all."

"With the lips," he said calmly, "there is no need to talk. We have come through much together. We have shared hope, and danger and sorrow and small triumphs. We have shared deceit and hardship. We have each put our honour into the other's hands. So much we have shared that there is little more, but that little the thing that makes us man and woman."

His hand began to move on her shoulder and she put up her own hand and held his wrist firmly. The chair creaked and she heard him make a dry sound in his throat and she knew that he had leaned towards her.

"Go, Mawzi," she said and the darkness and his near presence was stifling in the hot room.

"I cannot," he said and his other hand moved to rest on

her far shoulder and she knew that in the darkness above her face was his face. Oh God, she thought, what is it that makes them like this? But she knew that it was the same thing that made her wake at nights sometimes with a bitterness and longing in her . . . only for Mawzi she had nothing, nothing.

"Go," she cried angrily.

"I cannot," he said. She felt his wrist shake under her fingers and she knew his face was closer to hers because his breath touched her forehead as he said, "Through your shoulders I feel your heart beating, like the heart of a wild bird when it is held in the hand. There is no need for fear. See, I will calm the fear." His free hand moved from her far shoulder across her skin towards her heart and the touch was like the sudden sear of burning in her. As his lips came down to hers she twisted from him.

He came after her, his hands finding her body and his weight turning her across the bed as she half sat up. The thin blanket wrapped itself, constricting, round her legs and she kicked and struggled and her teeth bit into the hand that held her wrist. The sound of his pain was a sharp explosion of breath close to her face and she slid off the bed, hitting the small table and hearing the lamp smash to the ground. Free of him for a moment she pulled herself away in the darkness towards the door and she shouted. The shout was half-stifled as he found her and his hand came round her mouth and his free arm circled her waist, lifting her. They swayed together and fell, striking the table so that it grated across the floor. Her mouth was suddenly free and she shouted again. She fought and struggled against the grip of his arms. She heard him laughing deep within himself and knew that he was full of pleasure in this fight. And, as they swayed about the room with Mawzi seeking to imprison her arms and lift her towards the bed, there was only a great sobbing knowledge in her that she had not enough strength to fight him for long, and there was a dazed, confused weariness in her so that she could not tell whether she sobbed or shouted aloud or fought silently, striking at the hard body of darkness that crushed the breath from her. Suddenly she collapsed, exhausted by the struggle, and the sudden dead-weight of her body took him by surprise and she slipped to the floor. She lay there in a black tiredness

184

and she could hear him standing above her, breathing hard in the darkness and she knew that in a moment, when his breath eased, he would bend down and lift her and carry her to the bed. Her whole body shook with a great spasm of revulsion as she waited for the moment.

But the moment never came. The black nightmare blazed with a blinding whiteness. She looked up, a hand going feebly to her eyes at the cruelty of the staring light. She saw Mawzi standing above her and then, beyond him, the open door of the room and Major Richmond in a dressing gown on the threshold, his hand still held out towards the light switch.

Mawzi turned. His shoulders stiffened and his body hunched forward and he moved quickly towards Richmond.

"Get out!" he cried. "Get out!" His voice was shaking and tense like a master incensed by the interruption of a stupid servant.

As though the whole stifling nightmare had needed only this blaze of light to signal its climax of violence, Marion saw Richmond's eyes marking her beyond Mawzi and the angry jerk of his cheek muscles as though somewhere inside the flesh a mass of leather thongs had tautened. He stepped forward quickly. She saw his hand swing up and down and there was a curious wonder in her that the fingers were held straight and stiff, not bunched to a fist. The hard edge of his right hand struck Mawzi against the side of the neck. Mawzi gasped and toppled and then the major's left fist came up in a quick arc and struck Mawzi on the chin as he fell.

John moved aside a little and stood over Mawzi. Sergeant Benson had come to the open doorway behind him and beyond Benson she saw Abou who must have been roused by the noise.

"All right, Sergeant," he said. "Take him up to his room. Abou will give you a hand."

They came forward into the room and he moved away as they bent and lifted Mawzi. The man was shaking his head and sniffing. He was hard, thought John. Most men would have gone out cold. He watched them carry him through the door and he followed a few paces, rubbing the edge of his right hand which had gone numb from the blow.

185

"Leave Abou with him," he said. "And then get back on the main door."

They shuffled crabwise up the stone steps and John went back into the room, closing the door behind him.

She was still on the floor, half sitting, with her legs bent underneath her and her hands were raised cupping her cheeks. She was shivering and he could see her bare shoulders rise and fall as she breathed with the deliberate effort a person makes, after exertion or shock, to restore themselves, as though in the air itself was a great healing power.

The way she sat there raised a swift compassion in him, a tenderness towards her and an anger towards Mawzi that made him in that moment more vividly aware of her than he had ever been before. As he moved towards her, seeing the thrust of her sun-browned leg against the grey floor, the torn silk of her nightdress, and the distress in her face, he burned with anger against Mawzi. The silk and the flesh and the disorder of dark hair tightened something in his chest as though he strained against the pressure of a biting rope about him.

She looked up at him and one hand dropped to the bareness of her neck and he could see that she was trying to smile at him, to make some sign of thanks but was yet too close to what had so recently happened to be wholly aware that it was over.

He bent towards her and slipped a hand under her arm.

"Come up," he said gently, and he half took the weight of her body and stretched out his other hand to take her by the waist.

She stood up and breathed deeply and she said, "Thank you." He held her for a moment, steadying her. Then he withdrew his hands carefully as though he had built something to a delicate balance that any rough movement could destroy. He turned and saw her dressing gown on the floor at the foot of the disordered bed. He picked it up and came back to her and, standing by her side, draped it over her shoulder. As she moved into it she moved closer to him so that with all the naturalness in the world, as though they had both been waiting for it, yet both timid of any advance towards it, his arm was round her shoulders and she was

186

against him and had dropped her head against his breast.

"It's all right," he said and his arms tightened around her to contain the trembling of her body and he bent his head and let his lips touch the line of her forehead just below her dark hair, and the thing that was happening between them seemed so right and inevitable that there was no surprise in him, only a great warmth and desire to hold her in his protection. Very slowly she looked up at him and smiled and he knew that she was back and free of the horror and he bent and kissed her briefly on the lips and the kiss was between them so lightly and freely and then over that it was hard for Marion to know that it had happened.

"Get back into bed," he said and he moved away from her, one hand only on her arm and led her to the bed.

"In you get," he said, and he grinned reassuring, yet at the same time covering the newness that was between them, and his voice was like that of someone who half-bullies, half-jollies a child out of an unreasonable fear. "In you get."

She obeyed him, climbing into the bed while he righted the chair and picked up the bedside table. He turned back to her holding the broken table-lamp in his hand and he said, "Benson will fix you up with another in the morning. Is there anything you want now? A drink, maybe?"

"No, thank you." Stretching into the bed she was aware of a happiness in her which was so strange that she felt she would want more time than the world held to examine and enjoy it. He bent over her, pulling the edges of the bedclothes up and tucking it around her, and she had to laugh a little at his seriousness and the sudden feeling she had that she was a child being tucked away for the night, and her laughter made him pause and his face as he bent over her was close to hers.

This time, very simply, she pulled her arms from the covers and put them behind his head, drawing his face down to hers and they kissed with a full and ardent admission of everything that was between them and yet not ready for words, and there was an envy in her to hold him always, to have the hard, bruising weight of his shoulders and arms crush all thought from her. With his lips warm against her lips she could feel the wetness of the tears behind her eyes and

187

the slow tearing relief in her body as though, somewhere deep in the ice-bound stillness of her, there was a sudden movement and springing and a miraculous thawing that toppled icebergs and split the frozen stretches of loneliness which had been all she had known for years.

John drew away from her, standing up but leaving his hand in hers so that from looking up at him she turned her head slightly and kissed his palm before it left her.

He stood by her for a moment and there was a need in him to say something which had nothing to do with this, a need to break through to some point from which speech and movement would be easy, but there was nothing in him which could come to his tongue. He smiled at her and she smiled back and then he turned away from her and went to the door. With his hand on the switch he looked at her enquiringly and she nodded, asking for darkness. He switched the light off and went out.

He went to the main parapet door and tapped on it. Outside he heard Sergeant Benson stir and then the grate of the key in the lock. John stepped outside, but he motioned Benson not to shut the door.

"You took him up?" he asked and felt in his dressing gown pocket for his cigarette-case, absently forgetting it was not his tunic.

Benson fished into the pocket of his bush shirt and held out a packet of cigarettes. As John lit one he said to the sergeant, "Have one yourself. Tonight we can break the guard rules."

"Thank you, sir." Sergeant Benson lit himself a cigarette and standing by him John was glad of his simple, solid presence. It was hard for real thought to begin in him yet. He had to come to that slowly. Meanwhile, he was glad of the sergeant's company.

"He's pretty sick . . . real sick, I mean, sir. Vomiting. You half-killed him, sir." There was admiration in Benson's voice and acceptance, the final acceptance which no soldier gives to an officer until he has seen him in some kind of action.

"I should have killed him," said John. "But there would have been hell to pay."

"When I heard the rumpus, I couldn't think what was

going on . . . It was a good job I fetched you quickly, sir. Is the lady all right? I mean . . ."

"She's all right." John drew hard on his cigarette and he was thinking, this is something that common sense tells me is impossible, a madness, and yet I don't care. Why don't I care?

Sergeant Benson said, "The other one must be a sound sleeper. Not a peep out of him. He's an odd bird . . . They're a rum lot altogether if you ask me. He does nothing but read, read. If you walk by him he doesn't even look up. Like he was pretending he wasn't here. I suppose in Cyrenia he's a different man altogether. Mopey is the word for him here. Like when you take some wild animals and put them in a cage. They eat their hearts out. Some people, too, I suppose . . ." It was all right to talk, he knew that. On a late night watch when there was need to turn an officer out it was always all right to talk, to step a little outside your rank and be man to man for a change.

John stirred and dropped his cigarette to the stones, screwing the end out with the heel of his slipper. "I should keep this to yourself, Sergeant. If the men know, the islanders will know and we've got pressmen here tomorrow. The Governor wouldn't like any wild stories to be printed. Also," he laughed quietly, "I don't want it to be reported that I struck a prisoner, no matter how necessary it was."

"Of course, sir."

"I'll go up and have a look at Mawzi before I turn in."

"There's two of them. He's got Abou there, sir."

"It's all right, Benson. There won't be any more trouble."

He turned and went back into the tower and up the stone steps. There was a light showing under Colonel Mawzi's door and John opened it without knocking and went in.

Mawzi was sitting on his bed, drinking a cup of coffee which Abou had made him. Abou was by the window. There was a bowl of water on the table and Abou held a cloth in his hand.

Mawzi looked up at John and there was no movement in his face at all.

John said stiffly, "Colonel Mawzi."

"Yes?"

John said bitingly, "Colonel Mawzi, I am addressing you as the commanding officer of Fort Sebastian. Stand up when I speak to you."

Mawzi hesitated for a moment and then came slowly to his feet. The hatred in his face blazed suddenly.

"I am warning you," John went on steadily, "that in view of your behaviour tonight if you cause any more trouble I shall lock you in your room in solitary confinement for a week. Is that understood?"

Mawzi's nostrils narrowed and his mouth became a paper-thin line.

"You make yourself very clear, Major Richmond."

"Good. That is all."

John turned and left the room.

He went slowly across the dark landing and down the three steps to the level of Hadid Chebir's room. There was no light from under the door. How could the man, he thought, have slept through all this? First Sergeant Benson had heard the noise and had fetched him, and Abou had been roused by it; but this man slept on while his own wife was being assaulted in the room below him. It seemed unnatural. What was it Benson had said? That the man was moping, eating his heart out like a caged animal, pretending he was not on Mora . . . His mind went back to Oxford. It was odd, but since he had been here, so close to the man, he had not thought of their days at Oxford much. Now, puzzled and pausing before the door, his mind was full of Hadid Chebir. Once in *The Mitre* at Oxford he had heard another man unintentionally say something which had annoyed Hadid. The Cyrenian had turned on the man with murder in his eyes. The police had finally been called and both Hadid and the other had just escaped being rusticated for the rest of the term. What the devil would have been his reaction if he had caught Mawzi in the room below? Maybe he no longer cared what happened to anyone else. Maybe, the thought was a callousness in him which touched him to anger, the man had been awake and had just stayed on his bed, indifferent, pretending that nothing existed here, not even Mawzi or his wife. A quicksilver pride and a sharp, thoroughbred intelligence had been all the marks of Hadid. He saw little sign of them now.

On an impulse he put his hand to the man's door and went in. The room was in darkness. It was hot and so stuffy that he felt the windows could not have been opened for days. From the direction of the bed the faintest sound of breathing came to him. The man was asleep. How the hell could he be with all that had passed? Instinctively angry with the man, outraged almost by his sleeping, John flicked on the light. Let it wake him up, he thought. What the hell did he care? And he knew that somewhere at the back of his anger there smouldered the beginning of antagonism and rivalry because of the thing which had come between him and Marion. This was her husband, this was the man who should have been in her room full of protection and gentleness, full of . . . He went to the bed, frowning.

Hadid lay stretched out on top of the covers almost naked, a long length of pale brown body. His mouth was open with just the rounded edge of his tongue showing. The open mouth, stupid and lax, destroyed all the fineness of the face, turning intelligence to a dull idiocy. The body, too, was relaxed and heavy. He could have been something moulded from dark, soft clay, inert, and uninformed by muscle or bone. And John, who had helped many a fellow officer to bed after a mess party and looked in later to see how they did, recognized this familiar collapse of feature and body. With any other man he would have known that it was drunkenness that destroyed the sleeping personality of the flesh. But not with Hadid. Hadid never touched alcohol. Not even at Oxford.

He put his hand to the man's face and raised one of his eyelids. The pupil was small.

He straightened up, knowing now something that he had always suspected. The man was drugged. Somewhere, back in memory, he recalled Banstead saying that there was a rumour that Hadid took drugs now and then.

Looking down at Hadid, he felt sorry for him not angry. Years ago at Oxford he had been a young man, straight and fine-muscled, alive with grace and vigour. With him was his most pertinent memory of Hadid under the shower after a rugby game, water gleaming over his brown skin making a light and colour compact that you found only now and again

in the flesh of some of Velasquez paintings. He remembered
that moment under the showers so well because in those days,
inspired by his mother, and nursed, if a little hopelessly by
himself, had been the desire to be a painter . . . He loved
pictures; the El Grecos and the scabrous, nightmare Bosch,
the plaster whites of Utrillo and the primitive spring-bright
Italian colours that trembled all along the Uffizi galleries.
Each time he had seen Hadid under the showers and the
water light over his body he had known that, if he could have
been a painter, it would have been the body and the flesh he
would want to capture. He remembered, too, the incongruity,
ugly maybe for some, but for him so right in sharpening the
emphatic beauty of the rest of Hadid, of the irregular stain
of the large birthmark the man carried just to the left of his
navel.

Looking down at the man now, stretched long and dark
against the pale covers, his body naked except for the briefest
slip of cloth that had been twisted native fashion across his
loins and through his legs, John saw that the stomach flesh
to the left of the navel was smooth and brown, unmarked . . .
He stared down at the man, shock slowly mounting in him.

He leaned forward, unbelieving, suspecting some trick of
the bad light, or of his own eyes and memory. But there was
no mistake. This man carried no mark. Time and time again
he had stood under the showers with Hadid and seen that
white puckering, the blemish which to the body's perfection
had given more emphasis than perfection by itself could have
given.

This wasn't Hadid Chebir. This could never be Hadid
Chebir. Everything else, face, hair and figure, even the
texture of the skin was Hadid Chebir. But the man who lay
drugged on this bed was not Hadid Chebir.

He turned away, feeling almost that he had looked on
some indecency, and he was anxious to be out of this room.
He switched off the light, went down the steps and out past
Sergeant Benson who gave him good night. The sergeant
stared after him because the mutter from John's throat in
return to his good night had been that of a man miles
away in thought.

10

THE moon had long set when they left the house. The night was a warm cloaking darkness, full of a waiting silence, as though it were impatient and longing for the first bird sound or flicker of dawn to give it leave to go.

It would take them more than an hour to get up to the crater and by that time, Torlo calculated, it would be almost dawn. The light would be just right, dark enough to hide his approach to the cave and yet greying to dawn so that he could see to throw his hand grenades accurately. He had them in his pocket, four of them—though he knew that two would be enough to do the job. Still, they were old and, in case one failed to explode, he wanted to have a reserve.

He walked a little ahead of Arianna, neither of them talking, but he knew she was there, close behind him, as familiar with the path as he was.

Halfway up the long slope to La Caldera they paused for a rest. Torlo touched her arm and pointed northwards, out towards the sea. Far away was the regular lightening of the sky where the loom of the *faro* on the tip of San Borodon showed. Over there, thought Torlo, the dawn would soon break and the destroyer *Dunoon* would be under way and the Governor would come.

Before they moved on Torlo said in a whisper, "When we get to the top, go round and climb down by the pool. When I whistle, come. It would not be wise for us to go down the path together. If anything should go wrong, I would not wish thee to be found with me. But when I whistle all will be well for the grenade will be in my hand and will be thrown as I call thee."

The path was now no more than a dry stream bed running up past the highest terraces of vines and *platanos*. Arianna, moving surely in the darkness, not seeing the vines or the close-ranked growths of bananas, but aware of them, seeing everything in her mind, was thinking that after tonight, when the men were killed who had killed March, there would be less misery in her . . . always he would be in her heart, and always when she arranged the flowers in the church she would light a candle for him.

She heard Torlo's feet strike concrete ahead of her and knew that he was climbing the steps in the ramp alongside the great cistern that collected the water from the Caldera high slopes to feed the village during the dry months. Once, on a hot evening, although it was forbidden, she and March had come up here and bathed in the cistern . . . Her body stiffened with anguish as she remembered them together that evening.

When they reached the crater edge she was hot and sweating and one wing of her hair had come loose, clamping damply against her face.

Torlo put his hand to her arm and pushed her gently away. She left him and began to make her way quietly around the rim of the crater.

Torlo sat down by a boulder below the outer rim of the crater and lit a cigarette, keeping his head down and shielding the glow. He gave her good time to move around and make her way down to the pool. When he had finished his cigarette he nipped the glowing end out between his hard finger tips and then rose. The sky was beginning to grey in the east like the pelt of an old mule and, somewhere to his left, a cicada that had begun to call while he smoked was silent again. He went to the edge of the path down to the crater. The blackness below him was hard and unmarked, like the entrance to a great tunnel that bored into the heart of the world. Very slowly and cautiously he began to move down, keeping one hand on his jacket pocket to stop the movement of the grenades he carried. As he went he was smiling to himself for he was hearing himself describe this night. It was a story that could be told for the rest of a man's life. That one, they would say as he passed, is Torlo Zarate of Ardino; and the men would look at him with envy and the women would have a softness in their eyes and not notice the ugliness of his face for they would know that a man is truly the thing inside himself and not mirrored by his face . . .

His feet touched the sunbaked earth and grass at the bottom of the crater. He waited, listening. Arianna must be down by the pool now, not two hundred yards away. It was a pity, he thought, that when he threw the grenades the whole island would not wake to the noise. But here the bowl of the hills would trap it and the narrow gut of the cave would stifle the sound.

He moved carefully towards the cave, stopping now and again to listen. Instinct told him that with these men no care was lost. He understood now, too, that this matter of the prisoners at Fort Sebastian was of the greatest importance for why otherwise should these men be here so secretly . . . Let it be important, of the greatest importance then, for by that so much greater would his own importance be.

When he was ten yards from the mouth of the cave he stopped and crouched close to the ground. The greyness of the eastern sky had spread now like a rising tide and was lapping over the rim of the crater. Where there had been darkness unmarked was now a growing mass of shadows and he could pick out the shape of a tall agave silhouette not far from him, could see the outline of rocks and shrubs. Somewhere over by the pool a bird got up and went away into the night with one short, solitary call. He heard the soft beat of its wings overhead, and he smiled to himself for he knew that Arianna was there and the bird had known it.

He stared now at the rock face ahead of him. The bleached stems of the bamboo palisade shone whitely. The barrier to the cave mouth was about four feet high and there was a gap of two feet above it before the cave roof was reached. The screen had been built as a wind break not as a door. One could walk round either end and enter the cave. To toss his grenades over the top of the palisade was easy. There wasn't a boy on Mora who could not take a stone and at fifty yards hit a lead goat on any part of its body he chose. How else did one control goats?

Inside now they would be sleeping. They would have fetched their water for the coming day. They would be tired from their trip down to the cliff above the fort. Torlo could see them lying in there on the dry palm fronds, four men asleep and secure, or maybe one would be drowsily on guard, wishing for sleep, too.

He stood up slowly, his teeth biting with pleasure into his lower lip and he pulled out two hand grenades. He held one in each hand and worked them round in his palm so that his teeth would come easily to the pins. He took one step forward, his eyes on the gap above the palisade. He had a swift desire to yawn, not from tiredness but from rising pleasure.

He raised his right hand to his mouth and pulled out the pin, spitting it from him. He whistled and then he slung the grenade from him, the striker lever twisting in the air like a dead leaf. With the movement, though his eyes followed it and saw it curve over the top of the bamboos, the other grenade came up to his mouth. He threw it after its fellow and then dropped to the ground, sheltering behind a small boulder which he had marked for the purpose.

The thing that happened then was a delight to him. As the second grenade disappeared over the top of the palisade there came from the bowels of the cave a low, heavy crunch of sound, like some great jaw biting into an outer soft rottenness and meeting a hard core. Then the full blast of the two explosions mingled, bursting in the belly of the rock with a long, throaty rattle.

The palisade was swept away, the white shards of bamboo stick mingled with a cloud of dust and stones. Part of the cave mouth collapsed and rolled forward making a long slithering sound in the growing morning light.

Torlo stood up. From the greyness to his right Arianna appeared and came to his side. Together they looked at the half-blocked cave mouth. Somewhere inside a rock fell and then there was silence.

Torlo put out his hand and found Arianna's wrist.

"It is done," he said and he breathed deeply, the dust-filled air sweet in his lungs and the brightness of his future shining in his eyes.

"It is done," said Arianna, and very slowly she crossed herself. "And now I would look on them."

Torlo nodded, but before they could move towards the cave, there was a sound behind them and the sound leapt into Torlo's ears clear and full of meaning. It was the sound of a heavy boot striking against loose rubble, the sound a man makes who no longer cares for caution.

Torlo swung round, stepping in front of Arianna. Facing

196

them on the edges of the open space before the cave were five men.

Torlo cried, "Run!" to Arianna and pushed her away. His free hand came down, searching for the grenades that were still in his pocket. The man in the centre of the semi-circle raised his right hand. There was an ugly, muted explosion. The bullet tore a great hole in Torlo's left breast, spun him round and dropped him to the ground.

Arianna ran, swerving towards the cave mouth like a trapped animal. There was nothing in her except panic and the horror of seeing Torlo fall. A narrow break ran up the rocks at the side of the cave and she reached it and began to climb upwards, scrambling and fighting to escape.

Behind her the five men stood unmoving and Mietus, who had killed Torlo, raised his revolver again and fired at her as she was about five feet from the ground. The bullet smacked against the rock a foot from her face. Sharp stone splinters tore into her right cheek and Arianna fell. She hit the ground by the cave mouth with a crash and her right leg doubled under her awkwardly. She lay there without moving.

Mietus put his revolver into his pocket and walked over to her and the other men followed him. Her face was bleeding and her eyes were shut.

Mietus put up a hand and smoothed his worn, dusty-white hair. His mouth was tight with disgust.

"The light was bad," he said, more for himself than the others. "But I should not have missed. One forgets that a suppressor makes them pull to the right."

He squatted on his heels beside Arianna and rolled her to her back. Seeing her right leg lying awkwardly under her he straightened it and for a moment both his hands were on her ankle feeling it and moving it expertly.

"Broken, just above the ankle."

He stood up.

"What do we do with her?" asked Plevsky. He was a little dark blackbird of a man with a habit of working his tongue in his mouth as though he carried a bad taste always.

Mietus and the others looked at him; Sifal, brown-skinned, slender as a girl, but with too great a weight of stillness in him to give any man peace in his company; Roper, with the dissolute, battered face that had once been open and frank with charm, and Lorentzen, tall and wide-shouldered, awkward and unfinished-looking from the smallness of his head. And from the way they looked at Plevsky there was no doubt of their surprise at the stupidity of the question.

"She must go," said Mietus. "But first carry her into the cave. When she comes round there is something I want to know from her. Plevsky, you stay with her. We shall go back to the other place. If anyone should come we shall be there."

"Nobody will come," said Roper. "This crater could swallow a thunderstorm."

They carried Arianna into the shattered cave, laying her out on a heap of rubble, and then they dragged Torlo just inside the mouth of the cave.

"When she comes round," said Mietus, "make a signal and I will come down."

"Leave me some cigarettes," said Plevsky.

Lorentzen tossed him a packet.

Plevsky sat just inside the mouth of the cave and watched them move across the crater and disappear into the shrubs to the left of the path that led up to the rim.

The light was strengthening every moment now and on the high western ridge of the crater the first glow from the rising sun was touching the rocks with a soft silveriness that looked like mildew.

Plevsky lit a cigarette and looked at Arianna. Somewhere, years and years back in his life, he remembered a girl in Poland who had looked a little like this, dark, rich-bodied and with this peasant sturdiness. Then, seeing the fresh scarred sides of the cave, his mouth tightened a little. Why had he asked what was to be done with her? It was obvious. The man would have killed them all. What pity could the girl expect . . . ? They were lucky, he thought, very lucky . . . It was the kind of luck that Mietus was always having. It was Sifal, though, they really had to thank. Because of the interference to the reception on his set from the high crater walls he always had to climb to the ridge to open his nightly communication with Max Dondon. He had climbed up a little behind them that night and had seen this man at the path top looking down. Sifal had followed him to the house in Ardino, and then had come back to them. The rest had been easy. Two of them had gone straight back to the house and waited, while the others had hurried back to the cave to clear their stuff . . . How calmly Mietus had handled it, cold as ice, and seeming to know what would be in the man's mind . . .

Plevsky looked at the girl. Mietus knew from Colonel Mawzi that the soldier they had killed had gone to see a girl in Ardino. This was probably the girl, Mietus had said. She lay, breathing heavily, showing no signs of recovery yet. His eyes went to the body just inside the cave. Some flies, stirring now that the sun was beginning to flood the crater, hovered over the man's chest. Plevsky reached out to a couple of old, ripped sacks that lay mixed up with stone rubble and dust. He jerked them over the body and then settled himself comfortably back against the cave wall. The girl in Poland, he remembered, used to wait for him by the road bridge just outside her village. Once a week he came to the village on his rounds as a poultry buyer for his father's shop . . . He grunted to himself. It was all so far away that it was hardly worth thinking about.

Lying in bed, the reflected sunlight from the open window frame stretching in a long diagonal of gold across the floor to the door, Marion Chebir faced this new day aware of a strange combination of misery and happiness. She was courageous and forthright enough to face without any attempt at evasion the new facts which had come into her life. Yet, although the facts were new, she acknowledged that they had been slowly forcing themselves to life for many long months. Last night they had found their liberty. Last night a barrier which she had built around herself had been smashed down. She was no longer the creature her husband had created. For years she had known nothing except Cyrenia and her loyalty to it. Now, she saw the great evil of dedicating oneself completely to an idea. Ideas grew and assumed more importance than human beings. For the sake of liberty and national freedom men were assassinated and murdered. She, herself, had sat here in Fort Sebastian knowing that as the price of her freedom and as the preliminary payment for a military and political success in Cyrenia some of the soldiers around her, the cook, the sergeant, the guards who had become so familiar to her, would be killed. But that woman was now a stranger.

It had taken her two years to find her freedom and herself. Two years ago when Hadid Chebir had been killed in a minor skirmish, the prestige of the Cyrenian National Army had been low. The news of his death would have taken the heart from his hard-pressed followers. Colonel Mawzi had kept the death a secret, and a half-brother of Hadid, little known, but remarkably like him had taken his place . . . Out of the grief for her lost husband, out of loyalty and love for him, knowing that for him Cyrenia had meant everything, she had agreed to the deception, regarding it as her duty, as a trust which she must honour.

But grief passed, even the memory of love dimmed, and slowly she had felt herself more and more divorced from Cyrenia, more and more anxious to be left alone to find a new life . . . For the new Hadid—a husband in name only— she had no respect. Coaching him in the details of the dead Hadid's past had been a bitterness with her . . . And now it was not only the real Hadid who was dead . . . but the Marion who had loved him. All that was gone, all the past . . . finished.

Abou came into the room and placed her morning coffee on the table by the window. When he was gone she slipped into her dressing gown and went to the table.

What was it, she asked herself over her coffee and a cigarette, that finally wakened one? Not just a slow rebellion of the senses but always some quick knife-like thrust? She loved John Richmond. Through her love for one person she was now aware of all the others around her. Whether he loved her or not, or whether any part of his future would touch hers she could not say. Loving him was the important thing. She could love again and that was a new freedom and the scales were off her eyes . . .

Mawzi hated him and would make sure that he was killed. And not only his death, but the deaths of the other soldiers here whom she now identified with him became a horror in her mind.

200

At no matter what cost to herself, she decided now, there must be no more violence. Last night's kindling of tenderness and passion, brief—and maybe unpromising for her—had brought her wisdom. Through Hadid she had loved a country and an idea too much. So much so that she had become a monster. Only human beings were worthy of so much love. Quite calmly she knew that she would have to tell John Richmond about the coming attack. She would have to betray Mietus and Mawzi. No cause was great enough to claim the death of any man, unless that man sacrificed himself willingly and knowingly.

There was a knock on her door and, thinking it was Abou come to collect her coffee tray, she called, "Come in."

Colonel Mawzi came into the room. He crossed to the table in quick bantam strides and stood looking down at her.

"I realize," he said firmly, "that I am not welcome in this room."

Marion said, "That is a considerable understatement."

"Maybe. But it is necessary that we should understand one another——" He made a sharp movement of his hand as he saw her about to speak. "No, let me finish. For last night, I apologize. I was foolish and brutal. We have worked together for many years and in that time I know that I have had your respect and your loyalty."

"Not any longer."

"That is the point. I can do nothing about what has passed. I would not add to my foolishness by trying to excuse myself with you or to win back from you anything I have lost."

"Then why are you here?"

"To make sure that there is a correct understanding between us. To make sure that through my foolishness you do not fall into a greater one, a foolishness which would endanger you and many people who must still be loved by you."

Marion stood up slowly.

"Perhaps you'd better speak very plainly. What is it you think I am going to do?"

"You could go to Major Richmond and tell him the truth about Hadid and also about the plan for tonight. You could, if you were very foolish. It is the kind of thing an angry woman might do."

"And if I did this thing?"

Colonel Mawzi slid his hands into his tunic pockets and narrowed his shoulders and the frown on his face furrowed his bony forehead deeply. "You would not live long to enjoy your treachery. Wherever they took you, wherever they hid you, we would find you. You know that we have a long memory for traitors. Even after ten years when men have thought themselves safe we have found them. In the past you yourself have helped us to find such men. Hadid might die and I might die, but there will be others who will remember and go on searching, and finally you would die."

"When one has little to live for there is no great pain in dying," said Marion, but she knew that she no longer felt like that.

"True, but there are others who do not wish to die. You have a mother and father in England——"

"No!"

For a moment, like the bright flicker of a steel blade, Colonel Mawzi smiled.

"Yes. A mother and a father, a sister and a brother who are married and have children. If a traitor escapes us there is always his family. You do not believe this would happen?"

"Yes, I believe it would happen," she said quietly. Suddenly the future was vividly with her. She saw her mother with flour up to her elbows in the kitchen, rolling out pastry and humming to herself, her father feet up on a chair in the garden of a fine morning reading the *Sunday Express* before he began disbudding his chrysanthemums, her brother holding his son's hand as the child learned to take its first steps . . . Oh, God, no!

She turned away from Mawzi.

Behind her she heard him say, "I see that you understand. Good. But do not think that I trust you, even now. Tonight, if anything goes wrong, no matter what, I shall assume that in some way you have tricked us. But if all is well, then tomorrow you are free to return with us and from Cyrenia you may go where you wish. I give you my word for that."

She heard the door open and close and knew that he had

gone. She went to the window, resting her arms on the rough grey stone and stared out. The sunlight was full on the steep La Caldera slope. At the base of the ridge the poinsettia bushes were massed thickly, their flowers tipping the glossy green with flame. Higher up, sharp against the skyline, the stiff, archaic forms of prickly pear marched in an absurd caricature of human forms, swollen arms, small heads and padded hands dark against the sky. How often she had leaned on this window and watched the hillside until now she knew every stick and stone and bush.

Mawzi's words had put a frame round the thoughts that had been with her since waking. He, too, had wakened full of active, new thought and had been quick to come and warn her. Now, if she went to John Richmond with the truth there would be other deaths . . . She put her hands across her eyes, pressing them against her eyeballs as the beastliness was flashed across her imagination in a series of vivid, frightening pictures. Somewhere in England, some day, some night . . . there were a hundred ways they could do it. The scream of a car's tyres across the tarmac and a broken child . . . Her father's fishing rod and lunch basket under a willow beside the Evenlode and hours later downstream . . . "Oh God, no! No! No!" she cried to herself.

With the rising of the sun, the wind which had been light all night, picked up, freshening from the south so that the *Dunoon* fought a little against her bow and stern warps as she lay alongside the refuelling jetty. The wind streaming across the cod-drying grounds sucked up the salty, sickly smell. Lieutenant Imray, who was officer of the watch, noting the long streamer of mare's tail cloud coming off the tip of Tower Hill, told himself that it would blow for an hour and then fizzle out. Without turning, he said to the seaman behind him on the bridge, "Keep an eye on the Governor's place. I want to know when his car leaves."

"Aye, aye, sir."

Imray cleared his throat in a useless attempt to rid it of the disgusting smell of *bacalao*. It was the bloodiest smell, he thought . . . He looked at his watch. Seven o'clock. Somewhere now in Herefordshire Delia was back from exercising

203

the horses . . . bacon and eggs in the farm kitchen and the three spaniels sitting silent and obedient around her chair. There was a nip of nostalgia and love at his heart. He saw himself home on leave, getting the car out and away down the Oxford-Cheltenham road, like an arrow for Gloucester. The road came up in his imagination, vivid and clear, and he could hear in his mind the quick snap of the gear changing and the long, long whine of the engine on a hill . . . and the glorious moment when he swung into the drive up to the farmhouse and the gravel scrunched under his tyres and he braked hard to tear it into a furrow by the front door and annoy her father; and there she was in his arms . . . He sighed loudly.

Down below, Andrews stood in front of a small square of mirror fastened to the bulkhead and adjusted a pink eye-shade over his right eye. He grimaced a little savagely to himself as he noticed that the blue-brown edges of the black eye he was sporting still showed a little around the rim of the shade.

"If anyone asks," he said, "I'm suffering from con-junctivitis. In a way it's quite distinctive."

"A large steak is the answer, or a piece of raw liver," said P.O. Grogan. He sat at the mess table with a mug of tea and a cigarette.

Andrews sat down at the table and lit a cigarette from Grogan's. "The bastard," he breathed, "I could have finished him by myself. But she had to butt in. Perfidious."

"What?"

"Perfidious. That's not a cruiser class. That's a class of woman. I walk in there last night with a bottle of vino, a silk scarf I picked up cheap and love in my heart."

"And you come out with a black eye."

"She helped me to that—blast her! There he was sitting there, the big ape. Ma and Pa were all over him and she was purring away like a cat that's had the cream. Just got in on a banana boat he had, and there he was with his great banana fingers pawing around my girl . . . Alberto, that's his name, and he's just back from a long trip. And they're engaged. All this time they're engaged and she never said a word to me about him!"

"You'll find another. But this time pick one that doesn't work in the cod sheds. We'd all be grateful."

"In trouble friends are great comforts," said Andrews bitterly. "I'd have settled him only she had to go and throw her arms around me. I went out like a light. If we get shore leave in Mora I'll get drunk. It's the only way with a broken heart."

"Maybe I'll join you."

Andrews looked at Grogan sharply.

"What's eating you?" he asked.

"Not a broken heart. You can pick those up in any port. It's the missus's sister and her kids. They've come to stay with us again. He's a big, hulking pongo. Been posted to Malaya so the missus, bless her heart, invites her sister to stay with the kids while he's gone. Last time he was away for two years. Korea. Some lovely leaves I had. She's the weepy kind. Begins to think about him and then starts the water works. So many tears it rotted the lino in the kitchen, and God help me if I tried to say anything to snap her out of it."

"Fair enough, Grogy. We'll celebrate my broken heart and your rotten lino . . ."

Up at Government House, Neil Grayson was in his office, putting into his brief-case some papers he had to take with him to Mora. Outside on the drive he could hear the engine of the Governor's car ticking quietly. Behind him he heard the door open and close and without turning he knew that it was Daphne. The sound of her movements as she came up behind him sent a deep tremor of happiness through him. The rustle of her silk frock conjured up a warm, heart-reaching love in him, and in his imagination he was aware of her grace and the clean movement of her body, the carriage of her head and the long, moulded beauty of her legs and arms. He stood there without turning, to tease her, and then felt her hands rest on his elbows.

"Neil."

He swung slowly round, bringing her into the circle of his arms. God, she was lovely and he was in love, like a youth of eighteen and yet with all the stubborn vigour of a man, too. Whatever other people might say about them there was no escaping this. They were in love and he wanted no one else but her. He kissed her gently on the lips.

"How am I going to live for three days without you?" she asked.

He kissed her again.

"It'll soon pass. I'll phone you too."

"Darling," she said, "it's terrible the way I feel. I love you so much that it makes me feel guilty. Not for anything to do with us, but because the whole thing is so . . . Oh, Lord, isn't it awful to have so much feeling and not be able to put words to it." She laughed quietly, a little embarrassed and then said hungrily, "Kiss me. Really hard."

"We'll be caught. The Governor'll walk in here any moment." He was smiling.

"To hell with other people. Kiss me."

He crushed her to him.

When he let her go, she stood back smiling at him, and said:

"Now, I've got a surprise for you."

"Oh, something good?"

"I'm not going to miss you for three days. I'm coming to Mora with you."

"You devil—you got that kiss under false pretences. So you've talked your father into it?"

"Yes. I shall sleep on the *Dunoon*. There's no room at the fort—and anyway Daddy doesn't think it would be right. But, darling, during the day I shall be able to see you."

"And Teddy?"

"He grumbled. Doesn't like women on board—but he had to give in."

Neil took her by the arm.

"You'd better hurry. I can hear Sir George outside."

Five minutes later they were on their way down to the *Dunoon* in the car with Sir George Cator. Sir George was in a good mood. He liked going off on a trip and Mora was an island on which he had often wished to spend more time. It was a great pity, he felt, that more field work had not been done there on the flora and fauna with an eye on the old theory of a possible land connection between Europe and the Americas. For instance, this time he must get specimens of the unique tailless lizard to be found on Mora. In the West Indies he believed there was a similar lizard to be found . . .

In the head of the *barrancos* around La Caldera, too, there were exceptionally fine freesias, longer and stouter stemmed than any of the European varieties.

"You put in my camera, Neil?"

"Yes, sir."

"Good."

He'd take some photographs. Maybe he'd write an article for the Royal Horticultural Society's Journal. Happily, he breathed the warm morning air, oblivious of the smell of cod. Daphne looked well, blooming in fact. Never seen her look so well. The day before she'd played a round of golf with him on the Tower Hill course. Never known her so full of spirits . . . Some of the greens up there—his eyes had lifted to the cloud-ragged tip of Tower Hill—needed watering badly. The thing to do, of course, was to build a cistern like the ones they used for the bananas and vines. Expensive, though . . .

"What about the pressmen?" he asked.

"They'll be aboard, sir."

"We'll have to let them look around Fort Sebastian. But I've had a strict directive that they must not have any interviews with our charges . . . Should think Richmond will be glad of some company. His extra men are due here tomorrow, aren't they?"

"Yes, sir."

"Wouldn't have hurt to send a lieutenant with them. Would be good for him to have permanent company out there."

Sir George nodded to himself and began to hum gently.

Neil smiled to himself. The old boy was feeling good, obviously. He wondered what his reaction would be now if he told him that when he went back to England Daphne was soon to follow, would get a divorce from Burrows . . . that he was going to marry her? He'd go up like a rocket. He frowned. Daphne would have to handle that. Lordy, he hoped it went all right when the time came. Of course, nothing could stop them doing what they wanted to do, but Sir George could put a spoke in his wheel over politics if he wished. He could smash the whole thing for him if Daphne didn't handle it right. How much would that matter? It was curious how the emphasis had shifted for him lately. More than anything else he wanted her . . . Grayson, old boy, he thought, you've really slipped. Ready to give up everything for the love of a woman. Was that him now? He leaned back against the leather upholstery and glanced across at her. Unseen by Sir George, she caught his eye and smiled . . . Daphne, dear Daphne . . .

Teddy Burrows was on the bridge of the *Dunoon* as the Governor's car came along the quay. It was true that he had grumbled when Daphne had persuaded her father to let her come with them. But it was a perfunctory grumble.

The assurance he had felt last night while gambling with Daphne had gone. The morning had brought back his doubts —particularly her sudden wish to come to Mora. Was it because she wanted to be with Grayson, or was it just one of her spontaneous whims? The Lord knew. With this kind of thing you could argue anything whichever way you wanted to. You could tell yourself to be level-headed and sensible until you were blue in the face—but the truth was there was no escaping the agony of not knowing.

He was a forthright man, an honest man, and he had a feeling that there was no peace for him unless he went right to the heart of the matter and faced Daphne with his doubts —but how the hell could he do that merely on the strength of the letter? It would show such little faith in her. And yet until he knew one way or the other there could be no real peace for him. He would just go on swinging from one side to the other.

Going down to the quarter deck to meet Sir George, his eyes were on Grayson and just for a moment a great pang of jealousy and anger swept through him. If it were true—by God if it were true!

Daphne's voice came to him lightly:

"Stop frowning, Teddy. Aren't you glad to have me aboard? You and your old *Dunoon*. If you're not careful, I'll kiss you in front of all your men."

"Daphne, stop teasing Teddy," said Sir George. "Neil, take her below and put her in irons."

How could you tell, thought Burrows, forcing himself to smile at the old man's joke—how could you tell?

He excused himself and went back to the bridge. Before this trip was over he knew he had to be certain one way or the other. He began to take the *Dunoon* out, one part of his mind handling the routine automatically, the other part still concerned with Daphne. If it were true and she loved Grayson and—he forced himself to the thought—wanted a divorce, what would he do? God, it would break him up. But if that was what she wanted . . . Well, that's how it would have to be. He loved her very much, deeply, if not demonstratively, and anything she wanted that would make her happy . . . But by thunder, if it was going to be like that he'd give himself the satisfaction of having a go at Grayson. Just once . . . No one could blame him for that. But it wouldn't ever come to that. He couldn't imagine life without Daphne. Even if this thing weren't true, it had given him a jolt all right. A bloody big jolt . . . Made him think. In future he'd try to see things more from her point of view . . . He really would.

The *Dunoon* drew away from the quay and with the movement of the ship under his feet, he suddenly felt happier. The whole thing was nonsense . . . He was tearing himself to bits about nothing. Just a filthy letter written in spite.

About the time that the *Dunoon* was leaving Port Carlos harbour and taking the first lift of the Atlantic swell, John Richmond was swimming a few yards off the small beach below Fort Sebastian. Every morning since his arrival he had taken a swim here.

Lying on his back, looking up towards the grey-black length of Fort Sebastian, he could see no movement along the seaward parapet at all. The place looked ugly, artificial and remote against the blues and browns and yellows of the island. It was almost as though some child had taken a charcoal pencil and crudely blocked out a drawing of a fort on some bright holiday poster. High up over La Caldera a couple of fork-tailed kites were swinging in lazy spirals and along the Ardino road he could see the travelling puff of dust where some lorry bounced and rattled its way from the village.

From instinct, and with instinct strengthened by his army training, he liked to set down his problems clearly, make a frank appreciation of them and then decide on the best solution for them. There was nothing like army training for clearing the mind of a lot of rubbish and speculation. Find the point and stick to it. *The sole object of weapon training is to teach all ranks the most efficient way of handling their weapons in order to kill the enemy.* What could be more crystal clear and to the point than this, the first paragraph in all *Small Arms Training* pamphlets? Not an atom of doubt or muddle in it. There wasn't any situation in life that couldn't be covered by an operation order. At least, he smiled wryly to himself, it would be nice to think there wasn't. He turned over and porpoise-dived, going down deep until the pressure built up against his ears, and in the swaying, distorted green and yellow world he had the fleeting wish that he could go on and on and never come up, then there would be no operation order to make . . .

He came up and jerked his head to clear the water from his hair. He swam ashore slowly and waded out to his towel.

Here goes, he thought; you've mulled it over long enough. Now get it down in black and white. Question and answer.

Do you love Marion Chebir?

Yes.

How can you be sure?

How can you be sure the sun will rise tomorrow? I love her now and here. I know this for myself, just as surely as I know for myself the difference between a good and a bad painting.

Does she love you?

Yes.

Sure?

Yes.

What immediate steps do you propose to take about this situation?

John lay back on his towel in the sun. This was it, of course. The hardest question in the whole bag. What did he intend to do? He could go back to the fort now and find her, make his love clear and ask her to marry him. But that would also mean letting her know that he had discovered that Hadid Chebir was not the real Hadid Chebir. Where was the real Hadid Chebir? Dead or alive? He assumed he was dead, otherwise there was no need of this deception. He must be dead . . . his hand beat against the hot, dry sand in a gesture of irritation. But he couldn't be sure. This was where the muddle came in. This was what was making nonsense of any attempt to get a clear-cut plan.

John stood up, wrapped his robe about him and shuffled his feet into his sandals. The hard fact remained that he had to do something. He climbed slowly up the cliff towards the fort. In a little while he would take his morning walk along the parapet and his three charges would be there, in one or other of their familiar groupings. Marion's eyes would meet him and if she were alone they would talk. Just what he was going to say he had no idea.

In the Officers' Quarters he showered and then changed into a clean drill uniform for the Governor's visit. When he went out on to the parapet Colonel Mawzi was stretched out in a deck chair under the awning, his hands behind his head, staring out towards the cliffs and the run of coast that curved away to Ardino. Hadid Chebir was pacing up and down between the Bell Tower and the Flag Tower, restless, his hands behind his back. As he turned away from John after a brief "good morning" John could see the fingers of his clasped hands working nervously, energetically, and his walk was light and springy. He looked a new man, alive and vital, and charged with a force that longed for release, like a panther turning and turning about its cage, fired by a fierce longing for liberty. Whatever drug he took, thought John, it obviously left him full of vigour and confidence. The change in the man was remarkable.

Marion was reading in her chair by the Flag Tower. She looked up as John approached and, although her face was grave, she gave him a smile as she said good morning.

John put his hand into his pocket. He held out a key to her.

"Maybe," he said, "you'd like to have this."

She took the key and turned it over in her fingers, looking up at him questioningly.

"It's the key to your room. You can lock yourself in and sleep soundly."

She was about to say something when Hadid came up to them, half-swung round to continue his walk and then paused.

"What time do you expect the Governor, Major?" His voice was crisp, demanding almost.

"He should be here by eleven, maybe earlier."

Hadid nodded sharply and began to pace back towards Mawzi.

Marion said quietly, "You are very kind. Thank you."

Behind him John could hear the crisp beat of Hadid's feet on the wide flagstones. He said quickly, "While the Governor is here it will be difficult for me to see you alone. I want to, of course. You must know why——"

"Please . . ." There was a sudden look of misery on her face which stirred him, confusing him while at the same time it woke a great tenderness and anxiety for her in him.

"I know," he said, "the thing's all over the place. God knows there will be difficulties. But the fact remains that I love you and you love me. That's all that matters. Everything will work out right. We can free ourselves from all this, and I can take you away. For the moment nothing matters except one thing. I'm not making any mistake about that, am I? You do love me?"

For a moment she sat there, her eyes on him, and then he saw her shoulders shake a little as though a cold draught had swept over her.

"What's the matter?" he asked anxiously, and behind him he could hear the nearing beat of Hadid's feet.

"Nothing," she said suddenly and stood up. She was close to him, almost touching him and her eyes were full on his and he saw the mist of near tears in them. "I love you, yes," she said in a whisper and then she was moving away from him.

"Major."

Hadid's voice came from behind him.

"Yes?" He spoke to Hadid but his eyes were on Marion as she moved down the parapet towards the awning.

"There will be members of the press coming with the Governor?"

"I think so."

"Then I wish to make a statement to them."

John gave him his attention. "You will have to have the Governor's permission for that. You can ask him when he sees you."

"You think he will refuse?"

"I think he certainly will." John spoke curtly. "The whole idea of bringing you here was to stop you from making statements or speeches or carrying on any activity likely to make matters worse in Cyrenia."

Hadid recognizing the hostility in John thrust his head forward a little and a smile marked the lean face. He gave a little laugh and said, "I see, our Major Richmond is a trifle liverish this morning." He laughed again and turned back along the parapet. To avoid them all John went on past the Flag Tower and down the little stairway on the far side of the courtyard to his quarters.

Colonel Mawzi took his hands from behind his head as Marion reached the awning.

"You had an interesting talk with Major Richmond?"

Marion showed him the key in her hand.

"He gave me this."

"For your room, of course."

"Yes."

It was a little while before he spoke. Then he said, "You won't need it against me. Each man has one supreme foolishness in him. Mine is past."

Hadid came up behind them.

"This time tomorrow," he said, "we shall be free. It is hard to hold back one's impatience."

"This time tomorrow," agreed Mawzi, "you will be free." His hands had gone back behind his head and he ignored the two as he stared out at the cliffs.

Down in the courtyard Jenkins, the cook, and Abou had long finished their kitchen chores. They'd given themselves a ten-minute break for a cup of tea and now both of them were busy with brushes and buckets of white lime, painting the stones that formed a circle round the garden in the centre of the courtyard. The lime dried fast and staring white on the hot stones almost before the brush stroke was finished.

"Bull," said Jenkins across the bushes to Abou. "That's what they call this. The Governor's coming so everything has to be smartened up."

"Bull," said Abou smiling like an idiot old man.

"That's it, Abby. The Governor, so the Army thinks, will be bloody dim-witted enough to fancy it's always like this. Every bleedin' stone white, every man with a crease in his pants, every rifle with a clean bore, every pot and pan in the cookhouse shining like a mirror. There's been bull in the British Army since the beginning of time. I'll bet the bastard Ancient Britons had to put fresh woad on their faces, ribbon on the tails of their horses, and a polish on their Mark IV spears every time Queen Boadicea came into camp. Hardcastle!" He suddenly shouted.

Corporal Hardcastle—promoted to take Corporal March's rank—was walking from the gate to the men's quarters and had jerked an empty cigarette packet into the bushes.

"What's the matter, cookie?"

"Pick up that packet."

Hardcastle grinned and retrieved the packet which he had thrown down deliberately.

"There's one or two of those top leaves you haven't polished properly," Hardcastle said, tipping his head towards the top of the dragon tree.

"I'll put a polish on you in a minute!"

Hardcastle, grinning still, made an obscene gesture and disappeared into the men's quarters.

"Bloody bastard?" asked Abou watching Hardcastle disappear.

"That's right, Abby. You learn fast. That's what every mother's son of 'em is. Join the Army and see the world. Not them. Riff-raff. Joined up to get away from girls they put in pod, or to duck the police. Joined up 'cos they couldn't hold a job in civvy street. Or else they're milk-white National Service boys always grumbling 'cos army khaki rubs their delicate little crutches sore."

Sergeant Benson came across from the doorway to the stairs that led up to the Officers' Quarters.

"The major wants to know what you're putting on for lunch."

Jenkins straightened his back and rubbed a white-washed finger under his nose.

"Oh he does, does he?" He was in a good mood and this naturally made him belligerent. "Well it's boiled potatoes, bully beef, and a fig pudding. Very filling, all of it. Just the thing for a stinking hot day like this."

"That's not good enough for the Governor, and you know it."

"Well, it's what the men are getting."

"Then think again."

"Well, what about rump steak, cheese cauliflower, French fried potatoes and some fresh asparagus with butter sauce on the side. Or maybe, some cold lobster to begin with and then——"

"I'm in a hurry," said Sergeant Benson.

"I can't think why, Serg. There's nowhere to go on this island."

"Cut it out, cookie."

"All right, all right. Spanish omelette to begin with. Fried veal, beans and sweet potatoes. Best I can do. It would help, too, if I knew how many there would be."

"Tell you that later."

"Oh, yes . . . about five minutes before they want it! And then everyone stand by and watch me perform miracles."

"That's right," Sergeant Benson agreed cheerfully and moved away.

Jenkins made an angry sound in his throat.

"Bloody bastard also?" asked Abou.

"Yes. But he's all right. Can't help being a sergeant but he's all right. You see, Abby, in the British Army there's two kinds of bloody bastards. There's the kind you don't mind being in a tight spot with, and there's the other kind. Now, if you was in a tight spot with Benson you'd know one thing, you'd stand a chance of coming out of it walkin' and not on a stretcher. But with the other kind . . ."

Abou, slapping paint on his stones, listened to Jenkins talking away and some of it he understood and some of it he didn't understand, but the one thing that was clear to him without any shadow of doubt was that this was a good man with the right kind of fire in his belly, a man whom he loved but who, if necessary, he would kill with sadness and never forget.

11

H.M.S. *Dunoon* entered Mora harbour at five minutes past eleven. She dropped anchor watched by the islanders who crowded under the palms at the foot of the rough wooden jetty. Standing by the fort's jeep towards the end of the jetty were Major Richmond and Señor Aldobran. John had driven down by himself to meet the Governor. Sergeant Benson was in charge of the gate guard at the fort.

The Governor came ashore with Neil Grayson. After a few words with Señor Aldobran the Governor and Grayson got into the jeep and John drove them up to the fort.

"I've asked Teddie Burrows and Daphne to come up and have some lunch with us," said the Governor. "The pressmen will come ashore with him and they can have a look around the fort after lunch. How is everything? Under control?"

"Yes, sir. Except for one thing, which I would like to tell you about before you see any of the three."

"Oh . . ." For a moment Sir George's grey eyes were on John. "Trouble, eh?"

"Of a kind, sir."

At the gate the guard of honour was turned out, and then Sir George made a short tour of inspection before going up to the long mess room over the gate.

John poured sherry for the three of them, and the Governor said, "Well, let's have it, Richmond."

Standing by the window, nursing his glass of sherry, John told the Governor of the trouble between Marion Chebir and Colonel Mawzi the previous night. He avoided any reference to anything which had passed between himself and Marion; and then he described how he had gone up to see Mawzi and coming down had looked in on Hadid Chebir."

"I should explain, Sir George," he said, "that I was up at Magdalen at the same time as Hadid and knew him slightly. When I went in he was lying on his bed, more or less naked, and I should say drugged——"

"Drugged?"

"Yes, sir. I've had a suspicion he took drugs. How he got

the stuff I've no idea. But I imagine the stuff was smuggled in with their belongings——"

"But you checked their baggage?"

"Yes, Sir George."

The Governor frowned. "Bit of a slip-up, eh?"

"I'm afraid so, sir."

"Never mind." Sir George waved a hand. "That isn't the main thing, I imagine?"

"No, sir. At Oxford I'd seen Hadid under the showers naked many a time. One of the things I remembered about him was that he had an oddly shaped birthmark to the left of his navel. I'm absolutely certain of this."

"Well?" Sir George sipped at his sherry.

"This Hadid has no such mark. In other words, the man we've got here isn't Hadid Chebir."

"Good Lord!" Sir George made a violent gesture and spilled his sherry. "You're sure?"

"Absolutely. This man isn't Hadid Chebir. He never bathes. I think now that's because they know I was at Oxford with the real Hadid and might have spotted the absence of the birthmark. And from the relationship between him and Marion Chebir, I'm equally certain they're not man and wife. Mawzi would never have dared to assault her if this Hadid was her husband. There's never been any doubt that it was a love marriage, that she was absolutely wrapped up in him . . ." Though it was in the past, it was not something he liked to talk about for he could feel the slow twist of jealousy in him . . .

Sir George put his glass down on the table and wiped the spilled sherry from his hand with his silk handkerchief. He stood there, a short, grizzled figure, bushy grey eyebrows frowning and he looked from Grayson to John. Then he turned away from them and walked slowly to the fireplace and stood staring up at the oil-painting of General Cutts and rubbing his chin slowly.

Grayson lit a cigarette. To be present at a revelation like this was just up his street. Unless Whitehall sat on it hard, which he doubted, the press would get it and his name would be mentioned. When he got back home people would want to talk to him about it . . . and later, years and years ahead, he could see himself describing this moment in his auto-biography . . . serialization rights bought by *The Sunday Times*. Yes, this was the kind of publicity that helped a young man . . . Every little helped.

Sir George swung round slowly. "Has this Hadid ever recognized the fact that you knew one another at Oxford?"

"Yes, sir. But only in very general terms and made it clear that he didn't want to talk about it. I've no doubt that he's been well primed in the facts of the real Hadid's past."

"And where is the real Hadid? And why this deception? Have you thought about that, Richmond?"

"Yes, I have, Sir George. Before I came out here I was briefed by Banstead——"

"Banstead?"

Grayson said quickly, "He's Military Intelligence, sir."

"Oh . . ."

"He told me that the War Office weren't entirely happy about this Cyrenia affair," went on John; "that they felt there was something wrong about it somewhere. But that's all. They could give me no lead at all."

"They said nothing to me about this," said Sir George, stiffly.

"Understandably, sir. The whole thing was so indefinite."

"But why this change? Where for instance is the real Hadid?" Sir George came back and took up his sherry.

John hesitated for a moment. Then he said, "I don't know, sir. But my theory is that he's dead. It's the only way I can explain it to myself. I think he was killed some time ago in the Cyrenian operations. Maybe at a bad moment, when his death would have set their cause back good and hard. Mawzi covered up his death and they substituted this man."

"But you can't just find a man who looks like Hadid at a moment's notice. Particularly if you want to keep it secret."

"In this event they could. Hadid's father had a lot of children and not all by the same woman. This could be a brother, or a half-brother. The family likeness has always been strong . . . Hadid's father and Hadid were very alike. The rest of the children were always well in the background because Hadid was the one chosen to carry on the cause when the father went. If Intelligence went into it they could probably

218

discover that there were two or three brothers and probably all of them had a European education——"

"But there's the woman, his wife . . . why should she take part in this?"

"There'd be no trouble there, sir. She was very much in love with Hadid. He gave her everything she had; taught her everything she knew almost, and she devoted herself to his cause. When he was killed, she'd want his work to go on . . . she'd see it as her duty to keep Hadid Chebir alive and to avoid any setback to the cause . . . At least, she'd begin that way, though I've a feeling her fervour has worn off. In my opinion these three now are very much at odds with one another."

"It's plausible," said Sir George. "Yes, it's plausible. When the news of this comes out it could be a nasty shock to a lot of people in Cyrenia. What do you feel about it, Neil?"

"On a snap judgment, sir, I'm inclined to agree with Major Richmond's theory. I see no point in the deception if the real Hadid is alive. I remember, too, there was a time about two years ago when the Cyrenian National Army was pretty hard pressed. A lot of them were put in the bag and Mawzi and Hadid went underground for quite a while. The switch could have happened then and they went to earth while the new Hadid was groomed for his future rôle."

"Maybe you're right. Well, what do we do? Let Whitehall know and wait for their reaction?"

Grayson nodded. "I'll go down to the *Dunoon*, sir. We can send a cipher message through the Admiralty. I'll make out the message and only Teddy Burrows need know . . ."

"Yes, yes . . . This mustn't go beyond us." Sir George helped himself to another glass of sherry. "Damn it, there's always something. However, nothing we can do until we hear from London. The cat will be amongst the pigeons there." He laughed and cocked an eyebrow at John. "Well, my boy, this'll be a feather in your cap. All right, Neil, you get that message off, and bring Burrows and Daphne back with you for lunch."

When Grayson had gone, Sir George said, "Life's full of mysteries, isn't it? Trouble is we don't get enough time to deal with the really interesting ones . . . Though, maybe,

219

what I find interesting at my age wouldn't be interesting for you. Don't really care a damn, you know, about all this Cyrenian business—except officially. All this intrigue and manoeuvring for position. No way to settle it really. Time'll do that. Don't really care whether it's the real Hadid here or not. They're all trouble-makers. That's the point. Now, for a real mystery, take that dragon tree you've got out there in the courtyard. It grows here and as far as I know nowhere else but in the Canaries. Why? Can't find it in Europe, Africa or the Americas. Why? Couple of years ago I took some seed back to Port Carlos. Can't get it to germinate, though. Even sent some to Kew, but they had no luck . . . Strange."

Listening to the Governor, John found himself suddenly a little out of patience with him. It was no surprise to him that everyone could find a valid reason for their own selfishness. Life would be uncomfortable if one couldn't. But it really wasn't good enough to try and dismiss the Cyrenian business so easily. It really was a greater problem than trying to get the seeds of a dragon tree to germinate. The fortunes and hopes of thousands of people were involved in Cyrenia. The problem boiled down to countless small human problems . . . farmers who wanted to till their land in peace, petty officials who wanted some security of tenure, traders who wanted settled markets, soldiers who wanted to see some end to the risks they were taking . . . it was an impenetrable tangle of human activities and desires and he didn't see that Time was going to solve anything. Time would just alter the composition of the problem. The most one could do was to try and control the extremes of emphasis. That's why Hadid Chebir and Mawzi were here. If they went back to Cyrenia there would be bloody riot. But to see this and to contain it was only to have a firm grip on the collar of a mad dog . . . you could not hold it forever in gloved hands. Something had to be done with it. Mawzi and Hadid—whoever he was—couldn't be kept here for ever.

Following this line of thought and for a moment not averse from bringing Sir George back to the problem on hand, he said, "What do you think the Government will do eventually about our charges, Sir George?"

"Eh?" The grey eyes in the ugly face blinked and then Sir

George breathed deeply as he made the long voyage back from Kew Gardens. "Damned if I know. After all what can they do about them? Some things, you know, just don't have a solution. Perhaps you're a little too young still to believe that. But it's true. It's a human failing to think there's an answer to all problems. There just isn't. Why should there be? There's nothing neat and tidy about life wherever you look . . . You don't want to be deceived by all this talk of moral, political and economic progress. The only difference I've seen in my sixty-odd years is that life has got faster and louder and longer . . . And now, if you'll show me where my quarters are I'll go and have a wash before lunch. Neil should be back soon with Teddy Burrows."

The place they had moved to from the cave was a patch of acacia trees halfway up the side of the crater. The trees formed a barrier in front of a cleft in the rocks that ran back about twelve feet and was entirely in shadow. At midday Roper went down to Plevsky with food and drink. When he came back Walter Mietus asked him about the girl.

Roper shrugged his shoulders. "She's in some pain with her leg and a little delirious. But she has patches when she's quite clear in the head. Why are you keeping her?"

"I want to check the plan of the fort with her. I've had to go on what Mawzi has told me and what I can see with the glasses. These local people will know the place inside out."

"You think she will help you?"

Mietus, who was stripping and cleaning a Thompson sub-machine-carbine, looked up and nodded.

Roper lowered himself to a patch of loose shale at the side of the cleft and settled his back against the rock. He pulled out a packet of cigarettes and tossed one to Mietus. They smoked in silence for a while. Deeper in the cleft Sifal slept and Lorentzen lay at his side, his hands under his head, staring out at the green canopy of acacia leaves. The whole group were relaxed and unconcerned.

Roper said, "That bastard would have blown us to hell— I wonder why?"

Mietus, frowning over the return of the recoil spring to the sub-machine-gun, said, "He was her brother, I think.

From what Mawzi said about the soldier we killed I should say this was the girl."

"They'll miss them?"

"Not until tonight, and then it will not matter." Mietus finished assembling the sub-machine-gun and put it down by the pack at his side.

"You know," said Roper, "I knew a girl once who was a bit like her. Same kind of cheekbones and those sort of big, pouty lips."

Mietus smiled. "You and Plevsky, and Lorentzen there, you are all the same. Any girl always reminds you of some other girl, particularly if you haven't had any girl for some time . . ." His words trailed away and the smile went from his face, leaving it wooden. Roper knew what he was thinking about and, while there was no affection in him for Mietus, his respect for the man moved him to a concern that was almost kindness. He changed the subject.

"You've worked out the plan for tonight?"

"Yes. I'll brief you all when Plevsky comes up." He rose slowly to his feet and his shadow was dark across Roper.

"Where are you going?"

"To the top." Mietus reached down and picked up his revolver and field glasses.

Roper watched him go, passing under the acacias and then out of sight. Nothing worried him, he thought, because he had nothing to lose. He lay there, thinking over something Plevsky had said in the cave a little while before.

"There's no need to kill this girl, you know. She can't move far with her leg and she's delirious half the time. We ought to leave her here when we go. Somebody'll find her later. Why kill her?"

"She wanted us to die."

"That's over."

"Well, it's up to Mietus."

Yes, it was up to Mietus. And that meant she would be killed. Women meant nothing to him. Funny, she did remind him of some girl. God knows which one, though. He began to whistle under his breath, *In Dublin's fair city where the girls are so pretty* . . . Ah, Dublin . . . How far away was he, he wondered, from the nearest glass of Guinness? Then, his eye falling on the Thompson sub-machine-gun Mietus had been cleaning, he felt the memory of such a gun in his hands and the rapid kick against his belly as he fired from the waist. The gentle whistle died from his lips and he could feel the saliva gathering in his mouth as in his imagination he heard the wicked noise of the heavy .450 inch bullets smacking home . . . and it was my mother, he thought, who would make a parson of me and my father all for the law and here I am like an old adder in the sun.

From the ground to his side, Lorentzen spoke quietly, not moving, staring at the acacias and in a tone as though he carried on a conversation long begun and never finished: "You think some animals know?"

"Know about what?" Roper was used to Lorentzen's habits.

"About people who don't like them. If I go up to a dog it runs and runs. Always been like that with dogs. Horses is different . . ."

Roper smiled. "Animals are no better than people. Personally I've always thought dogs make bad judges of character. They judge by appearances. That puts you in a bad position right away."

"Yes." Lorentzen laughed quietly. "That's what it is about me. Pin-head, bean-pole . . ." He settled his long body more comfortably against the ground and sighed gently. "Nice and peaceful here. I'll be fresh and ready for tonight."

Up on the lip of the crater Mietus had found a place in the rocks from which he could look down on Mora and Fort Sebastian. He had his glasses to his eyes and was watching the *Dunoon*. A few local rowing boats were moving around it. A liberty boat pulled away from the destroyer towards the jetty. The white tops of the sailors' hats were spread over the boat like aspirin tablets . . . A shore leave party, Mietus guessed. He swung the glasses to the left, along the sea front and the still palms and then up the slope to the fort. There was some movement in the courtyard and he picked out the lorry and the jeep. On the parapet he found Colonel Mawzi and Hadid Chebir standing by the awning. He could not see Marion Chebir but assumed she was under the awning. It wasn't too easy to see in detail because of the heat haze that came up shimmering and swaying from the long La Caldera slopes below him. Much further round to the left was the open square of Ardino, the pink walled church catching the sun. There was no movement in the square.

Tomorrow, he thought, they would go down to the beach at Ardino. Max Dondon would be there on time with the flying boat . . . They'd pull away from the beach in one of the fishing boats (he must check with the girl about that) and then they would be off and all this affair over . . . In a few months there would be other things, and on and on and on, always the same sort of life. When you didn't care what happened to you, he thought, then things always went right. He wasn't worried about tonight. It was all planned; they would have the advantage of surprise and there would be no real trouble . . . Sometimes he could be frank with himself and admit that he would like to have real trouble. Real trouble might end everything for him . . . But until it did he knew that he had to go on and on. He wasn't the kind of man who could end things for himself. No power on earth he knew could make him take the revolver from his pocket and put it against his head. But some day or night, out of the anger of battle or skirmish, the bullet would come and complete the desolation which a rolling tank had started so many years before.

He lay there for a long while, watching Mora and the fort. The sun began to drop towards the sea and the parapet shadow began to lengthen across the courtyard of the fort. On the beach at Mora some of the sailors on leave were bathing. Distantly he could hear their laughter and shouts.

When he finally moved, his right leg was stiff and awkward from the long lying. He rubbed it as he made his way down into the crater. He went to the cave and not the acacias.

Plevsky was sitting well inside the cave out of the sun. Flies crawled over the sacking that covered the dead man. The girl was propped with her back against the loose stones and rubble that had fallen in a sharp moraine at the back of the cave. She was conscious and her eyes stayed on him as he came into the shadows.

He squatted by Plevsky and pulled a sheet of paper from his pocket.

"She has been conscious for long?" he asked in German.

"An hour."

"Does she talk?"

"No. I have no Spanish, but I have tried her with a little English. She says nothing. She is, I think, just a simple, stupid girl. And very frightened."

"So simple she would have enjoyed watching us all blown to hell."

"We killed her lover, no?"

"It could not be helped."

Mietus moved up closer to Arianna. Her face was dirty and cut. One wing of black hair fell across her forehead and she had her right hand on her ankle, leaning forward a little. Mietus put out his hand and took hers from her ankle. Her leg was swollen and mottled with bruises. She would be in pain. His eyes came up to her face and he saw fear mixed with sullenness.

Talking in Spanish, he said very deliberately, "Listen to me carefully. Who we are and what we do here is not for your understanding. One thing only matters. Do you wish to live?"

Arianna made no answer.

"Do you wish to live?" he repeated the question, his voice dull with patience.

For a moment Arianna's eyes went from him to the sack-covered heap at the cave mouth. When her eyes met his again they were narrowed by bitterness.

Mietus's hand came up quickly and slapped her across the left cheek.

"You understand my words. Answer. Do you wish to live?"

The pain from the blow made tears gather at the corners of her eyes.

"Yes," she said, "I wish to live."

"You shall if you answer my questions. But do not try to deceive me. To some of the questions I ask I know the answers so you will be unwise to try and deceive me—if you wish to live. How many boats will there be on the beach at Ardino at ten o'clock tomorrow morning?"

"Four."

"Is there one which will take ten people?"

225

"Yes."

Her voice was so low that sitting where he was Plevsky could scarcely hear her.

Mietus put the paper he held on her lap.

"You know Fort Sebastian?"

"Yes."

"This is a drawing of the fort. I shall point out the rooms and the various places and you will tell me if I have them right. Also you will tell me about the stairs that go up and down to the various rooms and about the passage-ways."

Mietus edged closer to her and took a pencil from the breast pocket of his leather jacket.

"There are many things about the fort I do not know," said Arianna.

"What you know, you will tell me."

"And how will I know that I will live?"

"I say you shall. Now, watch——" The pencil dropped and the point touched the paper; "——here is the main-gate. It has a little door cut into it?"

"It has."

"Inside there is a room to the right or left?"

"There is a big room to the left. To the right is a little place with a telephone."

Plevsky listened to them; question and answer, question and answer, and when it was all done he knew that the girl would die. Mietus was like that. These two had come to kill them. The man was already dead. The girl should have been dead, too, but Mietus had missed her. So now, he took advantage of the fact that his revolver with a suppressor pulled to the right. Mietus took advantage of everything. He was a machine . . . perfect. It was a pity about the girl. For hours he had watched her and he had remembered many things about the girl he had known far back in Poland . . . Odd, strange little things which he had not imagined could still be in his memory. For instance, he had remembered that the girl could stretch out her bare right foot and pick up a cigarette between the big toe and the others and he remembered, too, how on the farm she was without equal in sexing day-old chicks. He could recall the way her mouth puckered as she blew at the bottom fluff of the chicks . . .

226

Mietus went on questioning her and her voice came back, as thin as a reed trembling against a river current. Sometimes Mietus made a new mark on the paper, and then finally he stood up and tucked the paper into his breast pocket with the pencil.

He came across to Plevsky.

Plevsky said, "She has been useful."

"Yes."

"That is good. And now?"

"It is not safe for both of us to walk together in the open. Give me ten minutes, and then follow. Finish her before you leave. Here." He handed Plevsky his revolver with the silencer screwed to its barrel. Plevsky handed him his own revolver in exchange.

From inside the cave he watched Mietus move into the open, pass rapidly and quietly into the scrub and disappear. Plevsky looked at his watch. Behind him he heard the sound of the girl crying. He turned. She had her face in her hands and was sobbing and breathing hard against her sobbing. Her distress puzzled him. Either she cried because she knew she was going to die or because she thought she was going to live. He wondered which she believed. This sobbing, he thought, was a foolishness for it did her no good and made things awkward for him.

He went in to her and shifted his grip on the revolver so that he held it by the barrel. Her face was still in her hands as he stood above her. He reached down and hit her expertly with the flat of the revolver butt against the side of her head just above the left ear. She dropped back loosely against the pile of stone rubble. Her unconscious body sprawled awkwardly to one side so that the top button of her blouse burst and he saw the small bulge of flesh from her right breast pushed up by the pressure of her trapped right arm.

He looked at his watch, standing very still and not thinking about anything except the jerking little second hand of the watch. When the time was up he raised the revolver and fired two shots into the soft earth face at the back of the cave.

After dinner Sir George Cator went to his room to write up his report on his visit to Fort Sebastian. John and Neil

227

Grayson went up on to the parapet over the main gate and sat in deck chairs. The night was warm and still and the laughter and voices of the sailors on shore leave in Mora could occasionally be plainly heard. Other sounds carried clearly on the still air, the sudden acceleration of a lorry in the town, the hollow knock of oars in a boat and the distant sound of a goat bell somewhere up on the La Caldera slopes.

The two sat in silence, enjoying their cigars. After a while John said, "What do you think they'll do about Hadid Chebir?"

"The Government?"

"Yes."

"I should think that by tomorrow morning we'll get a message back asking for a full report and telling us to take no action yet. Eventually I think they'll give the news to the press and make sure it's known in Cyrenia. I can't see that it will do Mawzi any good there. Nobody likes to be deceived. And if the real Hadid is dead . . . well, feeling could turn against Mawzi for hiding it. This kind of thing is all right so long as it comes off . . ."

"It was a damned clever thing to do."

"He could never have got away with it unless the girl had agreed . . ." Neil sighed, stretched his legs and watched the rich cigar smoke float heavily away from him into the night. "Have you ever," he asked, "thought of going into politics?"

"No."

"You could easily when you've finished with the Army."

"Maybe, but it's not what I want."

"What is what you want?"

John smiled. "I don't know. To farm, go into business, buy paintings . . . I don't know. I'm the cabbage type really, I suppose."

Neil laughed. "After this business, you know, there's no doubt you'll get something. Sir John Richmond. The curious thing is that it'll come easily to you and you won't care a damn."

"It's what you'd like, isn't it?"

Neil twisted his head to watch John. "Yes, yes it is. Is it so obvious?"

"In a way. And I envy you for knowing. It must be a comforting thing to have settled what you want and where you aim to go. In some ways, I suppose, being ambitious is like being musical. Either you are or you aren't. I should say you'll get what you want."

"I mean to try, anyway. After this trip is over I'm leaving Sir George. Going back to London . . ." His words trailed away. He was thinking of Daphne and knowing he wanted to talk about her. Love, he supposed, did that to you, made you seek a confidant, made you anxious to have some excuse just to say the name aloud. Daphne . . . But he had enough sense not to say anything to Richmond. Neil could imagine how the easiness of Richmond's manner would change if he started to tell him about Daphne. Richmond just wouldn't have patience with it . . . Damned bad show, and all that. Love at Sorby Place was a matter of a good county name and a proper marriage settlement.

"One day you'll make it," said John. "You'll be Prime Minister and I'll see your photograph in the papers. Smiling on the steps of Number Ten. . ." But as he said it John felt the future cloak itself about him. Where would he be when he opened that newspaper? Not where so much, because it could be Nice, Tangier, Baltimore or Sorby Place . . . but with whom? Would she be there? He had no ambition in the sense Grayson understood the word. But he had this now. He knew what he wanted . . . He looked across through the velvet night to the silhouette of the Bell Tower, a silhouette cut with yellow window lights still. She was there and he longed to be with her. The longing was so strong that he almost rose . . . He wondered what Grayson would say if he suddenly confided in him that he had fallen in love with Marion Chebir? The man would be puzzled and, maybe, shocked. He could hear him. But why her? Why, when there are so many others who would give you all you want and fit so much better into your world?

Somewhere in the courtyard one of his men began to play a mouth-organ, very low and with long sad cadences.

In the Bell Tower Marion heard the sound of the mouth-organ. She stood at the window and the sudden drift of music gave her an unexpected clarity and made decision easier. All

229

day the thing had been clouded in her mind. But now it was abruptly clear. There was no relief in the decision because the end of thought left her free to an imagination which carried its own distress. But at last, she knew what she must do. Outside a man sat in the courtyard, cradling his instrument against his mouth and in the warm darkness there were all the other men . . . a body of humanity suddenly very near and important to her. And above them all was John Richmond whom she loved and for whom she was ready to admit that love was a supreme selfishness which had to be obeyed. She had known that with Hadid; knowing it again with John she acknowledged that it was only a matter of time before one gave way to the ruthlessness of loving. The time for her was now. All day she had argued with herself, and all day, deep in her heart she had known this moment of vital surgery must come. This, she told herself, was the true moment of Hadid's death. This was the moment when he and the last of her love for him ceased to exist and also all those loyalties which were not linked urgently and unavoidably with this place which held her new love. She was going to betray Mawzi and the false Hadid. By doing so she knew plainly that she could well be betraying herself, too . . . could be inviting the loss of all that she longed to save . . . All had to be risked. One life could not be balanced against another. The only logic and wisdom lay in preventing the immediate disaster. After that one could only pray for a miracle.

She turned away from the window. All she had to do was to unlock her door, go to the tower door and call softly to the guard and tell him to fetch Major Richmond. When he came into her room and began to speak the thing would be gone beyond her control.

She went to her door and felt in her dress pocket for the clumsy key. She opened the door and the light from the room behind her fell across the dark stairs. Someone moved out of the darkness into the light. It was Colonel Mawzi. He said nothing and in the silence she heard a soft scuffle from lower down the steps. Abou, like a polite genie, came into the light too, and stood with his head a little bowed, his eyes avoiding her Marion knew then that one or both of these men had been waiting out here ever since she had retired to her room.

Colonel Mawzi put out a hand and took her arm.

"This is an anxious night for us all," he said gently. "It is better that we should spend it together."

He moved, not pulling her, and she went with him, dumbly and blankly.

"Put out the light, Abou," Mawzi said.

As they moved up the stairs to Hadid's room, Marion heard the click of the wall switch from her room and then the soft scuffle of Abou's bare feet behind her.

In his room Hadid was lying fully dressed on his bed. He looked up at their entrance and said with almost boyish glee, "Only a few more hours."

Daphne had the small cabin which Marion Chebir had used during her voyage to San Borodon. She was in her dressing-gown, creaming her face, when Teddy came into her. The moment he entered she knew he was still restless and preoccupied. He'd been like it all day. Other people might not have noticed it but she knew him too well not to pick up the signs. He wandered round the cabin now and finally sat down and pulled out his cigarette case.

"Mind if I smoke?"

"You know I don't, darling."

Her back was to him. She heard the click of his lighter. She turned and looked at him steadily.

"What's the matter with you, Teddy?"

"Nothing. Just don't feel like bed. The press boys are in the ward room."

"You usually get on well with them."

"Not tonight." One hand fiddled with his lighter. She moved closer and took it from him.

"I'll have one, I think."

He held out his case. She closed her eyes momentarily as she drew at the cigarette.

"Come on, Teddy," she said easily. "Out with it. Something's on your mind. I know that Neil sent a special signal to the Admiralty——"

"The devil you do!"

"The whole ship's buzzing with it."

231

"Then it ought not to be."

"What is it—something gone wrong?"

"No."

"Then what is it?"

He didn't answer. He pulled at his chin with his blunt fingers and the familiar movement roused a swift affection in her. Years ago she had loved him, so she thought, in the way she now loved Neil . . . but somehow the thing had been lost. She had a sudden spasm of guilt at the thought that very soon now she would have to tell him about Neil. It would wound him terribly.

"Daphne . . ." he said and then cleared his throat and hesitated.

"Yes?"

"Daphne . . . I've been thinking. Maybe I made a mistake in staying on in the Navy. Yes, I was pure pig-headed about that."

"But you love the Navy."

"In a way. But I love you more." He looked away from her as he spoke.

"Teddy, dear——"

"Well, it's true. And I've been thinking—why don't I chuck the whole thing up? Go back to London. You'd like that, wouldn't you?"

"Why do you bring this up now?"

"Oh, I don't know. A chap gets to thinking about things. Seeing things clearly . . . from other people's points of view . . ."

She wasn't deceived by the casualness he tried to put in his voice. Every instinct in her was awakened. Outwardly very calm, she turned away from him and bent towards the mirror on the bulkhead and began to work the cream on her face into her skin. Inwardly she knew without doubt that somehow he must suspect something about Neil and herself . . . Not the truth, maybe, but something. He was a blunt, straightforward man. When he tried to be subtle he only succeeded in making things more obvious. There was a tremble of nervousness in her fingers as she worked at her face. He must know something. This talk of London and leaving the Navy . . .

232

"You'd like it," he repeated. "Kind of life you want. Enjoy it myself, too. Small house somewhere in Kensington, and me toddling off to the City. Always have looked well in a bowler and pin-striped trousers." He laughed and the sound cut into her, stirring a great tenderness for him in her. Oh, Teddy dear, she thought; it's all too late and hopeless.

"Yes, I'd like it," she said.

"Might even have some small place in the country . . ."

She patted at the skin under her chin. I'm growing old, she thought, and if it weren't for Neil it would be all I want. Just for a moment—because she hated the thought of ever having to wound Teddy—she wished there never had been a Neil, and then as quickly killed the thought. She wanted to turn and tell him the truth. But she couldn't. It would have to come, some day soon. She would have to tell him—but not at this moment. She had to prepare herself for it, lead him gently to it, not just blurt it out. It would be awful even so, but even worse if she did it now.

She turned and, seeing him sitting bulky and awkward, she went quickly to him and put her hands on his shoulder. She bent and kissed him. God forgive me, she thought; and she hated herself for the unhappiness which she carried for him.

"It's a lovely idea," she said. "But you sleep on it. After all——"

"But it's what you want, isn't it?"

"Yes, of course."

"Then it's settled."

He stood up, slipping an arm around her. "I'll get it fixed as soon as I can. Nothing to stop us. Nothing that I can see. Can you?"

She shook her head, unable to say anything and he kissed her gently.

When he was gone she stood in the centre of the cabin staring miserably at the curtained porthole. How can I tell him, she thought? How can I?

Until now she had been concerned only with herself and Neil. Telling Teddy had lain in the future, something that she accepted but hadn't vividly visualized. But now it was with

233

her. He had to be told. And this she knew was the hardest part of love; to take the knife and callously kill love in another; to take the knife and coldly cut away from him and from herself all that had been . . . She shut her eyes and her body shook suddenly. She would have to do it, but she knew that always the memory of it would make her hate herself . . .

In Mora, in the bar kept by the man with a twisted right hand, a hand that in repose was always begging, Andrews and Grogan were drunk. They were drunk like ships in good ballast, settled and riding steadily. They talked reasonably, though now and again a word became wild, slippery and untamed, but both of them ignored the rebellion in the other out of good drinking manners. A bottle of *fundador* was on the table before them, but each of them, cunning with the instinct born of many a monumental drunk, had already bought a spare bottle of brandy, which had been thrust awkwardly into a pocket, bulging the body like a great tumour. They knew that bars had a habit late at night of disappearing, that a man could find himself stretched in the bilge and rain water of a beached boat and only his own resources to provide him with drink, or that suddenly from the smoke and liquor haze one was alone and walking some dark, strange road and then the hand went to the pocket to find the familiar shape. Both of them knew, too, that the liberty boat would pull away from the jetty at midnight, and both of them knew that it would go without them. They smiled at each other happily, and Andrews said soberly, "That hand . . . it was probably twisted like that at birth. A difficult birth . . . obstet . . . tet . . . trically difficult, I would say. He probably hung on to the last moment and twisted his wrist." He adjusted his pink eye-shade and smiled.

"Who wouldn't," said Grogan and began to hum . . . *Every little boy and girl, born into this world alive . . . Is either a little Liberal or else a little Con-serv-at-ive . . .*

Just for a moment a touch of anxiety clouded Andrews' face. When Grogan began to sing it was a bad sign. Then he smiled. This was all right. It wasn't the *Wearing of the Green*.

234

When Grogan came to that . . . Whoa, boy, gale force eight, men o' war reef their upper topsails and all small smacks make for harbour . . .

One of their leave party came across to the table and muttered something about time to be getting back.

Grogan looked at him with a glassy stare, and Andrews with a pleasant and dangerous dignity said, "The history of your family, I should say, is of considerable interest. You want me to tell it to you? Geneal . . . genealogico . . ."

The other sailor smiled and said knowingly, "Ho, ho— like that, is it. One of these days you'll choke on one of them dirty great words."

Andrews began to get to his feet.

Grogan put out a hand and pulled him down. "Let me," he said.

The sailor wisely disappeared before Grogan could stand up.

To console themselves, the two filled their glasses again from the bottle.

12

An hour after darkness Mietus and his party left the acacia trees. In a long-intervalled single file they went up from the crater and bore right-handed around the crest until they were directly above the narrow spine of the ridge that ran down to Mora and Fort Sebastian.

Without any words between them Sifal unshipped the radio transmitter from his back and set it up on a bare plateau of rock. The other four melted into the darkness, forming a protective screen for him. An hour later the screen contracted around Sifal and the party settled itself below the lip of the small plateau, their backs against the rock base, their faces turned northwards towards Mora.

There were a few lights still showing in the town, lights also from the fort, and out in the harbour the lights from the anchored *Dunoon* made a ragged tracing of reflections over the water. The night was warm and still and heavy with the hot, perspiring breath of the earth. Far away to the north the faint loom of the San Borodon light began to beat against the blackness. At this time of the year darkness came late, and dawn early. It was already past eleven o'clock.

Sifal said quietly, "The reception was good. Max will be off Ardino at ten tomorrow morning." He spoke in German, for this was their working language. In his mouth the language had a singing, Oriental cadence that even now sometimes surprised Mietus. For some moments his words seemed pure sound, unintelligible, and then with a start one realized it was German he was speaking.

"Good," said Mietus, and then there was silence between them all. They waited now, he knew, for him. The men changed, he thought, from time to time, but the grouping and the silence and the waiting were always the same. Less than in the coming action he was aware that real pleasure lay in this phase, in this dark, silent hushed waiting. This was his world, they were his men . . . in him was power without impatience. He was intelligent enough to know that it was a poor kingdom, but he held it with pride because it was the only one he knew. Many a time he had waited for the moment when he would go down like a wolf at the head of a pack and, as always, the other, long-dead Mietus waited with him. Over the years he had learned to entertain this dead Mietus without bitterness, even with some affection. By now, if the moving, grinding bulk of the tank had not trapped him, he would have found a middle-age full of orderliness. He shut his eyes, seeing himself an architect in Dusseldorf or Hamburg, seeing his wife clearly with the high, marmoreal forehead and the blonde, vital threads of hair piled in Grecian loveliness . . . and the children, and the flat in one of the new blocks. And from the deep, sad, Teutonic romanticism in him he could say, I am a tree without seed. I am poor Walter Mietus whom war has half-destroyed; I am indeed a pitiable creature. And, as always, at this point he smiled and there was a vicious pleasure in him at his hopelessness, and he welcomed the mounting of bitterness directed against everything and everyone.

After a time he began to speak and there was an odd paternal note in his voice as though he were almost tender in

236

his concern for the men with him, but none of them was deceived by it for they knew that his real affection and tenderness was for the thing itself. He was concerned that this action should be unmarred by stupidities or hesitations. This love was professional and his anger against a false move could be fierce and cruel.

"The sun rises," he said quietly, "at five-fifteen. We shall go inside at four-forty-five. We shall leave here at four. Order; single file, myself leading, three-yard interval, Lorentzen and Sifal, you take the men in the guard room. No shooting unless it's absolutely necessary. We don't want the alarm raised until the last possible moment. Use a knife if you've got to kill. Plevsky and Roper—you go straight across to the men's dormitory. Hold them there and get their arms. Sifal and Lorentzen will bring their men across from the guard room and shut them in the dormitory with the others. Sifal and Lorentzen stay on guard there. The cook and the sergeant sleep separately in two rooms next to the cookhouse. Plevsky and Roper you get them, as soon as the dormitory is taken. If the alarm is raised and they come out before you've got the dormitory you'll have to drop them with your sub-machine-guns. Roper and Plevsky then take the courtyard stairs to the officers' quarters. The moment we're in I shall go straight up to the Bell Tower parapet and deal with the guard and release Colonel Mawzi and the others. If I can get the guard with a knife I will. If not my shot should be the first alarm . . ." His voice, quiet and unemotional, ran on, an even murmur of sound against the warm, dark night, and as he spoke he could see it all happening, living his words with a visual keenness that gave character and painted faces on the men in the fort below whom he had never seen. The guard on the parapet would be a fool like all guards, watching him come up the stone steps, wondering, puzzled and alarmed too late . . .

"Remember," he said, "the Governor must not be harmed. Remember, too, one quick death will show we mean business. The whole thing is simple and we shall have the advantage of surprise, but remember that nothing is certain. There is always some fool eager for a hero's death . . . Any questions?"

"The guard on duty just inside the small door?" asked Roper.

"I shall deal with him as we go in."

"All light switches are on the right inside the doors?" It was Lorentzen. "All?"

"Yes."

There were no more questions.

"All right," said Mietus. "We will check our arms before we leave here and I shall carry the spare arms for Mawzi, Hadid Chebir and Abou ..."

"Abou," Plevsky chuckled. "I had forgotten him. At least we shall get coffee soon after the job is done."

Mietus settled back against the rock and shut his eyes. There was no sleep in him, or in any of the others. They all lay there in silence, cradled by the dark night and their own confidence which they had learned to trust no farther than they could see. Mietus was right; nothing was certain except their own quickness and violence, and now that the moment of action was so close to them they were freed from thinking about it, able to relax and for this little while achieve an ordinariness of thought which for all of them was a kind of peace. Sifal was looking forward to seeing Abou. They came from the same hill village and were vaguely related which was not surprising in any Cyrenian hill village. He had been with Abou when Abou had killed his first man ... he smiled at the recollection of Abou standing, knife in hand, and written over his face his surprise that the thing had been so easy. Lorentzen, rubbing at a mosquito bite on his cheek, was thinking of a horse, an Arab mare that came to his whistle, would roll over and act dead at a sign from him, would stand, glossy, patient and proud, and he sucked his teeth contemptuously at the thought of other animals that shrank from him ... only the horse, moving like the wind with the blood-beating delight of hooves drumming and drumming on the hard sand, yes, only the horse loved him. And Roper, shutting his eyes, worked out a bridge problem, his extraordinary mind dealing the four hands, hearing the bid calls and seeing the cards flick down; while Plevsky, watching the lights from the *Dunoon*, remembered his father who used to carve little ships for him from the soft wood of fish boxes ... his father who had never seen the sea, and his mother who had been buried under the ruins of Warsaw . . .

Below them, distantly, the chalky lights of a lorry probed snail-like up the hill from Mora on the road to Ardino. As it passed at its nearest point to them they could hear very faintly the sound of men and women singing.

In the lorry drunk, roisterous, in love with the whole world, and ready to fight the whole world if it said a word out of place, were Grogan and Andrews. Neither of them was quite clear how he came to be in a lorry. One moment, they had been drinking in the bar and the next out in the street, staggering arm in arm and then suddenly surrounded by laughing men and women who had come to Mora for the day to watch the arrival of the *Dunoon* and the Governor . . . and now here they were swaying and lurching over the rough road, adrift on a great euphoric wave.

Arianna was adrift, too. She was the creature now of shock, of pain, and of horror. Awakening in the darkness of the cave was no more than the prolongation of a fearful nightmare whose elements mixed and shifted so rapidly that her fear became so physical that she shivered and trembled as though she had a fever.

Now and again she had moments of intense consciousness which, like some warm, green bud, seemed to peel away and reveal the bright blossom of understanding only for the flower to wither before she could really know it.

She felt the dry earth and stones under her hands and knew where she was. The darkness was no bar to her movement or vision for the day-bright picture of her horror and fear lived clearly in her mind. There, just down there, lay Torlo's body and even now she knew the galaxy of flies would be resting on the sack that covered him.

She pulled herself forward on her hand and knees and began to crawl towards Torlo. Her right ankle and foot flopped painfully against the ground. The bruise on her head throbbed and throbbed and made her hold her head down and sideways for relief. She moved and whimpered to herself like some maimed, fear-dazed animal. When her fingers touched the edges of the sack over Torlo she stopped and for

239

a moment she raised her head listening. The only sound from the night outside was of a cicada calling.

The men had gone. They had killed Torlo and they had thought they had killed her. She squatted back on one flank and felt the wound on her head. Maybe she would die, too. Maybe she was dying now.

She ran her hand over the sack and pulled it away from Torlo. In the darkness her hands went over him. It was as though he slept heavily and she shook him roughly and said his name. For a time there was a stupid mixture of understanding and not-understanding in her mind because he made no answer, and then, following it swiftly, came the clarity of knowing he was dead. She crossed herself and mumbled a prayer for him. Almost before the prayer had died on her lips she was bitter, bitter and angry, against the men who had killed Torlo and had killed March and had thought they had killed her. Her hatred of them was a moment of strength in her and of longing to reach and find them and to kill them. Torlo had promised her their death . . . She saw Torlo standing in the pale morning light, his arm swinging still from throwing the grenades. She put out her own hand now and shook him again, to wake him to come and kill the men with her. But Torlo slept. All right. Let him sleep. She would kill them herself. She would drag herself all over the island until she found them and killed them. Her hands, still on the stiff body, felt the bulge of the two spare hand-grenades in his pocket and she pulled them out and began to crawl with a feverish haste out of the cave, but her pace soon slackened as the rough stones and rocks cut into her elbows and knees, and she stopped, panting and suddenly sensible.

She dropped the two grenades into the front of her dress. Sitting up she tore strips from her underskirt and bound them around her knees. She worked with a slow, competent assurance, talking gently to herself. Her hands she left bare, they were hard and strong and had lifted stones and swung wood all her life.

When she was ready she began to crawl towards the path that led out of the crater. She went slowly, instinctively conserving her strength. Every little while the pain from her leg and the throb, throb from her head built up into a sobbing of breath in her lungs and she had to collapse, flat against the earth and wait for fresh strength to return to her. But each time she lay on the ground she could feel the hard pressure of the two grenades against her soft breasts, and each time she remembered March out in the fishing boat with them the day he had brought the grenades and taught them how to use them. With an agony of love and sadness she remembered asking him what the ring of red crosses round each grenade meant, the ordnance mark indicating that they were suitable for storage in tropical climates, and his answer that they were soldier's kisses for her, and then kissing her in front of Torlo which had made her brother angry. Poor Torlo . . . Poor March . . . But for them she would kill the men.

She eventually reached the top of the crater at twenty minutes past four. By that time Mietus and his party were on their way down to Fort Sebastian.

In the *Bar Filis*, Grogan and Andrews were making a night of it. Most of the Ardino folk with whom they had travelled back on the lorry had long disappeared. But still in the bar were Ercolo, the proprietor, who more years back than he could remember had learned the wisdom of only sleeping between midday and five o'clock, a handful of card-playing youths, an old woman without teeth and with a brown face, withered and wrinkled like a russet apple half a century old, and a fisherman who had come up late from lantern fishing for octopus and who now sat smiling amiably at all the noise. Drumming his heels against the front of the counter on which he sat was Ercolo's youngest son of five years who was getting an early and liberal education in his father's trade.

The two sailors were in that unsteady, romantic stage of drunkenness when, for the moment, they had ceased drinking and were content with the great, warm expansion of their souls and delighted with the nebulous golden light that flooded the world.

Andrews, still pink eye-shaded, had picked up Ercolo's mandolin from behind the bar and, half-supported by Grogan, was singing with Grogan coming in at the choruses.

Andrews had a fine, light baritone smeared now with the treacly, exaggerated notes of intoxication. As he played he sang to the old woman, winking and shaking his head roguishly.

Oh, Sir will you excuse me, for being out so late
And if my mother knew of it,
Full sore would be my Fate.
My father was a Minister, a good, kind honest man.
My mother was a dancing girl——
So I do the best I can.

The child on the counter beat his heels happily as Grogan came rollicking in with the chorus,

She'd a dark and roving eye,
And her hair hung down like glow-worms;
She's a rare sort,
A rakish sort.
She's one for a Fireship's crew . . .

They did an unsteady double-shuffle, collapsed against the bar and slid to the ground in a sitting position and the mandolin twanged away.

I eyed the wench full warily, for talk like this I knew.
She seemed a trifle overbold . . .

At the end of the third verse Andrews pulled himself up, laid the mandolin on the bar solemnly, and addressing the people present said, "Sorry folks. Must go and shed a tear for me old mother."

He gave a great shout of joy, staggered across the room, patted the old woman on the cheek, and disappeared. Grogan followed him, obeying the age-old drunken creed of friends in liquor that everything is done together.

Suddenly Andrews' head popped back through the door and he shouted with a grin, "Don't go away. Keep the cork out of the bottle!" And then he fell backwards through the door out of sight, singing——

Oh, Do my Johnny Boker—Come rock and roll me over. . . .

The laughter of the two sailors echoed wildly through the night.

In Fort Sebastian Sir George Cator was asleep. By his bedside was a copy of Jules Verne's *Twenty Thousand Leagues Under the Sea* which he had found in the long Mess Room. He was dreaming that he was taking a trip with Captain Nimo in the *Nautilus* and through the great plate glass window of the submarine's saloon they were watching a couple of coelacanths at clumsy play. He made little puppy noises of pleasure in his sleep.

Richmond was asleep, too. Soundlessly, dreamlessly. On his table the luminous dial of his wrist-watch shone palely, the faint light just touching the black shape of the revolver which hung on the wall at the side of his bed.

Neil Grayson was awake and thinking of Daphne. He lay in the darkness, smoking, wondering if she were awake too and thinking of him. As soon as it was daylight, he told himself, he'd walk down to Mora. There'd be a fisherman about who would take him out to the *Dunoon*. By now there might be a reply to his message to London about Hadid Chebir. All this, he knew, was really an excuse . . . he would stay aboard ship and have breakfast with Daphne. There was an impatience in him to see her, to hear her voice. He blew the smoke from his lungs luxuriously as he thought of her . . .

In his room Sergeant Benson was snoring lustily, flat on his back. The fort cat, an overfed tawny-coloured creature with one cropped ear, was curled in a ball at the foot of his camp bed.

In the next room Jenkins the cook was sleeping, too; but lightly, and he was dreaming with a fine smile on his face for he was at the village flower show and quite clearly no one else was going to come near him so far as chrysanthemums were concerned—best six blooms, any variety. Like bloody great coloured mop-heads. There was a murmuring, envious crowd around the exhibit, and he was sweating a little from the heat in the tent.

The darkness in the men's dormitory was lively with snores and gentle whistles of breath as they all slept.

Up on the parapet by the Bell Tower, the guard lit himself a cigarette and smoked openly, standing his rifle against the parapet.

Down at the main gate Corporal Hardcastle, Guard Commander for the night, was standing with his back to the gate, watching the courtyard. Above the black bulk of the dragon tree he caught the red glow of the guard's cigarette, wondered for a moment whether he would go up and brass him off and then gave up the idea and lit a cigarette himself. In the guard room three men, fully dressed, lay dozing on their camp-beds.

In the Bell Tower Colonel Mawzi turned away from the open window and looked at his wrist-watch.

"In ten minutes," he said quietly, "they should be coming in."

Marion, sitting on the end of the bed, shivered suddenly. She felt helpless and sick.

13

Two hundred yards from the end of the long ridge down from La Caldera, Mietus stopped. If they came down off the ridge by the fort they would have fifty yards of open ground to cover which was under observation from the parapet by the Bell Tower. It was still dark, but the darkness was losing its weight and density. Their movement across the open space might be seen.

He turned away right-handed, dropping off the ridge through a tangle of low cactus palm and poinsettia bushes. The others followed him like phantoms.

They hit the road from Mora to the fort about a hundred yards from the main gate. The road was dusty and swallowed even the whisper of their rope-soled shoes. Mietus put up a hand and eased the weight of the pack on his back. His hand came down and found the handle of the knife thrust into his belt. His sub-machine-gun lay cradled under his left armpit, nursed to a nice balance by his left palm. He drew the knife and pressed the blade against his sleeve to kill any reflection from it.

Fifty yards from the main gate he crossed the road and waited, beckoning to the others to close up on him. He stood at the foot of one of a row of narrow poles that carried the telephone lines from the fort to Mora. He looked at Sifal and then crouched. Sifal stepped on his shoulders, put out a hand to the pole to steady himself, and Mietus rose. Twelve feet above, Sifal's hand found the twin signal cables. He cut them with his knife and as the ends dropped with a faint whip of sound into the roadside bushes Mietus crouched and Sifal was on the ground.

Mietus paused. Away to the right over the sea there was the faintest lightening in the sky and, as though made restless by the nearing dawn, a seagull swept along the cliffs below them, unseen, but crying with a sad impatience for the light.

They moved on in single file to the main gate. A row of stones on each side of the gate had been white-washed for the Governor. The air was thick with the scent of jasmine that grew in a tangled bush against the wall.

Mietus stood close to the wooden gate and Lorentzen came to his side. Key in his left hand Lorentzen felt for the lock on the small door. His fingers found the round boss and slowly and carefully he fitted the key. It was a Yale lock. The days of forts were dead. The main gate would have withstood a battering ram, but they had cut a modern little door into the strength of the old oak timbers.

The key turned in the well-oiled lock. Lorentzen eased the door an inch open and stood back. For a moment Mietus paused and looked back at the men behind him. He could feel the cold, anonymous bitterness hard inside him as it always was at such moments. He turned back to the door.

With a long, easy movement of his right hand which held also his knife he swung it open, controlling it so that it did not slam back against the main gate timbers and he stepped inside. A weak bulb burned high up in the lofty vault of the gate arch. Corporal Hardcastle was standing directly underneath it, his back to Mietus. He died without fear or even a black moment of surprise. Mietus stepped up behind him and his right hand drove in a low arc so that the knife plunged diagonally upwards under the left shoulder blade and found his heart. There was a faint whistle of protesting breath from Hardcastle and he fell, dead almost before he reached the ground.

Without a look at the others behind him Mietus stepped over the body and disappeared into the gloom of the courtyard, circling quickly around the shrub and flower bed.

Roper and Plevsky followed him out of the gate arch and went quickly towards the men's dormitory on the far side of the courtyard.

Lorentzen and Sifal moved towards the partly open door of the gate room. They paused listening. No sound came from within. Faintly from the basement room of the Flag Tower came the steady beat of the petrol engine that worked the electricity plant. The sound was like the rapid beating of a heart in the darkness.

Lorentzen stepped into the room and his right hand went up for a second from the stock of his gun to flick on the switch. The room came up in a dim fog of light. The three men lay in shirt and trousers on their beds, their rifles against the wall behind each bed. Magazines and old newspapers littered a chair by the window. Dirty tea mugs stood in a row on a small table with an ashtray full of cigarette stubs. Over the middle bed was a coloured photograph of Marilyn Monroe.

A man, roused by the light, sat up in bed, scratching at his head and gaping in surprise. Sifal slid past Lorentzen and put the muzzle of his gun a foot from the man's face. Lorentzen took a step forward and kicked the other two beds. Slowly the men came up from their sleep, sitting up, and then one began to half roll from his bed. The movement was stopped by Lorentzen as he swept his gun in a short arc and said in English:

"The first one to be stupid gets this!"

"Eh, what the——" The beginning of protest and surprise in the man by Sifal died as the muzzle of the gun was jammed hard against his throat, driving him backwards so that his head hit the wall behind him.

"No noise!" said Lorentzen, his voice charged with husky threat. "Get up and come out. Be sensible and you won't be hurt."

The men, now fully awake and afraid, slid off their beds and stood stupidly, lost, fearful to make any movement lest it be the wrong one.

"You first——" Lorentzen nodded at the man by the bed nearest the door. "Then you. Then you." He stepped back towards the door and as the men moved forward one by one

Sifal moved round behind them. They went through the door, drawn towards the retreating Lorentzen as though he were some powerful magnet.

"Across to the dormitory," said Lorentzen. "Keep in a bunch. Slowly and no noise. If there's going to be a noise, I'll make it with this." The muzzle of his gun swung across them. But there was no need for threats now. On the ground before them was the body of Corporal Hardcastle. The dullness and surprise went from their faces. Their lips were tight, their face muscles hardened and Lorentzen knew that this was the dangerous moment. When a man sees his own dead, the fear in him stays but something comes up alongside it and the balance between obedience and revolt trembles delicately. Slowly, bunched together, the men began to move across the courtyard.

Meanwhile Roper and Plevsky had reached the dormitory. Because of the hot night the door was wide open. They went in and Plevsky switched on the light. There were only five men in the room. Their beds were spaced three along one wall and two along the facing wall. The overhead lights came up bright and strong. For a moment nothing happened and Roper, standing by the arms rack just inside the door, looked down the length of the room and felt the flick of distant nostalgia in him. Once he had been in this Army and lived in such a barrack room . . . the heavy boots by the beds, the web of blanco-ed belts and shoulder straps, the pictures pinned to the wall and the drab army blankets.

Somebody jerked up in bed and shouted angrily, "Put out that bloody light!" And then sat, rubbing his eyes and staring at Plevsky who had come forward to the head of the aisle between the beds. Other men came awake, grumbling and muttering: then taking in Roper and Sifal, and watching the slow arc drawn by their sub-machine-gun muzzles, the men were suddenly, curiously quiet.

"Keep quiet and stay where you are," said Roper evenly.

"Who the bloody hell——"

Plevsky's feet shuffled with the quickness of a ballet dancer and the man who had spoken was silent, open mouthed, as the muzzle rose and steadied a foot from his eyes.

"That's better," said Roper. "Now sit up on your beds

247

and put your hands behind the back of your heads. Be sensible and you won't be hurt."

Slowly the men did as he ordered.

From the open doorway behind them came the noise of the gate guard. They came into the room and Roper and Plevsky drew apart as they moved down the aisle.

"Sit on the ends of the beds and put your hands up like the others." Roper spoke as he backed towards the door, and then half over his shoulder he said to Lorentzen, "All yours now. Take the bolts out of the rifles in the rack and toss them out of the window." He nodded to a small embrasure cut in the outer wall a little to the left of the first bed.

Leaving Lorentzen and Sifal in the room he backed out into the courtyard with Plevsky.

Circling left-handed round the courtyard Mietus was hidden from the steps leading to the Bell Tower parapet by the shrubs and the dark mass of the dragon tree. When he came clear of the shrubs and tree he paused, looking upwards. The night was paling rapidly now and he could see the silhouette of parapet and Bell Tower against the sky. The long slope of the stone steps was in dark shadow. There was no sign of the guard at the top of the steps.

He crossed to the steps and began to climb them. When his head was level with the top step he saw the guard. The man was leaning with his back against the Bell Tower door, legs crossed and smoking. His rifle rested against the tower wall. He was staring straight at the top of the steps.

Mietus looked down into the courtyard. A light was shining through the dormitory door. He saw the bunched movement of men in the shadows, and then the blackness of their bodies against the doorway. Everything was in hand down there . . . noise now became less important. His eyes came back to the parapet guard. The man coughed gently against the cigarette smoke in his throat. Mietus came up two more steps but as he raised his foot to the third the guard saw him. The cigarette was jerked quickly away and the man bent for his rifle. In that moment, as the cigarette end cut a fiery parabola through the night, Mietus knew that the guard was more concerned with being caught smoking by his guard commander than with any thought of danger. He came quickly up two more steps, and now almost on the parapet level he fired from the hip.

The noise, brief but fierce, burst across the night wickedly. Every wall and parapet threw back the angry echoes and the courtyard caught the sound and slammed it from wall to wall in high, whining echoes.

The guard fell backwards against the Bell Tower door and his rifle crashed across the hard flag stones with a great clatter.

Mietus ran to him. Crouching at his side he began to search for the door key. He found it in his left trouser pocket and as his hand came free with it he could feel the warm tackiness of fresh blood on his fingers.

Neil Grayson, no sleep in him, had slipped out of bed and dressed. When the shots broke out, he was going down the courtyard stairs from the long mess room. For half an hour he had lain in bed telling himself to wait, not to be impatient, not to behave like a boy with his first love, but the longer he had lain there the stronger had become his desire to go down to the *Dunoon*.

He was half-way down the stairs, feeling his way in the darkness when the shots came. His whole body jerked with the unexpectedness of the sound and for a moment he felt his heart pound with the shock. He waited, but when no sound followed the shots, he moved on, pursing his lips angrily, imagining some fool of a guard who had loosed off in carelessness. Richmond would tear a strip off him ... particularly as the Governor was in the fort and would be awakened.

He pushed open the door to the courtyard and stepped out. As he did so he saw the lights from the inner windows of the men's dormitory and two men, caught in a triangular patch of light from the open door.

He skirted round the shrub bed towards them.

"What's happened?" he called.

The men halted in their movement along the wall. Their heads came round and the light from the barrack room slashed across the sides of their faces. Their faces were strange to Grayson, and with the recognition of strangeness there came a swift premonition of disaster in him. He saw an arm move upwards and instinctively he flung himself sideways.

A burst of .450 bullets whistled past him and smashed against the wall behind him. He crashed into the bushes of the little garden, rolled over and, pulling himself up, plunged through the bushes, making for the cover of the dragon tree. Its smooth grey elephant-hide trunk glimmered palely in the growing light. He flung his right arm across the trunk to swing himself round and into cover. But as he did so the sub-machine-gun roared behind him again. The shock of the bullets whipped sideways across his body, beating and pulping into his back. And great bark chips spurted from the smooth trunk in front of his face. He gave a long, moaning scream and dropped heavily, sliding downwards, his face rasping down the trunk of the tree.

Plevsky ran to him, took one look, and turned away, sprinting through the bushes to rejoin Roper outside the door of Sergeant Benson's room.

The door opened as he reached Roper. The light in the room was on and Sergeant Benson stood on the threshold in his pants and shirt. Seeing the two strangers full in the light from behind him he raised his service revolver. But his reaction was too slow. Roper, whose right hand had left his gun to reach for the door, converted the movement to a wild slash and the edge of his palm came down striking at Benson's wrist. The revolver dropped to the ground. Plevsky's gun muzzle was thrust into Benson's stomach. For a moment the three stood in a still group. Then Roper said:

"You were lucky my hand wasn't on my gun. Walk along to the dormitory, and don't try any tricks."

A yard to their right the door of Jenkins' room opened and he came out, rubbing the top of his head.

"What the hell's going on here? Anyone would think it was Guy Fawkes night . . ."

His back was to the three and before he could turn Plevsky and Roper had drawn back, pushing Benson ahead of them. Benson put out a hand and took Jenkins by the shoulder. The cook swung round, startled.

"Serg. What's——"

He broke off, seeing the two men behind Sergeant Benson.

"All right, cookie," said Benson grimly. "Keep your hair

on. There's trouble behind us and we've got to behave."

"The dormitory," said Roper.

Jenkins would have spoken again but Benson's fingers bit into his shoulder and he shook his head warningly.

The first burst of shots from Mietus wakened John Richmond. He was sitting up and grabbing for the light switch almost before he knew what had brought him out of sleep. There was silence now but the noise of the shots echoed in his brain. What the hell was happening? He slid out of bed and reached for his trousers. He pulled them on quickly over his pyjama trousers and then, as he put out his hand to get his revolver from the wall, there came another quick burst of shots.

He raced for the door and as he reached it a further burst of firing chattered into the night and he heard someone scream. Flinging the door open into the corridor he ran down to the bedroom where Sir George Cator slept. As he reached it the door opened and Sir George stood against the light in his pyjamas.

"What the devil, Richmond——"

"Stay where you are, sir."

He motioned the Governor back into his room and ran on. His mind was clear now and he could feel the pounding of angry alarm in him. The shots had come from a quick firing sub-machine-gun. A Thompson, he guessed, and at the same time knew that the only thing like it they had in the fort were a couple of Sten guns which hadn't even been issued to the guard.

At the end of the corridor, just before the entry to the long mess room, a flight of four steps went left-handed up to the parapet. John, the thought of his prisoners uppermost with him, went up the stairs two at a time and flung open the wooden door at the top which gave on to the parapet walk. For a moment he paused in the doorway, surprised that the night was gone and a cold, pearly pre-dawn haze was lightening the sky beyond the Bell Tower. Then, to his left, just turning the corner of the Bell Tower section of parapet walk, he saw four men running towards him. The first one was a stranger to him, but the three behind were Mawzi, Hadid

Chebir and Abou. He saw the leading man holding a sub-machine-gun and the others with revolvers in their hands. John fired at the leading man and stone chips kicked from the parapet at his side. Immediately the four dispersed, flinging themselves into the deep embrasures that were cut like small pulpits into the parapet wall.

John drew back against the angle of the stair door and called sharply, "Stay where you are, Mawzi. I'll drop the first one that moves."

For answer the stranger rose boldly from the cover of his embrasure and the machine-gun blasted. The heavy bullets splattered in a spray up the far side of the door and wood and stone chips flew from the wall. John felt them bite into his face and hands and the shock of the thudding bullets seemed to take his breath away. He drew back, slammed the door and pushed the bolt over.

As he did so the sub-machine-gun was fired again and the bullets smashed through the wood angrily. He heard them beat and whine in the dark vault of the stairs and one of the bullets singing off the stone wall seared across the side of his neck like a red-hot poker. The shock of the blow threw him off his feet and he fell backwards down the stairs.

For a second or two he lay winded and helpless. Then as he struggled up, groping for the revolver which had fallen from his hand, the door at the head of the stairs crashed open.

Momentarily he saw the stranger, pale blond hair haloed against the morning light, and Mawzi's dark face behind him, saw the raised Thompson gun and then heard Mawzi shout almost desperately——

"Alive! Alive!"

With a shout the man leaped the drop of the four steps and landed on top of John. Half sitting up John bunched himself against the shock and swung his left shoulder round to take the impact. Mietus thudded into him like a battering ram and they went over, rolling and struggling together across the corridor and slamming into the door of the long mess room. The door burst open with the weight of their bodies. Falling, they were for a moment separated. John struggled to his knees, saw the stranger rising also and drove his right fist hard into the taut, vigorous face. Mietus' head

252

went back. A spasm of angry breath was forced from his tight lips. Rising further, John struck again. The sub-machine-gun was on the ground a foot beyond the man. He jumped sideways reaching for it; but as he bent, his head turning towards the mess room, his eyes found a pair of feet just beyond the gun. Something hit him a crashing blow on the side of the head and he went down into darkness.

Spitting and shaking his head, Mietus pulled himself to his feet. John lay still on the ground. Beyond him stood Roper, the machine-gun in his hand still reversed, the stock raised as he stood over John. But there was no further movement from him. Plevsky slipped by them and at the bottom of the stair opening looked up and saw Mawzi halfway down the stairs.

"It's all right," said Plevsky. "He's out. Everything's O.K. below."

"Get the Governor. You and Roper."

Mawzi turned back up the stairs. Standing outside the door was Hadid Chebir with Abou. The light was strengthening fast now and the long ridge of La Caldera was clear right up to the crest.

"He's settled?" Hadid Chebir asked.

"Yes. The fort's ours. Nothing can stop us now."

"Nothing . . ." Hadid drew himself up, breathing deeply, taking the cold morning air as though it were wine. His face flushed with his exultation. "This day Cyrenia finds her full strength."

Mawzi nodded slowly. "And the name of Hadid Chebir will live forever, as only the memory of a martyr can. But a new leader, not a blown-up pig's bladder, will drive Cyrenia forward."

For the briefest moment, so brief that it was hardly enough to bring full recognition of the final insult and threat, Hadid looked questioningly at Mawzi.

Deliberately Mawzi raised his revolver and shot the man through the heart.

He looked down at him coldly for a moment and then, turning to Abou, said, "It is a pity that Major Richmond's only shot should have killed him."

Abou nodded.

14

ABOU finished dressing the flesh wound on the side of John's neck. He stepped back and handed him a glass of brandy from the bedside table. John, dazed and still thick in the head, drank and shuddered as the spirit bit into his throat. Silently Abou collected his clothes and laid them on the bed.

"Dress," said Colonel Mawzi from the door. He stood there, a short, alert figure, bantam-fresh and full of confidence, his arms folded across his chest and one hand holding a revolver.

John stood up and began to dress. He felt angry and disgusted with himself.

Colonel Mawzi watched him not without sympathy. He, too, had known the sickness of defeat. This man was a soldier, a commander, and all disaster in his command became personal to him. That was the way a good officer always felt.

He said, "A boat party has just begun to pull away from the *Dunoon*. It would be stupid for it to come up here. Two men could hold this place for days. Also, I imagine, neither of us wants any more casualties."

John, pulling on his jacket, spoke for the first time.

"What are the casualties?"

"Your guard commander, the guard on the Bell Tower and Sir George Cator's A.D.C."

John's face tightened angrily. God, what a mess.

"Is Sir George all right?"

Colonel Mawzi nodded. "He is a prisoner in the mess room. The rest of your men are under guard in their barrack room. You need not be ashamed of this . . . Surprise is hard to beat."

"What do you want from me?"

"You will go down to the *Dunoon* with a message to her commander. He must recall his men to the *Dunoon*, and his ship must remain at anchor until midday. You will, of course, return here after delivering the message."

"The *Dunoon*'s guns could blow this fort to pieces."

"True." Mawzi came a step into the room, leaving the door free for John to pass. "But at the first salvo I will shoot every one of your men in the barrack room. At the second the same thing would happen to yourself and Sir George. I am quite serious about this. Go up on to the parapet and you will see why."

John passed out of the room and down the corridor. Mawzi followed him and Abou padded along behind them.

The sunlight streamed down through the bullet scarred entrance at the top of the steps. Loose wood and stone chips grated under John's feet as he climbed the stairs.

The sun was bright over the eastern sea as he came out and the dawn wind was fresh and cool. Lying a few yards from the doorway, huddled against the grey parapet wall was the body of Hadid Chebir. John stopped, staring down at the body.

From behind him Mawzi spoke quietly. "I have had my casualties, too, Major Richmond. A serious one. Hadid Chebir is dead. But it makes no difference. He goes back to Cyrenia in triumph. Sir George goes with us, too."

Without turning John asked, "How was he killed?"

Mawzi came alongside him. "You ask? It was the first shot from your revolver."

John's eyes came up from the body to Mawzi. "You know that's a lie, Colonel Mawzi. My first and only shot went wide and hit the parapet."

Mawzi shrugged. "Did it? Abou saw Hadid die by your shot. So did I."

John looked at the revolver in Mawzi's hand which covered him. It was a German Mauser. He said nothing. His own revolver was a Service pistol .38. He understood very clearly what had happened. Mawzi was to be the new leader in Cyrenia. But he would have the power of Hadid's martyrdom behind him . . . His eyes met Mawzi's and he said coldly, "Make sure you get him back to Cyrenia, Colonel Mawzi. Make sure no one can ever prove that the bullet inside him came from your weapon. Even your people, I imagine, wouldn't take kindly to a manufactured martyr."

Mawzi smiled and made a little motion with his revolver towards the courtyard steps by the Bell Tower. "You can take the jeep," he said. "I am sure you will return. But if you should be tempted to stay I shall shoot three of your men."

John moved on along the parapet top towards the steps. As he neared them he saw Marion Chebir standing close to them. He came up to her and paused. For a moment their eyes met. He saw the fatigue and distress on her face and then a sudden, half-closing movement of her eyes, as though she would have shut them fully against this morning but couldn't, was being forced to watch and suffer it all. And John, without bitterness, but with a heavy confusion, thought: this is the woman I love, who loves me and yet stands on the other side of this disaster.

Ignoring Mawzi behind him, he said, "You knew this was going to happen?"

Marion nodded. "There was nothing I could do."

Momentarily the impulse was with him to loose some of the anger that turned inside him against her. One word from her would have kept Grayson and his two men alive, one word would have kept a man calling himself Hadid Chebir alive. Then, forcing down his emotion, knowing that he could not be mistaken, he told himself fiercely that if the word had not come from her there must have been a reason stronger than herself for it.

Behind him Mawzi said, "Hurry, Major Richmond."

He went down the steps to the courtyard and began to cross to the jeep. There was a man in a dark leather jacket outside the barrack room door. The muzzle of his carbine followed John.

A broken swathe of shrubs in the little garden caught John's eyes. He saw Grayson's body lying close to the smooth trunk of the dragon tree. The savage thought flashed across his mind that this was the end of all Grayson's ambitions. He'd planned and worked, and now this . . . Four feet up the smooth grey trunk, the wood was mangled and smashed from the impact of bullets and a thick, glutinous welling of red sap had run from it in a broad smear, and still ran . . . He went on to the jeep.

Under the gate vault, a tall man with a small head pulled aside the body of the guard commander and began to open the main gates.

Mawzi said, "Turn that boat party back and see that

Commander Burrows makes no mistake about my message. When you return leave the jeep outside the gate and come in with your hands above your head and keep them there until you have been searched."

John looked at the man and said nothing. He started the engine and drove towards the open gate.

He drove down the dusty hill to Mora and just before he reached the waterfront met Lieutenant Imray with half a dozen armed ratings. He drew up and Imray came to him.

"What the devil's happened up there?"

"Everything. Take your men back to their boat. All of them. I've got to see Burrows."

For a moment Imray wanted to question him but the look on John's face stopped the words in him.

At the jetty were a handful of Mora people and among them Señor Aldobran.

John called to him and said, "Señor, there's trouble at the fort. Tell all your people to keep to their houses until mid-day. They are not to go near the fort. If they do it could mean the death of Sir George Cator and also of my men. That's an order."

They pulled out in silence towards the *Dunoon*.

In the pines at Ardino where Arianna and March used to meet, Grogan and Andrews were drunkenly asleep. They snored and muttered and a half-full brandy bottle, tilted on the pine needles, caught the sun in a great diamond on its shoulder. Andrews lay unmoving, flat on his back. Grogan moved restlessly in his sleep. Something was digging into his right side and he turned over to his left. After a few moments something began to dig into his left side and he twisted over again. After a time he sat up, dazed with drink and sleep, half-opened his eyes and then shut them quickly against the blaze of the sun. Cautiously he partly opened his eyes again and squinted around him, one hand on his forehead, and swayed. He saw Andrews lying close to him, stared at him stupidly for a while and then as a great wave of nausea and head throbbing took him, he groaned and said, "Oh, Gawd ... Oh, Gawd ..." and flopped to the pine needles and lay on his back breathing heavily. Sleep, and drink, and the red mist of sun against his eyelids swept him up in a drumming, giddy spasm.

"And that's it." John stood up and going to the carafe by Burrows' bed poured himself a glass of water. He drank it and then breathed deeply. His throat ached but he was himself again. "Mawzi holds all the cards and if you make a wrong move it will put Sir George and my men in the soup."

Burrows was silent. He sat on the side of his bed in his cabin and frowned. He watched John take a cigarette from the box on the table and light it.

"And what do you think he's going to do—before midday?" he growled suddenly.

"Clear out. He'll take Sir George with him, and Hadid's body."

"How's he going to do that?"

"By air, I imagine. Flying boat. His men must have come in that way."

"How many men has he?"

"Five or six, I should think."

Burrows stood up. "I could blow that bloody place right off the cliff."

"But you won't."

"What happens to you?"

"God knows. I'm the man who's supposed to have killed Hadid. The Cyrenians will expect an answer to that one. The point is, however, until he's actually off the island we might get a break. Though I'm damned if I see what."

"Damn! Damn! Damn!" Burrows beat his fist into his palm. "I've got everything I want, but I daren't touch him. I'll send a signal through to the Admiralty, but a fat lot of good that will do. There's a code message here from them about the other business. No action until further instructions received. They're going to love me when they get my next message. Why in God's name do they send people like that out here with only a handful of men to look after them? Flying boats! It would have taken a R.A.F. squadron to watch that one!"

"You'd better keep a watch on the newspaper men you've got here. Don't let 'em ashore. Mawzi means every word he says."

"The clever bastard. Well, you can tell him I'll sit here until midday and watch him take my father-in-law off to Cyrenia. How's the old man taking it?"

"I haven't seen him yet."

"I can't see the Admiralty telling me to go in. They won't risk anything happening to Sir George. Poor old Grayson . . . what a bloody way to go."

He made a sudden angry, frustrated noise in his throat. "Sorry——" He looked sharply at John. "You're the one who's really in a spot. Isn't there a thing I can do?"

"Nothing. Just sit tight. And don't worry about me."

"Could be he'll take you back to Cyrenia. The Government will do a deal for you and Sir George."

John pursed his lips wryly. Mawzi would never take him back. Compared with Sir George he was small beer as a hostage. He knew exactly what would happen. Mawzi hated him. Mawzi didn't forget. But the odd thing was that in his own mind the personal importance of all this wasn't coming through. He'd made a mess of things. The responsibility for this was square on his shoulders, no matter what talk there might be about only a handful of men, of flying boats and all the other excuses. There was no room in his mind at the moment for thoughts about himself . . . They'd come later, nearer the time. But now he was only bitterly aware of the whole muddle and his self-anger . . .

He turned towards the cabin door. "I'm going."

Burrows nodded and for an instant he put his hand on John's arm.

Coming back from seeing John off, Teddy Burrows found Daphne in his cabin. She stood against his small sea-desk, a flowered dressing-gown belted loosely around her, her pale blonde hair alive with the sunlight that came through the porthole.

"Teddy," she said, "what's going on?"

"There's trouble at the fort," he said awkwardly, knowing that there was no escaping the truth, full of clumsiness

259

because he had no way of handling this gently. "Mawzi's taken it over. He had help from outside. But your father's all right, and will be . . ."

"But the shots? Has anyone——"

She came forward quickly. Her face was lifted to him, anxious and so dear to him that he knew that if it had been in his power to change things for her he would . . . He would have had Grayson alive, have faced anything rather than see her . . . God in heaven, what a mess!

"Two guards have been killed," he said thickly, "and Neil Grayson . . ." He held her hand, looking down at it, not wanting to see her face, for her sake and his sake. He heard the sharp passage of her breath and then the cabin was silent. He stood there holding her hand, keeping his eyes on the pattern of her dressing-gown, sparing her and himself.

There seemed no movement or sound in the cabin for a long time, and then very slowly her hand escaped his and held the stuff of his sleeve and her body was lightly against the bulk of his body and his arm went out and around her shoulders, drawing her closer and holding her. He felt her shake with a sudden spasm and he held her tighter.

"It's all right," he said. "It's all right . . ." The words were clumsy, no real meaning in them. But the tenderness in him was an agony as she trembled and her voice came muffled and faint to him.

"Oh, Teddy . . . Oh, Teddy . . ."

"Take it easy, old girl . . ." His hand came up to the back of her head and held her face against his breast. Everything would be all right . . . Against his hand that cupped her cheek he felt the touch of her tears and the love in him for her was a great strength and calmness so that the words he had used suddenly had a real truth and he knew that from now on everything would be all right because they would both make it so.

John Richmond got out of the jeep twenty yards from the main gate and walked towards the fort with his hands above his head. Mietus and Colonel Mawzi waited for him inside. Mietus ran his hands over him.

"Well, Major Richmond?" Mawzi asked.

"Lieutenant-Commander Burrows will remain at anchor until midday."

"Good." Mawzi looked at his watch. It was nine o'clock. He waved his hand towards the courtyard. "The mess room."

John went out into the sunlight of the yard and the two followed. Mietus was close behind him as he went up the courtyard steps to the room. A guard stood outside the door and opened it for them. Mawzi followed him in and Mietus came in and closed the door, covering them with his carbine.

Sir George, fully dressed now, stood by one of the windows overlooking Mora. He turned. Seeing the bandage around John's neck he said:

"You all right, Richmond?"

"Yes, sir."

"A mess, isn't it?"

"I'm afraid so, sir."

Colonel Mawzi came forward.

"We leave here in half an hour, Sir George. The *Dunoon* will remain at anchor until midday. We shall be miles away by then. I do not have to stress that any foolishness will only cause trouble."

"Yes, yes . . ." said Sir George. "We know all about that." He sounded testy and impatient and John could tell that, just as with himself the personal implications hadn't struck home yet, so it was with Sir George.

The Governor came by John, gave him an almost paternal pat on the arm and, facing Mawzi, said, "Nobody's going to be foolish. We don't want any more deaths."

Mawzi took out his cigarette holder and firmed a cigarette into the socket. He nodded approvingly. "You are a sensible man, Sir George. I shall try to make your stay in Cyrenia as comfortable as possible."

"I don't care a damn about that, Mawzi. It could be that your stay there won't be a very comfortable one. All the cards aren't in your hands, you know. Not by a long chalk."

"What do you mean?" Mawzi lowered his cigarette and frowned.

John stepped forward. He knew what was in Sir George's mind. "I think, sir," he said quickly, "that it might be wise——"

261

"Nonsense. Why shouldn't he have something to worry about?" Sir George jerked his head towards Mawzi, an ugly, turtle-like thrust. John could tell that the old man was hard with anger and he guessed that it was the deaths of Grayson and the other men in the fort that stirred him pugnaciously. "Major Richmond, here," Sir George went on, "was at Oxford with Hadid Chebir. He knew him quite well and the other evening in the Bell Tower he went into his room and saw him lying naked on his bed . . . The Hadid Chebir here is an impostor. The real Hadid Chebir has a birthmark on his stomach which this one doesn't have. My Government have already been informed of this, Mawzi. The moment they hear that you and Hadid Chebir are taking me back to Cyrenia they'll spread the news that the Cyrenian National Army is being led by an impostor, has been so led, in fact, for quite a few years . . ."

John saw Mawzi smiling. The old man should have kept quiet. This was doing no good at all.

Mawzi said quietly, "The thing you don't appreciate, Sir George, is that Hadid Chebir is not going back to Cyrenia. Not alive, anyway."

"He's dead?"

"Yes, Sir George. Major Richmond will tell you how he died. We shall take his body back. That is all we need. It will be buried and any false stories your Government circulate will be regarded by my people as the childish lies of a Great Power which has been humiliated by the incident here. Nobody will believe you or your Government and Hadid's body will never be examined by anyone."

"What is this, Richmond?" Sir George looked at John.

"Hadid is dead, sir. Colonel Mawzi claims I shot him. I did nothing of the kind. My belief is that Colonel Mawzi shot him himself, and always meant to the moment he knew this plan had succeeded. He means to be the new leader in Cyrenia . . ."

"That is true," said Mawzi calmly. "I shall be the new leader; but the memory and martyrdom of Hadid will be the strongest weapon in my hand. Nothing you say will be believed now. Sour grapes, I think, is the way you express it . . ." He paused for a moment, eyeing them. At the door

262

Mietus shifted his feet in a soft scraping sound on the boards. "The matter of a hero's death, Sir George," Mawzi went on, "is a question of timing. Two years ago when the real Hadid was killed our cause was in a bad way. His death then, had it been known, would have finished us, dispirited our tired supporters. So we substituted a half-brother of Hadid's. But now—at this moment of triumph for us, and humiliation for you—his death is superb. The loss of a leader in the moment of triumph is strength. Nothing that is said against him will be believed. I think all the worries, Sir George, are still on your side." He turned and walked towards the door. When he reached Mietus he paused and said over his shoulder, "We shall leave here soon. In the meantime I will have Abou bring you some coffee and toast."

When he was gone Sir George dropped to a chair and ran a hand wearily over his face. "I didn't know he was dead . . . They told me about our losses, but not that." He looked up at John thoughtfully, "What he said is right. No one would believe a word of our story."

"No . . . not once they're back in Cyrenia. But if we could prevent it; if we could keep Hadid's body and get the bullet from it that killed him . . . and if we had Mawzi, and . . ." John shrugged as his words tailed away. There were so many "ifs" and "ands".

In the cottage at Ardino Arianna lay on her bed in a feverish delirium. Her mother sat by the bed. Occasionally the old woman wiped the girl's face with a damp cloth and held a glass of water to her lips. Arianna stirred and now and again talked mutteringly to herself. The room was close and dark. Outside the sun beat down on the hard, dusty square.

There was the hollow beat of footsteps on the stairs and Ercolo came into the room. Unshaven and bleary-eyed he stood over the bed.

"She is still the same?" he asked quietly.

"The same. She talks wildly."

"I have sent someone to Mora. Señor Aldobran or the priest will come. They are as good as any doctor."

"I think of Torlo," said the old woman. "If it is from a fall she is like this, he may have fallen, too."

263

"A couple of men have gone up to look for him. It is easy to follow the way she crawled. It is lucky the sailors found her in the trees behind the bar . . . She could have lain there and died."

The old woman crossed herself.

Ercolo shook his head to get the drink from him and thought of the two sailors who had come staggering back into the bar just after sunrise, shouting something about a girl . . . reeling about the place wildly and finally pulling himself and the fishermen out and up the hill. The sailors had been no help in carrying her. They had fallen all over the place, laughing and singing.

"They have gone, the sailors?" asked the old woman.

"Yes . . ."

"The Holy Mother must have sent them. But it is of Torlo that I think. Even a goat can slip on Caldera."

Ercolo put a hand on her shoulder.

"They will find him and she will be well again. In a little while someone will be here."

He turned and left the room. Behind him the old woman dipped her cloth into a tin bowl of water, wrung it out and wiped Arianna's face again. The blood ran a little from the cut above the girl's ear and smeared the side of her face as the cloth slid over her smooth cheek.

Torlo, thought the old woman . . . A son was a son and she and her husband were old. One needed a strong son. This one would recover, for the women of Ardino were hard. Yes, this one would recover and leave them one day soon for some man. But Torlo . . . He could be lying dead up there. She crossed herself and began to say a rapid, mumbling prayer.

At a quarter to nine Abou brought Marion her coffee under the awning by the Bell Tower. He hovered for a moment like a shadow by the small table, pouring the coffee. Then standing back, folding his hands together, said, "In half an hour we leave, madame. The Colonel says you may bring a coat but no heavy luggage. It is a question of weight with so many."

"Thank you, Abou." She spoke without looking at him, her eyes on the waters of the small beach below the fort.

264

And she knew she sat here, watching the waters, because she could not bear to see the fort and the courtyard behind her. The sight of the dead was with her still and would be for a long time . . . And each death she acknowledged was on her conscience. She had been caught between two loyalties, not known how to change from one to the other and, when she had made up her mind, it had been too late. They were her deaths and she had to look away from them, but she knew they were there, could not erase from her mind the clear, brutal picture. The guard in the shadow of the Bell Tower, Hadid's body, the only one removed, but the blood drying on the grey parapet stones and in the courtyard . . . Behind her the breeze rustled the leaves of the dragon tree sharply and she knew what lay beneath it, could almost feel the slow ooze of blood and sap.

Abou said, "I see you have your light coat here, madame. If there is any other small thing you need from your room, I will fetch it. That way——"

"No thank you, Abou."

She knew that he meant to save her the need for going past the guard's body by the tower.

"I have everything I need." Her hand went out and touched the coat that lay over the deck chair by her side.

Abou bowed and moved away.

Everything. It was a large word, but for her it meant so little. For herself, anyway, she expected nothing, but for other people . . . for John Richmond and behind him so many others, maybe she still had something . . .

Restless she stood up and walked away down the parapet. As John had stood at the top of the steps and talked briefly to her she had been unable to guess what he was feeling. Did he hate her, or did he understand? She couldn't know. All she could know was her own feeling and her own love for him and this had become a hardness and resolution inside her. People made a mess of things. God knows she had, but even so one had to go on trying, trying and trying, right up to the last minute. Trying and hoping.

A flash of sun on glass drew her attention to the top of the Flag Tower. She recognized Sifal on the roof, elbows on the parapet, watching the eastern sky with a pair of field glasses.

She knew what he hoped to see. Sifal, Lorentzen, Plevsky, Roper and Mietus . . . she knew them all. And thinking of them the whole of her past, from the moment she had met the real Hadid took on the sudden colours of fantasy and the distortions of a dream. She should have stayed in Swindon and become an ordinary housewife like her sister. And now because it was clearly withheld from her she had an intense longing for ordinariness, for quiet and routine . . . to live with small cares and joys. Too late . . . and there were swift tears in her eyes as she remembered the tight mouth of John Richmond as he had turned from her and gone down the steps to the courtyard and across to the jeep.

She turned back to the awning and, although the morning was growing hot, she picked up her light coat and slipped it on, pushing her hands into the pockets.

15

IT was a three-ton lorry, recently re-painted a dark green, and the walls of the tyres whitened in honour of the Governor's visit. The back was open, though the arched hoops that carried the canopy were still in place.

The engine was ticking over gently and Roper was at the wheel. Lorentzen, who had opened the main gates, was now standing on the running board on the other side of the cab from Roper. His sub-machine-gun was slipped under one arm and he was smoking, blinking his eyes a little in the strong sun that poured down into the courtyard.

The body of Hadid Chebir, wrapped in three or four army blankets, was already lying on the floor-boards of the lorry.

Marion Chebir stood near by, her coat close around her shoulders as though she were cold, her eyes looking through the main gate towards the dusty road slope down to Mora.

John and Sir George Cator came down the courtyard stairs from the mess room, followed by Mietus and Colonel Mawzi. As they crossed the yard Sir George, seeing the body of Neil Grayson, bit his lower lip, and his face grew grim.

Behind them Mawzi said, "Major Richmond—go to the

barrack room. Tell your sergeant we're leaving. No doubt they'll break out when we've gone, but no man is to leave this fort until twelve."

They swung across the yard and Plevsky at the barrack-room door unlocked it at a word from Mawzi.

John called, "Sergeant Benson!"

The sergeant came forward to the door. Over his head John could see the other men in the room. They were very still and watchful.

Sergeant Benson said, "Sir?"

"Sergeant, Colonel Mawzi is taking us away. When we're gone, no one is to leave this fort until midday."

"Yes, sir." And then as Plevsky put his hand to the door, Benson went on quickly, "Sorry about this, sir. They were too quick for us."

"It's all right, Sergeant."

Benson stepped back as the door closed on him and Plevsky turned the key.

They moved on to the lorry, Plevsky following them and Abou came down the Bell Tower steps behind them and hurried across. Just for a moment his eye caught the damaged shrubs of the garden and he thought about his friend Jenkins. It was a good thing he still lived. He could not have been so happy himself had it been otherwise.

There were two bench seats, one on either side, at the back of the lorry. Sir George and John sat close up against the cab of the lorry. Marion took her place on the bench opposite them but a little lower down and Abou sat at her side, near the tail-board where Plevsky and Mietus stood holding on to the rear awning stay. Sifal sat on the floor-boards, his back against the tail-board, his feet drawn up and away from the long, blanket-wrapped length of Chebir's body. His sub-machine-gun rested across his hunched knees covering the inside of the lorry. In the cab were Roper, Lorentzen and Colonel Mawzi.

The lorry moved across the yard, under the shadowed archway and out into the sunlit space before the fort.

Mietus and Plevsky watched the sides of the road and the scrub-padded flanks of the slopes, not trusting any truce, their hands warm against their machine-guns. On the floor-boards the body of Chebir rolled a little with the motion of the lorry. Nobody spoke.

Sir George, holding to the bench with one hand to stop his body swaying, was wishing he was twenty years younger. As an old man, and a man of standing, he knew he would be treated as well as possible by Mawzi. Some time in the future he would be released as part of some political bargain. Whatever happened he was really of no importance except as a hostage. But in an affair like this there was always a delicate balance between success and failure. No game was lost until the final whistle went. If he had been younger, which means quicker and stronger, he would have waited for the fine chance which sometimes came to upset a balance. Back in the mess room where they had been left alone over their coffee he had said to Richmond: "If you get a chance, go for it. Don't worry about me." But for the life of him he could not see where any chance was to be given. As the lorry curved down the hill the *Dunoon* came into sight and he saw the movement of men aboard her. Teddy Burrows must be watching this, fuming with impatience. Teddy . . . He was a big, clumsy man, but the kind Daphne needed . . . Oh, she was a bit disappointed in him, he guessed, because he'd stuck to the Navy. But she'd grow out of that, even if she had to kick over the traces a bit first, but she'd grow out of it and find that Teddy was the right man. Funny, he'd imagined lately that she'd begun to take a little more interest in Grayson than he would have wished. Maybe that was why Grayson had decided to leave him . . . one of the reasons, anyway. Poor Neil . . . Who could have guessed that he would end like this? Suddenly he felt very old and very tired and sensed his anger turning against the stupidity of politicians and nations . . . Common sense, a little good-will, a little give and take, and there'd be no need for affairs like this. But it would never happen . . . and all over the world inoffensive soldiers finished up with a bullet in them. He stirred and grunted to himself.

The lorry rattled under the palm trees along the Mora waterfront. The beach and the boats were deserted. It turned right-handed into the heart of the town along the road that led out to the wide *barranco* running up to La Caldera.

268

John saw people watching from the windows and doorways. They were curiously still and unreal, like puppets in some miniature toy town. They went by the church and there was a sudden grey and white flurry from the pigeons on the baroque façade and he thought of the pigeons and doves at Sorby Place, and the thought was wry and bitter in him. He had dreamed of one day taking Marion to Sorby Place . . . a dream was all it would ever be. If he knew Mawzi the man would finish him off before he left the island. His eyes dropped from following the flight of the pigeons and he found Marion looking at him. She made no attempt to avoid his gaze and he looked full at her, knowing there was much he didn't understand about her, knowing that there must be an agony of confusion in her, knowing that there was never going to be any time for them to sort things out and come to the truth . . . but he went on looking because even though he was not sure of her he had no doubt about his own love. He could love her above everything she might be or do . . . that was the only truth that mattered, and he had discovered it far too late. He watched her now and knew that his face was as expressionless as her own because both of them were only living inside, and as he faced her the love in him became fierce and ruthless, acknowledging nothing else but itself, caring for nothing else but itself . . . and across the few feet that separated them he spoke to her in his thoughts, crying out to her that he didn't care a damn what she had been or what she had done or what was to be for him or for her because nothing mattered except that out of all the smallness and futility of his life he had found her if only for a brief moment, and the finding and the knowing was a richness that could never be denied in him.

The lorry changed gear to take the rise up the valley. The banana and vine terraces streamed by them and a pale cloud of dust trailed along the road behind them. They went sharp right at the Ardino turning and the road became steeper.

And then, across the lorry, his eyes still on her, John saw Marion's face slowly move to a new life. It was almost as though she had heard his thoughts, knew his feelings and had been waiting for them, living on the edge of hope but expecting nothing. He saw her eyes widen a little. Her head turned slightly towards Abou on her right and then back to him. So slow was the movement that it might have been brought about by the cant of the lorry as it took the steep rise. Then her head went further left and for a moment her eyes were off him and glancing downwards to her left side, to her arm. As clearly as though she had spoken he knew she was drawing his attention to something there on the seat.

Very gradually he saw her left hand slide out of the pocket of her light cream-coloured coat. It came out and for a moment it was fully exposed, the movement masked by her body from Sifal and the others at the end of the lorry, and then as slowly her hand slid back into the pocket. She had shown him the butt of a revolver.

He felt his heart leap and, scared of his face giving him away, he raised his hands with a tired gesture to his eyes and rubbed at them. When he dropped them and opened his eyes Marion had turned her head and was gazing away from him over the tail-board of the lorry. Sifal was looking at Abou, and Mietus and Plevsky watched the road and the scrub. John brought his head round and found Sir George's eyes on him. There was the merest shadow of a nod from the Governor and John knew that he had seen, too.

There was little hope, he knew, of Marion being able to pass the revolver to him. She must know that. But as clearly as though she had spoken to him he realized that she would be waiting from now on, waiting for the moment when he decided to take a chance and would be ready to cover him. And Sir George, too, would be waiting. What was it the old boy had said in the mess room? "If you get a chance—go for it. Don't worry about me."

He looked now with new interest at the guards. It would have to be one of them. He had to have a tommy-gun. It was his only hope. All of the guards carried them loose in their hands. It would mean a jump and snatch and a prayer that his moment of surprise would beat the movement of a trigger finger. And there would have to be cover close at hand to protect him.

He sat there thinking it out as the lorry whined in low gear down the hill towards Ardino. He could guess what was going to happen. They would go down to the beach and take

270

a boat. He remembered the morning days and days ago when March had driven him out here and he had gone down to the beach. He shut his eyes trying to picture the beach, and the path down to it.

He opened his eyes quickly as Abou suddenly gave a small cry. The man was pointing up over the right-hand edge of the cab. The others looked up briefly and John twisted round. Out over the sea at about a thousand feet a flying boat was coming round in a great sweep. Head screwed round John watched the flying boat plane down and then disappear below the cliffs beyond Ardino.

The road levelled out between low oaks and widely spaced pines, and a few moments later they were in the Ardino square. The lorry ran right across it, past the church and pulled up with its nose under the trees that flanked the beginning of the small path that led down to the beach.

Mietus and Plevsky jumped down and lowered the tailboard. Sifal stood up and covered John and Sir George with his gun. Marion climbed down and then Sifal motioned to Sir George and John to follow.

They stood in a little group at the side of the lorry and were joined by the three from the cab.

In the square some women had straightened up from the trough where they had been washing clothes. An old man was sitting on a stool outside the *Bar Filis*. Ercolo came to the door and began to walk slowly down to the lorry. He was followed by three young men from the bar.

Colonel Mawzi watched them crossing the dusty square. A few hens scattered before them and one of the women shouted something to Ercolo.

"Mietus—tell them to keep back and away from the beach."

Mietus moved forward, his tommy-gun held low, and Ercolo seeing the gun stopped, puzzled, a few yards from him.

"You have brought someone for Arianna——"

"Stay where you are," Mietus interrupted him in Spanish.

"But, señor——"

"Take these men back with you and stay in your bar. Anyone who leaves this square or tries to come down to the beach . . ." Mietus raised his gun significantly.

It was then that Ercolo saw Sir George and John.

Sir George said quietly, "Keep your people out of trouble. There is nothing you can do."

"Back!" Mietus took a step forward.

Ercolo hesitated and then turned and began to walk to the bar, the three young men following him. The women stood very still at the trough.

Colonel Mawzi turned to the group by the lorry.

"Roper and Plevsky, you carry the body." His voice was brisk, self-possessed. He gave his orders to the rest, impersonally, briefly, the whole movement long worked out in his mind. The flying boat was waiting and beyond it Cyrenia. His blood stirred with the thought . . .

Standing a little apart from the rest Marion said to him, "What is happening to Major Richmond?"

Mawzi's eyes travelled from her to John and he smiled.

"Only Sir George comes with us. We shall say goodbye to Major Richmond on the beach."

John knew what kind of goodbye was intended for him.

The party started off through the pines towards the top of the cliff above the beach. It was a narrow track and, John saw, with no cover on either side.

Lorentzen went first with Sir George close behind him. Then followed Sifal with John after him. Behind John came Mietus with Marion almost at his side. After them came Roper and Plevsky carrying the body, and Colonel Mawzi and Abou formed the tail of the file.

John watched Sifal ahead of him. The Arab was carrying his gun loosely under his right arm. The back of his head was close shaven and John could see the sweat on the walnut skin. Behind him he heard Mietus stumble and grunt.

They came to the cliff top and the beach was spread below them. A few boats were pulled just above high water mark. The tide was full in. A quarter of a mile out the flying boat taxied slowly against the wind and tide drift, keeping station in line with the beach. The wet black lava sand of the beach glittered under the fierce sun.

There was only one place and one hope, John had decided. The path went steeply and twisting down to the beach. Where it met the sand the dark cliffs curved round and broke

272

back in a cleft that was almost half-vaulted over by rocks that had fallen from higher up. He could see the cleft now as he followed Sifal down. In front of the cleft was a long barrier of black rock about three feet high embedded in the dry sand. If they could make the cleft, the rock barrier would give them cover. If they could make the cleft, and if they had arms they could possibly hold out for some time . . . God, it was a flimsy chance, so flimsy that he half drew back from any thought of making the attempt. One burst and both Marion and Sir George would go . . . A cold muscular shiver ran through him. He couldn't do it. They could never make the cleft.

From behind, Mawzi shouted, "Slower, Lorentzen."

John looked back. Roper and Plevsky had to take the path carefully with the body they carried between them. He saw Marion alongside Mietus. Her face was set hard, and he knew she was waiting and he knew that she understood clearly, too, what Mawzi meant by saying goodbye.

Mietus said harshly, "Keep moving. Don't turn round."

The file moved on.

They were fifty feet above the beach now. John marked with his eyes a spot at the end of the rock barrier where Sir George would have the least ground to cover to reach the cleft. And marking back he saw that this would bring him half-way along it and Marion at the path end of it. She had a revolver. Nothing would surprise her, but she would have farther to run than anyone . . . He couldn't do it, couldn't make her take the chance. But even as he told himself this he knew he was going to take the risk. She had given him the chance and the instinct for the gamble was in his mind and body like a drug because without it there was nothing . . . Not just his death, but the abandonment of hope when she had shown him the way.

The loose stones gritted and rolled under his feet. The palms of his hands were sweating and he rubbed them slowly across his tunic, drying them, knowing that when he grabbed for Sifal's gun there must be no slipping. A great black and yellow-tailed butterfly flipped erratically across the path and he saw Sir George's head turn slightly to watch it.

The long, slow Atlantic rollers ran lazily into the beach

and the noise of the water now was loud, seething and sucking.

Lorentzen jumped clear of the path on to the beach. He halted for a moment and looked back, and then began to plough awkwardly across the loose black sand, walking parallel to the black ridge of rock that fronted the cleft. Sir George followed him, his white jacket edges flapping a little in the sea breeze. John saw that the Governor had closed up a little on Lorentzen and suddenly he knew that if he didn't take the chance then Sir George would.

Sifal ahead of him jumped to the beach. His feet made a soft crunch in the loose sand. John jumped too, gaining a foot on him and ploughed forward shortening the distance between them. The soft sand would give little purchase for a leap and he wanted to be close. Over Sifal's shoulder he watched Sir George ahead of them. He marked a spot on the long length of rock and waited for the short, white-coated figure to come abreast of it. Four more steps . . .

Three . . . His feet slipped in the sand as he thrust forward.

Two . . . The sweat was thick on his palms again and he wiped them down the side of his trousers and, as his arms came up from the movement, he shouted fiercely:

"Now!"

He leaped forward and smashed his right fist hard down on the back of Sifal's neck. The man stumbled forward and, as he did so, John grabbed at his gun and jerked it free. Alone now, not knowing what was happening elsewhere, he fumbled at the gun to bring it round and into a firing position. Sifal rolled over on the sand in front of him, rolling and rolling desperately.

The sub-machine-gun came into his hands, bolt ready cocked, and his finger found the trigger. He fired at the rolling body, saw it leap and quiver, stopped firing and for a second was dazed by the harsh, beating echoes of the shots crashing back from the dark cliffs. And then, as though a mist had cleared from his eyes, he saw Sir George ahead of him, resting on his hands and knees in the sand. The Governor had jumped for Lorentzen and missed him.

Lorentzen, half-turned, had his gun pointing down at the Governor.

John fired, running sideways towards the rock barrier.

The cliffs echoed with vicious sound again and he saw Lorentzen double up. With John's second burst Lorentzen straightened and fell backwards spread-eagled to the sand.

"Into the cliffs," shouted John. He jumped for the rough sides of the low rock barrier and, as he did so, he saw the long file behind him, straggling across the beach and part way up the path. For a moment the whole scene seemed caught in slow motion. Roper and Plevsky had dropped the body and were in the act of straightening up. Mawzi and Abou were behind them trying to pass. On the beach Mietus stood with his gun thrust forward slightly, and Marion was swung partly towards the man.

Mietus fired. A row of stone chips flashed across the rock a foot in front of John.

Marion's hand came out of her pocket and, as the echo of rapid-firing shots died, there was the echo of a solitary shot. Mietus dropped his gun and his hands went to his side as he sank to the sand.

For a few seconds before he died Mietus saw them very clearly and very calmly. Sir George had picked up Lorentzen's gun and was climbing over the rock barrier towards the cleft. The British major was on top of the rock, firing up at the path, covering the girl as she stumbled across the loose sand and around the end of the rock barrier towards the cleft. The picture wavered a little, became misted and then was lost in a red blur, and as he went he was telling himself that this was what he had always known . . . one day out of the blue, out of the . . . blue. He dropped sideways and the scurfy blond hair was powdered with the black lava sand.

Moving backwards towards the cleft in the rocks, John blazed away at the foot of the path, seeing the four men a few yards up fling themselves for cover and from the tail of his eye watching Marion's stumbling run across the sand to the cleft.

Someone leapt from behind one rock to another at the foot of the path and a sub-machine-gun chattered and a great fan of stone chips and sand spurted between John and Marion. John fired at random, forcing the man to take cover, and jumped from the rock, catching Marion by the arm and half-

275

running with her, half-pulling her, scrambled for the cleft.

They flung themselves forward into the shadow and dropped to the ground. For a moment they both lay there, panting.

Against the high vault of the cleft where the loose rocks were piled came the sudden scream and whip of bullets and pieces of stones showered down on to them.

John lay for a second or two with his arm over Marion's shoulder, feeling the stones thud against his body. Then from his side he heard the answering chatter of a Thompson sub-machine-carbine, and then a sudden silence.

"Blast, the thing's stopped. What do I do?"

John sat up. Sir George was crouched to one side of the cleft just in front of them, frowning at the gun in his hand. A stone chip had cut the old man's face and blood trickled from it.

"Give me." John took the gun from him, cocked it, turned it to the right and shook vigorously. An empty case fell out.

"It's O.K. now," he said as he handed it back. "They often jam like that——"

Another scream and chatter of bullets whipped close over-head and drowned the rest of his words. The three of them crouched low and the spent bullets ricochetted among the rocks behind them.

In the following silence Sir George said, "Not too healthy. As you ran in here they came down to the beach and they're over behind that clump of rocks. Four of 'em. They've only got to keep up some covering fire while one of them climbs partway up the cliff. From anywhere up there the whole of this cleft is open." He put out his old hand, brown-splotched and veined, and touched Marion on the arm. "What you did was . . . well, first-class. Thank you."

Marion said nothing but for a moment she smiled. For the first time that day there was something like contentment in her. She looked at John and she knew he was feeling it, too. They were together.

John reached out for her hand and squeezed it. Then turning to Sir George he said, "Don't fire wildly. We haven't got much ammunition. Keep your eyes on the slope above their rock."

276

He edged himself forward across the sand and stones until he could get a view around the far end of the rock barrier. Nothing moved on the small sector of beach he could see. A little cloud of sand flies danced a few feet ahead of him. Distantly came the low, throaty growl of the breaking seas.

Somebody moved alongside of him and he knew it was Marion.

"Last night," she said, her voice unsteady and urgent, as though she fought to find some way to be even closer to him, "I wanted to come and warn you . . . but he guessed, he . . ."

"It's all right." He kept his eyes on the far rock. It was fifty yards away and these guns weren't too accurate at that range.

"All the time I've longed to be with you . . . to let you know . . . and this morning when they carried Hadid's body away they didn't see his revolver . . . It was against the parapet in the shade . . . Mawzi would never have trusted me . . ."

He put out a hand and tightened his fingers around her arm, feeling the shake in her. He could sense that she was very near the edge.

"It's all right, I tell you . . . whatever happens, it's all right . . ." They were words with little meaning, but it was his voice, he was speaking to her and his hand was on her arm . . . just touching her was enough.

Something moved by the far rocks and once more the bullets streamed into the cleft. This time they were lower and the stone chips hummed like angry wasps about them. There was a short silence and then another burst. John knew what was happening. Mawzi was keeping them down. Under Mawzi's covering fire one of his men would slip up the cliff and the moment their bodies were in view the end would come. John turned his head round and saw Sir George flat on his side, his old face screwed up in tight creases, and muttering angrily to himself. Another burst of fire splattered over their heads.

In the silence that followed Sir George pulled himself up a little and said sharply, "Good God—what's that fool doing?"

A wild shout suddenly broke out from up the cliff-side.

John looked up. Against the blue sky the staggering silhouette of a man was sharply outlined. He had his arms raised and shouted, wildly and angrily.

Mawzi, Roper, Plevsky and Abou looked up from their shelter and saw him too. Roper was a little apart from the rest, beginning to take the cliff climb that would give him a view of the cleft.

Mawzi raised his gun but even as he did so he saw it. Small and black against the pale blue sky, a tiny, dark ball that soared out and began to drop in a slow arc. Another followed it.

He shouted "Down!"

He flung himself against the base of the rock and saw the others drop too, their actions forced by instinct and years of experience.

Down they came, twisting and turning slowly, the two hand grenades which Arianna had tucked into the front of her blouse hours before, the two hand grenades which Andrews, full of drink, had noticed when he and Grogan had found her in the pines and which Grogan had taken from Andrews because he considered himself less drunk and, therefore, the proper man to be in charge of them. And now up on the cliff, wakened from his sleep after straying away from the pines and Andrews, Grogan watched the grenades fall and his mind was still reeling with the after haze of intoxication . . . Old Sir George lying in the sand being buzzed at with tommy guns . . . ! And the bloody major they'd brought from Gibraltar . . . ! And blokes spread dead on the black sands . . . ! "Aeeeeh!" he cried as the grenades fell; and he laughed as he remembered old Andrews staggering out of the pines, shouting, "Come and see. Come and see—I've found the only girl in the world with four charlies . . . Come and see."

On the sand below the first grenade exploded and two seconds afterwards the other one burst. The first grenade killed Abou, Roper and Plevsky and the second Colonel Mawzi.

John stood up slowly.

"Stay where you are," he said firmly to Sir George and Marion.

His gun at his hip he walked cautiously round the barrier and across the sand. To his left Sifal, Lorentzen and Mietus lay very still on the sands.

He skirted the rocks by the cliff path and climbed the boulder which had sheltered Mawzi and the others. He looked down. They lay twisted and still. The air was strong with the smell of explosives.

To his right a figure came half running, half shambling down the cliff path. He watched it curiously. Suddenly the figure stopped and bent over something.

Through the hot air into the silence of the beach came a cry, "Eh, what's this? Dead bloke in a blanket . . . What the hell . . . ?"

Grogan came running on, shouting, but his words were suddenly lost in a great roar of engines out at sea. The flying boat was moving swiftly, a blinding white bone of foam at her bows. John watched her go, watched her lift and slowly gain height and finally bear away to the south and out of sight beyond the far headland.

He turned back towards the cleft. Sir George and Marion had risen. She came slowly round the edge of the rock barrier towards him. As they met she put her arm into his and rested against him and he felt her body shake. He put an arm round her, holding her very tightly.

Behind him he heard Sir George say sharply to the man from the cliff top, "Who the devil are you, man? Never mind, never mind, you couldn't be more welcome . . ."

John stood there, his arm firm around Marion and the two men's voices were just a blur of sound . . . and vividly he knew all the trouble and fuss that would stem from this beach . . . the pressmen and the politicians, the enquiries and the high-level decisions, a whole weariness of time and talk . . . but, in the end, it would all pass . . . Everything would pass except this closeness to Marion, this fullness of contact. He looked down at her and she smiled at him.

That evening, as the sun was dropping behind the western flanks of La Caldera, Jenkins came out of his cookhouse carrying a tin of paint, insulating tape and a big ball of putty.

The sap was still running red from the dragon tree. He had been too busy all day so far to do anything about it. But now he had a little time to spare. He edged his way through the damaged shrubs, swearing gently at the way they had suffered and stood for a moment before the mangled grey trunk. He'd a grape vine once that some bloody fool had pruned while the sap was rising. Bled and bled and bled, the thing did, wept its bleeding heart out. It was enough to make you weep, too, the way some people carried on, taking a knife to things they didn't understand, bull-dozing around like a lot of savages . . . Well, there was nothing that could be done about some things, but a tree, now . . . he could fix it for another thousand years. A good gardener was worth five hundred soldiers . . . He set to work, swearing and cursing, as his hands moved patiently and skilfully to his task.

Popular POST

News of THE POPULAR BOOK CLUB — MAY 1959

"Altogether a glorious book!"

wrote **S. P. B. MAIS**

in the Oxford Mail

" The *Kon-Tiki* cameraman described this book as ' An African Kon-Tiki.' I found it even more exciting and better written. Amazing photographs ! Quite enthralling !"

JOHN L. BROM'S

20,000 MILES in the AFRICAN JUNGLE

Next month *you* will be enthralled by this gripping account of a brave man's journey into the inaccessible jungle. Here is big-game hunting with a difference ! For this man's weapon was a camera, his quarry— the jungle animals in their own savage environment. He also wanted to make contact with the native tribesmen, almost as wary and suspicious of the White Man as the shy animals themselves. How he succeeded is most vividly and excitingly described in words and magnificent pictures in next month's splendid choice.

MORE ABOUT THIS AMAZING JOURNEY INSIDE . . .

He braved the lonelines

PREVIEW OF NEXT MONTH'S CHOICE

I N THIS same small car, a man drove seven thousand miles into the African jungle before the loneliness sent him mad . . . Then John Brom took over. He drove the little D.K.W., which he named the "Flying Saucer," for twenty thousand miles over rough jungle tracks. The journey took nine months—nine months of continuously hard driving along a pot-holed, overgrown track few would call a road. He met with many adventures and had several narrow escapes both from animals and unfriendly natives. He had to cope with such hazards as running over a python and a head-on collision involving a fully grown antelope! Throughout it all, and despite the often oppressive loneliness, Brom retained his sanity *and* his sense of humour.

And, he never forgot the main purpose of his trip—to record on film some of the awe-inspiring magic of Africa, its feverish colour and excitement. Many of his magnificent photographs are included in the book.

THE WAGES OF FEAR . . .

One of Brom's adventures that will have you on the edge of your seat with excitement is the incident with the T.N.T. truck, which will surely recall to the reader the famous film *The Wages of Fear!* On a narrow, bumpy track, with no room to turn or to pass, Brom finds himself following an unsprung truck carrying seven tons of T.N.T. . . . How he dealt with that situation, and with the loquacious truck-driver who kept trying to tell him horrifying stories of explosions, is only one of the many incidents that must be funnier to remember than to experience.

ACCUSED OF CANNIBALISM . . .

Brom liked to repay the native hospitality with small gifts—tins of food or even bottled beer were always joyfully accepted. But one of these friendly gestures nearly cost him his life . . .

A tin of corned beef with a label showing a smiling black face led to Brom being accused of cannibalism by a Native King! Neither laughter nor earnest protestations would convince these primitive peoples that Brom was not carrying around tinned

that drives men mad!

Africans in his supplies. He was very lucky to make his escape from the enraged warriors.

FACE TO FACE WITH A GIANT GORILLA ...

"A few more steps and there, ten paces from us, a bush was shaking. Then a beating as of drums: the male had got wind of us, and was striking his chest with rage. There was a creaking and cracking of branches and two enormous, hairy hands parted the screen of foliage. A moment later, there was the great muzzle of the animal; it was looking straight at us from a distance of ten paces... I could see the reddish eyes, the yellow

teeth in the wide-open mouth, the almost human grimace, full of hatred."

This is how Brom describes his encounter with a gorilla—king of the volcanic summits of Africa. As you can see, he writes well on an incredibly exciting subject. The Popular Book Club is proud to offer you these fascinating glimpses into the strange world of Darkest Africa. You will be as impressed and fascinated by this unique story, as were the many reviewers who praised it highly.

"Brom's book, with its many pages of superb photographs of scenery, natives and animals, offers fine, serious descriptions no less than 'thrills' and entertainment." *Birmingham Post*

"Full of superb photographs, novel information about wild animals and wild men of all colours. It is written by a wise, amusing man totally free of sentimentality." *Radio Eireann*

> ## "ACTION, ADVENTURE & STRIKING PICTURES ..."

"Will delight the reader who seeks action, adventure and striking pictures ... there are few who will not get fascinated by Brom's sidelights on what is still a comparatively unknown continent." *Dublin Evening Herald*

"The illustrations give a rich and varied picture of Central Africa ... there are many splendid studies of animals ..." *Times Literary Suppt.*

"Marvellous photographs." *Sphere*

VICTOR CANNING

THIS MONTH'S AUTHOR

Published monthly by Odhams Popular Book Club (Odhams Press Ltd.), 9 Long Acre, London, W.C.99. May, 1959.

—twenty-five years of consistent success.

SUCCESS came very quickly to Victor Canning. His first novel was greeted with acclaim in 1934, and before he was twenty-five he felt certain enough of himself to launch out as a full-time free-lance writer. To-day, twenty-five years later, with many best-selling novels and popular short stories to his credit, he is still writing crisply and excitingly in a way that is often compared to John Buchan. Several of his books have been made into highly successful films. *Panthers' Moon* was the first. Then followed *The Golden Salamander* (you may remember the magnificent acting of Trevor Howard and lovely French star Anouk in this dramatic film) and *Venetian Bird* starring Richard Todd.

Victor Canning is married, has two daughters, lives in Kent and finds writing a full-time occupation.

> *May Choice*
>
> ## THE DRAGON TREE
>
> **by Victor Canning**
>
> Hodder & Stoughton 15/-   Club Edition 4/3

"THE EXPLOITS OF SHERLOCK HOLMES"

By ADRIAN CONAN DOYLE and JOHN DICKSON CARR

Here—by arrangement with our associates, The Companion Book Club, we are privileged to offer to "Popular" members this enthralling book at the special Club price of 4/9 (plus 9d. post) although originally priced at 12/6.

Sherlock Holmes's new exploits vividly described by his creator's son and his famous biographer, J. Dickson Carr. Watson and Holmes are together once more, in adventures all based on tantalizing references by Dr. Watson to cases that he mentioned but never fully explained. Here is a book certain to give enormous pleasure whether you are a fan of Holmes or fortunate enough to be discovering the world's most renowned detective for the first time. Beautifully bound volume, in black with scarlet foil and distinctive Holmesian dust jacket. **Don't miss this exciting offer!**

***A DOZEN THRILLING DETECTIVE STORIES for** 4/9

(Price elsewhere 12/6)   (Plus 9d. postage)

ORDER FORM

To: **THE POPULAR BOOK CLUB,**
Dept. P.Z.E.60, Odhams Press Ltd.,
9 Long Acre, London, W.C.99

PLEASE send me one copy of THE EXPLOITS OF SHERLOCK HOLMES for which I enclose P.O. value 5/6 (4/9 plus 9d. postage).

P.O. Number ....
Make P.O. payable to The Popular Book Club and cross | & Co.|. Do not send coins or loose stamps (not accepted under G.P.O. regulations).

BLOCK LETTERS PLEASE

        Mr.
NAME Mrs.......................................
        Miss
Full Postal
ADDRESS ....

...........................County ....